Addicted to You

Addicted Series

RECOMMENDED READING ORDER

Addicted to You

KRISTA RITCHIE
and
BECCA RITCHIE

BERKLEY ROMANCE
NEW YORK

BERKLEY ROMANCE
Published by Berkley
An imprint of Penguin Random House LLC
penguinrandomhouse.com

Library of Congress Cataloging-in-Publication Data

Names: Ritchie, Krista, author. | Ritchie, Becca, author.
Title: Addicted to you / Krista and Becca Ritchie.
Description: First Jove edition. | New York: Jove, 2022. |
Series: Addicted; #1
Identifiers: LCCN 2022014341 | ISBN 9780593549476 (trade paperback)
Subjects: LCSH: Sex addicts—Fiction. | Alcoholics—Fiction. |
Young adults—Fiction. | LCGFT: Romance fiction. | Novels.
Classification: LCC PS3618.I7675 A66 2022 | DDC 813/.6—dc23/eng/20220407
LC record available at https://lccn.loc.gov/2022014341

Addicted to You was originally self-published, in different form, in 2013.

First Jove Edition: August 2022
First Berkley Romance Edition: July 2023

Printed in the United States of America
13th Printing

Book design by Kristin del Rosario
Interior art: Broken heart on wall © Valentina Shikina / Shutterstock.com

To you, the reader:

When we originally wrote the Addicted series, we were in college with big, lofty dreams and hopes of Lily and Lo's story finding some people. It became so much more than just one romance between childhood friends, thanks to readers who wanted to see more.

It was about sisters, written by two sisters. It was about friendship, and the family you have and also make along the way. Rose's and Daisy's stories—the Calloway Sisters spin-off series—are woven so intrinsically into Lily's novels because we believe that one life does not stop while another goes on a journey. Every novel impacts every character. So the best way to read Lily's story and not miss a thing is by combining her series with the Calloway Sisters series in a ten-book reading order. It's the order we wrote the novels—all three sisters intertwined together.

This is the Addicted series. Ten books. Six friends. Three couples. One epic saga.

We hope these characters bring you as much happiness as they've brought us through-out the years.

As Lily would say, thankyouthankyouthank-you *for choosing them and us. Happy reading!*

All the love in every universe,
Krista and Becca

One

I wake up. My shirt crumpled on a fuzzy carpet. My shorts astray on a dresser. And I think my underwear is lost for good. Somewhere between the folds of the sheets or maybe hidden by the doorway. I can't remember when I took them off or if that was even my doing. Maybe *he* undressed me.

My neck heats as I take a quick peek at the sleeping beauty, some guy with golden hair and a scar along his hipbone. He turns a fraction, facing me, and I freeze. His eyes stay shut, and he groggily clings to his pillow, practically kissing the white fabric. As he lets out breathy snores, his mouth open, the strong scent of alcohol and pepperoni pizza wafts right towards me.

I sure know how to choose 'em.

I masterfully slip from the bed and tiptoe around his apartment, yanking on my black shorts—sans panties, another pair gone to a nameless guy. As I pick up my ripped gray tee, tattered and practically in shreds, the foggy image of last night clears. I stepped through the threshold of his room and literally tore my clothes off like the raging Hulk. Was that even sexy? I cringe. Must have been sexy enough to sleep with me.

Desperate, I find a discolored muscle tee on his floor and manage to tug it over my shoulder-length brown hair, the straight strands tangled and greasy. That's when I find my woolen hat. Bingo. I smack that baby on and hightail it out of his bedroom.

Empty beer cans scatter the narrow hallway, and I stumble over a bottle of Jack Daniel's, filled with black spittle and what looks like a Jolly Rancher. A photo collage of inebriated college girls decorates the door to my left—thankfully not the room I exited. Somehow I was able to dodge that Kappa Phi Delta horn dog and find a guy that *doesn't* advertise his conquests.

I should know better. I swore off frat houses after my last encounter at Alpha Omega Zeta. The night I arrived at fraternity row, AOZ was hosting a theme party. Unaware, I stepped through the four-story building's archway to be met with buckets of water and guys chanting for me to rip off my bra. It was like Spring Break gone awry. Not that I have much in the upstairs department to show off. Before I convulsed in embarrassment, I ducked underneath arms, wedged between torsos and found pleasure at other places and with other people.

Ones that didn't make me feel like a cow being appraised.

Last night I broke a rule. Why? I have a problem. Well, I have many problems. But saying *no* happens to be one of them. When Kappa Phi Delta announced that Skrillex would be playing in their basement, I thought the crowd would be a mixture of sorority girls and regular college folk. Maybe I'd be able to land a normal guy who likes house music. Turns out, the demographic centered on frat guys. Lots of them. Preying on anyone with two boobs and a vagina.

And Skrillex never showed. It was just a lame DJ and a few amps. Go figure.

Deep, *male* voices echo off the marble balusters on the balcony and staircase, and my feet cement by the wall. People are awake? Downstairs? Oh no.

The walk of shame is a venture I plan to avoid all four years of collegiate society. For one, I blush. Like intense tomato-red. No cute flushed cheeks. Just rash-like patches that dot my neck and arms as if I'm allergic to embarrassment.

The male laughter intensifies, and my stomach knots at the nightmarish image spinning in my mind. The one where I stumble down the stairs and all heads whip in my direction. The look of surprise coats their faces, wondering what "brother" of theirs decided to hook up with a flat-chested, gaunt girl. Maybe they'll throw a chicken bone at me, teasing me to eat.

Sadly that happened in fourth grade.

Likely, I'll sputter unintelligible words until one of them takes pity on my flaming red leopard spots and shuffles me out of their door like unwanted garbage.

This was such a mistake (the frat house, not the sex). Never again will I be forced to hoover tequila shots like a vacuum. Peer pressure. It's a real thing.

My options are limited. One staircase. One fate. Unless I happen to grow a pair of wings and fly out of the second-floor window, I'm about to face the walk of shame. I creep to the balcony and suddenly envy Veil from one of my newer comics. The young Avenger can vaporize into nothingness. A power I could surely use right now.

As soon as I reach the top step, the doorbell rings and I peek over the railing. About ten fraternity brothers are gathered on leather sofas, dressed in various versions of khaki shorts and collared shirts. The most lucid guy nominates himself for door-duty. He manages to stand on two feet, his brown hair swept back and his jaw intimidatingly squared. As he answers the door, my spirits lift.

Yes! This is my one opportunity to dash out unseen.

I use the distraction to glide down the steps undetected, channeling my inner-Veil. Halfway to the bottom, Squared-jaw leans on the door frame, blocking the entrance. "Party's over, man." The words sound cottony in his mouth. He lets the door swing shut in the person's face.

I hop over two more stairs.

The bell rings again. For some reason, it sounds angrier.

Squared-jaw groans and yanks the knob hard. "What?"

Another frat guy laughs. "Just give him a beer and tell him to piss off."

A few more steps. Maybe I can really do this. I've never been a particularly lucky person, but I suppose I'm due for a dose.

Squared-jaw keeps his hand planted on the frame, still blocking the passage. "Speak."

"First of all, does it look like I can't read a clock or furthermore don't know what *daytime* looks like? No shit, there's no party." Holy . . . I know that voice.

I stay planted three-quarters down. Sunshine trickles through a tiny space between the door frame and Squared-jaw's tangerine-orange Polo. He clenches his teeth, about ready to slam the door back in the other guy's face, but the intruder puts his hand on it and says, "I left something here last night."

"I don't remember you being here."

"I was." He pauses. "Briefly."

"We have a lost and found," Squared-jaw says curtly. "What is it?" He edges away from the door frame and nods to someone on the couch. They watch the scene like a reality rerun on MTV. "Jason, go grab the box."

When I glance back, I notice the guy outside. Eyes right on me.

"No need," he says.

I sweep his features. Light brown hair, short on either side, full on top. Decently toned body hidden beneath a pair of faded Dockers and a black crew-neck tee. Cheekbones that cut like ice and eyes like liquid scotch. Loren Hale is an alcoholic beverage and he doesn't even know it.

All six-foot-two of him fills the doorway.

As he stares at me, he wears a mixture of amusement and irritation, the muscles in his jaw twitching with both. The frat guys follow his gaze and zero in on the target.

Me.

I may as well have reanimated from thin air.

"Found her," Lo says with a tight, bitter smile.

Heat rises to my face, and I use my hands as human blinders, trying to cover my humiliation as I practically sprint to the door.

Squared-jaw laughs like he won their masculine showdown. "Your girlfriend is a skank, man."

I hear no more. The brisk September air fills my lungs, and Lo bangs the door closed with more force than he probably intended. I cower in my hands, pressing them to my hot cheeks as the event replays in my head. Oh. My. God.

Lo swoops in behind me, his arms flying around my waist. He sets his chin on my shoulder, hunching over a little to counter my short height with his tall. "He better have been worth it," Lo whispers, his hot breath tickling my neck.

"Worth what?" My heart lodges in my throat; his closeness confuses and tempts me. I never know where Lo's true intentions lie.

He guides me forward as we walk, my back still pressed against his chest. I can barely lift up a foot, let alone think straight. "Your first walk of shame in a frat house. How'd that feel?"

"Shameful."

He plants a light kiss on my head and disentangles from me, walking forward. "Pick it up, Calloway. I left my drink in the car."

My eyes begin to widen as I process what this means, gradually forgetting the horrors that just occurred. "You didn't drive, did you?"

He flashes me a look like *really, Lily?* "Seeing as how my usual DD was unavailable"—he raises his eyebrows accusingly—"I called Nola."

He called my personal driver, and I don't begin to ask why he decided to forgo his own chauffeur that would gladly cart him around Philadelphia. Anderson has loose lips. In ninth grade when Chloe Holbrook threw a rager, Lo and I may have been discussing illegal narcotics that were passed from hand to hand at her mother's mansion. Backseat conversations should be considered private among all car-participants. Anderson must not have realized this unspoken rule because the next day, our rooms were raided for illegal paraphernalia. Luckily, the maid forgot to search in the fake fireplace where I used to keep my X-rated box of toys.

We came away clean from the incident and learned a very important lesson. Never trust Anderson.

I prefer to not use my family's car service and thus embed myself further in their grips, but sometimes Nola is a necessity. Like now. When I'm slightly hungover and unable to drive the perpetually drunk Loren Hale.

He has knighted me as his personal sober driver and refuses to shell out money to any cab services after we were almost mugged in one. We never told our parents what happened. Never explained to them how close we were to something horrible. Mostly because we spent that afternoon at a bar with two fake IDs. Lo guzzled more whiskey than a grown man. And I had sex in a public bathroom for the very first time. Our indecencies became our rituals, and our families didn't need to know about them.

My black Escalade is parked on the curb of frat row. Multimillion dollar houses line up, each outdoing the last in column sizes. Red Solo cups litter the nearest yard, an overturned keg splaying sadly in the grass. Lo walks ahead of me.

"I didn't think you were going to show," I say and skirt past a puddle of barf in the road.

"I said I would."

I snort. "That's not always accurate."

He halts by the car door, the windows too tinted to see Nola waiting in the driver's seat. "Yeah, but this is Kappa Phi Delta. You screw one and they may all want a piece of your ass. I seriously had nightmares about it."

I grimace. "About me getting raped?"

"That's why they're called *nightmares*, Lily. They're not supposed to be pleasant."

"Well this is probably my last expedition into a frat house for another decade or at least until I forget about this morning."

The driver's window rolls down. Nola's deep black curls caress her heart-shaped face. "I have to pick up Miss Calloway from the airport in an hour."

"We'll be ready in a minute," I tell her. The window slides up, blocking her from view.

"Which Miss Calloway?" Lo asks.

"Daisy. Fashion Week just ended in Paris." My little sister shot up overnight to a staggering five-foot-eleven inches, and with her rail-like frame she fit the mold for high fashion. My mother capitalized on Daisy's beauty in an instant. Within the week of her fourteenth birthday, she was signed to IMG modeling agency.

Lo's fingers twitch by his side. "She's fifteen and probably surrounded by older models blowing lines in a bathroom."

"I'm sure they sent someone with her." I hate that I don't know the details. Since I arrived at the University of Pennsylvania, I acquired the rude hobby of dodging phone calls and visits. Separating from the Calloway household became all too easy once I entered college. I suppose that has always been written for me. I used to push the boundaries of my curfew and spent little time in the company of my mother and father.

Lo says, "I'm glad I don't have siblings. Frankly, you have enough *for* me."

I never considered having three sisters to be a big brood, but a family of six does garner some unique attention.

He rubs his eyes wearily. "Okay, I need a drink and we need to go."

I inhale a deep breath, about to ask a question we've both avoided thus far. "Are we pretending today?" With Nola so close, it's always a tossup. On one hand, she's never betrayed our trust. Not even in the tenth grade when I used the backseat of a limo to screw a senior soccer player. The privacy screen was up, blocking Nola's view, but he grunted a little too loud and I knocked into the door a little too hard. Of course she heard, but she never ratted me out.

There's always the risk that one day she'll betray us. Cash loosens lips, and unfortunately, our fathers are swimming in it.

I shouldn't care. I'm twenty. Free to have sex. Free to party. You know, all the things expected of college-aged adults. But my laundry list of dirty (like *really* dirty) secrets could create a scandal within my family's circle of friends. My father's company would not appreciate that publicity one bit. If my mother knew my serious problem, she'd send me away for rehab and counseling until I was fixed up nicely. I don't want to be fixed. I just want to live and feed my appetite. It just so happens that my appetite is a sexual one.

Plus, my trust fund would magically vanish at the sight of my impropriety. I'm not ready to walk away from the money that pays my way through college. Lo's family is equally unforgiving.

"We'll pretend," he tells me. "Come on, love." He taps my ass.

"Into the car." I barely stumble on his frequent use of *love*. In middle school, I told him how I thought it was the sexiest term of endearment. And even though British guys have claimed stake to it, Lo took it as his own.

I scrutinize him, and he breaks into a wide smile.

"Has the walk of shame crippled you?" he asks. "Do I need to carry you into the threshold of the Escalade too?"

"That's unnecessary."

His crooked grin makes it hard not to smile back. Lo purposefully leans in close to tease me, and he slips a hand in the back pocket of my jeans. "If you don't unfreeze yourself from this state, I'm going to spin you around. Hard."

My chest collapses. Oh my . . . I bite my lip, imagining what sex would be like with Loren Hale. The first time was too long ago to remember well. I shake my head. *Don't go there.* I turn around to open the door and climb in the Escalade, but a huge realization hits me.

"Nola drove to fraternity row . . . I'm dead. OhmyGod. I'm dead." I run two hands through my hair and begin to breathe like a beached whale. I have no good excuse to be here other than I was searching for a guy to sleep with. And that's the answer I'm trying to avoid. Especially since our parents think Lo and I are in a serious relationship—one that changed his dangerous partying ways and reformed him into a young man that his father can be proud of.

This, picking me up from a frat party with the faint smell of whiskey on his breath, is not what his father has in mind for his son. It is *not* something he'd condone or even accept. In fact, he'd probably scream at Lo and threaten him with his trust fund. Unless we want to say goodbye to our luxuries from our inherited wealth, we have to pretend to be together. And pretend that we're two perfectly functioning, perfectly well-kept human beings.

And we're just not. We're not. My arms shake.

"Whoa!" Lo places his hands on my shoulders. "Relax, Lil. I told Nola that your friend had a birthday brunch. You're covered."

My head still feels like it'll float away, but at least that's better than the truth. *Hey Nola, we need to pick up Lily from frat row where she had a one-night stand with some loser.* And then she'd look at Lo, waiting for him to explode in jealousy. And he'd add: *Oh yeah, I'm only her boyfriend when I need to be. Fooled you!*

Lo senses my anxiety. "She's not going to find out." He squeezes my shoulders.

"Are you sure?"

"Yes," he says impatiently. He slides in the car, and I follow behind. Nola puts the Escalade in gear.

"Back to the Drake, Miss Calloway?" After years of asking her to call me anything, even *little girl* (for some reason, I thought that would entice her to drop the whole act, but I think I only offended her instead), I gave up the attempt. I swear my dad pays her extra for the formality.

"Yes," I say, and she heads towards the Drake apartment complex.

Lo nurses a coffee thermos, and even though he takes big gulps, I'm certain that the caffeinated beverage does not fill it. I find a can of Diet Fizz in the center cooler-console and snap it open. The dark carbonated liquid soothes my restless stomach.

Lo drapes an arm across my shoulder, and I lean into his hard chest a tiny bit.

Nola glances in the rearview mirror. "Was Mr. Hale not invited to the birthday brunch?" she asks, being friendly. Still, anytime Nola goes into question-mode, it jostles my nerves and triggers paranoia.

"I'm not as popular as Lily," Lo answers for me. He has always been a much better liar. I blame it on the fact that he's constantly inebriated. I'd be a far more confident, self-assured Lily if I was downing bourbon all day.

Nola laughs, her plump belly hitting the steering wheel with each chortle. "I'm sure you're just as popular as Miss Calloway."

Anyone (apparently Nola too) would assume that Lo has friends. On an attractiveness scale, he ranges right between a lead singer from a rock band you'd like to fuck and a runway model for Burberry and Calvin Klein. Although, he's never been in a band, but a modeling agency did scout him once, wanting him for a Burberry campaign. They retracted the offer after seeing him drink straight from a nearly empty bottle of whiskey. The fashion industry has standards too.

Lo should have lots of friends. Mostly of the female kind. And usually they do come flocking. But not for long.

The car travels along another street, and I count the minutes in my head. Lo angles his body towards me while his fingers brush my bare shoulder, almost lovingly. I make brief eye contact, my neck burning as his deep gaze enters mine. I swallow hard and try not to break it. Since we're supposed to be dating, I shouldn't be afraid of his amber eyes like an awkward, insecure girl.

Lo says, "Charlie is playing sax tonight at Eight Ball. He invited us to go watch him."

"I don't have plans." *Lie.* A new club opened up downtown called The Blue Room. Literally, everything is said to be blue. Even the drinks. I'm not missing the opportunity to hook up in a blue bathroom. Hopefully with blue toilet seats.

"It's a date."

Silence (of the awkward variety) thickens after his words die in the air. Normally, I'd be talking to him about The Blue Room and my nefarious intentions tonight, making plans since I am his DD. But in the censored car, it's more difficult to start R-rated conversations.

"Is the fridge stocked? I'm starving."

"I just went to the grocery store," he tells me. I narrow my eyes, questioning whether he's lying to play the part of a good boyfriend or if he really did make a Whole Foods run. My stomach growls. At least we all know I didn't lie.

His jaw tightens, pissed that I don't know a fib from a truth. Normally I do, but sometimes when he's so nonchalant, the lines blur. "I bought lemon meringue pie. Your favorite."

I internally gag. "You shouldn't have." *No, you really shouldn't have.* I hate lemon meringue. Obviously he wants Nola to think he's an upstanding boyfriend, but the only girlfriend Loren Hale will ever treat well is his bottle of bourbon.

We stop at a traffic light, now only a few blocks from the apartment complex. I can taste freedom, and Lo's arm begins to feel more like a weight than a comforting appendage across my shoulders.

"Was this a casual event, Miss Calloway?" Nola asks. *What? Oh . . . shit.* Her eyes plant on the muscle tee I snatched from the frat guy's floor. Stained and off-white with God knows what.

"Umm, I-I," I stammer. Lo stiffens next to me. He grips his thermos and chugs the rest of his drink. "I-I spilled some orange juice on my top. It was really embarrassing." Was that even a lie?

My face flames uncontrollably, and for the first time, I welcome the rash-like patches. Nola gazes sympathetically. She's known me since I was too shy to say the Pledge of Allegiance in kindergarten. Age five and timid. Pretty much sums up my first years of existence.

"I'm sure it wasn't that bad," she consoles.

The light flickers to green and she redirects her attention to the road.

Unscathed, we make it to the Drake. A towering chestnut-brick structure juts up in the heart of the city. The historic

33-story complex boards thousands and teeters into a triangle at the apex. With Spanish Baroque influences, it looks a cross between a Spanish cathedral and a regular old Philly hotel.

I love it enough to call it home.

Nola offers a goodbye and I tell her thanks before hopping from the Escalade. My feet no sooner hit the curb than Lo clasps my hand in his. His other fingers run over the smoothness of my neck, and his eyes trail my collar. He sets his hands on the openings of my muscle shirt, touching the bareness of my ribs but also concealing my breasts from Philly pedestrians.

He observes me. Every little movement. And my heart speeds. "Is she watching us?" I whisper, wondering why he suddenly looks like he wants to devour me. *It's part of our lie*, I remind myself. *This isn't real.*

But it feels real. His hands on me. His warmth on my soft skin.

He licks his bottom lip and leans closer to whisper, "In this moment, I'm yours." His hands run through the armholes of my shirt and he settles them on my bare shoulder blades.

I hold my breath and immobilize. I am a statue.

"And as your boyfriend," he murmurs, "I really hate to share." Then he playfully nibbles my neck, and I smack him on the arm but fall victim to his teasing.

"Lo!" I shriek, my body squirming underneath his teeth that lightly pinches my skin. Suddenly, his lips close together, kissing, sucking the base of my neck, and trailing upward. My limbs tremble, and I hold tightly to his belt loops. He smiles, in between each kiss, knowing the effect he has on me. His lips press to my jaw . . . the corner of my mouth . . . he pauses. And I restrain from taking him in my arms and finishing the job.

Then he slips his tongue inside my mouth, and I forget about the fakeness of his actions and believe, for this moment, that he's truly mine. I kiss back, a moan caught in my throat. The sound invigorates him, and he pushes closer, harder, rougher than before. *Yes.*

And then I open my eyes and see the absence of the Escalade on the curb. Nola's gone. I don't want this to end, but I know it must. So I break the kiss first, touching my lips that swell.

His chest rises and falls heavily, and he stares at me for a long moment, not detaching.

"She's gone," I tell him. I hate what my body eagerly aches for. I could so easily hike a leg around his waist and slam him against the building. My heart flutters in excitement for it. I am not immune to those warm amber eyes, the ones that a functioning alcoholic like Lo carries. Endearing, glazed and powerful. The ones that constantly scream *fuck me!* That torture me from here until eternity.

With my spoken words, his jaw hardens. Slowly, he peels his hands from me and then rubs his mouth. Tension stretches between us, and my very core says to *jump*, to pounce on him like a little Bengal tiger. But I can't. Because he's Loren Hale. Because we have a system that cannot be disrupted.

After a long moment, something clicks in his head, horrified. "Tell me you didn't blow some guy."

Oh my God. "I . . . uh . . . "

"Dammit, Lily." He starts wiping his tongue with his fingers and dramatically takes what's left of his flask and swishes it in his mouth, spitting it out on the ground.

"I forgot." I cringe. "I would have warned you . . . "

"I'm sure."

"I didn't know you were going to kiss me!" I try to defend. *Or else I would have found toothpaste in that frat's bathroom. Or some mouthwash.*

"We're together," he says back. "Of course I'm going to fucking kiss you." With this, he pockets his flask and aims his sights on the entrance to the Drake. "I'll see you inside." He spins around, walking backwards. "You know, in *our* apartment. That we share, as a *couple*." He smiles that bitter smile. "Don't be too long, love." He winks. And part of me utterly and completely crumbles to mush. The other part is just plain confused.

Reading Lo's intentions hurts my head. I trail behind, trying to unmask his true feelings. Was that pretend? Or was that real?

I shake off my doubts. We're in a three-year-long *fake* relationship. We live together. He's heard me orgasm from one room over. I've seen him sleep in his own puke. And even though our parents believe we're one small step from engagement, we'll never have sex again. It happened once, and that has to be enough.

Two

inspect the refrigerator's contents. Champagne and expensive brands of rum cram in most of the space. I open a drawer and discover a pathetic bag of carrot sticks. As a girl who frequently burns off thousands of calories by grinding on pelvises, I need my protein. I've heard enough mean comments about my emaciated figure to wish for meat on my ribs. Girls can be cruel.

"I can't believe you lied about groceries," I say, irritable. I slam the fridge closed and jump on the counter. For however historic the Drake claims to be, the inside looks more like a modern escape. White and silver appliances. White countertops. White ceilings and walls. If it wasn't for our red and gray upholstered furniture and framed Warhol-inspired art décor, we'd be living in a hospital.

"If I knew I was going to make a pit stop at Douchebag Row, I would have bought you a bagel at Lucky's."

I glare. "You ate this morning?"

He gives me a *duh* look. "Breakfast burrito." He pinches my chin, still taller than me even though I'm on the counter. "Don't look so glum, dear. I could have always stayed at the diner while you found your own way home. Want me to rewind time?"

"Yes, and while you're leaving me to escape the frat house, you can go and pick up groceries like you told Nola."

He sets his hands on either side of me, my breath hitching. "I

ADDICTED TO YOU · 17

change my mind. I don't like that reality." I want him to lean in, but instead, he edges back and starts gathering liquor bottles from the white cabinets. "Nola needs to think I feed you, Lil. You're looking a bit skeletal. When you breathe, I think I can see your ribs." *Boys* can be cruel. He pours whiskey into a square glass beside me.

I purse my lips and open a cabinet above his head. When I slam it, he flinches and spills whiskey all over his hands.

"*Jesus.*" He finds a towel to dab up the puddle of alcohol. "Did Mr. Kappa Phi Delta not do his job?"

"He was just fine."

"Just fine," Lo says, his eyebrows rising. "What every guy loves to hear."

Red welts surface on my exposed arms.

"Your elbows are blushing," he tells me, a smile growing as he re-pours. "You're like Violet from Willy Wonka, only you ate a magic cherry."

I groan. "Don't talk about food."

He leans over, and I stiffen. *Oh my* . . . Instead of taking me in his arms—something I imagine in a momentary lapse of weakness—he brushes the bareness of my leg while grabbing his cell from the charging dock. I immobilize again. The touch barely fazes him, but my insides ripple in eagerness and want. If he was a no-named redhead with splotchy acne, I may still feel this way. Maybe.

Maybe not.

My fantasy tangles: Lo keeping his fingers on my knee. Roughly leaning over me, trapping me beneath his weight. My back arching against the cabinets—

"I'll order pizza if you go take a shower. You smell like sex, and I'm reaching my limit of inhaling foreign male stench."

My stomach collapses, and my fantasy poofs into reality. I hate picturing Lo and me unchastely together because when I wake up, he stands inches from me, and I wonder if he can tell. Can he?

I scrutinize him while he sips his whiskey. After a lingering moment of silence, his brows scrunch and he looks at me like *what the hell?* "Am I going to have to repeat myself?"

"What?"

He rolls his eyes and takes a large swig, not even grimacing as the sharpness of the alcohol slides its way down. "You, shower. Me, pizza. Tarzan eat Jane." He bites my shoulder.

I ease back. "You mean Tarzan *likes* Jane?" I hop off the counter, about to go wash off the frat house from my skin.

Lo mockingly shakes his head. "Not this Tarzan."

"Alcohol makes you mean," I say casually.

He raises his glass in agreement while I pad down the hallway. Our spacious two bedroom apartment masquerades as our lovers' den. Pretending to be together for three years hasn't been simple, especially since we started the ruse as seniors in high school. When we decided on the same college, our parents actually proposed our living situation. They're not very conservative, but even so, I doubt they'd understand or agree with my lifestyle, bedding more guys than is appropriate for a young girl.

My mother cited my eldest sister's college experience as reason enough to share a space with my "boyfriend." Poppy's random roommate brought friends over at all hours, even during finals week, and she used to leave her dirty clothes (including panties) on my sister's desk chair. Her inconsiderate behavior was enough for my mother to settle on off-campus housing for me and push Lo right into my bedroom.

It's worked out for the most part. I remember a weight rising off my chest once the doors shut and my family was gone. Leaving me alone. Letting me be.

I step into the quaint-sized bathroom and shimmy off my clothes. Once in the steaming hot shower, I exhale. The water washes away the smell and grime, but my sins are here to stay. The memories don't vanish, and I desperately try not to imagine this morning. Waking up. I love the sex. It's the after part that I haven't quite figured out yet.

I squirt shampoo on my hand and lather it in my short brown locks. Sometimes I picture the future. Loren Hale working for his father's Fortune 500 company, dressed in a tight fitting suit that chokes at the collar. He's sad. I never see him smile in my imagined futures. And I wouldn't know how to rectify it. What does Loren Hale love? Whiskey, bourbon, rum. What can he possibly do past college? . . . I see nothing.

Maybe it's a good thing I'm not a fortune teller.

I'll stick to what I know. The past—where Jonathan Hale brought Lo to informal golf games with my father in attendance. Me by his side. They discussed what they always do. Stock, ventures and product placements for their respective trademarked brands. Lo and I played Star Wars with our golf clubs, and they chided us when I bruised Lo's ribs, swinging my light saber too haphazardly and too hard.

Lo and I could have been friends or enemies. We always saw each other. At boring conference waiting rooms. In offices. At charity galas. In prep school. Now college. What could have turned into a cootie-driven relationship with constant teasing transformed into something more clandestine. We shared all secrets, forming a club with a two-person quota. Together, we discovered superheroes in a small comics shop in Philly. Something about Havok's galactic adventures and Nathaniel Grey's time-traveling plights connected with us. At times, not even Cyclops or Emma Frost could fix our troubles, but they're still there, reminding us of more innocent times. Ones where Lo wasn't boozing and I wasn't sleeping around. They allow us to revisit those warm, unadulterated moments, and I gladly return.

I finish scrubbing last night's debauchery from my body and slip my arms in a terry cloth robe. I cinch it around my waist as I head into the kitchen.

"Pizza?" I ask sadly, noticing the bare counters. Technically they're anything but bare, but I've become so desensitized to Lo's liquor bottles that they might as well be invisible or another kitchen appliance.

"It's on its way," he says. "Stop giving me those doe eyes. You look like you're about to cry." He leans against the fridge, and I subconsciously eye the zipper to his jeans. I imagine his gaze on the strap to my robe. I don't look up to ruin the image. "When's the last time you've eaten?"

"I'm not sure." I have a one-track mind, and it doesn't involve food.

"That's discomforting, Lil."

"I eat," I defend poorly. I see him pulling my robe in my fantasy. Maybe I should drop it for him. *NO! Don't do it, Lily.* I finally look up and he watches me so carefully that my face immediately begins to heat.

He smiles into a sip of his glass. When he brings it down, he licks his lips. "Do you want me to unbutton them, love, or should I wait for you to get on your knees first?"

I gape, mortified. He saw right through me. I'm so obvious!

With his free hand, he pushes his button through the hole and slowly unzips, showing the hem of his black tight boxer-briefs. He watches my breathing go in and out, jagged and sporadic. Then he takes his hands off his jeans and leans his elbows on the counter. "Did you brush your teeth?"

"Stop," I tell him, way too raspy. "You're killing me." Seriously, my *entire* body, not just my lungs, hyperventilates.

His cheekbones sharpen, his jaw locking. He sets his drink down and then zips up his jeans, fishing the button back through.

I swallow hard and tensely hop on the gray wooden bar stool. I run shaky fingers through my tangled, wet hair. To stop replaying the moment, I pretend it never happened and go back to our earlier conversation. "It's a little difficult to constantly stuff my face when we never have food here." We eat out *way* too often.

"I don't think you have a problem stuffing your face," he says, "just not with food."

I bite my gums and flip him off. His words would hurt more from anyone else. But Lo has his own issue that rests in the palm of his hand. Everyone can see it, and as I glance between him and the drink, his crooked smile hardens. He presses the rim of the glass to his lips and turns his back on me.

I don't talk to Lo about *feelings*. About how it makes him feel to watch me bring home a different guy every night. And he doesn't ask me how it feels to watch him drown into oblivion. He stifles his judgment and I withhold mine, but our silence draws tension between us, inescapable. It pulls so taut that sometimes I just want to scream. But I keep it inside. I hold back. Every comment that undercuts our addictions fractures the system in place. The one where we both live being free to do as we please. Me, bedding any guy. Him, drinking all of the time.

The buzzer rings beside the door. Pizza?! I beam and head over to the speaker box in the foyer, pressing the button. "Hello?"

"Miss Calloway, you have a guest downstairs. Should I send her up?" says the female security attendant.

"Who?"

"Your sister, Rose."

I internally groan. No pizza. Time to pretend with Lo again—even though he's fond of keeping up the charade when no one's around, just to taunt me. "Send her up."

Lo goes into roadrunner mode and zips around the kitchen, shutting liquor bottles into locked cabinets, pouring his drink into a tinted blue cup. I click the remote and the flat-screen TV blinks to an action flick. Lo plops on the gray-stitched sofa and kicks his feet onto the glass coffee table, acting like we've been immersed in the movie for the past half hour.

He pats his lap. "Come here." His amber eyes swim with mischievousness.

"I'm not dressed," I retort. And the spot between my legs already pulses too heavily to be in touching distance of him. The thought electrifies my nerves.

"You're wearing a robe," Lo rebuts. "I've seen you naked plenty of times."

"When we were kids," I retort.

"And I'm sure your breasts haven't grown since then."

My mouth falls. "Oh, you are . . . " I find a pillow on the nearby chair and start assaulting him with it. I get two good hits in before he swoops his arms around my waist and pulls me on his lap.

"Lo," I warn. He's been teasing me *all day*, making it harder than normal to withstand him.

He stares at me deeply, and his hand moves past my kneecap, edging up the robe, and settling on the inside of my thigh. He stops there, not making the next move. *Fuck.* I quake beneath him, needing his actions to go further. Not thinking, I place my hand on his and shift his fingers towards the throbbing spot. I push them inside of me. He stiffens.

Holy . . . My toes curl, and I rest my forehead on his broad shoulder. I hold his hand in a strong vise, not allowing him to do anything without my permission. Just before I go to move his fingers in and out, a knock sounds on the door.

I jolt awake. What am I doing?! I can't look at Lo, I let him reclaim his hand, and I scuttle off him.

Lo hesitates. "Lil?"

"Don't talk about it," I say, mortified.

Rose knocks louder.

I stand to answer, walking with more tension *everywhere* than before.

I hear Lo's footsteps behind me, and then the creak of the faucet as he turns the handle. I glance back and see him rinsing his fingers with soap.

I'm an idiot. As I turn the knob, I inhale, trying to wipe my mind clean of the bad combo: sex and Loren Hale. Having him as my roommate is like dangling coke in front of a druggie. It'd be easier if I let myself at him, but I'd rather not turn our relationship into friends with benefits. He means more to me than the other guys I bed.

The door swings open, revealing Rose: two years older, two inches taller and two times prettier. She waltzes into the apartment, her Chanel handbag swinging on her arm like a weapon. Rose frightens children, pets and even grown males with her icy eyes and chilling glares. And if anyone can unmask our false pretense, it will be my fiercest sister.

Right now, I pale at even meeting Lo's gaze, let alone pretending to be in a relationship with him. I don't ask Rose why she's arrived uninvited and unannounced. This is her routine. It's as though she feels entitled to all places. Especially mine.

"Why haven't you answered my calls?" Her voice layers with frost. She lifts her large, round sunglasses to the top of her head.

"Umm . . ." In the foyer, I dig through a basket of keys that sits on a round table. It usually houses my runaway phone that has found every opportunity to jump ship from my person, and it doesn't help that I don't carry a purse—an issue Rose likes to reignite. But I have no use for an item that I'll lose in a boy's apartment or dorm. Then he may find a way to return it, and I'll have to interact with him a second time.

Rose huffs. "You lost it? *Again?*"

I resign the search, only finding a few dollar bills, bobby pins and car keys. "I guess. Sorry."

Rose turns her vulture eyes on Lo, who wipes his hands on a dish rag and tosses it aside. "What about you? Did you lose your phone too?"

"No. I just don't like talking to you."

Ouch. I cringe. Rose sucks in her cheeks as red heat flushes them. Her heels clap against the hardwood floors, nearing him in the kitchen.

His fingers whiten against the plastic blue cup that hides his liquor.

"I'm a *guest* in your apartment," Rose snaps. "Treat me with some respect, Loren."

"Respect is earned. Next time maybe you should call before you stop by, or maybe you should start with *hey Lo, hey Lily, how was your day,* not demanding things like a royal bitch."

Rose whips her head to me. "Are you going to let him talk to me like this?"

I open my mouth but words are lost to uncertainty. Rose and Lo constantly bicker to the point of annoyance, and I never know which one to support: my sister, who can be so mean at times that she'll spew hate until it hurts, even at me—or Lo, my best friend and my *supposed* boyfriend, my one constant.

"That's mature," Lo says with distaste, "make Lily choose sides like she's a dog that has to pick a favorite parent."

Rose's nose flares in protest, but her yellow-green, cat-like eyes attempt to soften. "I'm sorry," she tells me, surprisingly sounding apologetic. "I just get worried about you. We all do." The Calloways do not understand the word *alone* or how someone could want privacy from their family. Instead of being the rich, neglectful parents, mine happen to be all-consuming. We had a nanny when we were younger, but my mother immersed herself in every aspect of our lives—too involved at times but also incredibly devoted and nurturing. I would love my family and their clinginess if I wasn't so embarrassed about my daily (and nightly) activities.

Some things need to be kept secret.

"Well, you see me. I'm fine," I say, refusing to glance back at Lo. Two minutes ago, I was about ready to do anything and everything to him. That *want* to be pleased has not diminished, just my stupidity to do it with him has.

Her eyes narrow to slits and she gives me a long once-over. I tighten my robe, wondering if she can tell how my body feels by looking. Lo sure as hell can.

After a short moment, she retracts her claws. "I didn't come here for a fight." *Right . . .* "As you know, tomorrow is Sunday, and Daisy will be here for the luncheon. You've *claimed* to miss the past few because of exams, but it would mean a lot to our sister if you could spare a couple of hours to welcome her home."

My empty stomach clenches with guilt. "Yeah, sure, but I think Lo may have plans already, so he might not make it." Good, at least I can bail him out of the obligation.

Rose's lips purse as she directs her irritation at Lo. "What is more important than accompanying your girlfriend to a family event?"

Everything, I imagine him saying. His jaw twitches as he

withholds a smartass retort. Probably dying to mention how this is a function that happens *every* Sunday, regardless if Daisy attends or not.

"I have racquetball scheduled with a friend," he lies with ease. "I can cancel if it means that much to Greg and Samantha." Lo knows that if Rose is fussing over the luncheon, then my parents will surely blow steam if I show up without him on my arm. They'll draw unreasonable conclusions—like he's cheating on me, or heading down his old childhood past of partying too hard. He still does (maybe even more) but it's best they not know that.

"It means the world to them," Rose says, as if she has the power to speak for other people. "I'll see you two tomorrow." She stops by the door and eyes Lo's jeans and plain black T-shirt. "And Loren, try to dress appropriately."

She exits, her heels tapping in the distance.

I let out a long breath and reorient my mind. An impulse to finish what I started with Lo eats at me, and I know better than to return.

"Lily—"

"I'll be in my room. Don't come in," I order. I downloaded a new video yesterday called *Master of You*. I planned to watch it much later, but I'm going to shift my schedule.

"What about when the pizza arrives?" he asks, blocking my path into the hallway.

"I won't be long." I try to slide by, but he extends a hand to the wall.

His bicep flexes at the movement, and I take a huge step backwards. *No, no, no.*

"You're aroused," he says, his eyes still on mine.

"And if you hadn't teased me, I wouldn't be in this position," I say, frantic. "If I still can't satiate this, I'm going to have to spend my afternoon traipsing around Philly for a guy wanting an afternoon quickie. Thanks a lot."

Lo grimaces and drops his hands to his side. "Well now I'm stuck going to your family's lunch, so I guess we're even." He turns his body, letting me through.

"Don't come in," I warn him again, my eyes bugging. I'm more afraid of what I'll do to him if he does.

"I never do," he reminds me. With this, he heads to the kitchen and waves tersely, downing the rest of his whiskey.

After my second shower and self-medication in the form of porn stars and an expensive vibrator, I tug on actual clothes: a pair of jeans and a maroon V-neck.

Lo sits in the living room, eating pizza and flipping through channels. A new glass of whiskey balances on his leg.

"I'm sorry," I apologize quickly.

His eyes briefly flicker to me before returning to the television. "For what?"

Sticking your fingers in me. "For getting you involved in Sunday's luncheon." I uncertainly take a seat in a red recliner opposite the couch.

He watches me like he always does, assessing my current state. He swallows his bite of pizza. "Honestly, I don't mind going." He wipes his fingers on a napkin and picks up his glass. "Better your father than mine."

I nod. So true. "So . . . are we okay?"

"Are *you*?" His eyebrows rise.

"Mmm-hmm," I mumble and avoid eye contact by grabbing a slice of pizza and scurrying back to the safety of my chair. Safe distance, check.

"I'll take that as a *weak* yes, considering you can't so much as look at me right now."

"It's not you; it's me," I say through a mouthful, licking sauce off my finger.

"Again, what every guy loves to hear." I can feel his eyes grazing my body. "I'm not even coming on to you right now."

"Don't even start," I warn, holding up a finger. "I swear, Lo."

"Okay, okay." He sighs. "You're going to The Blue Room tonight, aren't you?"

I jerk back in shock. "How'd you know?"

He looks at me like *seriously.* "You rarely go to the same club more than three or four times. For a while, I thought we were going to have to move one city over so you could find a place to . . . " He pauses, trying to find the words. ". . . fuck." He flashes that bitter smile.

"Very funny." I pick a pepperoni off the cheese. "Do you need a sober driver tonight? I can drop you off somewhere before I leave." I have no problem shooing away beer and hard liquor.

"No, I'm going to the club with you."

I hold in my surprise. He only ventures out with me on selective nights, and they vary too often for me to make sense of them. "You want to go to The Blue Room? You do realize this is a dance club and not some smoky hole-in-the-wall bar?"

He shoots me another look. "I'm well aware." He swishes the ice cubes around in his glass, staring at the liquid. "Anyway, it'll keep us from staying out too late and missing tomorrow's luncheon."

He has a point.

"You're not going to care if I . . . " I can't even finish the thought.

"If you leave me to go bang some guy?" he says, kicking his feet on the coffee table beside the pizza.

I open my mouth but lose my thoughts again.

"No, Lil," he says, "I won't get in the way of what you want."

Sometimes I wonder about his desires. Maybe he does want to be with me. Or maybe he's still pretending.

Three

I remember the first moment when I realized I was different from other kids. And it had nothing to do with boys or sexual fantasies and everything to do with my family. I sat in the back of my sixth grade English class, tugging down my plaid skirt required of all prep school kids. As the teacher left, a few boys scooted their desks to mine, and before I could form a reason for their closeness, they whipped out soda cans. Diet Fizz. Fizz Lite. Fizz Red. Just plain Fizz.

They took swigs and then left the cans scattered on my desk. The last boy opened his can of Cherry Fizz and smiled mischievously. "Here," he said, actually handing me the soda. "I popped your cherry."

The boys snickered and I turned the color of Fizz Red that stained a ring on my notebook.

In retrospect, I should have thanked them for buying all the Fizzle products. Every soda bought from the vending machine would line my pockets one way or another. They were probably the sons and daughters of oil tycoons, not nearly as exciting as being able to say that my father created the company that outperformed Pepsi last year. But I was too shy and mortified to do anything but sink further in my desk and wish for invisibility.

Lo can relate in some ways. He isn't faced with his family fortune on billboards and in restaurants, but every would-be mother knows a thing or two about Hale Co. products. Baby powder, oils, diapers, basically anything for a little newborn is created by the company. So Fizzle drinks may appear all over the world, but at least the Calloway name isn't scribbled on the label.

Only in my family's ring of socialites and business investors do we have to worry about teasing and reputations. Everywhere else, we're just two spoiled rich kids.

All throughout prep school, guys harassed Lo, calling him *baby*—not even close to being endearing. They even vandalized his gym locker by pouring Hale Co. rash powder on his clothes. Lo was an easy target. Not because he was skinny or short or shy like me. He had lean muscles to his name and even outran a soccer player. Lo chased him down the halls after learning he keyed his new Mustang.

But Lo only had one friend throughout his adolescence. And without a male entourage, he became enemy number one for other guys. An outcast to be picked on.

I regret most of my actions, and high school is full of wrong choices and bad decisions. Sleeping with someone who tormented Lo was one of them. I didn't care when it happened, but afterwards, I couldn't be more ashamed. I still am, and I wear it like a thick scar.

College changed everything for the better. Away from the small inclusive prep school, I no longer have to worry about gossip finding its way back to my parents. The freedom offers me more opportunities. Parties, clubs, and bars practically serve as a second home.

Tonight at The Blue Room, the ceiling glows with hundreds of glass bulbs. Midnight fabric drapes overhead, veiled as a night sky. True to its name, everything in the massive club is decked in a shade of blue. The dance floor blinks in teal and the upstairs furniture has navy velveteen chaises and buttoned chairs.

My black shorts stick to my sweaty thighs, and my silver halter dips low in the back but sucks to my clammy skin—the result of cramming two bodies in a bathroom stall. Blue toilet seats? Check. I thought I'd be floating on a high after having sex, but he barely satiated my desires. Plus, the heat makes me feel gross.

I spot Lo at the bar, his jaw tightening as he watches the bartender dart from one end to the other, the counter full of young patrons waiting to be served. Lo looks more peeved than usual, and I notice a blonde in a bandaged red dress sitting on a stool to his left, her long bare legs brushing up against his thigh. He acts oblivious to her advances, keeping his hardened gaze on the liquor bottles that tower behind the bartender.

"Come on, Lo," I encourage under my breath.

Then a guy sidles up and grabs my waist, dancing behind me. I ignore him, but he tries to move my hips while he rubs his pelvis against me.

The blonde beside Lo bites her lip and runs a hand through her hair flirtatiously. She leans in and says something to him, and I wish I was close enough to hear.

Lo's eyebrows bunch together, and I already see where the conversation is headed. He replies back and the girl's face twists in contempt. With venom in her eyes, she retorts something and departs with her blueberry martini in pinched fingers.

I curse and disentangle my dance partner from my backside. Quickly, I rush to the bar and replace the blonde. "What was that?" I ask.

"Go away. I'm busy and bodies are still here that you can fuck." He takes a large swig of beer, washing down his statement.

I inhale strongly, trying to let his comment brush off my shoulders. Trying to ignore his sudden moodiness. Some days, he can be sexy. Others, he can crush you with a glare. I narrow my eyes at the deep royal bottle in his hand that says *Berry Beer*.

"What the hell are you drinking?" It's been months since Lo has ingested anything weaker than port wine.

"All their liquor is fucking *blue*," he complains. "I'm not drinking blue whiskey. *Or* blueberry vodka."

At least I found the source of his agitation. The bartender approaches and I shake my head at him since I still plan on being the sober driver. He takes an order from a couple of other girls by my side instead.

I lean an elbow on the counter, facing Lo. "I'm sure it's not that bad."

"I'd offer you a sip, but I don't know where your mouth has been."

I glower. "I don't want your Berry Beer anyway."

"Good."

He chugs the bottle and motions for another at a lady bartender. She pops the cap and slides it over.

I take a quick peek back at the electric blue dance floor, and my eyes meet with . . .

Oh no. I spin back and plant my gaze on the racks of liquor and then bury my head in my hands. Maybe he didn't see me. Maybe we didn't make eye contact. Maybe it's all in my mind!

"Hey, can I buy you a drink?" He touches my shoulder. He's *touching* my shoulder. I glimpse from my palm to steal a glance at Lo. He looks detached from the situation, half his leg sliding off the stool, as though ready to go and give me space that he thinks I need.

"I didn't get your name," the guy adds. A redheaded girl beside me stands to leave, and I want to scream out for her to come back. *Keep your butt in that seat!* As she disappears, the guy scoots onto the stool, his body language open for me.

My luck has officially been thrown in the toilet bowl.

I lift my head, avoiding his bushy blond eyebrows and the

stubble around his chin. Yep, he's the guy I led to the bathroom. He's the one who locked the stall, pulled down my panties, grunted and heard me moan. At least he looks twenty-something, but I can't discern his exact age. I don't ask. In fact, I don't ask *anything*. My confidence has sputtered out with my climax, and all I feel is the heat of shame blooming across my ears.

I manage to mumble an answer. "My name is Rose." Albeit a lie.

Lo lets out a short laugh at this, and the guy puts an arm on the bar, leaning forward into my personal space to see my friend. "You two know each other?"

"You could say that," Lo says, finishing off another beer. He motions to the lady bartender again.

"You're not her ex or anything, are you?" the guy wonders, easing back just a little. *Oh yes, please go away.*

Lo wraps a hand around his new Berry Beer. "She's all yours, man. Have at her."

I am slowly dying inside.

The guy nods to me. "I'm Dillon." *I don't care. Please go away.* He extends his hand with a giddy grin, maybe expecting a round two. Thing is, I don't do round twos. Once I sleep with a guy, it ends there. Nothing more, ever again. It's a personal rule that I've sustained thus far. I won't break it, especially not for *him*.

I shake his hand, not knowing exactly how to shoo him off without being rude. Some girls have an easy time with saying *no*. Me on the other hand . . .

"What are you drinking?" He tries to flag down the male bartender who's busy with serving a group of girls. One wears a tiara and an *I'm 21!* sash.

"Nothing," I say just as a lady bartender in cut-off shorts and a cropped blue top stops in front of us.

"What can I get you?" she asks over the music.

Before I can add, *I don't drink* to the statement, Dillon says, "A rum and Fizz and a Blue Lagoon."

"We only have blueberry rum," she reminds him.

He nods. "That's fine."

She starts fixing up our orders, and I squeak out, "I actually don't drink."

His face drops. "You don't drink?" The disbelief makes me question my normality. I guess a sober body in a club is hard to come by. "So . . . " He scratches his stubbly cheek. "You're sober right now?"

I think I just died a second time. He thinks I'm a weirdo for having sober sex in a nightclub. My neck is turning violent red, and I want to stick my head in a hole. Or an ice bucket. "I drink," I mumble under my breath. "Just not tonight. I'm driving."

The bartender sets the blue cocktail on a napkin, and Dillon pushes it towards me. "Go ahead. You can always get a cab." Ulterior motives glimmer in his eyes. He's imagining what I'll do drunk, considering I wasn't too prudish sober. But that was before. And this is now—when my hunger to get laid has diminished considerably. At least with him.

"She doesn't want it," Lo snaps, clenching his fifth beer so tightly I think it might shatter.

"I thought you told me I could 'have at her'?" Dillon asks, using air quotes for effect.

"That was before you started fucking with my ride home. I need her sober, so go find another girl to buy blue volcanoes for."

"Blue Lagoon," I correct him.

"Whatever," Lo says into his swig of beer.

Dillon's eyes darken. "She has a mouth. Let her speak for herself."

Wow, this took a turn.

Lo rotates his body towards Dillon for the first time. "I bet you know all about that mouth, right?"

"OhmyGod," I mutter unintelligibly.

"Hey, don't fucking talk about her like that," Dillon tries to defend my honor.

What is going on?!

Lo raises his brows. "So now you're suddenly chivalrous, coming to her defense? You *banged* her in the bathroom. Don't act like you're the good guy in this situation."

"Stop, Lo." I shoot him a warning look that may be lost beneath my flushed cheeks. If he starts a fight, I'll be barred from the club.

"Yeah, Lo . . . *stop*," Dillon says in challenge. My face is so hot I think my skin might have second degree burns. Lo stares at Dillon for a long moment, unblinking.

"I'm not drunk enough for this shit," Lo announces. He rises from the stool and closes out his bar tab quickly. While I wait, Dillon clasps my wrist and I try to peel away.

"Can I have your number?" he asks.

Lo tucks his wallet in his back pocket. "She doesn't know how to say *no*. So I'm going to do it for her." *Thank you*. But instead of actually saying anything, Lo flips him off.

I don't look at Dillon. Lo. Or any other person in The Blue Room. I speed out of the club, wanting nothing more than to evaporate from the moment and flutter into the air.

After sliding into my sporty BMW, Lo silently joins me. The car ride home stays that way except for the sound of Lo unscrewing his flask and chugging it like he's been trapped in the Sahara desert for a week. We avoid talking or mentioning the bad night until we enter the apartment.

I throw my keys in the basket by the door, and Lo bolts for

the locked liquor cabinets. My hand shakes, and I tuck a flyaway hair behind my ear. I need a release.

The familiar sounds of clinking bottles fill the kitchen. "Do you want something to drink?" Lo asks, concentrating on his concoction.

"No. I'm going to call someone to come over. If they're still here in the morning, can you do the usual?"

He hesitates, and the bottle of bourbon freezes above his glass. "I may be passed out. I've been drinking shitty beer all night." Oh. He's about to get wasted.

"We have the luncheon in the morning," I say, my voice strained. Few things instigate a true fight between us, but I sense one brewing.

"I know. I'll be awake for it, but maybe not to help you. That's all I'm saying."

My chest heaves. "You're the one who ruined my night. You didn't have to come to the club with me and start an argument," I vent. "Now I'm the one who has to suffer because you didn't want to drink blue fucking vodka."

"Fine, go back to the club and be annoyed by that prick all night. I did you a favor, Lily."

Irrational anger surges through me and I push one of the stools hard. It knocks over and breaks a rung. I crawl back inside myself, instantly feeling bad about hurting a piece of furniture.

"Whoa," Lo snaps. "Don't Hulk Smash the apartment."

His addiction is screwing with my addiction. Alcohol trumps sex in this place, and that kills me. Or at least the part of me that *needs* a good lay, preferably one that lasts longer than five minutes.

I stare at the broken stool and feel so dumb. I squat and right it up. Mood swings. Lo understands what it's like to turn into a needy freak, but I still can't look him in the eyes.

"You're a big girl, Lil," he says after a moment of silence. I hear him stir ice into his drink. "If you want to hook up with someone then you should be the one to kick them out. I'm not stopping you from having sex."

I don't know why it feels like that or why his words upset me so much. I don't move until I feel Lo stealing my newly bought phone from my pocket. I frown as he scrolls through my contacts and lands on a number for a male escort service. He dials and presses the receiver to my ear while he sips his drink.

I take the phone from him and mouth, *thanks*.

He shrugs noncommittally, but the muscles around his shoulders tense. Without another word, he leaves for his bedroom. My nerves settle and the anticipation begins to build.

The line clicks. "Hello, how may we be of service?"

The alarm on my phone blares for the third time, an annoying harp melody that I seriously reconsider. I wiggle from my covers, careful not to hit the male body splayed out on the other side. I shouldn't have let him spend the night, but I lost track of time. Even though these . . . well, *sex workers* are on the clock, excitement fills their eyes at the sight of a young client who isn't middle-aged and obese. So sometimes *they* prompt the overtime, but this instance, it was my doing.

Will he want to stay for breakfast? I don't know sex worker protocol that well or what to say or do afterwards. Usually I have Lo bang on my door and tell the guy to beat it. Much easier. The digital clock on my white nightstand glows red. Ten in the morning. I have an hour to primp and shower for lunch at the Villanova mansion.

Quickly, I toss on a T-shirt that stops at my thighs and stare at my roadblock: a well-built, thirty-something male with tattoos sprawling along his torso. His limbs are tangled in my purple sheets, passed out from all the sex. Shouldn't he be used to it by now? You don't see me acting like I downed a bottle of sleeping pills.

"Hey," I say, timid. He barely stirs. *Okay, Lily, get it together.* If Lo believes I can do this, I surely can. Right?

I take a deep breath, battling the intense blush and nerves that threaten to rise. *Please don't start a conversation with me.*

"Hey!" I shake his legs and he lets out a long, bear-like groan. Yes! The sex worker rubs his eyes and props himself on his elbow.

"Whattimeisit?" he slurs.

"Late. I need you to leave."

He plops back on the mattress with a long whining noise. What was that? Did he just die? "Let me wake up, will you?"

"I have to be somewhere soon. You have to go."

He squints at me, the light too penetrating for his lethargic eyes. "While you get dressed, I'll make us some coffee. How's that?"

"I didn't pay you to hang around," I say, finding some confidence. Why is this so difficult? Are my requests that unreasonable?

He shoots me an annoyed look, and I instantly feel like a bitch. I shrink back.

"Noted." He stands to collect his jeans and button-down. *Yes, he's leaving.* But then, he stops and eyes the length of my body. I go rigid. "For someone who was anything but reserved last night, you look incredibly uncomfortable right now." He waits for me to explain.

I open my mouth and shut it, not sure what to say.

"Was the sex not up to your standards?"

I turn my head. "Can you just leave?"

"You're embarrassed? I don't understand . . . " Of course I'm *embarrassed*. I called a sex worker out of desperation, because it sounded nice, because I knew it would relieve something in me that ached for it. I wish I could be one of those girls who has the guts to do it because they're exploring their sexuality, but with me, I needed him to fulfill a desire, one that does nothing but torment me. And he's reminding me of everything I hate about myself. That I let my downstairs brain control my night. That I can't be a normal girl and just forget about sex for one *second*. Just one.

"Did I hurt you?" he asks, sounding concerned now.

"No," I say quickly. "It was great. I'm just . . . " *lost*. ". . . thank you."

My words spin his features into sadness. "If I leave, you aren't going to do anything . . . " He thinks I'm suicidal?

I inhale deeply. "I need you to go so I can head to a family event."

He nods, understanding. "Okay." He buttons the last of his shirt and adds, "You're fantastic in bed by the way."

"Thanks," I mumble, stripping my sheets.

The door closes, and my muscles don't relax like I thought they would. The conversation replays, and I feel strangely about it. He saw through me. Not many people do.

I don't have time to wallow in a self-deprecating puddle. The luncheon starts in less than an hour. I trip over a pair of sneakers on my way to the shower. While I wash off last night, I contemplate waking Lo. I'd rather let him sleep off his drunken stupor than force him to interact with my family.

By the time I hop out of the shower and change into a mint-green dress, I decide to check on Lo and make sure he's sleeping on his side. He rarely pukes when he passes out, but it doesn't mean it can't happen. Before I retreat from my room, I scour my closet for a rare purse. To avoid my mother's ridicule, it's best to be as normal as possible. I find a white Chanel with a gold chain (a birthday gift from Rose) shoved beside a broken pair of heels.

I unclick the latch. My runaway phone has reappeared, which is pretty worthless considering I already transferred my number and contacts onto a new iPhone.

I scroll through the old missed calls and few text messages that were delivered before I purchased my new cell. My heart stops as I open a text from Rose. Sent about the same time she last left my apartment.

> Jonathan Hale is coming to the luncheon. Tell Loren.—Rose

No, no, no. Lo maybe, possibly, could have stayed home today. I could have formed a weak "he's sick" excuse. Ditching on my family is a minor infraction. Ditching on his father is suicide.

Hurriedly, I toss the phone on my bed and head to his bedroom with less than half an hour to get ready. We're cutting this close.

I knock once and let myself in.

Unlike my bedroom, Lo's walls and shelves are covered with personality. Penn paraphernalia fits in nooks and crannies, like a red and blue clock and a Quakers bobble head. Photographs of us hang almost everywhere. Mostly for appearances' sake. On the dresser sits a framed portrait of Lo kissing my cheek. It looks forced to me, and little things like this make my belly flop, reminding me of our biggest lie.

My sisters believe I store my clothes in the guest bedroom closet for more space. In truth, I like staying in that minimalistic room. No photographs. Just brightly colored Leonid Afremov paintings of Paris. Though, sometimes they make me dizzy.

Lo lies fully clothed on his champagne-colored duvet. He's curled up on his side, and his light brown hair sticks in different directions. In his right hand, he cuddles an empty bottle of Macallan, a ten-thousand-dollar whiskey.

Five more liquor bottles scatter the ground. Some half-full, others dry. But those have to be from other nights entirely. He has a high tolerance, but not *that* high. All of these bottles would knock out a whole football team and probably kill him. I try not to think about that.

I go to the bathroom and wet a hand cloth with warm water. Back in his room, I sidle to his low bed, the mattress coming up to my legs. I bend over and press the towel to his forehead.

"Lo, time to get up," I say softly. He doesn't stir. This isn't the first time I've tried to wake Lo up for something important.

I abandon him passed out on the bed and race around his room, sweeping empty bottles and locking away full ones. When all the alcohol disappears, I turn my attention back on him. "Loren Hale!" I yell.

Nothing.

I try shaking his arms, his legs, his waist—anything that will make him rise to join the living.

Nothing.

He stays gone to the world and inside I'm cursing him for choosing this day to be so wasted. Time slips by, and my pulse heightens with every second. I can't leave him. Lo wouldn't do that to me, and if we go down, we go down together.

I unzip my dress and step out. In nothing but a pair of boyshort panties and a plain bra. At least I know what to do in these situations from his past experiences. Hopefully it will work.

With the little upper body strength I possess, I grab under his armpits and tug him off his bed. We both clamber to the floor, and he lets out a soft groan.

"Lo?!"

He sinks back into unconsciousness, and I quickly spring to

my feet and drag his heavy body towards the bathroom. "You. So. Owe. Me," I say with each jerk. The words aren't true. We've both banked enough favors that we no longer even count.

I kick open the glass door to the shower and pull him in with one last heave. His head lies in my lap, and even though I wear beige undies, I'm not too embarrassed. How can I be when he lies vulnerable in my arms? He may not even remember this in an hour. Better my underwear soaking than my dress.

I stay on my knees, panting as I reach up for the faucet nozzle. I turn the water to the coldest cold.

It sprays down on the both of us, and within ten seconds, Lo sputters awake, spitting out water from his mouth like I'm drowning him. I turn the water to a warmer temperature, and he tries to right himself, lifting his torso off my lap. He slips when he attempts to simply lean on the tiled wall.

His eyes close and open sluggishly. He still hasn't spoken a word.

"You have to bathe," I tell him from my corner of the shower. "You stink like booze."

He makes an incoherent mumbling noise, tightening his eyes shut. We don't have time for this. I stand, grab the shampoo and soap and return to his side while the water rains down on us.

"Come on," I breathe softly, remembering how he hates when I speak in my "normal" voice on bad mornings. Apparently it sounds like knives slaughtering baby pandas. His words, not mine.

He lets me pull his T-shirt over his head and barely helps me maneuver his arms through the holes. Water beads on the ridges of his abs, a runner's build that usually stays hidden beneath clothes. No one would expect how fit he is. Or that he does occasionally hit the gym. That's the best kind—the surprise of something *more* underneath something already handsome. I envy all the girls who get to experience that feeling for the first time with him. I shake my head. *Focus.* I train my gaze *off* the curves of his biceps and concentrate on his jeans. Without another thought, I unbutton them and yank down.

When the heavy, sopping denim sticks at his thighs, his eyelids flutter open. I blush uncontrollably even though this isn't the first time I've undressed him.

He peers down at me. "Lil . . . " he mumbles, sounding lethargic.

Okay, we do not have time for *this.* I yank. Hard. And they finally surpass his damn muscular thighs and to his ankles where the denim is much easier to manage. Now he's soaked in nothing but his black boxer-briefs, and I have to use all of my strength on the task at hand.

I take the soap and lather it into a loofa and wash across his lean torso, down his abs . . . umm . . . skipping that area . . . and to his thighs and legs. I don't have much time to wash his back, but I don't think it will be a problem.

The worst part is the smell. A bourbon scent emits from his pores, and after trying different soaps and colognes, we found some that work to mask the repugnant odor.

His addiction scares me sometimes. Alcoholism can destroy livers and kidneys, and one day, he may not wake up from a night of bingeing. But how can I tell him to stop? How can I judge him when I am nowhere near ready to let go of my crutch? So for right now, this is the best I can do.

I lather the shampoo into his hair while he keeps his eyes open, using his own strength to remain somewhat conscious. He's coming to, but I'm not sure he realizes where we are yet. "Have fun?" I ask while my fingers basically give him a scalp massage.

He nods slowly, and his gaze lowers to my bra—beige and now pretty much see-through. *Uh . . .*

I pinch his arm, and he lifts his head back to me. His eyes change, the amber color swimming and intensifying in the steam. He stares deeply, too intense. I hate when he looks at me like that. And he knows it. His hand rises and caresses the back of my neck. *Whaaat . . .* I shake out of my confusion and jerk away with a scowl. I don't have time to deal with his hungover, delirious moves.

He gives me a smirk. "Just practicing."

"Do you know what time it is?" I grab a plastic cup, fill it with water, and dump it over his head, not caring as the shampoo burns his eyes. He squints and mumbles a curse, but he's too tired to actually rub it off.

When the soap suds fizzle out, I drape his arm over my shoulder and lug his body to his bedroom. This time, he cooperates and helps me.

He collapses on the duvet, and I spend the next few minutes drying him off with a towel like he's my pet dog. He stares at the ceiling, transfixed. I try to talk to him, needing him responsive for the luncheon.

"We stayed out really late last night for Charlie's saxophone gig at Eight Ball," I remind him as I search in the drawers for a suitable outfit.

He laughs lightly.

"What's so funny?"

"Charlie," he muses with bitterness. "My *best* friend."

I swallow hard and take a deep breath, trying to keep it together. I can do this. I find another pair of boxer-briefs, slacks and a powder blue button-down. I turn back to him, debating on whether or not I'll have to see his junk.

His sopping underwear soaks his comforter, too wet to leave on with a pair of pants.

"Can you change yourself?" I ask. "I just want to limit the number of times I see your penis."

He tries to prop his weight up and succeeds, holding himself upright on the bed. I'm impressed. And also, sort of, starting to regret talking about his penis. Especially with the way he's looking at me. He blinks a few times before saying, "Leave them on the bed." I set the stack of clothes beside him and grab my dress that's slung over his desk chair.

Worry still beats in my chest. I enter my room and replace my soaked underwear before slipping into my dress. Is he going to be coherent enough to have a conversation?

In prep school, his father used to ground Lo as he stumbled home from a late night of drinking or when he found his raided and drained liquor cabinet. When Lo's grades started tanking, Mr. Hale threatened to ship his son to a military academy for young boys, thinking the structure would be beneficial for a rowdy teenager. I'm not even sure he connected the events and understood that Lo's real problem was alcohol.

In reflection, he needed AA or rehab, not a blue blood manufacturing camp. Instead, I gave him me: a scapegoat for his constant bingeing. That summer, we made the deal. And as soon as he told Jonathan that he'd started dating Greg Calloway's daughter, his slate wiped blank. Mr. Hale slapped him on the back, told Lo that I'd be good for him, and if I wasn't, he'd find a way to change his behavior. So we masked our lifestyles in order to continue them.

Even though Lo hardly became a model citizen in his early teenage years, my parents were overjoyed at the news of our relationship. The sound of a Calloway-Hale union surpassed the quality of the man on my arm. As if it's 1794 and our marriage will garner military power and land rights. Hello, we are *not* royalty.

With our new alliance, we lied for each other and hid our infidelities, playing the role of doting boyfriend and girlfriend. The deeper we sink, the harder it is to crawl out. I fear the moment where neither of us can breathe again—when someone discovers our secrets. At any moment, everything can crumble beneath us. The dangerous game both excites and terrifies me.

I return to Lo's room and relax when I see him fully dressed, leaning his side wearily against the bedframe. His shirt is unbuttoned and untucked.

At least he has pants on.

"Can you help me?" he asks casually. Without slurring!

I nod and take small steps towards him. I skim the hem of his button-down, and his hot liquor breath prickles my skin. To avoid any bubbling feelings, I make a mental note to grab a pack of mints before we leave.

"I'll be fine by the time we get there," he assures me.

"I know." I avoid eye contact as my fingers fumble with the button by his taut abs.

"I'm sorry," he says softly and then laughs. "At least I gave you something to fill your spank bank."

I sigh heavily. I don't *purposefully* fantasize about Loren Hale to get aroused. That would be way too awkward each time I meet his eyes. It's already bad enough it happens by accident. "You're not in my spank bank, Lo." I think he might complain or laugh, but he looks confused and kind of hurt. I don't have time to dig through the meaning.

"Sorry then," he snaps, agitated. He feels bad, and I suddenly wish I'd just played along. He loses his footing in his drunk stupor and falls back into the mattress. To catch myself from tumbling to the floor, I hold on to his arms tightly, but that sends me right into him. And when time starts to slow, I realize that my hand is planted firmly on his chest; my legs are pressed against his, and the only things that really separate us are his pants and my dress.

He breathes heavily, his muscles constricting underneath my weight. Something deep pulses in me, something bad. His hands stay on the small of my back, on the dip above my ass. And as he licks his lips, watching me peruse his body with eager, wanting eyes, I tap into the sensible part of my brain. I mutter, "Your dad is going to be at the luncheon."

His face blanches, and he lifts me up onto my feet like I weigh nothing. "We need to go," he says, leaving the last few buttons undone. He eyes the clock. "*Now*." His worry clears most of his hangover, and I hope that it will be gone by the time we reach Villanova.

Four

W e're ten minutes late, but we're not the only ones.
My father missed his flight from New York back
to Philly because his personal pilot had the flu. He
had to arrange a new one to fly his private jet. The whole ordeal
shouldn't take long, but my father requires a background check
on all his drivers. The new pilot will probably have to prove his
competence with at least an hour of test flights. My mother always meets him when he lands, so she's also MIA from this supposedly *important* luncheon.

But I'm not complaining. The extra time will help Lo become
a bit more responsive. We sit on the patio with a view of a large
infinity pool and yellow rose bushes. The mid-morning sun glints
against champagne glasses, filled with mimosas. Berries, cheeses,
crackers and petite sandwiches systematically line a white-linen
tablecloth. Everything stays in its proper place, on tiered platters
or doilies.

My stomach gurgles, and thankfully no one waits for our parents to chow down. Jonathan Hale hasn't arrived either, and he
claims he's caught in traffic, but I have a suspicion he's waiting in
his car, not wanting to be at the luncheon without my father
present.

Lo keeps his arm on the back of my chair, settling into the

charade. His closeness makes my body tense, and I end up sitting on the edge of my seat, as far away from *that* hand as I can be. Hopefully my distance is not too obvious. I ache to be touched more sinfully, but I know I shouldn't at this inappropriate time. And realize I *should* be near my supposed boyfriend. It's all so complicated.

"Pass the book over here," Poppy says, holding out her hand. Like the rest of the Calloway girls, my eldest sister stands out among crowds. A small mole on her upper lip screams Marilyn Monroe sexiness, and her skin looks far more tanned than the rest of ours, like a sun-kissed brunette. When I meet Poppy at malls or outlet stores, she turns heads. Sometimes I do too, but I think it has more to do with my chicken legs—so skinny they could crack like a wishbone. Not attractive, I know, my mother usually reminds me.

Daisy slides her modeling book to Sam, who passes it to his wife. Poppy grins as she flips the pages. "These are gorgeous, Dais."

The compliment doesn't faze my youngest sister. She's too busy munching on tiny sandwiches like she hasn't eaten in the past month.

"How was Fashion Week? Meet any cute boys?" I bat my lashes, trying to be funny but probably looking goofy and awkward.

Daisy snorts. "I think Mom ruined any kind of game I could have." She ties her brown hair into a pony, making her unblemished skin and narrow face look all the more striking.

"Wait? Mom went with you?" I shouldn't be too surprised. Our mother tagged along to every single ballet rehearsal Rose had, even skipping family meals to watch her practice. She could have easily joined the cast of *Dance Moms*.

"Uh, *yeah*," Daisy says. "I'm fifteen, remember? Hell would freeze over before she let me do Fashion Week by myself. How did you not know that?"

"I'm kind of out of the loop."

"*That* is the understatement of the century," Rose says.

Poppy smiles. "Don't be mean, Rose. You're going to scare Lily off for another two months." We all know who the nice sister is. Still, I can't help but love Rose more. Maybe because we're the closest in age or because she actively tries to be a part of my life. I see her more than I do anyone else.

Rose sips her mimosa with tight lips.

Daisy points an accusing finger at me. "You haven't been to Sunday luncheon for *two months*?" She scrutinizes me, as if searching for any visible wounds. "How are you not dead?"

"I ask the same question all the time," Rose cuts in, "seeing as how I get crucified if I miss one."

"The perks of dating a Hale," Poppy says, this time sounding bitter too.

Lo's fingers tighten on the notch of my chair at the sound of his name.

My throat tightens. Poppy spent years convincing our parents to accept her boyfriend and welcome him into the Calloway brood. Since Sam had barely six figures to his name, my parents feared he wanted Poppy for her inheritance. So my father hired him at Fizzle even though Sam only had a high school diploma and a resume with Dairy Queen as his sole employment. Eventually, my father learned Sam's benevolent intentions and approved of their marriage. And subsequently my mother did too.

Now a small munchkin with Sam's dark hair and bright blue eyes runs somewhere around here. Poppy smiles often and has more maternal affection than our own mother, but she won't ever forget the judgment they cast on Sam or all the hassle, even if their intent was pure.

Her resent ricochets back to me since they'd swiftly embraced my relationship with Lo.

"If I could change my name I would," Lo says, the room blanketing with even more uncomfortable tension.

Poppy says, "Which one?" And the mood begins to lighten. The girls laugh at Lo's expense, but laughter is better than taut muscles and furtive glances. Lo has never been too keen on his full name. One reason why Rose always calls him Loren.

"When did you get so funny, Poppy?" Lo asks, tossing a grape in her lap. I'm surprised he chooses not to banter back with a flower insult, considering my mother named all four of us after plants. It's only embarrassing when we're all together in public, so I can deal.

"Resorting to food fights already, Loren?" Rose interjects. "The luncheon hasn't even officially begun."

"Now you know why they don't care if we bail for months," he tells her. "Mystery solved."

"Can I see Daisy's book?" I ask Poppy.

She hands it to me across the table and it knocks into the stem of my champagne glass. I curse under my breath and jump up before the orange juice stains my dress.

Lo quickly grabs a napkin, standing with me. He rests a hand on my arm and dabs the spill around my chest, thinking nothing of it. I guess no one else would either because we're together (not really), and my mind has begun a serious free-fall. A server enters with more towels, and I am burning too much to actually move.

"I'm sorry." Who am I apologizing to? Myself for being clumsy?

"Ohh, Lily is turning into a rose," Poppy teases.

Rose shoots her a glare at mentioning her name within a slight insult, and I only redden further.

Lo sets the napkin on the table, and whispers in my ear, "Be cool, love. It's just a little spill." He smiles in amusement and his breath tickles my skin. I practically ooze into his arms. He kisses me on the lips, so light that after his mouth has separated from mine, all I can think about is it returning.

The staff zips in and out of the patio, cleaning the mess around us like worker bees.

When everyone settles and I reattach my head to my body, I stiffly sit back down, and flip open Daisy's book. Lo leans into me to peek at the pictures, his thigh meshing against mine. *The photos.* Yes. I blink, focusing. In most of them, Daisy stands against a white backdrop without any makeup. Beauty shots, I suppose. I turn another page and my mouth falls.

She's naked! Or nearly naked. She stands with five-inch heels and wears a men's suit jacket. Nothing else. The shot focuses on her long bare legs and the sides of her breasts. She has slicked-back hair in a tight ponytail, and her makeup makes her look twenty-seven, not fifteen. Daisy's hips bend awkwardly in the pose, the only indication that it's high fashion and not *Penthouse*.

Lo whistles a long note, sounding as shocked as I feel.

"What's wrong?" Daisy asks, careening her head to try and see the photo.

"You're not wearing anything." I hold up the book so she can see which photo we're discussing. She stays perfectly calm, not even embarrassed. "I have underwear on. It's nude though."

"Did Mom see this?"

"Yeah, she suggested I try to book mature photo shoots. It'll increase my value."

Her value. As though she's a pig up for auction. "Do you like modeling?"

"It's fine. I'm good at it." *Okaaay.* That is not the answer I wanted to hear, but I'm not her mother. I skip these weekly events for a reason, and attaching myself to situations won't help me ease out of the Calloway household unseen.

Lo rubs his mouth, finding the right words. "You're fifteen,

Daisy. You shouldn't be taking off your clothes for cameras." His fingers brush against my shoulder, and he whispers in my ear, "You didn't even do that."

As if I've set the sexual standard. I gape and pinch his thigh. He cups my hand, intertwining my fingers in his, and even if I should pull away, I don't want to.

Rose cuts in, "Don't big brother her when you can't even remember her birthday, Loren."

Lo's jaw locks, his cheekbones sharpening. He reaches for his mimosa and then grabs my purse, searching the handbag for his thin flask.

My mind goes suddenly blank as the staff starts shuffling inside. I tap Lo on the arm, and he follows my gaze, stiffening to stone.

Our parents have arrived.

For the past twenty minutes, Lo and I have avoided our parents' focused attention. My mother fixates on Poppy's toddler, who busted her front tooth last Wednesday on the sidewalk. If I have to hear the words *plastic surgeon* one more time, I may need four mimosas and an attractive male server.

Jonathan Hale and my father whisper at the head of the table, enjoying their own private conversation. If their isolation bothers my mother, she doesn't let on. She fingers a string of pearls on her bony collar and listens intently to Poppy.

"How is Penn?"

I jolt at the question, immediately reanimating from my stupor. Since Rose attends Princeton, it's safe to say my father is speaking to Lo and me.

"Hard, lots of studying," Lo says briefly. His arm curls around my waist. I'm too nervous to be lusting after him.

"Same," I murmur. In my family, I'm "the quiet one," so it's easy to get away with monosyllabic answers.

My mother perks at the start of a new conversation. "Lily, my little pansy, how have you been?"

I grimace, glad she didn't actually name me Pansy. I can't believe that was even an option. "Fine."

"Are you two taking any classes together this semester?" She fingers her champagne glass, red lipstick staining the rim.

"Just one. Managerial Economics and Game Theory." As Business Majors, Lo and I are bound to share some classes, but we try to sparse those as much as possible. There is such a thing as too much Loren Hale.

Jonathan sets down his glass of whiskey. The irony is not lost upon me. "How are you doing in it?" he cuts to the point, eyes right on his son. Both Jonathan and my father look dapper in Armani suits, their hair not yet grayed and their strong jaws cleanly shaven. The difference lies in their features. Jonathan stares like he could rip out your heart. My father looks open enough to run in for a hug.

"I have an A," Lo says. My brows shoot up in surprise. An A? I'm barely passing, but Lo's naturally smart, almost never needing to study.

Jonathan glances at me, and I immediately start sinking in my chair—as though his pupils are too powerful to make contact with. "You look shocked. Is he lying?"

"What? No, I-I," I sputter. "We don't talk about grades . . . "

"You don't believe me, Dad?" He touches his chest. "I'm wounded."

Jonathan settles back in his chair. "Hmm." *Hmm?* What does that even mean?!

My father tries to lighten the suffocating atmosphere. "I'm sure Lily is keeping you focused on the important things."

Lo grins. "Oh, she definitely is."

"Gross," Rose deadpans. If only she knew he was talking about booze and *not* sex. My mother gives a circle of disapproving looks, full of the same ice that Rose inherited.

"Any graduation plans yet?" my father asks.

I think about Lo's future again, wearing a tight suit, working for his father, his lips pulled into a perpetual frown.

"We still have a year to decide," Lo answers.

"You both need to start formulating a plan," my father says, sounding critical.

A plan. I've been so focused on Lo that I haven't even begun to imagine my life past college. Where will I be? *What* will I be? White empty space fills the void. I'm unsure of what picture to paint.

"We just want to give school our full attention. Grades are really important to us." *Yeah right.*

My father folds his napkin on the table, about to switch topics. "Jonathan and I were discussing the upcoming Christmas Charity Gala sponsored by Fizzle and Hale Co. The press has been buzzing about the event for weeks, and it's important that everyone is present to show support."

"We'll be there," Lo says, raising his glass.

"Any news on a ring?" Poppy asks with a teasing smile.

"I'm still twenty," I remind her, shrinking. My mother missed the opportunity to call me Violet.

"You don't have *any* news?" Rose questions, her face sharpening.

I frown in confusion and shake my head. What is she going on about?

Her lips tighten in a thin line and she whispers to Poppy, who quickly whispers back.

"Ladies," my mother chides. "Don't be rude."

Rose straightens and sets her frosty gaze on me. "I think it's odd that you've been drinking orange juice and water."

"I'm driving," I tell her. What is with everyone and my choice to be sober? When did it become *abnormal* to refuse alcohol at a meal?

My mother huffs. "That's what Nola is for, Lily."

"Anderson as well," Jonathan adds.

Anderson the Nark. *Never.*

"Well, I have a reason to believe your choice of drink has nothing to do with driving," Rose says. *What?!*

"What are you insinuating?" My heart beats wildly. Please don't let it be what I think. Please, please, please. Lo squeezes my hip to reassure me, but whatever is coming is bad.

"Yes, Rose, what are you insinuating?" My mother comes to my defense.

"I have a friend who goes to Penn. She saw Lily walking out of the pregnancy center last month."

Last month . . . oh, jeez. I cover my eyes with a hand, and slouch so low in my seat, I'm practically eye-level with the table.

My father chokes on his drink, and Jonathan has gone very, very pale, a feat I didn't think possible for his Irish skin.

"Is this true?" my mother asks.

Yes.

I open my mouth. I can't say the real answer. *Yeah, I went there. I visit the health clinic to check for STDs every couple days, okay? And I take pregnancy tests. I am safe and I know it. Most people can't say that.*

Or the whole truth, *one afternoon the pink plus sign actually haunted me. They sent me to the pregnancy center for an ultrasound. False alarm, thankfully.*

"Lily, explain," my mother nearly shrieks.

Lo stares at me for a long moment before he realizes I have no capacity to form words, let alone lies.

"It was just a scare," he says and turns his attention to Rose. "It's funny how you choose now to bring this up when you've known for a whole month."

"I was waiting for Lily to tell me herself. I thought we were closer than this."

My lungs collapse.

"Why wouldn't you tell *me*?" my mother asks.

I swallow hard.

"Or me," Poppy says.

Daisy raises her hand and points to herself. "Me too!"

I press my fingers to my eyes before waterworks kick in. "It-it was nothing."

My mother's nose flares. "Nothing? An unplanned pregnancy is not *nothing*."

Dad cuts in, "You have your entire future ahead of you, and children will change the way your life works forever. You can't undo that." Yeah, I'm pretty positive a kid would hinder our lifestyles, a reason why I've been so careful thus far. I don't have the heart or strength to tell them everything. That if the pink plus sign stuck around, the kid wouldn't even belong to Lo.

I stand up quickly, my head pumping with helium. It floats but I still manage words. "I need some air."

"We're outside," Rose says.

Lo rises from his seat. "Air that you don't breathe." He places his palm on the small of my back.

"Loren," Jonathan growls.

"*What?*" he growls back, his gaze falling to his father's whiskey, envy and bitterness clouding his amber irises.

"It's been a long afternoon," my father says. "Lily looks pale. Take her inside, Loren."

Before anyone changes their mind, Lo ushers me through the French glass doors and into the nearest bathroom. I collapse on the toilet seat.

"Why would she do that?" My chest constricts with each breath. I tug at the tight fabric of my dress that suctions to my ribs. What if her friend saw me walk out of the sexual health clinic instead? How do I explain checking for STDs?

Lo kneels in front of me and presses a warm washcloth to my forehead. A flashback hits me—of doing the same to him. In less than a few hours, we've switched places.

"Rose can be cruel," Lo reminds me.

I shake my head. "She was hurt." And this is how Rose Calloway retaliates against someone who's affected her. "She wanted me to tell her first." I rub my eyes, trembling. How will Rose take the knowledge that I sleep around? Will she hate me afterwards? I have no clue. Predicting her reaction has caused restless nights, and so I decided it's safe to just keep my nighttime activities to myself. I thought it would be easier on everyone.

"Breathe, Lil," he whispers. When I inhale and exhale in synchronization, he deserts the washcloth for his flask. After a couple swigs, he wipes his mouth with his hand and rests against the sink cabinets.

"This is getting harder." I stare at my hands, as though they hold my intangible lies.

"I know," he breathes. I wait for him to say the words, *I'm done pretending.*

Instead, we eat the silence. The swish of his alcohol and my sniffles are the only music to our misery.

Someone knocks on the door, and Lo stuffs the flask back into my purse.

"Lily? Can I talk to you?" Poppy asks.

Lo glances at me for what to do. I nod. And he goes to the sink, putting his mouth underneath the faucet. He spits water back into the bowl and then opens the door.

Poppy gives him a warm, maternal smile. "Your father wants to talk with you. He's waiting in the parlor."

Lo practically slams the door on his way out.

Poppy fiddles with her fingers while I stare at the black marble floor. "I didn't know Rose was going to say anything. She told me this morning, and I thought we'd have a chance to talk to you before announcing anything to Mom and Dad."

I unclip my heels and set my toes on the cool marble, not strong enough for words.

Poppy fills the void. "Rose is going through a tough time. She sees Daisy with her modeling career, you have Loren, and I'm busy with my daughter." She pauses. "You know Calloway Couture was just dropped by Saks?"

I frown deeply, not realizing.

Rose built Calloway Couture with our mother as a little side business when she turned fifteen. Years later, it's grown into a profitable fashion line that Rose can call her own. I never ask about her months or her life. Yet, she always finds the time to ask about mine.

"I've tried to call you," Poppy continues. "For two months, and you haven't answered. Lo hasn't answered. If Rose doesn't stop by and assure me that you're alive, sometimes I wonder . . . " Her voice turns grave. "I can't help but think you've eliminated us from your life."

I don't dare look at her. Tears prick my eyes, burning, but I hold them back. *It's easier this way,* I remind myself. *It's easier if they know nothing. It's easier to disappear.*

"I was in college too, and I know your social life and studies can take precedent over family, but you don't have to cut us out completely." She pauses again. "Maria is three. I'd love for you to be a part of her life. You're good with her—whenever you're around." She takes an unsure step forward and reaches out for me. "I'm here for you. I need you to know that."

I rise on two shaky legs and let her wrap her arms around my shoulders, squeezing me tightly. "I'm sorry," I murmur. She sniffs, her tears falling on my back. After pulling away, I inhale. "Thanks, Poppy."

Her words defeated me, tearing down any ounce of resilience. I have nothing left to give, no comfort to spare. I feel like a shell, waiting for the hermit to return home.

Five

Days move by in a sluggish haze filled with random bodies and carnal highs. I try to keep to my word and answer my sisters' calls (I still screen my parents'), but at times, my runaway phone acts like an angst-ridden teen and goes missing. Usually, I'm too self-absorbed in bodily pursuits to care.

I also have one valid excuse to keep my phone off.

Class.

Business and economics courses at Penn hijack my time. Maybe I should've picked an easier major, but my talents start and stop at being able to woo a boy into bed. And most girls can easily succeed where I do.

Life would make more sense if I happened to be a prodigy in art or music. I'd have a direction, a purpose. Then maybe my future wouldn't look so blank.

Since my artistic gifts peak at stick figures and whistling, I'm stuck with statistics. At noon, I sit beside Lo in the very back auditorium row. Managerial Economics and Game Theory—it really does exist. And I understand about 1.111% of the professor's dry lecture.

Lo kicks his feet on the empty chair below while I feverishly take notes on my laptop, my fingers pounding against the keys.

After a few minutes, I feel note-fatigue. It happens. So I pop up another window and search my favorite sites.

My eyes widen in glee. Kinkyme.net just uploaded a video featuring a pro soccer player (a porn star) and a fan (another porn star) in sultry positions. I tilt my head as he caresses her neck and takes her in the gym shower. Ooh, steamy.

The footage rolls on mute, of course, but my breathing shallows as his muscles enclose the fan-girl into the corner, trapping her beside the hot, wet tiles.

Laughing erupts, and my head shoots up from the computer, my face flaming in retaliation.

No one stares at me.

In fact, eyes plant on the professor. He makes another joke about Ke$ha and glitter, a humorous digression. I swallow, *okay*, my mind is playing tricks on me. I minimize the porn and expand my notes again.

Lo gnaws on the end of his pen, not aware of the students or the professor. He reads the latest *X-Men* comic on his iPad and nurses a thermos in his other hand.

"You're not borrowing my notes," I remind him in a whisper.

"I don't want them." He takes a large swig of his alcoholic beverage. I think I saw him concocting an orange, lemon and whiskey mix this morning, something nauseating.

My brows scrunch. "How do you plan on studying?"

"I'll wing it."

That's what he always says. I hope he fails. *No, I don't.* Yes, I do. Sort of. While I'm saddled with anxiety, he leisurely relaxes in his seat.

"You really want to piss off your father?" I ask. At last week's luncheon, Daisy told me his father took Lo aside and laid into him about grades and being safer with me. She said she saw "spit fly," which could be entirely true. I've seen Jonathan Hale grab the back of Lo's neck like a pup, pinching so hard that Lo squirmed in pain until his father released the hold. I don't think he realized the amount of strength he was using or the hurt in Lo's eyes.

"He'll find something to be angry about, Lil," he whispers. "If it's not school or you, it's my future and Hale Co. He can't send me to fucking boot camp if I flunk, not when I'm an adult. So what is he going to do to me? Take away my trust fund? Then how will I support my future wife?"

I can't see that future. The one where our lies go as far as marriage. And by his bitter tone, I doubt he pictures it too. I lick my dry lips and return my attention back to the professor. I've missed a good chunk of information with that one conversation, and I don't have any friends in the class to ask for notes. I start typing hurriedly again.

After a couple minutes, Lo sighs in boredom and nudges my side. "Have you had sex with anyone in this room?"

"Why do you care?" I try to multi-task and concentrate on the lecture too. The little tab at the bottom of my screen also distracts: *Pro Pleasures Fan, Watch Full Video HERE.*

"I'm about to fall asleep."

Huh? I concentrate on highlighting a line in my notes. "Then why'd you even come?"

"Attendance counts ten percent. I can actually control that part." He leans his shoulder into me, his warmth entering my space, his hard bicep on my soft. A breath dies in my chest. "You didn't answer my question."

My eyes dart around the hundred bodies compacted into the auditorium-style room. I land on a short guy with a fedora, brown hair peeking beneath. Two years ago. His apartment. Missionary. I spot another with nearly black hair tied into a tiny pony. Five months ago. His beat up VW. Reverse cow-girl. The moments bleed into my brain, replaying. My heart quickens at the images, but my stomach sinks at the answer to Lo's question. In a hundred person class, I've slept with *at least* two guys. What does that say about me? *Slut, whore.* I hear the condemnation.

Yet, I glance back at that little tab on my computer, my chest fluttering in excitement.

"So?" Lo presses.

"I don't know," I lie.

An eyebrow quirks. "You don't know?" Before I can unmask his expression, he smiles with that familiar bitter amusement. "That's hilarious."

"You need to get laid," I shoot back. *Think about your non-existent sex life for a change.*

"And you need a drink."

"Ha. Ha."

"You started it."

I bang on my keys and he edges out of my space, the weight of his arm gone. The warmth replaced by cold. I inhale strongly and try not to think about the emptiness in my belly or the spot between my legs.

My finger slips, hitting a random button.

"Ahhh, baby, right there, right THERE!"

The entire room goes silent. And heads turn to the back, towards the source of the sexual noises, towards *me*.

Oh my God. My porn stays in the tab, but the sound heightens as the pro-athlete reaches his climax. Her moans. His groans. I click buttons as fast as my finger will allow, but my computer expands the porn window and says *Not Responding* every time I try to exit out.

Lo presses his knuckles to his lips, trying desperately to hide his grin.

"Take me in the ass. Please, please!!! Ahhh!" the girl cries.

RESPOND!!! I internally shriek. No, my computer has decided to rebel against human intelligence. So I slam the screen shut and close my eyes, praying for my teleportation power to kick in. I know it exists.

"aaaahhhhHHHH!"

I bury my head in my arms. Finally, the noise dies off, leaving the lecture hall in dead, awkward silence. I peek up from my arm-fort.

"I have a virus," I mumble and cringe, too embarrassed to rephrase it to *my computer* has a virus.

The professor's dark eyebrows draw into a hard line, not pleased at all. "See me after class."

People steal glances back at us, and the exposure sends my skin into red disgrace.

Lo leans in again, but his masculine presence no longer tempts me. I feel like I've been electrocuted. "I didn't know you watched anal porn."

He tries to cheer me up with the words, but I can't even laugh. An army of fire ants just crawled across my body. "I'm dead," I mutter, and a horrifying thought hits me. "What if my parents find out?"

"This isn't high school, Lil."

The words don't make me feel much better. I stare at my palms and retreat inside myself. My shoulders curving forward, my head slightly bent.

"Hey." Lo gently turns my chin to meet his gaze, one full of understanding, narrowed with empathy. I begin to relax. "He's not going to call your parents. You're an adult."

It's hard to remember that when my parents cling to my future with such diligence and force.

"How often do you do it in the ass?" Lo banters with a crooked grin.

I groan and bury my head into my arms once again, but my lips upturn in a small smile. I hide that as well.

After another half hour of fearing my computer and producing paper notes at a snail's pace, the class ends. People take the opportunity to glance my way as they stand to leave, like they want a full mental picture of The Girl Who Watches Porn (In Class).

I rise and my hands shake by my sides. Lo passes me my backpack, and I sling it over my shoulder. His palm brushes my waist, for a brief second, as he says, "I'll see you later. Maybe we can grab lunch during your break."

I nod, and he pulls away, leaving me to wonder whether that was real or fake. Whether he meant to really touch my hip or if it was an unconscious movement, trained from all these years of pretending.

The scary part, I almost hoped it was real.

I watch him disappear with an old JanSport backpack, nearly empty. No notebooks. No pens. No computer. Just an iPad, a phone and a thermos in his possession. He walks without worry or care, tapping the height of the door frame on his way out. Something about his self-assured nature, his unhurriedness, mesmerizes me.

"Name?"

I break out of my trance. The professor stands at his podium, waiting for me.

"Your name?" he asks again, just as tersely. He slides his laptop into his briefcase. Students for the next period begin to filter in, and their instructor starts erasing the whiteboard that's scrawled with economics problems.

I near the podium. "Lily Calloway."

"Lily," he says dryly, taking his briefcase from the table. "If you can't bring a clean computer to class, then you need to take notes with a pen and paper. Next time this happens, I'll be enforcing this on everyone. You don't want to be the girl who ruins this privilege for the whole class." No, I do not. I only have one friend, already isolated as it is, but that doesn't mean I want to make any enemies.

"I'm sorry," I say.

He nods and walks off without another word.

Six

The clock ticks past midnight by the time I trudge into the Drake's lobby, my heels clapping on the creamy marble floors. My muscles ache from being wedged in a coat closet at the ballet theatre. I stayed seated beside Rose and Poppy for a total of ten minutes. Then I disappeared in search of a guy who eyed me at the ticket booth. After the hookup, I returned to my seat and they hardly noticed that I bailed on our planned sister-time. I spent the rest of the ballet imagining the male dancers with me—taking them home after the show ended. And when the curtains closed, a huge part of me wanted to go find one, but I was with my sisters. I was sitting with them, thinking about sex. I was an idiot.

I enter the golden elevator and press the highest number, my back aching. Did he have to slam me into the hangers?

Before the elevator closes, a man rushes in, slipping his fingers between the doors. They bounce back at his touch.

He pants heavily, out of breath, and I watch as he runs a hand through his thick brown hair. He presses the button to the floor below mine, and the elevator rises.

I check for a ring. None. His charcoal suit looks expensive, his gold watch validating my suspicions. Late twenties, early thirties.

Lawyer, I predict. But I don't care much about it. Not when the shape of his body appears to be hard, toned and powerful.

This is the easy part. Not knowing him. Letting my passions consume me for a single instant. This is what I do best. As my confidence soars, I shut my eyes, inhaling a deep, thoughtful breath.

With his hot gaze, he skims the length of my bare legs, which peek beneath an elegant white, backless dress. I slowly peel off my black coat and shift suggestively. He has a view of the very small of my back, the part bare and eager to be taken hold of.

I rest a hand on the elevator wall, my breath low and strained. And his body slides against me, those large palms on my slender hips. I lower one to my thigh, to the place between my legs. And he grows. A sound sticks to my throat, and I keep my hands on the wall. He finds his way into me. *Yes.*

His fingers tighten around my waist, cinching my dress, pulling it higher. One of his hands holds my shoulder to drive deeper. And with one last thrust—

Bing.

My eyes snap open, and I turn bright red from the fantasy I created. That guy has no idea that I pictured him unchastely with me. I stand by the wall, my hands bunched in my coat pockets, holding in that strained breath.

And the man—he doesn't look back, doesn't even acknowledge my existence—slips out of the elevator doors, which have burst open.

My fantasy built the tension, but it never released it. As the doors shut, I bang the back of head on the wall. *Stupid, Lily.*

I reach my floor and walk down the hall. Right now, I wish I could revert back to my high school self. Where I had sex maybe once a month. Most hours were filled with porn and my imagination. Now, very little excites me, and when I find something that does, I think about it constantly. I can barely even last a whole day without being gratified by a set of hands and a male body thrumming against mine.

What's wrong with me?

I throw my keys in the basket, hang up my coat and kick off my heels, trying not to think about what just happened. The smell of scotch lingers in the air. As I head to my door, I pass Lo's and suddenly stop.

"Hey," a girl giggles. "Don't . . . " She moans. *Moans.*

What is he doing to her? The creepy thought loiters, and I bite my nails, picturing Lo.

His hands on my legs, my hands on his chest, his lips against mine, mine against his. *Lily*, he breathes, bringing me close, his hold so very tight. He looks at me with those amber eyes, narrowed with passion. And he knows just what to do to make me—

"Oh . . . God!" She starts screaming as he finds the right spot. He must be good in bed, and I find myself wishing she'd go away. What does it matter if he has a girl in the room? I told him he needed to have sex. And he's having it. I should be happy he's finally getting laid.

But I'm not swallowing a happy pill right now.

I bottle my feelings that begin to brew and confuse. I slip into my room, ready for a shower. My phone beeps, and I open the text.

> Don't forget, we're dress shopping tomorrow. Thanks for coming tonight. Love you.—Poppy

Dress shopping. Oh yeah. For the Christmas Charity Gala. Even months away, the girls want to find perfect outfits for the event. Including jewelry, heels and clutches. The whole ordeal will take hours, but I'll be there.

Thump, thump, thump.

Lo's headboard. Into my wall. A ball tightens in my throat, and I scroll through my list of contacts, hesitating on the escort service. After the last sex worker turned a physical day into an emotional one, I've avoided any interaction with paid-to-screw men.

I toss my phone on my purple comforter.

Thump, thump.

Shower, I try to remind myself. Yes. I head to my bathroom.

Thump. Thump. Thump.

Good God.

I turn the nozzle to hot, shed my clothes, step in and shut my eyes—trying to think about anything other than sex. And Loren Hale.

Seven

I sit on a Victorian chaise in the dressing room lobby, surrounded by too many mirrors and too many racks of dresses, some costing more than bridal gowns.

While my sisters try on long, draping beauties in deep wintery colors, I protect the dozens of shopping bags from the jewelers and shoe stores. After choosing a plum gown with lacy sleeves—my first choice—I no longer have to agonize over what to wear to the Charity Gala. I happily sit outside, stealing glances at a cute guy one chaise over. He twists a ring on his finger and checks his watch, waiting for his wife in a curtained dressing room to the left of Rose's.

I am not a proponent of infidelity, adultery, cheating, you name it. I've never intentionally hooked up with a married man, and I don't plan to now, but staring . . . that's not against my rules.

Anyway, I can't help it. His whole jaw is lined with scruff, the kind you want to run your hands on. His light green eyes stay in his vicinity. For the best, I suppose, but a huge part of me wants him to look over. To stand up and come—

"This is so ugly."

I jump as Daisy emerges from her dressing room. She pads to the set of mirrors in the lobby and does a little spin. I cringe.

Yeah, the big bow situated on her butt is not helping. Neither is the puke-green color.

"It's hideous," Rose agrees, pushing back her curtains and joining us.

"Oh, I like yours," Daisy exclaims.

Rose takes the time to check out her velvet blue dress in the mirror. The fabric cinches at the bust and hugs her slender frame perfectly. "What do you think, Lily?" We've made up since the "pregnancy" debacle at the luncheon. Rose apologized during breakfast one morning at my apartment. She brought over everything bagels, my favorite, and subsequently, I said I was sorry too. For not being around more. That's how our relationship goes. I disappoint her. She forgives me, but never forgets, and we move on.

"It looks beautiful on you, but so did the last fifteen."

Poppy's voice trickles from her dressing room. "Put your arm in here. Stop being so difficult." She sighs exhaustedly. After a couple seconds, she enters the lobby with a squirming little brunette girl.

"Aw, Maria, you look so cute," Daisy says, touching Maria's lacy pink dress with white tights. Poppy finally coaxes Maria against her hip, settling down.

"What do you say?" Poppy tells her daughter.

"Thank you, Auntie." She puts her thumb in her mouth, and Poppy immediately takes it out.

"You're too old for that."

She's three and in the Calloway clan, potty training, walking, reading, spelling, writing must all be achieved before the average age, lest we turn into normal people.

Rose inches closer to me, away from Maria, who makes her grimace. Her hatred of children is actually amusing. I smile as she suffers, and when she notices it, I suspect a wave of bitchiness headed my way.

"Who are you bringing?" she asks.

Oh. Not too bad. "Lo, of course." My smile widens. "The better question is who *you* are going to bring." Rose constantly fights for the right to go stag, since no guy can ever live up to her impossible standards. But our mother insists on dates, believing that if you arrive without a man, you look cheap and unwanted. Something that I disagree with—Rose even more vehemently than me. Fighting our mother exhausts me, and for Rose to back down, my mother must have brought the waterworks. Rose hates tears almost as much as she dislikes children.

"I'm working on it."

She usually takes Sebastian, her go-to arm candy, but apparently he's ditching her this year for his boyfriend. I listened to her rant about it all last week, and I think she's out of fire to reignite the same conversation.

Daisy chimes in, "I'll probably bring Josh."

I frown. "Who's Josh?"

She pulls her brown hair into a pony. "My boyfriend. Of *six months*," she emphasizes, her voice still light.

"Sorry," I apologize. "I just . . . " Am never home to see her. Or him. And I don't listen well.

"It's okay."

I know it's not.

She shrugs and disappears into her dressing room to take off the green monstrosity.

Rose shoots me a cold glare. "Who do you think she's been texting all day?"

She's been texting? "Dad?" I try.

Rose rolls her eyes dramatically.

Maria throws her ballet flat at me. Jesus!

"Maria!" Poppy exclaims.

Rose laughs loudly. I think this is the first time a child has made her smile. And it was by abusing me with a shoe!

"They're stupid!"

I gape. Did she call me stupid? Is everyone really that mad at me? Even a child?

"Don't use that word," Poppy scolds. "Tell Lily you're sorry."

"I hate shoes!" *Okay, good.* At least someone still hasn't fallen out of love with me. "Stupid, stupid, stupid!"

"What about these." I point to a box of glittery silver flats with pink clips. Maria's eyes widen and she calms. I smile. "Are you sure she's not Rose's kid? Toss her some Prada and she shuts up."

Rose's laughter dies down. "Funny."

Poppy says, "I'm going to take Maria to the bathroom." *She's going to spank her.* My mother used to threaten with a wooden spoon. Those hurt, you know. They're pretty damn scary, and I learned to quiet in public places, fearing the wrath of my mother and the swat of a utensil. "Can you watch my dressing room, Lil? My purse is in there."

"Yeah, sure."

Once she disappears from sight, Rose moves a few bags and finds a seat next to me. "Is it Loren?"

I frown. "What?"

Her yellow-green eyes meet mine. "Is he keeping you from us?"

My stomach churns with acid. Lo keeping me from them? I want to laugh or cry or scream, anything—maybe, just maybe, even shout the truth. *I can't fit you into my schedule, not when it's booked with sex, not when you wouldn't understand.*

"It's not Lo. I'm just busy, sometimes even too busy for him."

"You're not lying to me, are you?"

I look at my hands, a small tell, but I doubt she'll pick up on it. I shake my head. "No."

After lingering silence, she says, "I told Mom that Penn would be too hard for you. Of course she didn't listen. You weren't the model student at Dalton."

I laugh—that's an understatement. "My grades sucked." Dalton Academy rode me hard, in many ways. Without my family's achievements, I wouldn't have been accepted to an Ivy League. That much is clear.

"I remember filling out your applications," Rose says with pursed lips, but there's a shimmer in her eyes, as though the moment is a fond one for her. I barely remember it. I must have been surfing the internet, looking at porn. Thinking about sex.

"You did a good job," I say. "I got in."

"What did it matter? You chose Penn, not Princeton." She stands and pretends to admire herself in the mirror, but I can tell she's trying to hide her real feelings. We fought a lot when I made the decision to go to college with Lo and not her. She never talked about being roommates with me, but Poppy later told me that Rose had already begun picking out dishware and furniture for an apartment off campus that she hoped we would share.

At the time, I blamed my choice on Lo, telling everyone that he hadn't been accepted to Princeton. Of course, he was, but how could I enjoy my freedom and live in close proximity to Rose? I couldn't. She would find out about all the boys. She'd be repulsed by me and cut me from her life for good. I can't take that rejection or criticism. Not from her. Not from someone I truly adore.

Very softly, I say, "I'm sorry." I feel like all I do is apologize.

Rose looks blank. Completely shut off. "It's fine. I'm going to try on that black dress." She slips into her curtained room, leaving me alone. Well, not totally alone.

I glance back at the other Victorian chaise.

My heart sinks. Empty. He's gone. Great, now I don't even have someone to ogle.

My phone vibrates in my jeans. I pluck it out and frown at the unknown number. Hmm. I open the text.

> Want to hang out?—215-555-0177

Must be a guy I drunkenly gave my number to after we hooked up. I usually keep personal information to myself, considering it provokes attachment and stalking.

My lips grow into a smile, wondering who could be on the other line. The excitement actually takes me by surprise. If I was drunk when we met, I probably won't remember him. Anonymous. Technically, it'll be like a first encounter.

I make my choice.

> Where do you want to meet?

Eight

The next morning, I wake to a splitting headache and the spins. Turns out, I vaguely remembered the guy from my text, just not enough to warrant a good mental picture. He likes booze and peer pressured me into doing tequila shots. But I still remember the thrum in my chest, the beat pulsing as I reached his door, as I knocked and waited for him to answer, to let me in and do *it* as many ways as his body would allow. Anonymous sex—not knowing what the guy will look like on the other side—hooked me so, so very much.

As I lie still, coming down from a serious high and left with a hellish hangover, I wonder about Lo. I haven't seen him since my porn blared across the lecture hall. I spent my lunch break cramming for a quiz and couldn't meet him on campus, and Saturday was filled with dresses, shoes and sisters. I don't even know what he did or where he was, not uncommon. We're not together *all* the time, anyway. We do separate on occasion. I think.

I drag my body from the bed, throw on a baggy T-shirt and jean shorts. I want to ask him about that girl he brought home. Maybe he'll tell me what he did to her. Would that be weird?

As I exit into the hallway, I stop at the sound of faint laughter, emanating from the kitchen. *Girl* laughter.

My frown deepens. Is this the same girl? No, it can't be. My stomach knots. Is it? Hesitantly, I move closer and then go still at the doorway.

"You're a good cook," the girl says, her voice familiar.

I don't know why I assumed he would have a one-night stand like me. Why would I assume that? So she stayed the night. Friday *and* Saturday.

Lo mills around the kitchen, fixing two bloody marys and scrambling eggs on the stove. I scrutinize the girl who sits cross-legged on the bar stool, wearing his muscle Clash T-shirt. Her big breasts peek out on either side, and I can see her red panties beneath the charcoal-gray fabric.

She's a natural blonde, her hair wet like she just showered. And even without makeup, she resembles a girl next door, someone you'd bang and then take home to your parents.

I feel even more nauseous.

Lo scrapes the eggs onto two plates. When he looks up, he finally notices me lingering like a creep. "Hey, Lily." He points to the blonde. "This is Cassie."

Cassie gives me a small wave. "Hi."

I smile back, but I shrink inside like a wilted flower. She's nice too.

"Do you want breakfast?" Lo asks. He acts as though this is a normal routine. Him, bringing home a girl. On a first name basis with her. Since when do we know the names of our guests? Never. Okay, well that's more my rule, but I thought it would extend to Lo too. It has since we've been in college.

"No," I mutter. I gesture to the hall behind me. "I'm going to . . . "—*go shrivel in self-pity*—"take a shower." I dart into the depths of the hallway, retreating to the safety of my room. Okay, that was weird. I was weird. The whole situation was extremely weird. Is that how Lo feels about me when I bring men home? I shake the thought off. Of course not. I don't display the guys and test them out to see if they're boyfriend material. I ditch them almost immediately.

Only one thing can take my mind off Lo. I change quickly into a black day dress and comb my hair, which thankfully doesn't look too greasy. After spraying perfume and slipping into a pair of wedges, I grab my phone and let three texts, all anonymous numbers, guide my fate.

Unfortunately, I must enter the kitchen to reach the foyer and then the front door. I try to put invisible blinders up as I walk through, my target on the exit. *Go, go, go!*

"Where are you going?" Lo asks, his frown apparent in his voice.

"Out." I grab a set of keys in the basket and then drop them back in. I don't need to drive him anywhere since he has Malibu Barbie on his hip. So I'm getting drunk today. Maybe I'll call a cab as well.

"Did I do something?" Cassie's loud whisper echoes from the kitchen before I leave.

I'm waiting by the elevator when Lo appears around the bending hallway. I still can't meet his eyes. I'm unjustifiably angry, which makes everything so much worse.

"What's wrong with you?"

I push the glowing button three more times.

"Lily, look at me." Lo grabs my arm and pulls my body towards him. I finally take in his warm, amber eyes, full of confusion and scorn. "What the hell is going on? You're acting weird."

"Are you dating her?"

His brows furrow with hardness. Does he think I'm jealous? *Am* I? Oh jeez. "That's what this is about? I've known her for two fucking days," he says. "You're the one who told me that I needed to get laid, remember?" Yeah, can I rip out that girl's vocal cords?

"I remember, but I thought you'd have a one-night stand and be done with her." Wow, that sounds bad.

"I'm not you."

My chest constricts. Everything hurts more than it should. He's said far truer and meaner things to me. I avoid his gaze once more, my eyes planted on my feet.

His hand goes to my shoulder. "Hey, I'm sorry. Can you just talk to me, please?"

"I'm scared," I say, the first thing I can think of. I don't really know what I am. Confused, angry, upset. But excuses start tumbling from my lips, excuses that I've engrained in my head like a machine reading code. "What happens when she wants to meet your father? What happens if she starts telling people she's dating Loren Hale, and that person happens to be friends with Rose?" I don't care about any of that. The charade can go to hell for what it's worth. I just don't like seeing him move on without me.

"I'm *not* dating her," he emphasizes.

"Does she know that? Because she seems to be very comfortable for only knowing you two days." She's wearing his shirt and sitting half-naked on *my* bar stool. I want to kick her out. I want to get *Rose* to kick her out because she'll do a hell of a lot better job than me.

I am being irrational. And rude and so, so hypocritical. I need to get out of here.

"She's not moving in, Lily. She spent the night, that's it."

"Twice!" I shout. "And she's eating breakfast with you. *You* made her breakfast." He usually makes *me* breakfast. Not random girls.

"And not everyone acts like a scared little mouse after sex," he says cruelly. My face twists in hurt, and he grimaces. "Wait, I didn't mean . . . "

"Just stop," I say, holding up my hand. The elevator dings and the doors slide open, but his fingers still wrap around my wrist, so I don't leave just yet.

His voice lowers, the doors shutting. "You're a permanent fixture in my life. You're not going anywhere." Why does he have to say it like that? Like I'm some chandelier hanging out while he slips a ring on another woman's finger.

I shove him off now. "I know we're not together, okay?"

"Lil—"

"She's going to ruin everything!" It hurts to see him with her, playing house. That's our routine. I smack the button hard. Get me out of here.

"At least tell me where you're going."

"I don't know."

"What do you mean?"

I scoot into the elevator, and he sticks a hand on the frame, the doors refusing to close me in.

"I mean, I don't know. I'm not going to a club. I'm meeting up with someone spontaneously. Probably at a motel or his place."

"What?" His chest collapses and lines crease his forehead. "Since when do you do that?"

"Since yesterday."

His jaw clenches in reproach. "Are you taking the car?"

The elevator buzzes angrily since he has the doors propped open for so long. I push his arm off and he takes a step back. "No," I tell him. "It's all yours. I plan on drinking."

"Lily," he says. "Don't do this."

The elevator doors begin to close.

"Lily!" He tries to stick his hand in, but they shut before he can. "Dammit," I hear him curse, leaving me with one last view of him inhaling a sharp breath. I should revel in the fact that I'm scaring him as much as he's scaring me, but I can't.

Nine

took the car. Maybe Lo's pleads bled into my brain, subconsciously affecting me. Or maybe I just really didn't want to drink. Whatever the case, my BMW sits outside of a dingy apartment complex. Smoke wafts in a guy's bedroom, filling my lungs whole. He kisses with rough, wet lips, his mouth sucking my neck. I want to be intoxicated by the moment. I wait for it to carry me away. He's decent looking, in his late twenties, I suppose. Not fit, not toned. But he has cute eyes and dimpled cheeks.

The seventies shag carpet, dirt-orange walls and lava lamp distract me. As my knees dig into his hard mattress, I stare off, my mind drifting, his hands not doing their job and my head not staying in the game.

I think about Lo. I think about the past. I think about him with Cassie and why it hurts so much. And then a memory floats right into me.

Lo tossed me a blanket in his father's den, and I wrapped myself in the fuzzy fabric while he loaded the first season of *Battlestar Galactica* into the DVD player.

"Do you think we can finish the season before Monday?" I asked.

"Yeah, you can crash here if it takes that long. We have to find out what happens to Starbuck."

I was fourteen, and my parents still thought I cherished Lo like one would a cootie-ridden boy next door. I was far from that place, but I let them believe so anyway.

And then his father stopped by, standing in the crevice of the doorway with a crystal glass of whiskey in hand. The mood shifted. The air sucked dry, and I could practically hear our hearts beating in panicked unison.

"I need to talk to you." Jonathan Hale kept it short, running his tongue over his teeth.

Lo, fourteen and gangly, stood with tight eyes. "What?"

His father glanced at me, his cutting gaze shriveling my body into the enormous leather couch. "Out here." He clamped a hand on Lo's shoulder, guiding him into the darkness.

Their tense voices reached my ears. "You're failing *ninth* grade algebra."

I don't want to remember this. I try to concentrate on the guy in front of me. He lies on his back and brings me above him. Mechanically, I begin to unbutton his jeans.

"That's not my report card."

"Don't bullshit me."

I want to forget, but there's something about Jonathan Hale that stirs my mind, something off. And so I relive it. I remember. In their moments of silence, I pictured a stare-off between them. One that only fathers and sons with tempestuous relationships can share. Full of hatred and unspoken truths.

"Fine, it's mine," Lo said, losing the advantage.

"Yeah?" his father sneered. Their shoes scuffled, and something slammed into the wall. "Don't be so fucking ungrateful, Loren! You have *everything*."

The image hurts, and I shut my eyes, pausing for a minute. I actually stop pulling down the guy's pants.

Jonathan growled, "Say something, now's your chance."

"What does it matter? Nothing's good enough for you."

"You know what *I* want? To be able to talk to my associates about you, to gloat and tell them how my son is better than their little shit. But I have to shut my fucking mouth when they bring up achievements and academics. Get your act together or I'll find a place that'll make you the man you should be."

The guy sits up. "Hey, you okay? You want to switch positions?"

I shake my head. "No, no. I'm fine." I straddle his waist and run my fingers along his chest, sliding down his boxers.

Jonathan Hale's shoes clapped off in the distance, and Lo didn't return to the den for what seemed like ten more minutes. When he finally came back in, his eyes looked red and swollen and puffy, and I stood up and walked towards him, letting my emotions guide me.

In the present, I sit up. "I'm sorry," I mumble, sinking into myself. I grab my clothes, put them on as quickly as possible and hightail it out of his place. He's not the right guy. I need another. Something more.

He calls after me, but I don't listen. His door shuts on my way out, and the cold air rushes into my body, waking me up but sending me back at the same time. My car sits in the rear of the parking lot of his apartment complex. I walk quickly, but my pace doesn't carry off the memories. They stay.

"Let's watch the movie." Lo didn't look at me.

I only knew one way to make a person feel good, something I believed was better. Impulsively, I reached for his hand. I held it, and he frowned, staring at me like I'd grown horns. But at the same time, his reddening eyes looked eager to take hold of something other than the pain that plagued him.

The parking lot. I yank open the door to my BMW and fumble with my phone, finding some numbers I haven't exhausted yet. I set up a few random meeting places. Yes. Yes. Yes. No.

I kissed Lo's lips. Softly, gently. And then I led him to the couch where our hands roamed more hungrily, our bodies moved more passionately, needing to feed our temptations and close out everything else.

We had sex for the first time. The *only* time.

Afterwards, Lo drank himself to oblivion. And I sprawled out on the couch, making a promise with myself to never sleep with Loren Hale ever again. To never cross that line. Once was enough. It could have ruined our friendship, but we acted as though nothing transpired, as though the moment came with heightened spirits and unleveled heads.

I won't make a mistake that can cost us what we have. So I pocket my phone, put my car in reverse, and make new plans. Ones that involve blank faces and unpainted canvases. Ones that don't involve him.

Ten

The next few days blur. I manage to avoid Lo each time I arrive and depart from the apartment. On the occasions that I sleep at the Drake, I wear earbuds to deafen Lo and Cassie's love-making noises. Mostly, I spend the night somewhere else, any place that involves anonymous sex and the surprise of a mystery man.

My new discovery invades my waking hours. If I'm not scrolling through tons of unknown numbers, I research Craigslist for anyone willing to hook up. I have yet to use the online resource for a lay, but the allure brings me back. With only a screen name to go off of, I find myself imagining the person on the other end. What they look like. What I could do to them in bed.

The more Lo pulls away, the more I turn to sex, the only thing I can reach for. It feels like he's wedging a large space between us. He hasn't asked me for a ride in a whole week, and we've stopped discussing our nightly plans together. I used to be able to draw up his schedule as fluidly as my own. Now, I couldn't tell you if he made it to bed last night without passing out.

I lie on my purple sheets, contemplating my very small existence and staring at the sun. It crests the sky, shining bright rays through the slits in my blinds. An arm drapes across my bare back. I don't want to wake him. Hopefully his eyes will flutter open while I feign sleepiness. I've been up since five in the morning, thinking and gazing at the same spot. The sun. The window. My life.

Bang! The noise from my door jolts me. "Lily!" Lo knocks again, his fist slamming into the white wood.

My heart lodges in my throat. I put a pillow over my head, spinning and crashing in a post-drunk tidal wave. The door clicks, and I curse the fact that Lo has a key.

My groggy male guest props himself up. "Who are you?" he asks with a yawn.

"Don't talk so loud," another voice groans. *What?!* I did not . . . Did I? There are *two* guys in my bed! I didn't . . . I couldn't have had sex with both of them. I search my memories, but I blank when I reach my anonymous "date" at a bar. Booze forgives all transgressions, but it doesn't help with the morning after.

My limbs have petrified.

"Both of you, get the fuck out," Lo sneers. "Now!"

Quickly, the two guys shuffle for their clothes, pulling on articles while I disintegrate into my sheets and cower underneath another comforter. When they finally disappear, silence blankets the room.

Usually whenever Lo kicks a guy out in the morning, he's so blasé about it. Sometimes he even offers the poor guy a cup of coffee before he leaves. This is not normal.

While I avoid his gaze, Lo paces, and I hear the crinkle of plastic. I peek from my sheet-cave.

He's cleaning?

I use a part of the sheet to cover my chest and straighten up. "What are you doing?" My voice comes out small and choked. He doesn't answer. Instead, he stays focused on tossing the empty beer bottles into a black trash bag along with many articles of clothing. *Boy* clothing.

For the first time in days, I actually *look* at my room. Layered in different underwear, spilled with bottles of booze and tainted with white powder on my vanity—it's disgusting. My floor hides beneath mounds of debauchery and sin. Half the sheets pile on the ground, and used condoms scatter my rug. It feels like I woke up in someone else's bed.

"Stop," I tell him, shame sending tears. "You don't have to do that."

He tosses an empty box of condoms into the bag before looking up at me. His expression remains inscrutable, scaring me even more. "Go take a shower. Get dressed, and then we'll go."

"Where?"

"Out." He turns his back and continues trashing my things. I've cleaned his room countless times, but he was always unconscious to the world when I did it.

I wrap my purple sheet around my body and waddle towards the bathroom. After I shampoo my hair and lather soap on every inch of skin, I step out and pull on a terry cloth robe with slippers. I pad back. A full garbage bag sits by the open door, and outside the archway, I hear the faucet running in the kitchen.

I change in the closet, throwing on a comfortable black cotton dress, not knowing the proper attire for wherever we're headed. I can't make a guess on the destination either. My head sits as numb and cold as my body.

When I enter my room again, Lo stands by the door, the trash bag gone. He gives me a quick once-over while I tie my hair into a small pony, my fingers trembling. "Ready?" he asks.

I nod and follow him out, grabbing the keys. As I walk, I notice all my aches and pains. Blackish, yellow spots bruise my elbows and thighs, probably knocking into things last night and not remembering. My back hurts too, like I hit a doorknob or something. Tears prick my eyes, which stay nice and pink while I refuse to let the waterworks escape.

"Where are we going?" I ask again, sliding into the driver's seat since Lo can't.

"The health clinic. You need to get tested."

My stomach caves. Right. Tested. "You don't have to come."

I watch him try to find an appropriate answer, but he ends up muttering, "Just drive."

I put the car in gear and head down the familiar roads.

"When's the last time you've been to class, Lil?" he asks softly, staring out the window, watching the buildings blink by.

"Last Wednesday." *I think.*

"Yesterday?" The spot between his eyebrows wrinkles.

"It's Thursday?" I say, startled. Why did I think it was Saturday? My hands begin to tremble again, and I tighten them on the leather steering wheel. Hot tears scald on their way down, betraying me. "I just got a little mixed up." How did I even come to this place?

"I know."

I inhale a strained breath and turn the car down a couple more streets before parallel parking. I lean over to open the door, but Lo puts his hand on my shoulder.

"Can we talk for a second?"

I tense back into the seat. My eyes glue to the unlit dashboard. Is this my ultimate low? I thought the pregnancy scare was the most terrifying moment of my life, but waking up in bed with two guys I don't remember—that will haunt me. How can I be missing *days*? As if sex and liquor stole them from me . . . maybe drugs participated in the thievery too. I can't even remember.

I wish I was Lo. I don't think that often, but right now, I envy his ability to be a "functioning" alcoholic, one that doesn't get aggressive or physical or lose memories. He drinks all day and all night, only suffering the repercussions when he surpasses his tolerance and blacks out.

He keeps his narrowed gaze on me and lets out a heavy breath. "You remember when we first arrived at Penn and we both went to that freshman pajama party?" Ah, yes, the Pajama Jam. The blistering memory brings a heavy frown to both of us. "You found me blacked out on the floor in the morning."

He censors the image. Where his cheek was covered with vomit. Where I lifted him in my arms and thought, for the most horrifying moment, that my best friend had finally succumbed to his greatest flaw.

Lo's voice deepens. "All I can recall is waking up in the hospital, feeling like a fucking twenty-ton truck ran me over."

"You'd just had your stomach pumped," I remind him.

Lo nods. "I could hear you arguing with the nurse about calling my father. You insisted that she keep the matter private since I was eighteen."

I had to pretend to be his sister just to enter his hospital room. So stupid. Everything. That whole night. Right now. But to rectify what's been done, what we've solidified, is beyond my power. Part of me will always believe that we're past change. Maybe we've already accepted that this is how we'll live and this is how we'll come to die.

My eyes burn at the thought of the two guys in my bed. But I don't want this to happen again. That, I do know.

"We made a deal after that, remember?" he continues, carefully choosing his words. "We said that if this is going to work—you and me, Lo and Lily doing whatever we want, being who we are—then I'd have to know my limits and never exceed them. I honestly never thought . . . I never thought it would be a problem for you too." He runs a shaky hand through his hair and takes a deep breath. "I didn't know that sex addicts could have limits, Lily, but somewhere . . . somewhere you crossed a line. And you're scaring the shit out of me. I haven't been able to get ahold of you in days. When I pass out, you're not home. When I wake up, you're usually gone. This was the first time I've seen you, and . . . " He rubs his mouth and looks away.

My heart beats so fast. I don't know what to do or say. Tension stretches between us, not the good kind, and it hurts to touch it.

His voice lowers while I press my palms to my hot tears. "I don't have any right to tell you to stop. That's not what I'm trying to say, but for this arrangement to work, you have to know your limit. *This,* hooking up with guys in motels, not answering *my* calls, and"—he stumbles on the words again—"fucking . . . *two* guys. That has to end. What if they hurt you?"

I close my eyes, the tears spilling out the creases. "I don't remember them."

"You were drunk," he realizes, his features darkening. "What's after this? Orgies? Sexual humiliation?"

"Stop." I rub my eyes, cringing at the images.

"Where's your head at?" he murmurs.

I can't do this again. "I'll stop, not the sex, but the motels, the unknown texts, Craigslist—"

"Craigslist?!" he yells. "What the fuck, Lily? You know who solicits for sex on those things? Child molesters and perverts, not to mention it's fucking illegal."

"I didn't use it!" I shout back, my cheeks flaming. "I was just looking."

He holds his hands out, takes a deep, meditative breath, and balls them into fists. "Did you feel like you couldn't talk to me?"

I've never had a problem unburdening myself on Lo. It's what we're both good at, but turning to anonymous sex felt like a natural progression once our dynamic started to shift. "Things were changing," I mutter so softly that I think he's missed the words.

When he doesn't ask what I said, I suspect he heard. "I know I can be a royal asshole. But I love you. You're my best friend and the only person I've ever told that I have a problem. It doesn't matter if we're in a fucking fake relationship. We're supposed to talk to each other. Come to me before you go off the deep end, okay?"

I wipe the last of my tears and sniff. "How's Cassie?"

"She hasn't been in the apartment in days, Lily," he says, reminding me of all the time I lost in my hazy state.

"What happened?" My chest lightens, and I hate that I'm taking pleasure in his aloneness.

"There's this girl who ran out of my apartment." He pauses. "She looked like a bat out of hell. She barely combed her hair, not unusual for her"—he shrugs—"but she seemed pissed, and the only difference in our relationship had been this *new* blonde girl on a bar stool. So I dumped her, figured it may solve a problem or two." He waits, tilting his head at me while I process what he just said.

My chest swells.

"Did it?" he asks.

I should be the better person and say *no*, let him have a normal life with a beautiful blonde bombshell. But I've never been good at the morality bit. "Maybe."

He actually smiles and rests a hand on my neck. He kisses my forehead before I can form thoughts, and when he pulls away, his lips brush my ear. "I'm here for you. Always."

I take a deep breath, his words enough to guide me into the clinic with my head upright and my shoulders back. I'm going to be okay. Whatever happens, at least Lo will stay by my side.

. . .

After the health clinic, Lo mixes himself a drink at the counter while I make plans to study for an upcoming exam, popping open my laptop and spreading out my notes on the bar. Once I find two weeks of neglected practice problems for economics, I realize how far behind I truly am.

There is an upside. I'm clean. Free of diseases and complicated decisions. Like rehab or abortion clinics. I choked Lo to death when the test came back, hugging the life from him as I cried in relief. I don't know what I would have done if he didn't know my secret—if I was alone with the knowledge of my problem.

Long before we started our fake relationship, I helped hide Lo's addiction on every occasion. I would smuggle him into one of my guest bedrooms at Villanova until he slept off a hangover. I'd kick bottles of Jim Beam and Maker's Mark underneath his bed before the maid lurked around and his father inspected the stateliness of his son's things.

Back then, he would lie to my sisters about my weekend plans. Most were spent at parties hosted by public school kids. Screwing boys from different schools helped diminish rumors about me at Dalton. I was calculated in the selection.

Then one chilly night in October, I crawled through Lo's window. With Jonathan Hale at a conference in New York, I could have used the door, but ever since I watched *Dawson's Creek* I believed there was only one way to make a proper entrance.

I was seventeen and tear-streaked, and I just had sex. Lo sat on the hardwood floor, his phone in one palm and a Glencairn whiskey glass in the other. He jumped to his feet as soon as he saw my matted hair and smudged mascara.

"Who was it? Did he hurt you?!" Lo frantically scanned my body, looking for wounds.

"No," I said with a grimace. "He didn't . . . it's not him."

Leaving Lo confused, I walked to his desk and picked up the bottle of Maker's Mark. He grabbed it from my hand before I could even uncap it. "This is mine," he said.

"So now you don't share?"

"I never do."

I rubbed my arms, feeling empty and cold. He kept staring at me as if his intrusive gaze would open me up. I guess it kind of did.

"The party was pretty lame," I muttered under my breath.

"Apparently enough to make you cry," Lo said bitterly. He cringed at the sound of his own voice and took a swig from the bottle. Then he stepped forward, eyes softening as he rubbed his mouth. "You know you can tell me anything, Lil. I'm not going anywhere."

Lo knew most of my dirty secrets by then. The sex. The porn. The constant self-love. But telling him about *this* had been the hardest part of our friendship. It felt like admittance to something unnatural.

I sank down on the mattress while Lo stood holding the bottle by the waxy red neck, waiting for me to start.

"It was fine. The sex was fine."

Lo rubbed his temple in distress. "Lily. Spit it the fuck out. You're driving me crazy."

I stared down at the floorboards, unable to meet his eyes, and said, "Afterwards, I thought it would be the same. But as I was grabbing my clothes, he stopped me."

I glanced up and Lo's cheekbones looked like sharp glass. I continued quickly before he cut me off with a slew of vulgarities. "He didn't hurt me. He just asked me a question."

I took a shallow breath and twisted the bottom of my shirt in my hands. Then I opened my mouth and struggled to produce the rest, eating air.

"Should I guess?" Lo asked. His chest rose and fell with hurried concern. Before I could respond he was pacing the length of the room and spouting off questions. "*Were you a virgin? Have you done this often? Do you want to do it again?*" He stopped and ran a shaky hand through his hair. "What the hell did he ask?!"

"Want to fuck my friend?" I said in barely a whisper.

Lo dropped the bottle and it landed in a loud *thunk* on the hardwood floor.

"I thought it would be fun. He left and his friend came in. And that was that . . . " My bottom lip quivered as the shame wedged a crevice in my heart. "Lo," I choked his name. "What's wrong with me?"

He came closer and bent down to my height on the bed. Carefully, he cupped the back of my head, his fingers intertwining in my brown locks. His deep amber eyes filled mine. "*Nothing* is wrong with you," he said. He brought my head to the crook in his shoulder, his arm encasing me in a comforting hold, and held me for a while.

When he pulled away, he brushed my hair behind my ear and asked, "Are you scared of getting hurt?"

"Sometimes. But it doesn't stop me." I blinked back tears. "Do you think . . . do you think I'm like you?"

We had never openly acknowledged his dependence on alcohol before, or how he abused the drink more than any average teenage boy.

He slowly ran his finger over the lines in my palm before he looked up at me with haunted eyes. One kiss on the head and then he straightened up. With a tight voice, he said, "I found my old Amazing Spider-Man edition the other day. We should have a reading marathon." I watched him tensely walk to his cedar chest, unclasping the brass locks.

That night, he never truly answered me.

But I got it anyway.

That was the first time I realized I wasn't just another promiscuous girl in school. I didn't just have sex for fun or because it made me feel empowered. I liked the high, the rush, and how it seemed to fill an emptiness that kept growing inside of me.

Eleven

At night, I return to clubs and bars, my regular dwellings, without formulating anonymous meetings. Surprisingly, Lo accompanies me most of the time, drinking at the bar while I sneak to the backrooms or toilet seats to hook up. Still, I crave the adrenaline rush and thrill of daytime anonymity. I fear these past weeks pushing my addiction to a new extreme has ruined me a little.

I try though. I've deleted all my unknown numbers and anytime the urge to log into Craigslist surfaces, I think about the terrible morning waking up in bed with two faceless men. It helps.

I zip up a black nighttime romper when my phone buzzes. Normally, I would chuck it at my pillow and let the ring die out, but this is Lily 2.0.

So I press the green button. "Hey, Daisy."

"Lily!" She sounds as shocked as I am that I answered.

"What's up?"

"I need a favor," she hesitates to continue.

I guess I'm not really the go-to sister for favors. Rose would be the first one to call, literally willing to drop her entire day's plan if we need her to. Then Poppy, almost as sisterly, but she has a daughter that eats her time and blocks out her schedule. I'm the least reliable, least available, least everything sister.

"So," she eases in, "Mom and Dad are going at it. They've been screaming about the decoration budget for the Christmas Charity Gala. I know Mom's going to come up and start rehashing their argument to me, and I'd rather not be involved." She pauses. "Do you think I can come over and stay the night in the guest bedroom?"

I frown, wondering if she already asked Rose, or even Poppy and Sam, who have plenty of extra space. Will it be rude to question? I think it will, especially if she's reaching out to me. I take a trained breath. "Sure."

She squeals. "Thankyouthankyouthankyou! I'll be over in a half hour." *That soon?* The line clicks, and I glance at my room . . . the guest bedroom. Where she'll be sleeping. Shit.

"LO! LO!" I scream, frantic.

Ten seconds later, he runs into the room, eyes suddenly sober. "What's wrong?" he says, panic-stricken.

"Daisy is coming over."

His muscles slightly relax, and he combs shaking fingers through his hair. "Jesus, Lil. I thought you were hurt. Don't call my name like that unless you're bleeding."

"Did you hear me?" I say. "Daisy is coming over. And she's *spending the night*."

His eyes darken. "Why didn't you ask me first?"

My cheeks heat. "I-I didn't think. She asked and I said yes." Oops, I forgot about Lo. I *also* forgot that everyone thinks I sleep with him, which is so not the case. "It was a subconscious reaction, and I didn't want to be rude."

With a sigh, he rubs his eyes and then scans my room. "Strip your bed, throw the sheets in the washer, and hide all of your porn. I'll lock up the booze."

We split up and focus on our specific tasks. Twenty minutes later, the guest room turns clean and presentable for Daisy. Trying to fish out the panties under the bed ate up most of the time. The doorbell rings, and I close the washing machine and start the cycle.

When I enter the kitchen, Lo and Daisy are already talking. My presence breaks their chit-chat, and I smile. "Hey, Dais." I give her a hug.

"Thanks again for letting me crash here," she says, taking off her designer tote bag and setting it on the bar stool.

"It's no problem."

"Do you want anything to drink?" Lo asks, his eyes glittering with mischief. He always offers a guest a drink so when he pours himself a glass of alcohol it doesn't seem too suspicious. He glances at me with a crooked grin, knowing I'm in on the secret.

"Water is good," she says. "Is it weird not having staff?"

"You mean serving yourself?" Lo calls from the fridge. "It's backbreaking pain." He grabs a thermos from the shelf and slides Daisy a water bottle.

"Don't be an ass," I tell him.

Lo snakes an arm around my waist, drawing me to his chest. His lips tickle my ear. "Never," he breathes, his eyes drinking me in.

My entire chest constricts. *This is not real. He's playing a part. That's all.*

"So this is your apartment," Daisy says, and I break from Lo. She wanders away from the bar and scans the living room to the left and the hallway to the right. Not much else. She inspects pictures that line a bookshelf towards the living room. I forgot Daisy has never been here before. I talk to her the least, mostly because she's the youngest and not very involved in my life. I guess the only way to be close to me is to inject yourself in my world because I won't make the move to enter yours. That's horrible, isn't it?

"If you two have kids, you so have to burn this one," Daisy

says with a laugh. She holds up a photo of Lo sticking his tongue in my ear while I shriek in disgust. Out of all the pictures, she's chosen one of the few that wasn't staged. We were sixteen, a time before we started our fake relationship.

"Have you not heard of a wet willy?" Lo asks, taking a large swig from his thermos. He sets it down on the counter and approaches Daisy, taking the photo from her. His smile widens, filling up his face into something beautiful.

"You're supposed to lick your finger," Daisy protests like he's a moron, "not put your tongue in her ear."

"I agree," I say, even though I don't, not really. My body heats at the image of Lo so close to me, the whole ordeal sexier than I'll let on.

"Oh, you do?" Lo says, with the tilt of his head, an eyebrow quirks up, unbelieving. "If I recall, you were not complaining that day." He stalks towards me. "You were all flushed."

"I'm always flushed," I retort, my breath hitching as he nears, his lips pulling in that playful smile. I point a threatening finger at him. "Don't."

My back hits the counters, trapped in the corner, and I wonder if this is real or if I'm lost in my head, fantasizing. I don't want to find a way to escape his hold, and I forget about my sister, who remains near the living room, scoping out years of history—fake and real—on shelves and tables.

"Take it back," he demands. "You liked it."

"I did . . . not," I breathe. He sets a hand on either side of the counter, on either side of *me*, blocking me in with his build.

I blink. I'm dreaming. I know am. This isn't real. Lo looks me over, undressing me with his intrusive gaze, and when his eyes meet mine, I feel as though he knows I'm confused about his true intentions. And that makes this game all the more fun for him. At least right now he seems to be enjoying it.

Suddenly, he kisses me. Deep, hard. Oh . . . *this* can't be just in my mind.

My back digs into the counter, but he wraps an arm around me, bringing me to his chest, tugging me closer than close. His body melds against my legs and torso, and I succumb to his tongue that finds mine. His large hand caresses my neck, and I submit to our eagerness as he drives closer, to the fire that ignites us both.

And then he pulls away, and his tongue slips into my ear. I squeal, awakening, and shove him off.

He laughs, full-bellied laughs, and turns his back on me to pick up his thermos. His lips are red and mine sting and puff from that *intense* kiss. All to prove me wrong, I suppose.

"That was not necessary," I tell him.

"Now you're going to tell me you didn't love my tongue in your mouth? I know you'd like way more than that. Maybe my tongue licking your—"

"Stop," I say, my body tightening. I glance over at Daisy, who flips through a photo album in the living room. When I turn back to Lo, my jaw has officially unhinged. He purposefully wipes his sweaty brow with the hem of his black tee, just so I'll catch a peek of the prominent ridges in his abs. My breath deepens, hot and bothered, but I would be this way if anyone did that to me . . . I think.

He edges over again and loops a finger in the waistband of my pants, tugging me to him. "Relax, love," he whispers, playing into the performance. "I can finish you off later." He sucks hard on my neck, and a sound catches in my throat.

Okay, this is too much. I shove him off, too hot to even shoot him a warning glare about taking the charade too far—about teasing me again. Lo is too good at hitting my tender spots. And then I remember Cassie, her cries, as though Lo is more masterful than he's ever admitted. Is he really that good in bed? *Don't go there, Lily. There's no coming back once you do.*

My nerves still thrum from the aftermath, and he subconsciously licks his bottom lip, leaning against the counter as he watches me grow redder. Even that pulses the place between my legs, making me crave something more. Something further than just kisses and fondling. Oh God.

Daisy returns from the living room with an uncomfortable look. I sincerely hope she didn't witness *any* of that. I'm an awful sister. Truly horrible. "I actually don't want to be in your way," she confesses. "I'll just stay in the guest room and watch TV if that's all right?"

"That's fine, Dais." I show her to the guest bedroom, pressing a finger to my tingling lips on the way. She disappears inside and throws her bag on the bed. I close the door as I exit, and Lo stands right there in the hallway with a foot against the wall. He nods to his room—the one we're supposed to share every night.

I follow and he turns the lock once we're inside.

On the dresser, I dock my iPod and put the speaker on a low tune but loud enough that I ease at the idea of speaking freely. These walls can be thin. Case in point, the *thump thump thump* of Lo's sexual adventures with Cassie.

Tinted glass cabinets engulf an entire wall. Seven of the twenty have secret locks that only open with a magnetic key. I would say he's paranoid, but last winter, I had to explain to Rose why a dozen quarter-filled tequila bottles were shoved underneath the sink. One of Lo's worst weeks, and I haphazardly tried cleaning up after him. Not well enough, apparently.

Rose didn't question my story, only complained that I hadn't invited her to our Mexican themed blowout. I should laugh at the ludicrous lie—that we actually have friends to call—but I sadden at the thought of Lo drinking enough alcohol in one week to satiate an entire house party.

He pulls out a glass and a bottle of an amber-colored liquid.

I climb onto his bed, my heart racing from earlier. It shouldn't. This is Lo. We're supposed to be together. We're supposed to be affectionate, but yet, I can't stop replaying what happened. I can't stop blushing or heating or wishing he'd just take me right here. *No, no, no. Don't go there.*

I rest my back against his oak headboard. "Can you make me something?" I ask, my voice raspy. I clear my throat. Jeez, what is wrong with me? I'm usually not this uncomfortable with Lo, but this situation mounts my anxiety and my desires. I cross my legs and swallow hard.

His eyes flicker to me briefly, and he tries to hide a knowing grin. He clinks another crystal glass to his and sets them on his desk. I watch as he unlocks a second cabinet, with the mini-fridge hidden inside. He scoops out ice and effortlessly pours the liquor without pause or spillage. When he finishes, he walks around to my side of the bed, not sitting next to me. Instead, he hovers with both glasses in hand.

"Are you sure you want this?" he asks huskily, and part of me wonders if he's talking about more than just the drink. *Yes, I want all of it.* I blink, no, he has to be talking about the alcohol. *Stop fantasizing, Lily.*

"Why wouldn't I?"

He licks his lips. *Stop doing that.* I hold in a breath. "It's strong," he says, watching me closely. Too close.

"I can handle it."

Lo puts the glass in my palm and stays towering over me, the authority something new, something I'm not used to. I kind of want to stand and take control of the situation, but Lo blocks me from setting my feet on the ground.

He tosses back half his glass in one gulp, the liquid sliding down easily. He waits for me to taste mine before he finishes off his own. "What are you waiting for?"

My heart to stop pounding. I take a small sip and cough. Holy hell. I choke into my fist.

"Hey, go easy," he tells me. "Do you need some water?"

I shake my head and stupidly take another sip to try and help the burn. Instead, that goes down just as rough.

He takes the alcohol from my hand and sets it on his night-stand. "No more for you."

I keep hacking into my fist and curse myself for trying to relax with alcohol. I should have known Lo would concoct something semi-toxic, too potent for any normal, sane human being.

When I settle down, I inhale a deep breath and slouch. "Are you going to sit down?"

"Why does it matter whether I sit or stand?" he asks, not moving one bit.

"You make me nervous."

"Scared I'll jump you?" he wonders with a devious smile, still drinking. He's finished off his and has already started on my drink.

Yes. "No."

"Then I don't see a problem with me standing here." His eyes do that thing again, the one where they scan the length of me, as though imagining what I look like bare and wanting.

To ignore him, I examine all of his memorabilia tacked on the walls and set on the shelves. The only time I venture in here is to help wake him up or to make certain he's not passed out in vomit. I hardly pay attention to the decorations. Some of them only stay here to assemble our mountain of lies.

Framed comics line the wall directly in front of me, hanging above his desk. All Marvel: *Avengers*, *Spider-Man*, *X-Men*, *Cable* and *Thor*. The bottom corners are signed from our numerous trips to Comic-Con in San Diego.

Last year, we stopped attending the comic book convention when I slept with Chewbacca, or at least a fan dressed as the *Star Wars* character—one of my more embarrassing conquests. Lo didn't have a splendid time either. He drank something Captain America gave him. Turns out the Cap imposter wasn't too noble, having spiked his booze with roofies. Nerds can be vicious too.

"You remember when you slept with Chewbacca?" Lo must have followed my gaze to the same poster. He heads to his desk to make another glass.

I shoot him a look. "At least I didn't accept drinks from every masked superhero that approached me."

"Yeah? Well at least I'm not into bestiality."

My eyes narrow and I grab a pillow off the bed, chucking it at him with all my might. I would *never* be into something like that. Gross, gross, gross.

Lo dodges the pillow but it collides with a bottle of bourbon, knocking it over like a bowling pin and toppling it to the floor. Lo's face darkens in contempt. "Watch it, Lily." He picks up the bottle, unbroken, and reacts as though I hit his child.

I don't say I'm sorry. It's just alcohol. And he has plenty more. When my eyes plant on a shelf by his head, my heart nearly drops. "How long has *that* photo been there?" I spring from the bed. He should have burned it!

He carefully returns his bottles to a safe location and cranes his neck to see what I'm fussing over. I'm so embarrassed by the photo that I shove him from the desk and spread my arms out, failing at blocking his view since the picture sits above me and he far surpasses my height.

He laughs at my lame attempt and plucks the frame off the shelf with ease. I try to reach for it, but he hoists it high above, teasing me further.

"Toss it out," I demand, my hands flying to my hips, just so he knows I mean it.

"It goes with the posters," he muses, his eyes twinkling at the memory that's encapsulated within the frame.

"Lo," I whine. He's right that the photo fits in with the others. Also at Comic-Con, Lo and I stand beside cutouts of Cyclops and Professor X. I wear nothing more than a pair of latex pants, a shiny black bra and long plastic blades from my knuckles. I look more confident than I let on, mostly because Lo begged me to stop hiding behind his back. It was his fault I was scantily clad in the first place. He insisted I join him as his favorite X-Men's love interest. So he dressed up as Hellion—the young New Mutant with telekinesis—in a spandex, red and black suit, and like a good friend, I played the part of X-23 for the day, the female clone of Wolverine.

I hate that the photo is in a room with dozens of empty memories. A few frames over, we're holding hands underneath the Eiffel Tower during a family trip to France. Fake. Another, he kisses me in a gazebo. Fake. I sit on his lap during a boating trip in Greece. Faker. Why do we have to tarnish the real memories in our friendship by placing them with phony ones from our pretend relationship?

"Please," I beg.

"Where am I going to get better proof that we're a couple?" he protests, inching towards me just to make this even more awkward. My back hits his desk, and I hope to God we're not reenacting the earlier kitchen scene. But then I kinda do.

"Technically . . . " I say, eyes on his chest, ". . . this is *my* room too."

"Yeah?" He sets the photo back on the shelf above me, and before I can turn and snatch it, he clasps my wrists in a tight hold. He stretches my arms behind my back. Oh my God.

"Lo," I warn.

"If this is your room, then make me believe it."

"Shut up," I say instantly. I don't even know why.

"That's not very convincing."

Is he being serious? "This is *my* room," I say adamantly, wondering if that's enough.

"It is?" he plays along, edging closer. "You don't seem so sure."

I try to reclaim my hands, but his grip tightens and he widens his stance so his feet trap me against the desk. Yes, this is just like the kitchen, only worse (or better) because I am not in control without my arms. Not one bit.

"Step back," I try to sound forceful, but it comes off too raspy and too wanting.

"Why do you think this is your room?" he asks. "You don't sleep here. You don't fuck here. You don't eat or drink here. What makes this yours as much as it is mine?"

"You know why," I breathe. *We're pretending, aren't we?* I'm so confused. What is he to me right now? Friend, boyfriend, something else entirely?

"Once you stepped through that threshold," Lo says, "you entered my place." His hot, bourbon-scented breath hits my neck. "Everything in here belongs to me."

My head lulls dizzily. I hate that I haven't had sex today. I hate that my body wants Loren Hale. And maybe even my mind too.

I try to concentrate. I have to. "Take it down," I say again.

"No, I like that photo and it's staying there."

Why does he care so much about that stupid picture?!

Before I ask, he spins me around and leans my stomach against his desk but keeps my wrists in his hands, pinning my arms to my back. I try to wiggle out of the hold, but he presses his body to mine, in a position that I've fantasized so many times. Just like this (maybe not the submissive part), but with him behind me, his pelvis grinding into my backside. I gape, internally dying. Luckily he can't see my open-mouthed expression.

I draw in a tight breath. "You're being mean," I tell him. He knows I haven't had sex. When we were eighteen, he asked me what it felt like to go without climaxing for a day, and I told him it feels like someone is burying my head under the sand and pulling my limbs so tight they become taut rubber bands, waiting to be snapped and released. The cravings feel like drowning and being lit on fire at the same time.

He said he could relate to the paradox.

"I know you're enjoying this."

Yes, very much so. "Lo," I breathe. "If you're not going to have sex with me, you need to back away. *Please.*" Because I don't think I can say no. My body wants him so badly that it trembles beneath his weight, but my head has become far more resilient. He's just teasing me. That's it. And I don't want to wake up feeling ashamed about not stopping. He doesn't like me like that. He couldn't want someone like me.

He lets go and takes three steps back. I massage my wrists and set them on the desk, not facing him just yet. I collect my bearings— the places inside of me way too tempted right now. When I muster the courage, I spin around, my eyes livid. "What the hell is wrong with you?" He can't use sex against me, not like that.

His jaw locks, and he spends a great deal of time pouring his next drink. He takes two large swigs and refills it before even beginning to answer me. "Don't be so serious," he says lowly. "I was just playing around."

His words send arrows into my chest. It hurts. I know it shouldn't. I wanted him to say, *it was all real. I meant it. Let's be together.* I know that now, even if being together will bring a whole new set of complications. Instead, he reinforced our façade. It's all a lie.

"You want to play around?" My body thrums with heat. I storm over to his liquor cabinets, find the magnetic key and open them up quickly.

"Hey, hey, hey!" Lo shouts. I barely pull out two bottles before he has his hand on my wrist, knowing I'm either about to trash them or chuck 'em out of the window. I haven't decided which yet.

"*Lily.*" He growls my name like it's the most profane word in the dictionary. We're both furious, and I feel justified in it. I don't look away. His face sharpens, and I can almost see the gears cranking in his head.

"Let's talk, Lo," I say tightly, not moving yet. "How is what I'm doing any different than what you just did to me?"

He inhales a deep breath, eyes narrowing. As always, he calculates each word before speaking. "I'm sorry, okay? Is that what you want to hear? I'm sorry that you can't handle being touched by me. I'm sorry that the very thought of fucking me disgusts you. I'm *sorry* that every time you're horny, I'm here."

And there goes my breath. I don't understand what he's trying to tell me. Does he want me or is he pissed that I'm a sex addict? I carefully set the bottles down on the desk and disentangle from his grasp. I slip into his bathroom and lock the door just as he nears it.

"Lily," he calls.

I lie on the cold tiles and close my eyes, trying to clear my mind. I'm starting to wonder how much I can take of this—of not knowing the truth of our actions, of our relationship. It's driving me insane.

My body shudders, a small withdrawal from the lack of stimulation today. I keep my eyes shut and try to sleep it off, but the knob jiggles with the click of the lock. The door opens and Lo pockets a bump key.

I don't move from my resting place, and I train my gaze on the white ceiling.

Lo sits next to me and leans against the Jacuzzi tub. "You shouldn't be worried if Daisy heard us. Normal couples fight."

Right, the charade. Silence thickens, and I'm proud of making him suffer a little.

He shifts on the ground and pulls his knees up, arms loosely wrapping around them. "When I was seven, my father took me into his office and pulled out this small silver handgun," he says and pauses, rubbing his mouth with a small, dry laugh.

I keep my expression blank, even if the story interests me.

Lo continues, "He put it in my palm, and he asked me how it felt to hold it. You know what I said?" He glances at me. "I told him that I was scared. He smacked me on the back of the head and said, 'You're holding a fucking gun. The only people who should be scared are the ones on the other end of it.'" He shakes his head. ". . . I don't know why I just thought of that, but I keep remembering all of it. The way the gun felt heavy and cold in my hand, how I was so terrified of the trigger or of dropping it. And there he was . . . disappointed."

I sit up and scoot back on the other wall to face him. He looks visibly upset, and that's as much of an apology from Loren Hale as I'll ever need. "You never told me that story before."

"I don't like the memory," he admits. "As a kid, I felt this overwhelming sense of admiration towards the guy, and now it makes me nauseous thinking about it."

I don't know what to say, and I don't think he wants me to reply anyway. So the quiet passes once again. A shudder runs through me, even as I try to suppress it.

"Are you withdrawing?" Lo asks, his eyes heavy with worry. "Do you need something? Like a vibrator?" That's *not* awkward . . .

I shake my head and clench my eyes closed as the pain in my extremities intensifies from being riled up without release. They pull tight and sharp. I'm a rubber band that can't snap.

"Can you talk to me?" he says, irritated.

"A vibrator isn't going to help," I say, opening my eyes.

"Why not? Are you out of batteries?"

I return the smile, even though I'm not in the mood. "It's just . . . not enough." He gives me a weird look. "It's like keg beer."

His nose crinkles. "Copy that." He scans my body, and I look away from the intrusiveness of it, his gaze heating me quickly.

"I'm going to just . . . withstand it for tonight."

"You could go out," Lo suggests. "If Daisy wakes up and looks for you, I can tell her that you had . . . an emergency study group since you're failing econ."

"I don't even believe that. It's fine, Lo."

"I've been a jerk, so I want to help you," he says in a breathless tone. "And there's only one obvious solution."

My forehead hurts from frowning so hard. Is he really going *there*? Does he want to have sex with me? For real?

"We can get you wasted so you won't care about having sex. Then you'll pass out and Daisy will be long gone tomorrow."

The suggestion takes me aback because it's not what I expected or kind of wanted to hear. I would have liked him to say, *sleep with me, I want to be with you, for real*. Hell yes, I would have replied. Even if monogamy scares me more than anything, I would try it. For the whole purpose of having Loren Hale. I think I've always wanted it. With him. But I'm not so sure he feels the same. This is a letdown, but at least it's a solution. "That's a good idea."

"Yeah?" Does he seem bummed out by my sudden acceptance of it? I can't tell. "Well, good thing I know someone who's an expert in the field of alcohol. He can set you up real nice."

"Just tell this guy not to make me so drunk that I puke," I warn.

"Barfing is unacceptable, got it." We rise from the floor and reenter the bedroom, and I lose my shakiness to a smidge of excitement at something new—with him mostly. I usually don't drink at all throughout the night. Lo's never told me outright, but I can tell he likes me better when I'm sober. Maybe so I can drive and help him regain consciousness, but sometimes, I think it's more than that.

I sit on the edge of his bed and cross my ankles. "Are you going to make me something that I can actually drink?"

"I think I have flavored rum somewhere. It'll be easier going down." He spends a few minutes concocting a *very* large drink, filled in an over-sized, super-wide water bottle.

"Ugh . . . " I hold the cold concoction. "Am I going to die?"

"There's more Diet Fizz in there than rum, I promise."

I take a tentative sip, and when it doesn't burn, I take a much larger one.

His smile grows. "Good?"

"Tastes like coconut."

"That's the rum." He plops on the bed beside me, and he has a much smaller glass of whiskey in hand, being economic with his sips. In a matter of minutes, I down the whole drink but barely feel a thing. Maybe it hasn't kicked in yet.

I glance at Lo. The way he watches me with rapt attention sets my whole body aflame. I just want him on me. In me. Dear God. "More," I tell him. "Maybe I should take some shots."

"I don't know your limit," he says, standing. "And the whole point of this isn't to get you sick." He fixes another mild drink. I can barely look at him without imagining his body on mine.

I join him by the desk and grab a shot glass. "I need something with a higher alcohol content." Before he can protest, I pour some of his whiskey into a shot.

"A whiskey shot?" he says with raised eyebrows. "Really? You're going to fucking gag, Lily."

I narrow my eyes in challenge, and then throw back the liquor in my throat.

I gag. But I do manage to swallow it down without spitting it back up.

He cocks his head to the side like *told you so.*

I touch my neck. "That was horrible. I think my insides are burning." I try to clear my throat.

"Now you're just being dramatic."

He pours me a shot of something clear and then something else and holds both of them up. "Vodka. Cranberry juice."

I nod and drink the first and wash it down with the second. Ah, much better.

He shakes his head at me. "You done?"

I run my eyes over his abs, and the spot between my legs clenches. *No, no, no.* "Another."

I barely hear him mutter, "This is stupid." Hey, it was his idea, but I can tell he's rethinking it. A lot. An hour later, one more drink and a few more shots, I head to the bed and the whole world sways. Whoa.

I think it's hitting me.

I fall backwards onto the mattress. I can't see my feet. Everything swirls, and I no longer . . . even a little . . . care about sex. Hell, I don't think my body is capable of moving on its own accord right now.

I lie supine on the bed and stare at Lo as he shambles about the room, cleaning up spills and shutting away bottles.

"Lo . . . ren," I say his name, which feels funny on my tongue. "Ren . . . lo." I smile stupidly.

"I'm glad you find my name as amusing as the rest of your sisters," he says, locking the last of his cabinets. Then he sits beside me while I shut my eyes. "How do you feel?"

"Spinning," I murmur.

"Don't think about it," he instructs. "You think you can crawl underneath the covers?"

"Hmm?"

Everything starts fading. And I drift into the blackness.

don't know what time it is. All I know is that there's a monster rumbling in my stomach, and it wants out. I'm underneath Lo's comforter. I don't remember even getting here or putting my head on his pillow. Lo sleeps on the other side, facing towards me, but he keeps his hands to himself.

I debate whether I'm really sick or not. The effort to walk to the bathroom sounds strenuous and painful and way too taxing on my head and body. But I am past nauseous right now. And then my stomach contents start rising.

I have to get up.

Hurriedly, I race to the bathroom and pull open the toilet seat. Everything I drank appears in the bowl like a magic trick.

"Lily?" Lo flips on the bathroom lights. "Shit." He runs a washcloth underneath the faucet and then kneels behind me.

I can't stop vomiting, but each time I do, I start to feel somewhat better.

He rubs my back and pulls strands of hair out of my face. After a few minutes, I start dry heaving, no longer actually puking anymore. He flushes the toilet and wipes my mouth for me with the cloth.

"I'm sorry," I mumble, about to set my cheek on the toilet seat. Instead, he gently leans me into his chest, and I rest my head against him.

"Don't apologize," he says, sounding pained.

"Lo?" I whisper.

"Yeah?"

"Please . . . don't move, okay?" The thought of standing or shifting my body at all may just send me back to the toilet.

"I won't." He wraps his arms around me, keeping me warm on the cold tile. We stay like that for quite some time. And I start to fall back asleep, my eyes heavy. And then I hear his voice, so soft that I think I've made up the words.

"I should have just had sex with you."

Twelve

The morning sunshine burns my vision. I squint and scoot up, trying to right my world. *Where am I?* is the first, scary thought that I process. I take in the champagne comforter, my two legs underneath it, my hair pulled back into a nice pony, and little flashes of last night course through me.

Lo carried me from the bathroom to the bed, tucking me in and keeping my nasty hair out of my mouth. Last night, I think I snatched a bottle of whiskey right from his hands. Even as he protested, I guzzled the liquor like an idiot. I'm *that* kind of drunk.

I let out a tired, mortified groan. When an antagonizing voice doesn't make fun of my bear-like noise, I frown and glance at the right side of the bed. Empty, except for an unmistakable butt print. *He has a good ass.* I stuff my face in the pillow and groan louder. I hate that I think that.

I try not to dwell on whatever stupid things I said or may have done while intoxicated. I rub my eyes and sit up, but a piece of paper safety-pinned to my shirt, which is actually *his* shirt, distracts me. *He changed my clothes?* I think at first. Must have puked on the other tee.

My cheeks rose as I pluck the paper off and scan it. The letter is scrawled so fast it looks half in cursive. My eyes widen in horror.

"What the hell?"

Parents are here. Get the fuck up.

What are my parents doing here? Do they know Lo and I aren't really together? Do they think Lo's an alcoholic? Are they going to send him to rehab?

I stand on two quaking feet and find a glass of water and four aspirin on the desk. Gratefully, I pop them and begin to search for clothes I can wear. His closet doesn't have a wide selection, but I store a few emergency outfits just in case of the worst.

I hop into a lavender day dress that will impress my mother, considering my greasy hair will dock me a couple of points. After brushing my teeth four times, rolling a stick of deodorant on and pinching my cheeks for natural blush, I gain the courage to leave the sanctuary of Lo's bedroom.

I take a sharp breath, voices echoing off the hallway walls from the living room.

"Where is she, Loren? The morning is almost gone," my mother complains. I wish he could use the "she's ill" excuse, but for the Calloways, ill requires a hospital visit and an extended stay. Otherwise, you're fit to enter the world of the living.

"I'll go check on her," Lo says, voice tight.

I step into the living room as he rises from the gray couch. "Ah, there she is," my father exclaims with a bright smile. My mother and Daisy sit on the gray-stitched couch, both sporting pretty floral dresses. Everyone stands as I enter, as though I'm a queen or something. But then I spot the Hermès suitcases and luggage bags leaning against the wall. They're a matching set. Lo's and mine.

What the hell is going on? They know, don't they? They're sending us away! Maybe to a far off rehabilitation center. We'll be apart. Alone. For real.

Just as I put a shaking hand to my mouth, seconds from puking again, Lo rushes to my side and speaks. "It's your father's birthday weekend."

I try to breathe. My eyebrows shoot up in surprise.

My mother fingers her pearls, which choke her bony neck. "For goodness' sake, Lily, I've been reminding you for months. We're taking the yacht to the Bahamas to celebrate."

I've never been good with dates or other peoples' schedules. I turn to Daisy, who seems to be looking everywhere but at me. "Why didn't you tell me?"

Lo's cheekbones sharpen, his jaw clenching, and I realize I've missed something. Daisy clears her throat, but her eyes train on the carpet. "I knew you would have made some sort of excuse . . . and we all agreed . . . " she trails off.

It hits me. She lied. She didn't want to be here last night. I wasn't really on her list of sisters to call for help. This was a setup.

"We knew you would forget," my mother clarifies. "This is an important trip for your father. He's been working hard, and we want our *entire* family present. If that meant having Daisy spend the night so you can't run off in the morning, then so be it. But now you're awake and we have to go. Rose and Poppy are already waiting at the plane." I assume we have to fly to Florida in order to take the yacht to the Bahamas.

My head spins, excuses resting on the tip of my tongue, anything to avoid a family event. Even if it is my father's birthday, they should have never tricked me into going.

Lo runs his hand along my arm. "You okay?" he whispers so only I can hear. Maybe he thinks I'm going to throw up again.

I nod even though the news slapped me in the face.

He says, "Put on a smile. You look horrified, Lil."

I do as he requests, offering my mother a small one. Her

shoulders stay tense, but her lips twitch in acceptance. Good enough.

It isn't until we leave the apartment that it dawns on me. I haven't had sex in over twenty-four hours, and Lo hasn't consumed his usual amount of alcohol, since he watched me all night. And we're about to be sequestered on a boat. With my family.

This just got a whole hell of a lot worse.

Thirteen

I try thousands of excuses before boarding the yacht. Lo and I planned a double date with Charlie and Stacey. I'm failing economics (true) and I need to cram for the upcoming exam (truer). None stick.

After I puke over the side of the boat, I admit to being hungover and layer on the "drank-too-much-wine-last-night" defense. My mother looks less than thrilled by my behavior, but it gives me free rein to openly sip Lo's hangover brew. I never ask what's in the brown liquid, lest I barf again.

He nurses a glass of Fizz in his right hand. I accompanied him earlier when he slipped the bartender five hundred bucks to serve him three-fifths bourbon whenever he orders soda. That also covers the liquor bottles he requested to be sent down to our cabin. He's a stealthy one.

I admire the tenacity, but I'm not feeling incredibly supportive. I lie on the yacht's sun deck with a nauseous belly and a pounding migraine. I put a towel over my head to block the radiating sun from my tender eyes and pull a corner up so I can vaguely see my surroundings. The rays beat on my fair skin. Even after applying SPF 15, I know I'll roast in the heat. And I secretly hope I'll burn. Maybe it'll get me off this fucking boat.

"Feeling better?" Poppy asks, dragging a lounge chair next to

Lo's. I make a great effort to *not* stare at his abs and toned body that bakes in the sun. He probably won't get much of a tan because he has on SPF 90.

Poppy spreads out her Ralph Lauren towel and puts on large, engulfing sunglasses and a floppy hat before sitting down.

"No," I tell her. "Where's everyone else?"

"Still eating lunch inside. Are you sure you don't want anything? I can bring you a sandwich."

I groan at the thought of potent smells.

"That's a definite no then."

I nod. "Definitely no."

Rose and Daisy have both earned official Brutus badges for tricking me when Rose announced my "pregnancy" scare secret, and my mother keeps shooting me sharp looks. She probably hopes I'll turn to stone.

"Do you think they'll notice if I jump overboard?" I ask, sitting up and plugging my nose before taking a much larger swig of the hangover drink. I stifle a gag. Gross.

Lo doesn't say a word because he's fast asleep, his Fizz-bourbon still wrapped in his fingers. I wonder if he stayed up all last night, taking care of me. I gently pry the glass from his clutch so it doesn't spill all over him.

"It's not so bad here," Poppy says, cracking open a hardback. She relaxes, and if I was her, able to enjoy the sunshine, to read, to stare off and drift and dream about anything, I'd think this was pretty lovely too. But as I gaze at the wide, vast and endless ocean, I imagine my body rocking on someone else's. I re-create the blissful feeling of reaching the highest peak in my mind. The elevator. The man in a suit. Thrusting. It's all planted there, telling me to feel a familiar sensation again and again and again.

But I can't. Not here. And so I'm left craving something that will never come.

The sliding door *whooshes* open, and Rose walks out with a tequila sunrise. She spends a great deal of time bringing her lounge chair in front of everyone's, the legs scraping against the hard floor. When it's just right, she spreads out a light blue towel and sits, facing me.

"Do you want me to get you one?" she quips, raising her alcoholic drink.

"Very funny," I say, my stomach gurgling, still unsettled.

Lo could have easily downed fruity drinks all night without too much suspicion, but he hates sweet mixes. And he'd rather not draw any attention to himself. He puts away drinks so quickly that people are bound to be suspicious or worried that he's returning to those old, inebriated, party-filled years before we got together. Of course they never really ended, maybe the prep school parties, but not the drinking. No one knows that though.

"Did he get you drunk?" Rose wonders, eyeing Lo's sleeping body like she could stick him with voodoo needles.

"No," I lie. "He actually tried to get me to stop." Semi-true.

Rose looks doubtful and she kicks his lounge chair, waking Lo up from his nap.

He jolts, startled. "What the hell?"

"Rose," I say with the shake of my head. "He was tired."

"Really? I hadn't noticed."

Lo pushes his hair back with his hand and mutters a few insults under his breath. Then he raises his lounge chair to a sitting position. "Look what the wind blew in."

"What?" Rose snaps.

Lo's eyebrow rises, confused. "What *what*?"

"What did the wind blow in? Finish what you were saying if you have the balls."

"You're right, I've lost my balls. You win." Lo scans around his area for his drink. I hand it to him, and he looks appreciative that I kept it safe. He chugs down half.

He doesn't need to finish his statement. I'm almost positive he meant to call her a bitch, or at least implied it in the vaguest way possible.

Poppy says, "I think you're getting burned, Lily."

Oh great. My plan to burn alive has been ruined by Poppy's maternal worry.

She tosses me a bottle of suntan lotion.

"I'm fine, really. I burn and then tan. And I need the color." I push my aviators further up my nose.

Rose snorts. "That's the dumbest thing I've heard in a while."

"That's not true," I retort. "I'm pretty sure Maria said something about the color of the sky actually being orange. And you were there."

"I'm excluding children from this."

Lo smiles. "Ooh, Rose, showing favoritism towards children. What is the world coming to?"

She glares at *me*. "I still hate that you brought him. Poppy had enough sense to leave her husband and child at home."

Lo finishes off his drink. "I'm right here, you know."

Rose ignores him, waiting for me to respond.

"It's not like I have a child that Lo needs to look after. If Maria wasn't born, Sam would be here, right, Poppy?"

Poppy looks impassive. "I'm not getting into this." Sometimes, being Switzerland during family tiffs is super annoying for everyone else.

Lo sets down his drink and then picks up the suntan lotion. I think he's going to apply more to his Irish skin, but he stands and then pushes my legs up to my chest. He straddles my lounge chair, not noticing how his movements cause my chest to cave, my breathing to shallow and my heart to race.

With only a thin bathing suit on, I feel ready for something more. The sun soaks my skin, the heat intoxicating, dizzying my thoughts, a headiness I drift in. My toes curl inward as I try to suppress my feelings, which will surely volcano sooner or later. I need him. I need to release all of this, but I don't know how to ask without it being awkward. This is so different than supplying him with scotch and rum. I'm asking for his *body*. That's not okay.

"I can do it," I say, my breath ragged as he pops the lid.

Rose adds, "This doesn't make me like you any better, *Loren*."

"I know," Lo says, his back to her. "And frankly, I don't really care, *Rose*." Yeah, emphasizing her name does not have the same effect. Lo squirts lotion in his hand, and I recoil.

"Really, I can do it myself."

His eyes widen like *we're supposed to be together, dingbat*. Oh right. "Let me get your shoulders." He scoots forward and takes my arm in his large hand. His fingers knead into my tender skin.

My eyes shut while he rubs the lotion lower on my ribs, lifting a side of my bandeau black bikini top to apply beneath the hem. He can feel the way my chest rises in and out, my breathing heavy and strained.

He turns my body around and leans my stomach on the lounge chair. Then he hovers forward and starts spreading lotion along my shoulder blades and lower back. He unclips my bandeau, and I fade away with his touch. *Holy . . .*

The sliding door *whooshes* again. "Can I help any of you?" a server asks. He wears a white collared shirt and black pants, the yacht service uniform. In his late twenties, he has golden hair and an angular face, making him too angelic, too handsome and too desirous for my throbbing body.

"I'll take a drink," Poppy says. *No. Make him leave!* "What do you have?"

While he starts listing off the expansive menu, Lo presses his thumbs down in a massage pattern. Oh . . . that feels good.

I grip the towel underneath my head, my body starting to build towards something bad. I want to tell Lo to stop, but I'm not sure I can say the words without being breathless.

I clench my teeth as his fingers dig deep and then lightly flutter over my skin, playing with my needs. I hate him right now. I hate how I want this so, so badly.

My gaze finds the attractive server, and I lose it. I keep my back from arching, my body from bucking, and I snap my eyes closed before they roll back. A muffled noise escapes, and I think my sisters have missed it as I begin to come down. But when I open my eyes again, more than embarrassed, the server briefly meets them, scanning the length of me. Knowing.

I bury my face in my towel. *Disappear*, I order.

"You," I hear Lo's voice.

The server's shoes clank on the floor, coming towards us. Oh my God?! What is Lo doing? "What would you like?"

"Stop staring at my fucking girlfriend," Lo says, topping it off with a bitter smile. "That'd be great, thanks."

"Lo!" Poppy shrieks.

Rose is actually laughing. The world has gone mad. And I refuse to look at it, hiding underneath the covers, topless, my chest still pressed on the lounge chair.

"I wasn't staring," the server refutes with a tense voice, unmasking his emotions. "If you want something, I'll gladly get it for you. If not, I'm going."

"Great," Lo says. "I'll take a Fizz."

"You mean a bourbon and Fizz?" he retorts in challenge. Oh shit.

"No, I mean a regular Fizz."

The server says, "But you've been drinking bourbon all day, Mr. Hale. Are you sure you don't want another one?"

"You've been drinking hard liquor *all day*?" Rose says, her voice suddenly flat.

"No," I refute before Lo can. I peek from underneath my towel and glare at the server, finding some internal confidence for Lo's benefit. "You must be mistaken. I've tasted his drink."

The server eyes me for a long time, trying to read my expression, and I try to soften my gaze, as though telling him it will be worth his while. Or something. Anything. I mean, I moaned while *watching* him spout off menu items. And he saw it. That's all I have to go on.

"Right," the server says. He glances back at Lo with a knowing, satisfied look, thinking he'll bed me later and really show up this rich prick. I don't want him to, and I fear that he actually will. And I'll let him. "I'll get your drink—"

"Don't," Lo says, clipping my bandeau back. "I'd rather not drink spit with my Fizz, and we all fucking know that's where this is headed. So leave."

Poppy says, "You can cancel my order. I think it's for the best if you stay inside."

The server nods and disappears at her wish.

I stand immediately. "I'm going to the bathroom and maybe to the pool." The words sound static and hurried, but no one questions them, except Lo. He collects his things and follows me indoors and to our cabin.

I don't look at him. I head to the tiny, tiny bathroom and turn the one-person shower to freezing cold.

I hear clinking, and I glance back just as he gulps straight whiskey from the bottle. He licks his lips and wipes his mouth with the back of his hand, pissed. When his eyes meet mine, he finally says, "Did you orgasm?"

My entire body flushes. "Not really," I mumble.

He nods to himself, staring dazedly at the ground. "Did you get aroused from me or him?"

I frown. "Does it matter?" I already feel awful about the whole event. "You shouldn't have been teasing me like that, Lo. I'm already tense as it is."

"I was trying to help," he snaps.

"By making me want to have sex on the sun deck?!" I shout. "That's *not* helping. You made the situation worse."

His face twists in anger and hurt. He plops on the edge of the double bed and puts the bottle to his lips again. Then he says, "If you have sex with that fucking asshole, we're done."

I hesitate by the bathroom. "What?" My voice goes small. For some reason, I think he's talking about our friendship. His glazed, reddened eyes tell me so.

He lets his words hang in the air while I internally freak out, imagining a world without him. So very alone.

"What do you mean, Lo?" My heart hammers.

"We're done," he says. "You really think your family will accept the fact that you cheated on me with the staff? No, we'll have to break up."

Our fake relationship, that's what he's talking about. I exhale. "I'll be careful."

His eyes narrow, heated. "So you're going to sleep with him?"

I shrug. "I don't have much of a choice."

He shakes his head. "Un-fucking-believable." He stands up and takes his bottle with him, turning his back on me.

"You don't understand," I start, quickly trying to defend what my body craves. "I can't stop thinking about it, Lo. My legs are shaking. My hands are shaking. I feel like I'm being set in a blender. I just need someone . . . "

"Stop." His voice sounds pained again. "Just . . . stop."

I'm so confused. "What do you want me to do? I can't go without it. You're drinking!" It's so unfair. "Why can't I have sex?"

"Because we're supposed to be together!" he yells. "You're supposed to be *my* girlfriend." Before I can ask him to elaborate, he goes to the door, purposefully trying to avoid my questions. "I'll be at the pool."

Fourteen

I spend most of the day shivering in a shower, trying to force myself to forget Lo and the male server and body parts. Self-love does nothing but frustrate me, and I sink to the cold tiles, crying the pain away.

Lo confuses me. Does he want to be with me? Or is he just afraid I'm going to ruin our lie? I can't find the meaning to his words, no matter how hard I repeat them.

I skip dinner, but Rose barges in my room and knocks on the door. "What are you doing in there?"

I shut off the faucet and wrap a towel around my wet, wrinkly skin. When I step out of the bathroom, she appraises my state. I mutter, "We had a fight."

"You and Lo?" Her eyes harden. "What'd he do?"

I shake my head. "I'm not even sure." Tears build again.

"That asshole," she says before going to my suitcase. "I knew something was wrong at dinner." Did he look trashed? My heart sinks at the thought of Lo drinking himself into oblivion because of me.

"How so?" I ask.

She finds my charcoal bathing suit and hands it to me. "He was really quiet," she says, actually not making a snide remark.

"He excused himself early, and I saw him sit on the deck and watch the sunset."

"Oh," I say softly. I finger the bathing suit. "What's this for?"

"Poppy, Daisy and I are going to the hot tub. I thought you should join."

"I don't feel well—"

"I know, but maybe being surrounded by other people who love you will help."

I'm not talking about my broken heart. My hands tremble even as I hold the cloth, and I don't know how much more I can take without having sex. I need to find the server, but Lo's expression stops me from making a move. I don't want to betray him, and if there's something there—just a chance that it exists—I don't want to ruin it. Not for anything. But I worry that I may.

I don't have the strength to argue with Rose. So I begin to dress in the bathing suit, dropping my towel.

"Is the fight serious?" she asks, sitting on the bed with crossed legs.

I shoot her a look. "Don't act so happy about it."

"What? I'm not enjoying your sadness, but I'm not going to pretend to be upset if you two break up."

"Why do you hate him so much?" I tie the straps around my neck.

"I don't hate him," she refutes. "He annoys me, but I don't *hate* him. Maybe dislike." She runs her fingers over the nautical bedspread. "I don't think he's good for you. Is it so bad that I think you can do better?"

"No," I whisper, fully dressed now. "But Lo and I . . . " I try to find the words. "We may not be good for each other, but sometimes I feel like he's the only guy who could ever love me." And that's the truth. Because who would love this? A girl who sleeps around. A whore. A slut. Trash to be disposed. That's what everyone sees.

"You think too lowly of yourself," Rose says, standing. "If you don't love yourself, Lily, how can anyone love you back?" She wraps an arm around my shoulder. "And you don't need a guy to fulfill you. I wish you would remember that."

And I wish that were true.

The stars twinkle overhead as all of my sisters soak in the warm, bubbling hot tub at the bow of the yacht. For this quiet hour, it seems like we're the only ones who exist.

Thirty minutes in and I already know this is a bad idea. The jet behind my backside does nothing but lead my fantasies to dark, sensual places. And my mind has drifted so frequently that I'm surprised I haven't fallen asleep and been afflicted with a hot sex dream.

All that keeps me present are my sisters' numerous games, like "Never Have I Ever"—in which I learned that Rose and Daisy are still virgins. Good for them. Thankfully Rose steers the conversation away from Lo and relationships. Mostly, I listen to Daisy talk about her week in Paris and the cute models, which also does not help my cause.

Then, I hear the clap of shoes across the wooden boards. I glance over my shoulder, and I try not to audibly sigh or moan or do anything at the sight of the attractive server. He sets down four towels for us and makes eye contact with me, clearly a signal, before he departs.

So this is it. I want to say no, but I'm afraid of what will happen if I don't have sex. And Lo hasn't offered. So . . .

Here I go. I fake yawn. "I'm going to head to bed, girls," I tell them, climbing out.

Rose watches me. "You'll be okay?"

I nod. "Yeah. I need to talk to Lo anyway."

"If you need backup, I'm happy to lend my nails," she says with a smile.

I share it easily. "I'll be sure to call you if I need them."

That's all it takes. I slip inside the yacht, where the server lingers by the bar, talking softly to the older bartender. He gives me a once-over and then I head downstairs, looking back to make sure he follows me.

He does.

Each step down towards the cabin rooms, I sense my looming fate. Am I going to ruin our fake relationship? Lo's paranoia ekes into my brain. What if I ruin our *friendship* over this? Or any possibility of a future, of something more together? I shake it off. This is like any other day. Lo will be happy that I feel better, and he'll be glad that I did it unseen. Nothing will change. *Nothing will change,* I repeat.

And then I freeze at the bottom. Lo sits outside our room, empty-handed. His head hangs low, and when he sees me, he jumps to his feet. I fossilize and feel the server's body-heat right behind me.

Lo doesn't even look at him. He keeps his hard gaze right on me. "I need to talk to you."

Talk. I don't need talking. I need something else. "I'm busy." *Just say it! Tell Lo you want him and end this.*

I'm a coward.

His nose flares. "Please."

I glance back at the server, who seems to be piecing together our relationship, trying to figure out what kind it is. Very, very unconventional, that's what.

I am awful at saying no. So even though my body protests with all its might, I nod and slip into my cabin, Lo shutting out the server behind us.

I feel like I have to justify my actions again. "Lo, I really need this. I'm sorry. I am." I inhale a strained breath. "I just don't know what else to do." I keep talking, afraid of what he has to say, so my words tumble out. "I can't stop thinking about it, and I know it won't stop until it happens."

"Sex or sex with him?" He points to the door. "If you really want him, Lily, then go. Have at him. Make him come, make him scream, if that's what makes you feel better, then do it."

"Wait," I say, my head spinning. "Wait, that's not. No . . . " I swallow. "It's not him. It's just the sex." I fiddle with my fingers, much more nervous than I've ever been with him. This is not pretend. What we're saying to each other—this is very real. "I'll start shaking if I don't find a way to satiate this. It's like . . . it's like there's something wrong in my head, and the only way to be at ease is to do it. You understand . . . don't you?"

He rubs his lips. "Yeah, yeah, I get it."

I inhale, thinking he's going to let me go without the added guilt. "So we're okay then?"

He blinks in confusion. "What?" And then he realizes what I'm asking. "Fuck no, Lily. I'm not saying it's okay for you to have sex with him."

My eyes glass. "Why are you doing this to me?!" I scream. "I've never once ripped a glass out of your hands. I'm sorry you hate this guy, but there's no one else. You want me to sleep with the old bartender? He's my father's age!" I do have some standards.

He scowls darkly and then touches his chest. "I'm clearly an option, and yet you *still* can't ask me. I don't fucking get it. Am I that revolting to you? You would rather go through withdrawals and bang some asshole than sleep with me?"

I gape, choked for a response. He wants to sleep with *me*? "I'm not going to use you like I do these other guys," I murmur.

"Goddammit, Lily," he curses. "I am standing here telling you that I want to have sex with you, and you still can't accept it. Was it that terrible the first time, is that it?"

"What? No . . . " The first time was wrong, impetuous and rushed. Back then, we were just kids trying to make each other feel better. If we have a second time together, I don't want it to be like that. "You shouldn't have sex with me just because I'm withdrawing. We're friends," I tell him. "You're not going to be another name on my list of guys for the week. Okay?"

His nose flares, breathing heavily. And he starts closing the distance between us.

"Lo," I warn.

"Have you ever thought about it?"

I watch his feet near, my pulse racing.

"Have you ever thought about me inside you?"

I almost stumble back, but he hooks an arm around my waist.

"Have you ever thought about us together?"

I can hardly breathe. "Together?"

"Where I don't share you with any other man."

All the time. "Yes." I keep expecting to wake up.

"If I could be enough to fill you, would you let me?"

I look at him. "Yes."

"Then let me try," he says, his hand cupping my face. "Let me try to be enough for you."

"That's a big undertaking," I tell him, my body swelling.

His lips brush mine as he whispers. "I'm big enough to take it." Oh . . . "Let *me*. Help *you*." He places my palm over his swim trunks, right on his crotch. *Yes.*

"I didn't know you wanted to . . . you never said anything," I stumble. My lungs struggle for air, three years of tension bursting.

With a shuffled step, he draws me even closer and then guides me backwards to the bed. "How the hell could you *not* know?"

"I'm dirty," I refute, hot tears brimming. "You don't want me."

His face twists in pain. "I don't think that. Neither should you." His lips graze my neck and then find my ear. "Lil, I want you to ask me. I need you to."

He presses his forehead to my temple, gently edging me closer to the mattress, his hands tight on my hips. I continue to struggle for breath. I know what he wants now.

He wants this to be real.

So do I.

"Help me," I say, breathlessly.

He grips the back of my neck, hard, plunging his tongue in my mouth. My legs hit the mattress, and my back slams into the bed. He lifts me up, all while keeping his lips hungrily on mine.

Bottles clatter to the floor, and Lo doesn't pull away to retrieve them. His hand kneads my breast, my top coming off. I grip his bare back, clutching for support. I try to flip over so I can be on top, but he refuses my demands, keeping my body trapped beneath his weight.

I succumb to his hardness and the way his rough movements dominate my bones. He lifts my leg around his hip but keeps my other on the bed.

I usually take control, pouncing on my prey, but here, every action has equal intensity. My fingers run through his soft hair, and his mouth sucks on my nipple, his tongue swirling around while I buck against him. Oh . . .

"Lo," I moan. I can't do this much longer. He's too far away. There's too much distance. "Closer."

He pulls my arms above my head, stretching me, and I cry out, my toes curling. "I need you. Please . . . ahh . . . " I'm in my zone.

He sheds his shorts, and I try to climb on him again, but he returns to my arms, pulling them once again. He stares deeply into my eyes, his body melding perfectly into mine. "I'm not one of your conquests," he says in a throaty voice. "I know what you want, and you don't need to take it. I can give it to you."

His fingers slide beneath my bikini bottoms, finding the sensitive place. They slip in and out quickly—so fast. I shudder and moan and try to speak but words don't come. I've reverted to caveman talk in grunts and groans and shrieks.

"Stay still," he orders, stepping off the bed, which rises without his weight. He walks across the room, completely naked, and fishes out a few condoms from his suitcase. I drink in his whole body. Even his cock . . . wow. That has definitely grown since the last I saw it.

He rips open the condom, climbing back on the bed. Unbearable seconds tick by, and I squirm, impatient.

He smiles and kisses me again, long and hard. Ah . . . I shudder. And then he fills me. His hips grind against mine, and he presses down with each thrust, getting as close as possible. I shut my eyes and turn my head, a natural reaction as I float away with the overwhelming sensation.

He grips my chin, still moving against me, and turns my face to his. "Look at me."

My eyes snap open, and his words send my body in a tailspin. I cry out. "Lo . . . " I grip his back tightly for support. "More."

He pumps, and his amber eyes stay on mine as he drives in and out. In and out. Deeper and deeper. I am lost to his scotch-colored irises. To the way he stares into me. No one has ever looked at me like this.

Everything bursts.

I'm flying into the most blissful feeling in the world.

I never want to come down.

Fifteen

Most nights, I pass out after sex, relying on sleep to avoid any communication with the other guy. As this bliss seeps away, I can't close my eyes. My head spins from the event, desperately trying to quantify what just happened.

Lo silently climbs off the bed and tugs on a pair of black boxer-briefs over his bare ass. He rescues a fallen bottle of bourbon and a glass from the counter. I tighten the navy sheets to my chest, and he hops on the bed, the mattress bucking underneath me.

More gently, he takes a seat at the foot.

He wants to talk. I suppose I do too. I think it may be where we went wrong the first time.

"Thanks," I say first.

His eyes flicker from the dark liquid to me. "I didn't do it all for you, you know?"

"I know."

He licks his lips. "Where is your head at?"

"I'm confused," I say truthfully. "I think I've been confused for a long time. I haven't known if you've been playing into our lie or if you really mean to touch me the way you do." Saying that feels really good.

He looks at me deeply. "I've wanted to have sex with you again since the first time," he admits. "But you had all these rules, and I didn't want to be the clichéd horny guy trying to abuse your addiction. So I was waiting for you to *ask* me to do it again."

I frown. Why didn't I? "I thought it was part of the lie. I thought you were just pretending." How could I know that he wanted more?

His jaw locks and he shakes his head. "I've never pretended, Lil. We've been together, even if you thought it was some fucking lie. We just weren't having sex." He stares at his glass. "On bad days, I'd touch you more than I should, I admit. Like when Daisy spent the night, but I was hoping you'd finally open your eyes and realize that I was there. You didn't have to suffer or go be fulfilled by some other guy. I was right in front of you."

"I just thought you were teasing me."

He nods. "I know. It didn't work how I planned." He swishes the alcohol in his glass, staring. "I understand your addiction, and I'm only bothered by the other guys when I tempt you to that place. I blame myself for making you aroused, hoping that you'll finish with me. But you never do, and in the end, some lucky bastard gets what I want. I had everything with you, the good and bad parts of a real relationship, except the sex." He inhales deeply. "I wanted it, but not on your terms."

"You've been waiting around for six years," I say, staring off. Six years of miscommunication. One of us could have opened up. Instead we let the tension build between us, growing a lie.

"The worst part was hearing you." He shakes his head. "You know, I'd stay awake, listening to you, wondering if your cries would turn terrified, wondering if some guy decided to take advantage or hurt you. But I can't . . . " He pauses on the words.

But I know. "You can't tell me to stop." Because it's hypocritical. He won't quit drinking, not for me, not for anything.

"Yeah." He inspects me from a distance, taking in my body language after sex. "How was it for you?"

Amazing. "Do you want a rating or something?" I try to lighten the mood.

His face sharpens, all hard lines, all ice, all Loren Hale. "I'm open to criticism." He finishes off his drink.

I can't rate him. He's literally not quantifiable on any chart. I have never trusted someone to take control and to do it so passionately. "You're enough," I tell him, my voice small, "but I can't lie to you. I worry that in the future, you won't be. And then what? I've never been committed to one guy, Lo. For you, I'd try, but . . . what if I fail?"

"You'll still be having sex," he says. "You'll just be having crazy, mind-numbing sex with me. Every day. On your terms. And if you slip up, it's okay."

"No," I immediately refute. "No, it's not. If we're together for real, I can't cheat on you. That's not okay." I realize I have to try. No matter what, I have to try to make this work and to find everything I need within Lo. I think it's possible, but it may be hard sometimes. "I'm going to need you, do you understand?"

Lo nods. "Of course, Lil."

"So on the days that you drink yourself to sleep before eight o'clock, what am I supposed to do?"

"You're making a compromise, and it's only fair that I do the same. We'll work out our schedules." He rests his hand on my ankle, sending shivers up my spine. "I want to love you more than I love this"—he waves his bottle—"and I don't know how else to do it unless there's something to lose." The stakes have become much greater. If I fail, that means I cheat on him. If he fails, that means he may drive me to cheat. Either way, we'll be alone and empty. We've never entertained the idea of being together, in part because we were never ready to make small sacrifices, like less drinking, no more one-night stands. I'll need to find the thrill elsewhere.

Three years later and drowning in lies, we're suddenly prepared to lose everything for the chance at something real.

"So this is it then." I skim his features, the firmness of his chest, the darkness in his expression and the wanting in his eyes. "We wake up tomorrow and become an actual couple. No pretenses. I stay monogamous to you, and you cut back on the drinking to help me. Are you sure you want to do this? There's no going back. If we break up . . . " *Everything will change.*

"Lily." He sets his glass aside and scoots closer. He cups my face in his hands. His closeness still makes my heart flutter like I've never been touched by him before. That's a good sign. "We're terrible at so many things—remembering important dates, college, making friends—but the one thing we've always been halfway decent at is being together. We owe it to ourselves to try."

"Okay," I say in a small breath.

His smile grows and he kisses me hard, cementing our new deal—or breaking our old one. He directs my back into the nautical comforter, and I happily wrap my arms around him, holding on tight and never letting go.

Sixteen

The rest of the trip, I no longer question the validity when Lo reaches out for my hand or when he slips his arm around my waist. It's all one-hundred-percent real affection that I can enjoy without constant confusion.

Back in Philadelphia, the clouds replace the sun and the most tropical it gets here are the little umbrellas in fruity drinks. Reality sets in along with the fall season, exams looming as close as the Christmas Charity Gala. Now that I'm back to the land of male bodies, I try to train my mind on Lo and no one else. Not the hot dog vendor on the street or the lawyers entering and exiting the apartment complex.

I can't cheat on Lo, but sometimes the *cannots* turn into *maybes* which become *okays*. And I'm at a loss of how to control that kind of cascade once it begins. Good thing economics steals my thoughts off Lo and even sex.

I slam my head against the fat textbook. "Die, numbers, die."

Alcohol bottles clink in the kitchen, a familiar sound that now drives me insane. I blame college. "Lo," I call from the living room. "Have you done this homework yet? Can you help me?" I must be desperate if I'm requesting his support.

He laughs but doesn't bother to answer me. Just lovely. I'm going to fail. Like I need another reason for my parents to hound me. The world lies to you. They say that you become this independent, self-sufficient creature when you turn eighteen, severing the familial ties once you enter collegiate society. But in our economy, nine times out of ten, you're financially dependent on them until you join the real workforce. Even I—daughter of a multibillionaire tycoon—have to rely on family for support. There's something vitally wrong with this system, and I don't have to be fucking good at economics to know it.

I bite my fingernails to the beds and smack my book closed. I watch Lo lean two hands on the counter, his shirt riding up and his eyes narrowed at his computer screen. He clicks some buttons, staring intently at a webpage.

I start to picture him walking towards me, eyeing me the way he did while at sea. He knows me well enough to take the lead. And he does, willingly, spreading my legs open . . .

Lo straightens up and shuts the laptop, his movement waking me from my fantasy. Okay, I can't concentrate on profit margins when all I can think about is something a little more nefarious.

Quietly, I pad over to the kitchen, where Lo mixes a drink. He cuts back on quantity, not quality. Bourbon and whiskey, his favorite dark-colored liquors, spread across the counters in droves.

I hover by the fruit bowl and lamely act like I'm examining the apples. In the past two weeks since we've been back in the city, I haven't figured out how to approach Lo without feeling weird. I'm not the type to come out and say: *Hey, Lo, can you please sleep with me?* The thought of uttering those words sends red spots to my skin. Doing it with strangers is different. I never have to see them again, and I rarely use words. I give them a deep, sultry look, and they follow me wherever I go. Using that Venus fly trap technique with Lo feels cheap and overwrought. So instead, I stand here awkwardly.

I don't want to ask for sex like I'm ordering something from a bar. Why can't this be easier?

I try to avoid the uncomfortable conversation with a question. "You do realize we have a test in a week? Are you going to even study?"

"I'll wing it." Relaxed, he sips his drink and leans his elbows on the counter. He tilts his head, watching me closely.

Maybe that was a bad question to ask. Now I feel nervous for the both of us.

About this time, I'd be sporting a glittery tank top and heading for a club, even if it's only the evening. Now that I'm monogamous, I only have one option, and he happens to be fulfilling his own obsession by downing a bottle of bourbon.

Should I even pull him away from that? Does it make me the needy, selfish person in the relationship?

"Lily."

His voice cuts into my thoughts. I stop pacing. Holy shit, when did I *start* pacing?

"You okay?"

"I'm fine." I go back to the fruit.

"You seem awfully fascinated by those apples."

"Yep."

"Okay, enough." He sets down his glass and edges close to me. "Ever since we returned from the Bahamas, you've been nervous and jittery whenever you *obviously* need sex. You do realize you used to tell me when and where you would have sex every night?"

"That was before it was with *you*," I defend.

"So this should be easier," he says, perplexed.

"It's not. I don't like asking for it. The guys I bed want to have sex with me." I cringe. That didn't come out right. "What I mean is," I say hurriedly as my arms flush, "they're actively looking for a hookup too. Not relaxing on the couch or surfing the internet. I don't want this to be a chore or for my problems to invade your personal life."

"I assure you, having sex is not a chore, especially not with you. As for your problems, well, that's what being in a relationship is about, Lil. Your problem is now my problem. In fact, it's almost always been my problem. Now I just get the reward instead of watching some douchebag take it."

"But you don't need me to drink. You don't have to ask me to fix a whiskey sour. Your addiction doesn't infiltrate my life like mine does yours."

"Yes it does, just in other ways. And do you really think I walked into this blind?" He twirls a piece of my hair in his finger. "I know how much sex you have. I know that when you're not having it, you're browsing porn. I'm not an idiot, Lil. I've been your best friend for years, and I haven't lost that knowledge now that I'm your boyfriend."

He makes solid points. "Okay, but I still feel weird asking for it."

Lo hooks his fingers in the waist of my jeans, eyeing the sliver of skin that peeks beneath my blouse. "Then don't," he tells me, his hand spindling across the small of my back. "If you want me to choose when we do it, I can. But I didn't want to take that from you."

His hand rises up my spine and he skillfully unclasps my bra. I stagger back in surprise, heat blooming on every part of me. He hooks his arm underneath mine, putting me in a lock so I can't squirm away. Our bodies touch from top to bottom, his hard chest against my soft. I can barely breathe.

Lo presses his lips to my temple and then he whispers, "Do you trust me?"

I swallow hard, trying to focus. *Do I trust him?* "Yes," I say. "But . . . you can't wait too long." My words tumble out, more frantic than I anticipated. "It has to be more than two times and spaced out. When I get stressed, I may need more and—"

His lips find mine, shutting me up. My shoulders droop and I melt almost instantly. He loosens his hold so my arms can fly around his neck. We're dancing. And yet, our feet don't move, but I feel lighter than air, suspended above the clouds while performing the waltz *Beauty and the Beast* style.

Gradually, he breaks the kiss and keeps his forehead to mine. I sway from the aftereffects. My lips on his. The surprise of it all.

"You're not losing anything," Lo tries to assure me. "You're gaining spontaneity. How did that feel?"

I open my mouth but can't form the words.

His grin widens, satisfied. "That good, huh?"

"Mmm-hmm." I've resorted to mumbles.

"You could be doing dishes in the kitchen," he whispers, his lips tickling my ear, "and I could come right up and. . . . "

His hand slides down my back and below my jeans, in between my thighs . . .

I'm sold.

I remove my shirt, my bra already unclipped. And he easily lifts me up and places me on the counter. I see something in his eyes—a desire that I hadn't noticed before. It's filled with determination, as though convincing me that he's enough.

I hope and pray and wish that he is. Only time will tell.

Seventeen

The smell of garlic bread and tomato sauce stimulates my hunger. I wiggle in my seat and tug on the hem of my black cocktail dress that rides up my thighs. Since starting college, the nicest place I've dined at is a pub that serves expensive cheeses and pistachios. The only instances when I read menus with a minimum hundred buck taste-testing course are during family dinner parties, my mother forcing me into high heels and pinching my arm to smile.

The incredulous stares are not helping me feel any more welcome. Middle-aged and elderly aristocrats shoot judgmental glares our way, waiting for us to dine-and-dash at any moment. Lo must sense the unkind speculation from our ages. Wrinkles have permanently creased his forehead.

He made the reservation a week ago, citing that we need to have our first "real" date. I sip my wine slowly. When he ordered us the house Merlot, I held in my surprise. He hasn't had wine— what he refers to as "subservient" alcohol—in months. And even though Nola drove us to La Rosetta, Lo rarely orders alcohol for me. Of any kind.

Now an official couple, I thought I'd stop overanalyzing his gestures, but I start thinking way too much, mostly about the differences in our relationship. Sometimes I wish for a remote control to pause my brain. Just for a moment of peace.

The waiter returns with a basket of "premium" bread. Those were his words when he talked about the loaf, and he looked all snotty about it too. Maybe he expected our eyes to widen in realization that we were at an *expensive* restaurant—with *premium* bread and pricy ravioli, a place not built for young adults with ones or twos beginning their age.

"Are you ready to order?" he asks with sucked in cheeks, reminding me a little too much of my mother.

I bounce between Capellini alla Checca and Filetto di Branzino. Pasta or sea bass? Lo notices my indecision and says, "Give us a few more minutes."

The waiter shifts his weight. Uh-oh. I know that look. He's about to get mean. "This isn't a Mexican restaurant where you can eat free chips and then leave. The bread costs money." *Oh, the premium bread costs money! Who would have thought?* "You have to order eventually."

Lo snaps his menu closed and he spreads his hands out on the table, gripping the sides. He looks about ready to flip the damn thing over. *His father would*, I realize. The thought steals my breath. I don't want to compare them. Ever. "I said 'give us a few more minutes.' Did I ever insinuate that I wouldn't pay?"

"Lo," I warn, his knuckles whitening. *Please don't flip the table.*

The waiter glances at Lo's hands and then the manager finds his way to our table. Eyes from other linen-lined booths and candle-set tables have drifted over to us, staring at the spectacle.

"Is there a problem?" the manager asks, slightly older than the waiter, both dressed in uniform blacks.

"No," Lo answers first, peeling his fingers off the table. He takes out his wallet. "We'd like a bottle of your most expensive champagne to go. We'll be leaving after that." He hands the manager his black American Express card.

The slack-jawed waiter straightens up. "That's the Pernod-Ricard Perrier Jouet. It's over four thousand dollars."

"That's it?" Lo says with the tilt of his head, feigning shock.

The manager places a tight hand on the waiter's shoulder. "I'll get that right out for you, Mr. Hale." Ooh, he even used his name from the credit card. Bonus points for him. He ushers the waiter out of our sight, and Lo looks about ready to break the neck of a chicken—or the man who just shuffled away with his tail between his legs.

"So we're not eating here," I say, adding up what just happened.

"Would you like to eat here?" he almost shouts, unbuttoning the top of his black-collared shirt.

"Not really." My cheeks blossom with an ugly red tint the longer people stare.

He rolls up his sleeves. "I had no idea that respect needed to be earned in a fucking restaurant."

"Can you stop messing with your shirt?"

"Why?" he asks, calming down. He scrutinizes my body language. "Is it turning you on?"

I glare. "No. It looks like you're about ready to run into the kitchen and beat the crap out of our waiter." Which is comical. Lo avoids most fights and would be more apt to scream in your face, verbally attacking, than throw a punch.

He rolls his eyes but stops messing with his sleeves per my request.

Only a minute passes before the manager returns with a gold bottle and the American Express card. Lo stands, gestures for me to rise, and he grabs both and shoots everyone a scalding look on his way out, even the manager who did nothing more than apologize and offer a grateful thanks.

I slip my hands into my long woolen coat. "Nola isn't supposed to be here for another hour," I tell him.

"We'll walk for a while. The taco stand is ten blocks away. Think you can make it?"

I nod. My short heels already stick in divots along the cracked sidewalk, but I try not to fuss about it. "Are you okay?" I ask him. The bottle swings in his hand, but he reaches down for mine with the other, holding tightly and warming my chilly palm.

"I just hate that," he says, wiping his sweaty brow. "I hate that we're still treated like children even though we're in our twenties. I hate that I had to pull out my wallet and buy respect." We stop at a crosswalk, a big red hand flashing at us, telling us to stay put. "I feel like my father."

His admittance takes me aback. And his cheekbones sharpen, making my stomach somersault. He looks far more like Jonathan Hale than I will ever confess.

"You're not him," I whisper. "He would have flipped that table over and then left the staff to clean his mess."

Lo actually laughs at the image. "Would he?" The sign changes to *walk*, and we cross the halted traffic, cars lined on the street with bright headlights shining forward and backwards. Just like that, the mention of his father drops in the air, lost behind us.

I spot the taco stand in the distance, lit up with a string of multicolored lights. A small park resides across the busy street, and a few college-aged kids surround a surging fountain, chowing down on burritos. I suppose we fit in with this demographic, but wherever Lo and I go, I always feel like an outcast. Some things never change past high school.

"Are you cold?" Lo asks.

"Huh? No, I'm fine. My coat is fur-lined."

"I like it."

I try to hide the smile. "Check the tag."

He swiftly falls back with furrowed brows and takes a peek. "Calloway Couture?" He joins my side again. "Rose designed it," he concludes. "I take it back. It's ugly."

I laugh. "I can get her to design you a sweater vest."

"Stop," he says with a cringe.

"Or a monogrammed shirt. She'll put your name right over the heart, *L-O-R-E-N*—"

He pinches my hips, and I shriek and laugh at the same time. He guides me to the taco stand, his lips by my ear the whole time, whispering some R-rated things that he would like to do to me for being so bad.

"Can we skip the tacos?" I ask, suddenly hot.

His grin lights up his face. He turns to the vendor, not feeding into my desires. Yet. "I'll have three chicken tacos. She'll take beef with extra lettuce." He knows my order by heart, not surprising since we eat here regularly, but now that we're together, it seems sexier.

"You want hot sauce on those chicken, right?"

"No, not today."

I frown. "You always get hot sauce."

"And you hate spicy food."

WhaaatOhhhh. It clicks. He plans to kiss me sometime soon. *That*, I like. We pick up our orders, pay and settle down across the street on the fountain ledge.

He gently rocks the champagne cork from the bottle and it sighs once released. He pours each of us enough to fill our two flimsy Styrofoam cups.

Around the same time, I take a big bite of my taco, and sauce dribbles from the end and down my chin. Hurriedly, I find a few of the napkins that haven't blown away, but I fear Lo has already witnessed my embarrassment.

He tries hard not to smile. "I do remember you being in cotillion. Or was that a dream?"

I snort, not helping my case. "Hardly. I had to dance with Jeremy Adams all night and he was a whole head shorter than me. Since *someone* chose to go to the ball with Juliana Bancroft."

He takes a large bite of his chicken taco to suppress laughter.

"I still don't understand why you did that to me. She was horrible." I take a big gulp of champagne, the bubbles tickling my nose. I already feel more relaxed. Liquid courage, something Lo knows a little about, but I predict that he'd be just as brazen without the added consumption.

"She wasn't that bad," he says, scooping fallen chicken from the tray back into the tortilla.

"She filled my locker with condoms."

"You don't know that was her."

"I slept with her boyfriend. If I had known she was dating some guy from a public school twenty miles out, I would have never touched him."

I avoided sleeping with guys from Dalton Academy. I hardly wanted a slutty reputation, so I chose my conquests very, very carefully. But obviously not *too* wisely or else I would have noticed his lie when he claimed his single status. Lady Luck had been somewhat on my side though. Juliana never told anyone what happened because she didn't want people to know she was dating "lower" in the first place. A small plus to the horrible ordeal.

"It could have been any other girl," Lo still refutes. I think partly to rile me. He picks up his champagne cup.

I gape. "The condoms had glittery stickers all over them. Who else in high school had a Lisa Frank fetish? She even carried around a binder with a rainbow unicorn and she was in *ninth grade*. So not only was she cruel, but she was vain enough to practically sign her name across the crime." I pause. "You know the sad part of that story? I actually used those condoms."

He snorts on his champagne, choking on the alcohol.

I pat his back. "Take it easy there. Maybe you should switch to something you can handle. I'm an alcohol aficionado. You should listen to me." I flash a smile.

"Is that so?" he says, his face red from hacking up a lung. He takes another sip to clear his throat.

"So why did you take Juliana?" I wonder. "You never answered."

He shrugs. "I don't remember."

"And I don't believe you, Loren Hale."

"Use my full name, Lily Calloway, its authority is lost on me." He flashes an equally smug smile.

"You escorted me to plenty of balls before that one," I remind him. "So what changed?" I shouldn't nag, but my curiosity prevails over my sensibility.

He sets his empty tray aside and holds the champagne bottle between his legs. I wait while he thinks about the right words, on how to frame his answer. He picks at the flowery gold paint. "The night before Juliana asked me, I came home trashed. I paid off some guy to buy me a bottle of Jim Beam. I spent that afternoon drinking in the back of our old elementary school." He rolls his eyes. "I probably looked like a fucking delinquent. I was bored. And I guess that's not even a good excuse anymore. My father saw me stumbling in, and he went off on some tangent about being unappreciative." His eyes narrow at the brick walk. "To this day, I remember what he said. 'You can't even fathom how much I've *fucking* given you, Loren. And this is how you repay me?'"

I'm afraid to touch Lo. He's in some kind of trance, and if I put my arm around him, he may jerk out of it, sullen and unhappy. He may be both regardless.

He continues with a heavy frown, "I listened to him rant for an hour. Then he started talking about you."

"Me?" I touch my chest, not believing I could enter this kind of conversation.

He nods. "Yeah, he said you were too good for me, that I would never be able to grow up and be with a girl like you. I was young, rebellious, and when he said *go*, I yelled *stop*. When he said *Lily*, I shouted *Juliana*."

"Oh," I mumble, not realizing how deep-seated the truth really is.

"For the record," his voice lightens, "I was miserable all night having to listen to her go on about her horses. And if I remember correctly, you did use Jeremy's short height to your advantage."

My ears heat and redden at the memory. I use my hands as blinders to shield my mortification. "You're not supposed to find my past conquests amusing," I whisper-yell, still blocking my peripheral vision.

His lips quirk. "I love all of you." He raises my chin with a finger and kisses me so delicately that I wonder who the man is on the other side of me. The tenderness draws me in, and I lose breath in the short moment.

I break away first, not sure if I can last kissing him like this without the promise of wild, passionate sex. He raises his eyebrows, putting his cup to his lips, grinning. Yes, he knows exactly how I feel right now. I'm so transparent.

I change the topic to keep from oozing into the fountain.

"Poppy keeps asking me about your birthday. She wants to meet all of our friends at the party they're *supposedly* throwing for us—Charlie and Stacey especially."

He remains calm. "What did you tell her?"

"I told her that she'd hate the party. Too many drunken college students, and she'll have to meet them some other time. She bought it pretty quickly. Besides, she has no reason to believe we'd create fictional friends."

"I wish you'd chosen a better name than Stacey. I don't know any Staceys that I'd ever be friends with."

"That's name prejudice and immature."

"There's no such thing as name prejudice, but I don't doubt it's slightly immature. I have many faults."

"About your birthday"—I stay on track—"since you're not passing out at noon, can I actually take you out to celebrate?"

He rips off the last of the champagne label. "I don't think so."

"Come on. We can dress up in costumes and go to a party."

"Why can't we just stay at home, drink and have sex?"

"We do that every day, Lo," I say irritably. Since we've been together, my late night clubbing customs have disappeared. Unlike Lo, I'm not used to being cooped up in the apartment so much. "There have to be some perks to having a birthday on Halloween."

He takes a swig from the champagne bottle, thinking. He wipes his mouth with the back of his hand. "I guess we already have the perfect costumes."

I grin and then immediately frown. "Wait, what costumes?" My stomach flops, and once my embarrassment begins to set in, his face lights up. Oh, I hate him. "No, not the same ones we wore to Comic-Con." My skimpy X-23 outfit! And his tight, equally revealing Hellion suit. The picture framed on his wall.

"You want to go out so badly, that's my condition."

He's trying to see how much I want it. I inhale deeply. I'll wear a cape in the front or something absurd to cover me. "Fine. You have a deal."

"We like making those, don't we?"

I suppose we do.

Eighteen

"Take these numbers into account, not these." My tutor gives me a concerned look. "Do you follow?"

My eyes grow wide. "I'm going to fail. Again."

He taps the eraser of his pencil on the thick economics text and stares at the numbers. His lips draw into a thin line, trying to figure out how to tutor the stupidest girl at Penn. I'm hopeless. It took three more days of solo-torture before I sucked up my pride and emailed Connor to tutor me.

Now I have company in hell.

"Try this one, Lily." He slides the book to me and points to a big paragraph. Words. Too many words for something involving numbers. Why can't economics choose between the two? Having both numbers *and* words in an equation sends a splitting migraine to my skull.

I struggle for another five minutes before I throw my pencil down in a huff. "I swear I'm not doing this on purpose," I say quickly. "And I know you're probably wishing I chose someone else."

He leans back in the rickety old library chair. We're holed up in a tiny study room with a whiteboard, a long table, a light fixture and one glass wall to remind us that other people do exist.

The perk: I can scream in obnoxious frustration and no one will hear my cries but Connor.

Time ticks by, and the sun has already bailed on us. I'm probably keeping my tutor from his dinner or evening plans. I glance occasionally at his thick, wavy brown locks and deep blue eyes, scoring high on the Guy-I'd-Like-to-Fuck chart—or the chart I used to have before I entered a monogamous relationship.

The collar to his navy peacoat is popped, the first sign of his preppy status. Honestly, I hoped for some dweeb with glasses and acne. Someone who wouldn't entice me so much.

"How did you learn about me anyway?" he asks, intrigued. "Referral?"

"You were listed as a tutor on the economics departmental website. I just kind of went for the coolest name. It was between you and Henry Everclear." No girls, or else they would have been my first choice.

"So you went for Connor Cobalt." He smiles in amusement. "Connor isn't my real first name. It's Richard."

"Oh." My arms heat. "I guess that's not as cool." I could smack my head at my reply, wishing for something pithy or witty. Instead, I get *dumb*.

"What's your full name?"

I glance warily at the clock on his phone, resting on the table beside my book.

He follows my gaze. "I won't charge extra."

I flush further. I've definitely heard *that* before. "I don't want to keep you from your plans."

"Oh no," he says with a laugh, setting down his Starbucks coffee. "I don't have any plans. I'm actually kind of glad you're a little slow. I've been tutoring freshman A-type personalities for the past few months and they whiz through my problems in under twenty minutes. I need tutoring hours for my resume. The MBA program at Wharton is pretty competitive and any extracurricular helps."

I should take offense to that, but I can't argue with the truth here. I am struggling. "Well, I may be a lost cause."

"I'm the best tutor at Penn. I bet you a thousand dollars I'll have you at least capable of passing your next exam."

I gape, disbelieving. "That's in two days."

He doesn't even blink. "I guess we're going to be cramming for the next forty-eight hours." He checks his watch and simultaneously picks his coffee back up, taking a sip. "You never told me your full name by the way. It can't be worse than Connor Cobalt." He flashes a pearly white smile—like the blinding ones that surrounded me in prep school.

"Lily Calloway."

His head jerks back in surprise. "You wouldn't happen to be related to Rose Calloway?"

"Sister."

He grins again. I wish I could tell him to stop. After years of pretending and lying, nothing screams "fake" more than overzealous smiles. "She's on the Academic Bowl for Princeton, right? We compete against them all the time. She's wicked smart. I'm surprised you didn't ask her to tutor you."

I laugh dryly. "I think you'd have to be built of armor to learn anything from Rose. She's a tough teacher."

His eyebrows rise as he finishes off his coffee. "Is that so?" He's too curious for his own good.

I decide to save him and turn back to my books. "So are you really prepared to lose a thousand dollars?" He may be keen on racking up hours for his resume, but I actually need to learn this stuff.

"My pride is on the line. It costs more than a thousand dollars." He checks his Rolex watch again. "Do you have a Red Bull at your place?"

Wait? Is he inviting himself over to tutor me?

He sees my confusion as he starts stacking textbooks together. "Library closes in ten minutes. I wasn't kidding about cramming for the next forty-eight hours. It's either your place or mine. But I have to warn you, my cat hates girls, and I haven't cut her nails in a few weeks. So unless you want to be jealously assaulted by Sadie, I suggest your apartment."

I prefer the Drake anyway. With Lo around, I have less chance to do something moronic. Like listening to my lower brain.

"My place is fine." I sling my backpack over my shoulder as we leave. "But I live with my boyfriend, so we'll have to be quiet."

He whistles. "A junior and shacking up already. That explains a lot."

He holds open a glass door for me, but I freeze before stepping onto the campus quad. "How so?" Do I wear everything right on my chest? Or is Connor Cobalt so arrogant he believes he has me all figured out in a short study session?

"A lot of girls here are from family money—"

"Wait," I stop him before he continues. "How do you know I have money?" I glance at my wardrobe. Nothing on me screams distastefully wealthy. I wear a pair of Nike sneakers, track pants and a Penn sweatshirt. If Rose saw my style, she'd have a hernia.

"Calloway," he says my name with a laugh. "Your daddy is a soda mogul."

"Yeah, but most people—"

"I'm not most people, and I make an effort to know names, especially ones that matter."

Uh, I have no idea how to respond to *that* conceitedness.

He leads me outside into the chilly night. "Like I was saying, most rich girls all tend to do the same thing. Find a guy at an Ivy

League who will be incredibly successful, marry early, and have their future set without having to do the extra lifting—straight As, stellar recs, full CVs. I'm not judging. If I was a girl, I'd probably be on the same path. Hell, I'll end up marrying the type."

What a horrible generalization. Not all women would throw away their careers at the chance of being taken care of by a man. I could punch him or vomit. Either one seems like an appropriate reaction. I bet he also believes women should only pop out babies. God, Rose would scratch out his eyes if she heard him.

But I'm not as bold as Rose, and it's too late to find another tutor. So I bury my thoughts and follow this asshole outside.

Lo!" I shout, walking through the door with Connor trailing behind. "Lo!" When he doesn't answer the third time, I presume he's left the apartment entirely. I shoot him a text and hope he's not too sloshed to feel the vibration.

We set camp at the bar counter. I pore through three different books, making slight progress but not enough to count as a success. On the problems Connor dishes out, I get twenty-five percent correct. That number has yet to fluctuate.

Two cases of Red Bull and a pepperoni pizza later, it's eleven o'clock and Lo still hasn't returned home. My phone sits lamely on the counter, and I glance at it, expecting to see a missed call. I told Lo about my tutoring session, and we went wild this afternoon. Maybe he thought he satiated me enough, so he planned to ditch me tonight and do his own thing.

I bite my lip. Worry starts to set in a few minutes later, and concentrating on the problems becomes near impossible.

"Maybe he just lost track of time," Connor says, watching me check my phone repeatedly. "I think someone is throwing a highlighter party on campus tonight. Lots of the underclassmen I tutor were talking about it."

"Upperclassmen don't go?"

"Not usually. We're more focused."

I try not to roll my eyes. Another wide generalization. Lo would hate this guy. I must still look anxious because Connor closes our books.

"I'm sorry," I tell him. "We can call off the bet. You don't need to lose your money because I can't concentrate."

"I've never failed on my tutoring promises. The bet still stands. You'll pass your exam, Lily. I'm certain of it." That makes one of us. "Now, you're obviously really concerned about your boyfriend. Until we find him, you're not going to learn anything, so where do you think he could be?"

Huh? He's offering to help me track down my boyfriend? I blink away the strangeness of Connor Cobalt and try to concentrate on Lo. Where would he be? That's a good question. He partied himself out his first two years of college and has recently stuck to bars. Usually he arrives home at a reasonable time so he can drink heavy liquor here and pass out.

If I'm not driving him, then he has to be somewhere on campus. "You said that the highlighter party was on campus?" I ask.

"It's outside on one of the quads."

"We'll start there."

S trobe lights flicker across a grassy field. Bodies pump together to the hypnotic beat of house music. We approach at a distance. Most people wear white clothes with streaks of paint and marker that glow in the black lights. They run around and grind, almost animalistic in the cold night.

How will I be able to find Lo in this mess?

Before we integrate with the bumping and sweaty crowds, a petite redhead clenches my elbow. "Hey, you'll need this." She passes me a white tee. I frown as she hands Connor a much bigger size from the cardboard box by her feet. He doesn't seem fazed as he unbuttons his dress shirt and pulls the other over his head, handing her his button-down.

"I'm not getting that back, am I?" he asks her with a flirtatious smile, or maybe it's just a nice one. It's hard to tell with a socialite like him.

Her eyes flicker roguishly, and she grabs his wrist. With a black magic marker, she scrawls her number on his palm. "I'll keep it safe for you." She puts her arms through the holes and wears the button-down like a light jacket.

Holy crap. I have to commend her. That was sexy.

Connor just smiles—calm and collected like it's completely normal to search for his tutoree's lost boyfriend and be hit on by a pretty redhead at a party.

Keeping my shirt on, I yank the white tee over my clothes and pull my hair out of the collar, layering up. Then we enter the madness.

Some guy with a neon green wig runs at me screaming like a banshee. He brandishes a giant pink highlighter and streaks it right across my boobs. That's lovely.

Connor finds my hand and tugs me in a different direction. "What does he look like?!" he yells over the blasting music that vibrates my feet.

I dodge a purple highlighter that heads for my bare arm and pop up Lo's picture on my phone.

"I know this guy!" He points to the screen. "He's in my International Affairs class!"

I suppose that's not that big of a coincidence. Business majors have to take all the same upper-electives. "That's good! Should we split up?!" A girl squeals beside me and draws a yellow line right across my ass. Seriously? I'm not even wearing white pants. The marker stains an ugly brown color on my jeans.

He scouts the party and nods. "I'll be on the side with the canvas and paint!" *There's paint around here?!* Yeah, he can take that area. "You check out the keg."

Good, he sends me to the one place Lo will probably be if he attended this crazed party, even if he considers keg beer to be the equivalent of cat piss. Huddled around the keg, people with markers are sparse, which leaves college students who came for free beer.

A lanky guy covered in neon blue paint does a keg stand, his shirt flopping over his head and revealing patches of curly hair on his chest. He chugs the bitter drink, and it takes only a couple minutes to deduce that Lo isn't here.

I should have known. Cheap alcohol and ear-splitting music have not been part of his ritual since he was nineteen. While Lo may not have fully matured yet, his indulgences have.

I try calling him again, but it goes straight to voicemail.

"Lily?"

I frown and spin on my heels to face the male voice. I don't recognize him until I spot his highlighted fraternity shirt: Kappa Phi Delta. The frat house Lo picked me up at.

His blond hair blows in the wind, but the cold misses me as my whole body heats in an uncomfortable embrace. I guess I'm the real jerk in this scenario since I ditched him so quickly after the one-night stand.

He notices my confusion and points to his chest. "Kevin." He nods to the keg. "Can I get you a drink?" Translation: *Do you want to do it again?*

Before I decline, Connor bounds over, face flushed from fighting through tangled bodies. His white tee is splashed in a variety of neon paints and streaked with highlighters. Someone missed the shirt, and his elbow glows bright pink. "I didn't find him," he tells me.

"Connor Cobalt!" Kevin exclaims.

Oh my God. They do not know each other. Where am I?

Connor turns and his grin widens as he sees Kevin. "Hey, man!" They exchange the bro-hug: a handshake, squeeze, lean in and slap on the back. I never understand those.

"I'm surprised to see your ass here," Kevin says with a smile. "I thought keggers were far too inferior for Connor Cobalt." Glad to know other people find his full name fascinating.

"Actually, I'm on the clock."

"You call this tutoring?" Kevin's eyes drop to the number written across Connor's hand. "Damn, man, maybe I should adopt your methods. All I get out of my hours are headaches." He glances at me, noticing my lingering presence. "Oh, this is Lily." Obviously Kevin idiotically spaced out when Connor acknowledged me earlier.

Connor frowns deeply and tilts his head towards me. I want to smile. *Yeah, you don't have me all figured out.*

"Yeah, I know," Connor says. "I'm tutoring her. Econ."

Kevin presses two fingers to his lips, trying to suppress his amusement. "You mean, you're 'tutoring' her, right?" The douchebag even uses air quotes and nudges Connor's shoulder suggestively.

My nose flares and heats again. I'm standing right here!

Surprisingly, Connor's face contorts in disgust. He brushes Kevin's shoulder off like he may have infected him. "No, I mean I'm actually tutoring her, Kevin. We're here to find her boyfriend. She can't get ahold of him." He turns a fraction, closing off his body to his . . . friend? I can't tell anymore. Connor is an enigma.

He says offensive things and then becomes affronted when someone else dishes it out—though less subtly.

Kevin doesn't take the hint. "Yeah, my brothers told me about him. He came to collect her the morning after at the house."

I watch as Connor opens his mouth, but I don't let him speak.

"I was single," I defend myself, even if my rash-like mortification spreads. Mixed with neon highlighter, I must look like a freak. "And just so you know, you were an awful lay." I turn to go and then on second thought—I whip around and slap the Solo cup from his hands. The frothy beer soaks the grass and Kevin rolls his eyes as if this isn't the first time a girl has assaulted his keg beer.

I inhale a strained breath and march away, pushing past people, not even caring when someone smears green on my cheek. Whatever. Nothing can make this night worse.

Connor catches up to my side as we find a break in the bodies, but I keep my speedy pace towards the parking lot.

He says, "I was about to tell him he's a moron, but I think your method was far more effective."

I laugh and wipe off stray tears that somehow escaped between now and then. When did I even start crying? The whole night has twisted my insides, and on top of everything, I didn't find Lo.

What if he's passed out at a bar? What if he's stumbling on the streets or getting his stomach pumped in a hospital?

My voice grows small. "I don't know where he could possibly be."

"He's probably fine, Lily."

I shake my head, distraught tears building. "You don't know him." I bite my bottom lip to keep it from quivering.

Connor grimaces in sympathy. "How about we go back to your place and I'll wait with you until he returns?"

"You don't have to do that," I say, sniffing. "I've already wasted enough of your time. This goes beyond tutoring me."

"Yeah, it does," he says with a nod. "But this is the most interesting thing that's happened to me in six months, which was the last time Sadie scratched my date. And"—his eyes shift to the ground—"I guess I know why you'd be worried about a guy like Lo. He smells like booze almost every time he does show up to class."

I frown. He doesn't show up often? I know he's not the model student, but the way Connor talked, it made it seem like Lo skips more than he attends. As for his smell, Lo takes more precaution with our families—extra mints, showers, cologne. During school days, he cares less.

No one has ever confronted me with Lo's problem before. I stumble for words before landing on something that feels semiright. "He usually answers his phone." It feels good not denying the truth to someone, even if that someone is as random as Connor.

We walk towards my BMW. "You must really wish I picked Henry Everclear."

"Actually, no." We both slide in the car, and I man the steering wheel. "I like the challenge. I'm in the top five percent of my class. Top one percent of my major. All I need is that extra something and Wharton won't be able to resist me."

I put the car in gear and head out. "Let me guess. Reforming the girl who is failing economics is your extra something?"

"I wouldn't have put it so blunt, but yes."

I try not to laugh. Connor has no idea how frank he can be. I switch lanes. "About Kevin . . . " I feel like I need to defend myself further. I'm not sure why.

"You don't have to explain," Connor tells me. "People have fun. I get it." He taps the door handle to the beat of the soft rock song. "Goddamn, you live far away."

I stop at a red light. "It only feels like that in traffic." After a few more jerky stops, we arrive at the apartment complex. I walk briskly to the elevator with Connor on my heels. I try to hide my nerves by crossing my arms.

We fly up multiple levels, the numbers blinking above. I glance at Connor. "You have . . . " I motion to my ear. Bright orange paint crusts the top part of his.

He doesn't go to rub it off, only smiles. "I'm covered in paint. Don't worry about my ear."

"Have you been to a highlighter party before?" What else could explain his clear composure throughout the crazy ordeal? He barely batted an eyelash when girls started grabbing his ass. He has two sets of pink handprints on his butt to prove it.

"Nope. I've heard about them though. It was interesting."

The bell dings, and I try to figure out what would stir Connor's stoic exterior. Maybe *not* being accepted to Wharton. Yeah, I can imagine that not going over too well.

I fumble with my keys and unlock the door. "Lo!" I yell into the living room. Connor closes the door behind me, and I storm through the apartment, hoping to find Lo in the kitchen fixing a drink.

It's empty.

I try his bedroom, not even bothering with a courtesy knock. I swing the door open, and my stomach drops. "Thank God."

Lo lies facedown on the bed, fully dressed and accompanied by three brown liquor bottles. I don't know or care when he returned home. The fact that he's present and not dead on the streets relieves me.

I approach him and say his name a couple of times to test his level of consciousness. With my pent up frustration, I shake his shoulder. He still doesn't stir. Carefully, I roll him onto his side and press the back of my hand to his clammy forehead. He's warm but not enough to run a fever. Alcohol poisoning. My other fear.

"Is he okay?"

I jump at the voice, momentarily forgetting Connor. He leans a hip on the door frame, looking impassive as he watches me take care of Lo.

"He'll survive," I say. "Thanks for your help."

He shrugs casually. "It's good for me. I've been so holed up in the library for the past four years that I've forgotten what real problems look like."

Riiight. I brush off his hundredth offensive comment of the night. "I'll see you tomorrow then? If you still want to tutor me."

"For the fifteenth time, *yes,*" he says. "You need to work on your listening skills. I'll see you at six."

I frown. "Isn't that a little late?"

He flashes one of those prep boy smiles. "Six in the morning."

Oh. I glance at the digital clock on the desk. "That's in five hours."

"Then you better get to bed." He looks inscrutable, glimpsing at Lo one last time, and then slips out the doorway, leaving the apartment.

Lo is dead to the world, and I decide to sleep in the guest bedroom. I curl in my purple sheets and realize that I've been so concerned for Lo's safety that I haven't thought about sex at all tonight.

Nineteen

Connor arrives promptly at six with steaming coffee and a box of croissants. Unlike me, no dark circles shadow his eyes, and he saunters in, all too chipper. He must run on five hours of sleep.

"Are you on drugs?" I ask. "Adderall?" Lots of college students abuse stimulants to study, basically performance enhancers for the intellectual elite.

"Absolutely not. You can't taint natural genius." He pauses. "Have you tried it? It may work for you."

"You do realize you just insulted me?" I finally "out" his rudeness.

He rips a croissant in half and smiles. "I apologize," he says, *unapologetically.* "I was just trying to be helpful. Some people can concentrate better on Adderall. It's not for me, but maybe for you?" Strangely, rephrasing the question helps mild the insult. That may be one of Connor Cobalt's intricacies. Or just a gift.

"No drugs," I tell him, never liking stimulants, downers, or any narcotics. I have an addiction already—I don't need another. "I want to do this the right way, even if I'm not a natural born genius."

"Then let's get to the books."

We study a few more hours, and I retain the information this time, working on problems while Connor busies himself by making me flashcards. His handwriting is neater than mine, and I'm sure he's already inflated himself with that knowledge.

When he finishes his last stack, he peeks at the clock on the oven. Studying eats time like a beast, so I'm not surprised it's already noon. "He's still asleep?" Connor asks, sounding surprised.

It takes me a moment to realize he means Lo. We've dodged the subject since Connor stepped through the doorway with sweet smelling coffee and baked goods. He asked if Lo was okay and that was that.

"He's passed out," I correct him. "He'll probably wake up within the hour."

"Does he do that a lot?"

I give him a noncommittal shrug, not wanting to discuss Lo right now. Thankfully, he catches the hint and flips open my notebook to review my problem sets.

Twenty minutes later, we order Chinese for lunch. As soon as I hang up the phone, the toilet flushes in the other room. I focus on the sound of heavy, sluggish footsteps. I have zero interest in speaking with Lo, only to get slurred responses with irritable jabs.

I turn to the books, pretending that Lo hasn't risen from bed, and ask Connor to explain chapter four to me again. Lo must hear another guy's voice because only seconds pass before he braces the sunlight that streams through the kitchen windows.

Connor's words taper off as Lo lumbers in. His matted hair sticks up in different directions, his complexion peaked and clammy, and the pungent smell of scotch permeates around him. If he was a cartoon, he'd be Pepe Le Pew with a smoky cloud circling his body. I should have helped him shower or at least tried to change him out of his clothes last night. He would have done the same for me.

Lo runs a hand through his hair and shuffles to the coffee pot. His eyes briefly flicker to the bar where we sit. "I know you," Lo says, filling a mug.

"International Affairs. You sit in the very back. I'm in the very front."

Lo turns his head a fraction to catch my gaze, his eyebrows rise like *do you hear this guy?* Yep, been there already. "Right." Lo opens a cupboard and pulls out a bottle of Baileys Irish liqueur for his coffee. "You're the guy who sets the curve." He says it like it's a bad thing, but he doesn't see Connor beaming beside me.

"I'm tutoring Lily for her econ exam tomorrow."

Lo shuts the cupboard, and I see his neck flush red. He hesitates before facing us fully, leaning against the sink.

"You know about the exam, right?" I ask Lo. I can easily see that he forgot.

"Yeah," he says into his mug, taking an extended sip.

"Are you in the same class?" Connor looks all too eager. "I do group tutoring too."

"I'm maxed out on studying. You help Lily." Lo finishes off his coffee way too quickly. Then he opens the refrigerator and grabs a carton of eggs, preparing his hangover cure.

Connor nudges my shoulder. "Back to work. You're at a sixty, minimum. I need you pulling out an eighty average on these problems."

"But I thought we're just trying to get me to pass."

"I always deduct ten points for nerves."

The blender cranks up, and Lo hunches over, using one arm to hold the lid and the other to support his weight on the counter. In effect, he looks about ready to melt into the floor or fall asleep again.

He barely acknowledges me. Maybe he thinks I cheated on him. I don't even know how much he trusts me around other guys. We rarely leave the apartment to test those boundaries.

Or maybe it's just guilt—at not being coherent to answer my phone calls. I suppose that makes more sense.

After Lo concocts his hangover cure, he disappears back into his bedroom. I try to concentrate on studying, and then the Chinese arrives. I sigh at the sound of a food break.

"How long have you been dating him?" Connor asks, using his chopsticks to grab a noodle from the container. He has perfect chopstick form. I wouldn't be surprised if he spoke seven different languages too.

I stab my orange chicken with a fork, stalling as I decide which answer to give him. The fake one: *three years*. The real one: *three weeks*.

I have yet to lie to Connor, and I'd rather not start. "We've been friends since we were kids, and we moved in together when we started college. But we just started dating a few weeks ago."

"Wow, your parents must be pretty cool to let you live with a guy friend. Mine have strict serious-relationship-only requirements. Like marriage serious. They don't want any girl mooching off of me until I put a ring on it. So Sadie's my only female companion."

"You're single then?" I sip a Diet Fizz.

"Happily," he says with a nod. I try to imagine what type of girl Connor would seek, but she seems unfathomable—like a hazy picture with only her brain showing. Regardless, he has plenty of options. Very attractive, extroverted girls fondled him at the highlighter party. I guess being good looking, approachable, well-dressed and friendly goes a long way. Even so, he recognized their flirtations but never participated in them.

"Are you gay?" I blurt without thinking. What's wrong with me? I busy myself with a big bite of orange chicken, stuffing my mouth to fill the awkwardness.

He shakes his head, not insulted. Nothing ruffles him. "Girls. Definitely girls. But you're not my type. I like someone who can intellectually spar with me."

I need to start a drinking game. I'll take a shot every time Connor finds another creative way to call me dumb. On second thought, I'd probably die from alcohol poisoning.

After we finish our Chinese, I clean up and Connor instructs me to type and retype my notes until it sinks in. Being on the computer is dangerous. While the silent minutes tick by, I sometimes forget Connor hovers beside me. The subconscious urge to log onto porn sites creeps into my fingers.

When I was much younger, my downward spiral began with small compulsions, like mustering the nerve to click into an X-rated site. Gradually, I started moving forward. Porn sites became dirty chat pages, five minutes became an hour, and I obsessed about my next opportunity to surf the internet—like a young boy's fixation with *Halo* and *Call of Duty*. Porn is my time bandit, stealing days from me, causing me to be late to family functions and class. Even though I feared my sisters finding out—or God forbid, my mother—I returned without pause.

I lose sleep to my behavior, and still, I can't stop.

"I don't hear typing," Connor scolds in a light tone.

I pound the keys loudly, hoping it'll incite him. He blithely resumes "grading" my problem sets, which just means he's scribbling a bunch of red marks all over the paper.

The last video I watched involved my favorite couple: Evan

Evernight and Lana Love. They role-played—Evan as the cop, Lana as the speeder. He climbed out of his car in his full, blue police uniform, fingers hooked on his belt. And then he set a meaty hand on her silver Lexus, bending down into her space, her window lowering.

"Lily," Connor calls.

I jump. "Yeah?" I squeak, not making eye contact. He can't read my mind. He can't see where I've just been. I sink into the bar stool.

"You stopped typing again, and you were breathing all weird. Everything okay?"

No. Sex literally invades my brain like enemy troops. I spring to my feet. "I-I have to talk to Lo. Can you give me ten minutes?"

I expect anger, but he nods casually. "Take your time. You're useless until you can focus."

My brain barely processes the insult as I beeline for Lo's bedroom. Forget knocking. I storm through and shut the door behind me. I keep my hand on the brass knob, half of me still undecided about being here. My cowardly side says to go back to the kitchen and wait for Lo to talk, to apologize, to do something before I confront him with simmering heat in my pupils.

But here I am. Not able to move forward. Not able to flee. Lo meets my gaze, rubbing a towel through his damp hair. He looks like a member of the living again, dressed in clean jeans, a black crew neck tee, color returning to his cheeks and his eyes not so glazed.

His amber irises hold me in a trap, and I forget why I bombarded through in the first place. Was it for sex? No, not when we haven't discussed his disappearing act last night.

"Done studying?" he asks and tosses the towel on his leather desk chair. His muscles stay taut.

"No. I'm taking a break." I can't separate from his gaze and leave. Nor can I ask the festering question.

Lo just stares at me. He grits his teeth and veins pop from his neck, not out of anger. I see his restraint, trying not to burst out in a series of unfiltered words. He swallows and glances towards the wall of cabinets where his crutch hides. I can almost see him counting in his head before he turns his attention back on me.

"Say something," he breathes.

I blurt, "I didn't have sex with him. Or anyone else."

His face breaks into a million shards and his chest rises. Pained, he puts a hand on his desk chair to steady the blow in his body. I guessed wrong—that's not what this is about.

He holds the bridge of his nose, cringing. "Did you think I was obsessing over that? Wondering if you screwed your tutor?"

"I wasn't sure." I bite my fingernails. "So . . . you didn't think I had sex with him?"

His eyes fall to the floor, and then very softly, he says, "I wouldn't have blamed you, if you did."

My lungs suffocate underneath invisible weight. Tears prick my eyes. He wouldn't care if I slept with someone else? He expects it.

"I should have been here," Lo explains, more to himself. He keeps shaking his head, probably wishing to reverse time and strangle the boy who passed out too early, who wouldn't answer my calls. "If something happened, that's on me, not you."

"Please don't," I say, bracing my body against the door. It keeps me upright as much as the chair does him. "Don't give me a free pass to cheat on you. If I cheat, it's real. If you're not here, it's real. You want to save me from the guilt if I sleep with someone else? Well, you can't."

His eyes grow red. "I'm not any good at this." Not good at a relationship? At being with me? At trying to drink less? He doesn't elaborate what *this* actually means. So I'm left to guess. He finds a beer in his drawer and twists off the cap, a surprising choice considering the low alcohol content. Weirdly, it's almost like a peace offering, an "I'm sorry" for Loren Hale. Only he can apologize with alcohol.

"Why didn't you answer my calls?"

"My phone died sometime during the night. I didn't know it until I woke up." He motions to his desk where his cell docks in the charger. Then he edges closer to me and pries my hand off the door, intertwining his fingers in mine. He spends an awfully long time staring at the way they lace together.

"Where were you?" I breathe.

He licks beer off his lips. "A bar a couple blocks down the street. I walked." He leads me into the middle of the room, my feet gliding with his. Something's wrong. I see the cold, jagged pain in his eyes, so deeply cut that it can't be all from guilt— from me.

He turns up a pop ballad and then draws me close. He lifts my arms around his shoulders and then slides his hands on my hips. Lo sways to the beat, drifting, but I plant straight in reality while he tries to forget.

"What happened?"

He looks right at me and says, "Nothing." I almost believe him. His brows even furrow a little, appearing confused.

"Maybe you'll feel better if you tell me," I whisper.

He stops moving, and his eyes cloud. Lo stares up at the ceiling for a moment, shaking his head before letting words slide off his tongue. "I called my mom." Before I can ask, he says, "I don't know why. I don't know . . . " His nose flares, holding back an avalanche of emotion.

I wait for him to continue, even though a weight bears on me and my breath has been lost to the past. He knows the question I want to ask.

Quietly, he says, "You were at the library, and my mind started going. I just, I don't know. I looked up Sara Hale on the internet and found her number." Even after their discreet divorce, she kept Jonathan's last name to retain some of his fortune. He constantly complains about it, but there's nothing he can do now. She walked away with a billion dollars in assets and a chunk of the company as a shareholder.

"Are you sure it was the right number?" By his staggered breathing, the call must have gone badly.

He nods, his gaze flitting around the room. He looks lost. I keep my hand in his, but he's somewhere far, far away. "I don't know what I planned to say," he tells me. "Maybe I should have started with, 'Hey, thanks for getting knocked up just to marry my dad and take his money' or 'Hey, thanks for nothing.'"

"Lo . . ."

"You know what I said?" he laughs, tears building. "*Hi, Mom.* Like she means something to me." He rubs his mouth in thought, and he lets out another short laugh. "After all these years of being satisfied with not knowing a thing about her, I finally call. And she says, 'Who is this? Loren? Don't you *ever* call this number again.' She hung up on *me.*"

My mouth drops. "Lo, I'm . . . " *sorry*—for what? His mother being a freeloading gold digger who willingly handed her child off after a billion-dollar settlement? "It'll be okay. You're not missing anything good. She's a horrible person."

Lo nods. "Yeah . . . yeah, you're right." He inhales a deep breath. "I shouldn't have called her. I wouldn't have gotten so trashed. I just wanted to stop thinking about it."

I squeeze his hand. "I know."

"Come here." He draws me to his chest and then kisses my

forehead. "I'll do better. I'll try harder for you." He rubs my back, keeping me in the warm embrace for quite some time. I want to live here. In his arms. Where I know it's safe. "We're okay?" he asks softly.

"I think so." I take a peek at the clock. Connor must be waiting, counting the seconds, each tick another point off my future exam.

Lo places his hands on my neck and inspects me closely. "You're shaking."

"I'm fine." I glance hesitantly at the door, wanting to do things with Lo but not having the time. Not with my tutor in the kitchen.

Lo suddenly understands my reservations. "I'll distract him for twenty minutes, and you can stay in here and watch something. I'll bring you a tape from your room."

"Really?" My face brightens.

He breaks into a small smile for the first time today, genuinely happy to help. "Really, really. Any preferences? Role-playing, oral, BDSM?" He goes to the door, about to dig through my porn videos.

"Surprise me."

His grin widens. Moments later, he returns with three DVDs. His eyes dance mischievously as he hands them over. Scanning the titles, I find the source of his amusement.

"Anal?" I say, smacking him on the arm with the plastic cases.

He kisses me lightly on the cheek and gives my butt a small pat. "Don't have too much fun without me." He stops by the door. "Anything I should know about your tutor before I talk his ear off?"

Now I can't help but laugh. "He says mildly offensive things. He thinks he's smarter than everyone on the planet—that's not an exaggeration. And he knows Rose."

His eyebrows shoot up. "How does he know Rose?"

"Apparently, they met at an Academic Bowl competition. I don't think they talk or anything, so you're in the clear."

"Good to know." He creeps out of the room, leaving me to my own devices.

And I let all my troubles float away, even Lo's story, last night's events and my impending failing grade. For this small moment, I just feel good.

Twenty minutes later and down from my high, I feel stupid. For taking a porn break during a study session with my tutor. The only way I justify my actions and not turn into a cherry red tomato is by remembering that I wouldn't be able to memorize facts without feeding my compulsion.

I wash my hands, grab a Diet Fizz from Lo's fridge, and gently close the door behind me. In the hallway, Lo and Connor's voices breeze through, making me stop by the wall.

"Definitely B," Lo says. "A, C and D don't even make sense." Is he studying or talking about breast sizes?

"That's right." Connor sounds proud, a reaction that I couldn't squeeze from him. *Definitely studying.* "Good job. You know, you're not half bad. If you weren't so lazy, you'd probably reach the class average." *Reach the class average?* Even though Lo barely mentions his grades, I thought he was doing better than that. Like gold-star-worthy scores.

"Do you think I'm too dumb to notice that you just called me an idiot or do you just not care?" Lo asks.

"Honestly," Connor says, "I don't care."

"Huh . . ." Lo mutters. I imagine his forehead wrinkling as he tries to process Connor Cobalt and his blunt (sometimes incorrect) honesty.

"Lily was pretty worried last night. We wasted a lot of studying hours looking for you. Where'd you end up going?"

"Wait," Lo says in disbelief. "*You* helped look for me?"

I had the same reaction when Connor offered to search for Lo. It barely fazes Connor that accompanying someone he hardly knows to hunt for a drunken boyfriend isn't at all ordinary.

"Yeah," Connor says. "We tried the highlighter party on campus, but you weren't there. I ruined a pair of pants doing it. Girls always go right for my ass. I don't get it."

"Lily didn't hit on anyone, did she?"

I should be hurt that he doesn't fully trust me. But I'm glad he's cautious of my fidelity. It means he cares. And it'll make me try harder to be faithful.

"Why would she do that?" Connor asks. "You two are together, right?"

"Newly together. We're trying to work through some things." Wow, Lo doesn't lie. Does Connor Cobalt have magic truth dust that he sprinkles on people? Or maybe it's too hard to lie to his brutal honesty.

"So, where'd you go?" Connor nudges.

"A bar down the street."

I wish I could eavesdrop for another twenty minutes, but I do need to pass the class. I pad further down the hallway and make my presence known.

Lo spins around on the bar stool, holding the neck of his beer. When Connor turns, I notice an identical Fat Tire in his own hand. He can drink and study? Is he a superhero or something?

"Feeling better?" Lo asks with concern, hinting at a lie he must have used for Connor's benefit.

"It was probably all the caffeine," Connor tells me. "If you're not used to Red Bull and coffee together, it can upset your stomach. I should have brought some antacids."

The tops of my ears warm in a rash-like red, never wishing to hear someone talk about my indigestion—fake or not. And the fact that Connor's tutoring methods involve cycles between caffeine and antacids is mildly disconcerting.

"You're flushing oddly. Do you have a fever?" Connor asks, not embarrassed by anything. Maybe he thinks other people are immune to that sentiment too. For me, not so much. My shoulders cave forward, like a turtle creeping back into its shell.

"She does that a lot. You embarrassed her," Lo says with an edging smile. Attention to my humiliation only brightens my shade of red.

"Can we just . . . go back to studying?" I pop open my Diet Fizz and sit on the other stool beside Connor.

"I like that plan," Connor says. He turns to Lo. "You want to join? You could probably use it. You're looking at a high sixty. And high or not, an F is still an F." *A high sixty?* I frown. I should have known Lo wasn't doing well in class and that he frequently skips others. The signs are there, but I'm too preoccupied in my own business to notice. Now that I do, I'm at a loss of how to help. I'm not even sure he'd appreciate my prodding.

"I guess I have nothing better to do," Lo says.

I hide my surprise, which quickly turns to pride. I want nothing more than for Lo to succeed, and that actually means he has to try on his own terms. Baby steps.

By the evening, my skills rest at a solid C status, and Lo is in the mid-B range. Connor looks pleased and actually smiles when he grades my problem sets now. Lo pries off the top of his twelfth beer, not hiding the fact that he consumes alcohol a little too regularly. When he switches to bourbon, he rejects his thermos and pours it into a clear glass. I thought Connor would make a comment about Lo's drinking habits, but he never says a word. The only time he brings up alcohol is to ask for a second beer.

Twenty minutes later, Connor gathers the work books together in his arms, balancing a large graphing calculator on top.

"How much do I owe you?" I ask, fumbling in the basket by the foyer for my checkbook.

"Save your money. I'd rather write these hours down as voluntary. It gives me more community service credentials."

Lo smiles into a sip of bourbon, more amused than peeved. In fact, he's taken the rude comments pretty well. Maybe he finds Connor endearing like me. Or as endearing as a pretentious honor student can be.

"Halloween is tomorrow," Lo addresses Connor. "Do you know any good costume parties? Lily wants to go to one."

He's considering going out? I almost jump up and down in excitement. "It's Lo's birthday," I add quickly, too thrilled to hold it in.

Lo shoots me a dark look, but I smile. Nothing can bring me down. Not if we're *finally* going to a party as a couple.

Connor flashes his pearly whites. "Your birthday is on Halloween? That's fucking awesome. As for parties, I know about five people throwing them." Not surprising. Connor has made it quite clear that he has *many* connections, pocketing them everywhere he goes. "I wasn't planning on going since most of the hosts are affluent pricks, but I'll make an exception and take you both to the least shitty of the bunch."

"Why make an exception for us?" I ask. Then my face lights up. "Am I your favorite student?"

He shakes his head. "Hell no. But you did pad my resume, so don't go finding another tutor. And honestly . . . " His eyes dart between Lo and me with a growing smile. "Fizzle and Hale Co., you both still haven't realized who I am. And I have a good feeling you wouldn't give a shit if you knew." He wanders, books in arms, towards the door. "Good luck tomorrow. I'll call you, Lily, about the party."

Lo turns to me and with the tilt of his head, he says, "Who the hell is Connor Cobalt?"

I feel like I should know.

Twenty

One Google search later, we find information regarding our new friend.

Richard Connor Cobalt is the son of a multibillion-dollar corporation that owns smaller companies involved in paints, inks and magnets. Unlike Hale Co., Cobalt Inc. brands their products with smaller subsidiary names like MagNetic and Smith & Keller Paints. So I feel a little less stupid for not realizing his family's prestige.

And Connor is right. His wealth doesn't change my perception of him. He may be using us to solidify a spot at Wharton, but he does so through tutoring, not badgering me for a reference from my father. If anything, I think more highly of him. He could ride his name all the way to the top. I'm sure he does take advantage of his connections, but there's genuine hard work and drive to be the best.

Also, if Connor willingly spends 48 hours cramming for a *random* girl, without monetary compensation, I wonder how many close friends he actually has. Maybe none.

After my test, I take a seat in a comfy, slightly overused chair in the chatty study lounge. I dial my sister's number.

One ring passes before she answers. "What's up?" Background noise crackles through the speaker. "Hey, watch it!" Rose yells at someone. She puts the receiver back to her ear, her voice more present. "Sorry. I'm walking on campus, and some asshole threw a Frisbee at me. I'm wearing heels and a fur coat. That does not scream, *I want to play.*"

"He probably thought you were cute," I say with a smile.

"Yeah, well I'm not a dog that will jump up at the sight of a toy." She sighs heavily. "Why'd you call? It must be important."

"It's not," I say.

"I just assumed, since you were the one to initiate the call." She sounds a little distracted.

"If now's a bad time, I can call later."

"No, no, no. I'm just crossing traffic. Cars will hit pedestrians even if we use crosswalks. You know how it is." That I do. Reckless driving and too many bodies trying to reach the other side of the street—it makes for a very dangerous combination.

"Well, I decided to hire a tutor for econ."

"Oh, that's great. How'd your exam go?"

"Eh, not sure. Hopefully I passed." I bring my feet up on the chair cushion. "You know the tutor though."

"What," she deadpans. "Who?"

"Connor Cobalt."

She shrieks. I have to hold the phone away from my ear. "That motherfu—" She continues her string of expletives, ending with, "asshole, he's tutoring you?"

"Yep."

"You know, my team beat him at the last Academic Bowl tournament, but he was obsessed with the fact that he knew some 18th century British philosopher who influenced Freud. He wouldn't shut up about it." She's foaming at the mouth. "He's so annoying, but you probably already know that."

"Mmm-hmm." Better not take sides on this one.

"You should dump him and find someone else." She pauses.

"It'll probably do wonders to his ego. You know, I'm always available."

At this, an incoming call starts ringing, disrupting my talk with Rose. I glance down and see CONNOR COBALT in big letters. Uh . . . "Hey, Rose, I'll have to call you back. We'll talk more later. Someone's on the other line."

"Lo? You're seriously going to hang up on me for him right now."

"No, actually it's—"

She gasps. "No. You are *not* ditching me for Richard."

I laugh at his real first name. "I'll talk to you later. He probably just wants to know how I did."

"*Lily*," she warns.

"Bye, Rose," I say quickly, switching lines. "Hi, Connor."

"Estimated grade?"

I sigh. The exam was hard, and I have no idea whether I passed or tanked. "An A," I joke.

He sounds like he's walking hurriedly on campus, places to go, people to see. Hey, kind of like Rose. I inwardly smile. "You'll make an A in econ when I piss glitter, but if you feel confident about it, that's what matters."

"Thanks, Connor."

"About tonight, I'll swing by your place around ten, and my driver can take us to the party from there . . . " His voice trails off, distracted. "Hey, Lily, your sister is calling me." Oh my God, she is not.

"I hung up on her to talk to you," I say quickly. "How does she even have your number?"

"She probably called someone who has it," he says, not sounding surprised at all. "I should answer this."

"Good luck."

"I'm not scared of her," he laughs. "See you tonight, Lily." My phone beeps, going silent.

Lo exits the classroom from across the hall and waves to me. I stand and follow him out of the building. We make a conscious effort to not talk about grades or the exam, lest it ruin the mood and Lo's birthday.

When we reach the Drake, I hide inside the guest room, clumsily putting on my old superhero costume. I avoid all mirrors. The leather fits more tightly than I remember and my whole midriff is exposed to the world.

I sit on the bed, hunched over to hide my skin.

The door creaks and Lo sticks his head in. "Hey there." He enters, proudly adorning red spandex with black sides, a large belt around his waist, and a giant X on his chest. He looks bad-ass, especially with the way the sleeves are cut at the bicep, showing off his sharp muscles.

"You look like a wilted flower," he tells me. Before I can protest, he lifts me by the hips off the bed and holds my wrists from covering my bare stomach. "You're hot, Lil," he whispers in my ear and then kisses my temple.

"Where's my cape?" Despite the soft kisses on the nape of my neck, I can't think of anything but the outfit.

"X-23 doesn't have a cape." He sucks my ear lobe, and his hand slides down the leather, to my thigh and then . . .

I gasp. "Lo . . . " I grip his arms tight and bite my lip.

He twirls me around and aims me towards my floor-length mirror. Sneaky. "If you're uncomfortable, you can change. I'm not forcing you to wear it, *but* you do look beautiful. See."

I stare at the long plastic "knives" poking out between my fingers. I can't see my ribs, which is a plus. Like I need any skeletal jokes during Halloween. I suppose the outfit makes my breasts look a little bigger than normal. But I still don't like the way the leather rides up my crotch. There's nothing I can do about that now, and I want to try to be confident in my skin for Lo. It's his birthday after all.

"I suppose a cape would be sacrilege," I say.

He spins me back and kisses me hungrily, his fingers leading a fiery trail down my bare stomach. I pull away as they dip below my latex pants again.

"Lo," I say in a ragged breath. "It took you an hour to put your suit on." Lo gained muscles in the past few years, and while I was glaring at my costume on the hanger, he asked me if I had any oil so he could slip on his outfit more easily. He ended up rubbing Hale Co. baby oil all over, but it slid on, the oil doing its trick.

Another change from the last time—his lower area seems to be way more prominent. Or maybe I refused to look last time. I try to avert my eyes, but I can't help but stare every so often.

Like right now.

He smirks. "Afraid it may disappear?"

My arms blush. "Um . . . no," I mutter. "I'm actually wondering if your suit will rip if you get . . . uh . . . you know."

"Hard." Oh God.

His grin widens as I turn my head, trying desperately to restrain any longing that pulsates within me. I want to jump him right now. I do. Truly, I'd love to rip off his suit, but Connor is supposed to be here in less than an hour and I have little time to force Lo's body back into the unruly fabric.

"I'll try to contain myself," he says with a lingering smile. "But there is something I can do without taking off *my* clothes."

Huh? My brows relax as he drops to his knees. His hands slide down my hips on his way to the ground. Holy shit.

He glances up with his bedroom eyes, his tongue licking his

bottom lip, and his heady gaze electrifies my body. He uses one hand to cup my bottom and then folds my latex pants down and down and down. Oh . . . my . . .

He pushes my legs, so I fall into my mattress, and he spreads my feet wide open. He still kneels at the foot of my bed, and I grip a handful of his hair, tugging his head back. His firm hands stay on my knees, and neither of us makes a move yet.

I know what he's about to do. He refuses to remove his eyes from mine, almost challenging me to be the one to look away. I don't. From my sexual interactions with Lo, I've come to enjoy this the most—the staring, the locked eyes, the feeling of being connected beyond intertwined limbs. I've never had that before.

Not with anyone but him.

"Breathe," he tells me.

Right as I focus on inhaling, he runs his hands up my thighs, to my hips, and I buck at his touch. "Lo . . . " I shudder, and he breaks his gaze to kiss my throbbing spot.

I clench his hair tighter, losing air to these feelings.

I don't see how this can ever become old.

Twenty-one

Connor's driver, Gilligan, looks nothing like the famed television character. Big boned, bald and more suited to be a bodyguard than personal chauffeur, he passively carts us around Philly, not saying much of anything.

Connor uncorks the second bottle of champagne and replenishes my glass. Every time I take a sip, my plastic blade hits me in the nose. Lo has a much easier time as he grips a flask that's filled with less bubbly liquor.

The birthday present I gave him clashes with his Hellion costume. Regardless, Lo wears the necklace that almost looks like a beaded rosary, except instead of a cross there's an arrowhead at the end. Something I found when we took a trip to Ireland, only twelve at the time.

Lo subconsciously touches the necklace as we bump along the street. I smile, glad it means something to him as much as it does for me.

I look back at Connor. "Do you always ride around in a stretch limousine?" I run my hands over the polished black leather seat.

"Don't you?"

Lo holds my waist, touching my bare hip as he draws me to his body. He chimes in, "Oh yeah, we take limo rides around

Walmart's parking lot just to show regular people what money looks like. Don't we, dear?"

My eyes bug at Lo's sarcasm. "We have Escalades," I say, trying to recover, disentangling his hand from my hip, even if it kills me. His playfulness—while incredibly sexy—will most definitely make Connor uncomfortable. He's our first real friend, and Lo is about to get us tossed on the street.

Connor puts an arm across the top of the stretched seat, wearing a cape, a cloth mask over his eyes and a plastic sword. Zorro. "Most people disapprove of the limo, but those people aren't the ones I'm trying to impress. Do you see how many people this can hold? Plus, I'm facing you. I don't even have to strain my neck to talk. Those things are valuable to me."

"I can get along with that." Lo sets his mischievous eyes on me. "What about you, love?" I thought the teasing would stop after we solidified our relationship. This kind of taunting, I like way too much, and he knows it. He snakes his hand on my knee, running it up my leg, too casually to be taken as something overtly sexual. For me, he may as well have dropped on his knees a second time.

I mouth, *stop*.

He mouths, *why?* And he breaks into a gorgeous smile. Lo looks to Connor, but he tightens his fingers on my thigh. "You want to hear a story?" *Where is this going?*

Connor raises his glass. "I'm all ears."

Lo's eyes flicker to me, too briefly to make sense of his intentions. "Fizzle has company tours all the time, you know, the ones where they show the history of the soda and then let you try all the imported flavors."

"Sure, I toured the factory with my ninth grade class."

"It's not real, that place. It's not really where they make the drinks."

Connor nods. "I suspected."

"Well, Lily and I were twelve and her father left us in the museum area."

The memory floats to the surface. I smile and add, "He thought we'd be occupied by tasting all of the sodas."

Lo looks to Connor. "But Lily had a better idea. She said the real factory was a street over."

Connor's brows shoot up. "You went to the actual factory by yourselves? How'd you get in?"

Lo cocks his head at me. "Want to take this, love?" His hand sinks down my inner thigh.

My breath hitches, not able to form actual words.

"No?" He grins and adds to Connor, "She told them her last name and said her father wanted her to take a mini-tour. When we went in, we darted off in another direction." He ran so fast. He always does. I struggled to keep up, and he'd slow or run loops around me. As the security started gaining on us, he lifted me on his back. I held tightly to his neck, and he sped towards a giant, spinning vat of dark liquid. We hid out for a little while, and when the footsteps died in the distance, he concocted a masterful plan.

"Did you get in trouble?"

Lo shakes his head. "No, her dad has a heart of gold. He was actually flattered that we wanted to see the factory. If he'd known what I did, maybe he wouldn't have been too kind. I found some alcohol around the place." Correction: *He took out his flask.* "And I dumped it into the syrup."

"Shut up," Connor says. "You spiked the soda recipe?"

"They probably couldn't taste it. There wasn't really that much compared to the amount of syrup, but I take pride in the fact that a handful of people got a little something extra because of us that day." He turns to me, and I think, maybe, he may kiss me. He has that look in his eye, the one that trails the fullness of my lips, the one that could tip me over the seat and give himself over to me. And then his phone beeps, breaking the connection.

I sigh, a little deflated. It's not mere coincidence that the phone all of a sudden rings. My parents and sisters have been trying to wish him a happy birthday since this morning, but Lo would rather listen to the incessant beeping than confront them—or have a prolonged conversation with Rose.

"Just answer them," I urge.

Lo glances at the screen, and I peek over his shoulder, seeing a photo of his father.

His face sharpens. Unlike my family, he never rejects his father's calls. Sometimes I think it's more than fearing the wrath of Jonathan Hale. I know, somewhere deep down, he loves his father. He just doesn't know what type of love it is or even how to process it. Lo puts the phone to his ear. "Hey."

In the quiet of the limo, I hear Jonathan's rough voice through the speaker. "Happy Birthday. Did you receive my gift? Anderson said he left it in the lobby with the staff."

"Yeah. I meant to call you." Lo glances warily at me and takes his hand off my leg. "I remember you drinking it when I was younger. It's great." His father gave him a bottle of fifty-year-old scotch, Decanter or Dalmore or something. Lo tried to explain the value of it to me, but it whizzed right over my head. I couldn't stop thinking about how perfect and wrong the present is and if his father knew it too.

"The next time you come over, we can break it open," he tells him. "I have a couple cigars here too."

"Sounds good." Lo shifts his shoulder, closing me off.

"How has the day been for you so far?"

"Okay. I aced an econ exam."

196 · KRISTA RITCHIE and BECCA RITCHIE

One of Connor's eyebrows arches, disbelieving.

"That so?" His father also sounds unconvinced. I must have been the only one who had any faith in Lo's grades.

"I can't really talk now," Lo tells him. "I'm with Lily. We're headed to a Halloween party."

"Okay. Be safe . . . " He pauses, as though he has something else to say. After a long moment, he adds, "Have a great twenty-first, son."

"Thanks."

His father hangs up, and Lo acts casual as he pockets the cell. He tightens his arm around my shoulder, bringing me closer. But his muscles stay taut, a subtle difference that also punctures the amusement in his voice. "Maybe you should just tell your sisters that I said thanks. Send out a mass text or something."

"Why can't you do that on your own phone?"

"Because they'll reply back and then I'll have to reply to that, which sounds exhausting."

"He has a point," Conner tells me.

Uh, shouldn't he be siding with me? He's *my* tutor. "Don't tell me *you* find small talk draining. That's your thing."

Connor cups his champagne glass. "It sounds exhausting for *him*. I'd enjoy a talk with your sisters."

"By the way," I say. "How was your conversation with Rose? You're still in one piece, so I presume it went well."

Lo chokes on a sip of whatever's in his flask, and I pat his back. "Excuse me," Lo says. "You talked with Rose? Like had a fully formed conversation?"

Connor nods. "I even invited her tonight."

Lo groans. "You did not invite the ice queen here."

"Hey," I shoot back. "That's *my* sister. She has a good heart." I pause. "You just have to be liked by her first."

"Or be related to her," Lo points out. True.

"So she's coming?" I wonder, kind of nervous. I'd rather not explain Lo's intoxication to her, especially since he's supposed to be reformed from his boozing, careless days. It's his birthday, and she'll add that to his list of negative attributes and reasons why he's not good for me.

Connor says, "She's not coming." Is that disappointment in his voice? "She said she'd rather skin my cat." He smiles. Like *actually* smiles at that. Oh my God, were they flirting with each other over the phone?

Lo relaxes and mutters, "Thank God."

Connor nods to me. "By the way, what are you supposed to be?"

Am I going to get asked that all night? I guess I should prepare. I flash my plastic claws. "X-23."

He squints, confused.

"The girl version of Wolverine, technically his female clone."

"Oh. Okay, cool. You kind of look like a hooker with knives though." *What?!* That is not helping my confidence. "Lo, you need to prepare yourself for this party. So many guys are going to hit on her."

Just when I thought I snuffed out my insecurities.

Lo gives me an encouraging squeeze on the shoulder. The thought of guys everywhere used to be exciting—a playground for my compulsions—but now, I couldn't be more scared. Maybe a party is a bad idea.

To Connor, Lo says, "Good, it'll give her practice saying *no*." Oh, that was mean. I push him off, untangling his arms from mine. He focuses on tipping bourbon into the tiny opening of his flask, not caring anyway. He would have before he talked to his dad. He might have teased me back and whispered something dirty in my ear. Now, his mind has switched tracks.

"I can say *no*," I defend with an unconvincing mutter. I haven't tested this theory since we've started dating.

Lo caps his flask and looks to Connor. "If you see her flirting with someone, just yank her off him."

"Lo," I warn with wild eyes. What the hell is Connor going to think? That I really am a whore with claws?! My entire body heats and I struggle not to bury my face into my hands.

"You two are so weird," Connor says, very casually.

Being called weird by Connor is like a unicorn calling a horse magical. It makes no damn sense, which is why Lo and I break into smiles, even if Lo's mood has somewhat shifted since the phone call.

Abruptly, the car jerks to a stop. Gilligan mumbles out a "we're here" and unlocks the doors. I press my nose to the window, ritzy suburbs right in view. A glowing mansion sits at the top of a steep hill, lighting up the dark sky. Out of all the parties, Connor said he picked the one that would have the best food. In the same sentence, he mentioned that I looked like I needed a good meal.

More cars roll up to the circular drive, and we climb out to confront the hoopla. A fountain crests the center, red, bloody water spurting from the stone. Zombies are staked in the green lawn, so life-like that I thought the gory limbs and droopy mouths were facilitated by paid models. Upon closer inspection, they're nothing but silicone, prosthetics and paint.

We follow Connor up the stone stoops, and he bangs a bronze knocker. While we wait for an answer, more people gather behind us.

The door whips open quickly, loud music booming from inside. George Washington or possibly Mozart stands in the archway, holding a champagne glass. A white pill fizzes at the bottom of the gold liquid.

"Connor Cobalt!" He grins and sways on his feet, the white wig slightly off-kilter.

"Hey." They go in for the bro-hug. "Who the hell are you supposed to be?"

"Thomas fucking Jefferson."

"Of course," Connor says with a sarcastic smile. Thomas Jefferson doesn't pick it up, and before hanging around Connor, I wonder if I would have noticed it. Connor motions to Lo and me, and I grip onto Lo's hips, hiding my exposed midriff behind half his body. "These are my friends. Lily and Lo."

Thomas Jefferson narrows his eyes at Lo and I duck further behind his back. "What are you?" he wonders. "Mr. Spandex?"

"Clever," Lo says with a glare.

"They're X-Men," Connor clarifies.

With this, Lo grabs my wrist and pulls me into view. He plants a hand firmly on my waist, as if this guy will know the New Mutant couple.

Thomas Jefferson stares at my long claws. "Right!" He claps his hands in recognition. "Wolverine Girl."

"There's no such thing," I correct him. He gives me a funny look, and Connor sighs, slight impatience cracking his leveled exterior.

"Can we only be invited inside if you understand our costumes?" Connor asks. He cranes his neck to look past the host's shoulder. "Because I think I spot a Sweeney Todd in there, and I know for a fact you've never heard of him."

"Huh. Connor Cobalt. Always got to be right." He swings the door and mockingly motions us inside. His staff must have evacuated for this college party, not wanting to be swept up in a hurricane of puke and candy corn.

Unfazed by the insult, Connor steps into the massive grand foyer where crystal chandeliers twinkle from the ceiling. Partygoers go up and down the marble staircase and further into glowing rooms, cobwebs strewn across door frames. People stumble around and sway to hypnotic music.

I step through the doorway, and then Thomas Jefferson blocks off the entrance before anyone else can cross.

"I don't know you," he says to the people behind us. "Or you." The door slams. He traipses back in and passes Connor. "Freeloaders," I hear him say, as though Connor will nod in agreement. He doesn't do anything but pluck a steaming pumpkin mug off a goblin's tray. Now those hairy things *are* models, waddling about with warty faces.

Unlike the highlighter party, Solo cups are replaced with champagne glasses and pumpkin mugs. Little baggies of pills and powder are clandestinely passed from palm to palm. I grew up with these blowouts—rich teenagers needing drugs to satiate the endless expanse of time. As if they reanimated straight from the pages of Bret Easton Ellis' *Less Than Zero*.

Drugs have never been my problem, and maybe I should feel a sense of gratitude that my compulsion is less dangerous than shooting liquid fire into my veins. Sex is a part of everyone's life, addicted or not.

Drugs aren't.

Alcohol isn't.

You can spend years without both, but most people never become lifelong celibates. Every time I catch a girl tucking a baggie into her bra, eyes glazed and gone, I feel a pang of jealousy. Why can't I have an addiction that people understand? It's a vile thought—to wish for an addiction many die with. I'd rather have none at all, but for some reason, I never allow myself that option.

Before I made sense of my compulsions, I would spend hours lying in bed, emotionally drained from my ping-ponging thoughts. One minute, I vehemently defended my actions inside my mind. It was my body. Sex made me feel better and stopping would cause more problems than continuing down the destructive path. The next minute, I cried for hours and convinced myself to quit. I told myself I didn't have a problem. I was just a whore looking for a way to justify my constant sexual thoughts. Sometimes I tried to stop. I trashed my porn and refused my body the luxury of climaxing.

But I couldn't stomach the withdrawals, and those fruitless goals quickly ended. I always found a reason to start again. Maybe that's my biggest fear—that I'll find one excuse to move on from Lo. And I'll be compelled to take it.

Lo dashes off in front of me, and I run to keep up and hide behind his back. A gaggle of hippies in flowery mini-dresses bombards Connor. He nods and smiles perfunctorily, and it sets off a wave of giggles.

He'll have to fend for himself. I trail Lo into the kitchen, where bodies compact near the silver stove. They flick on the gas and light cigarettes from the flames. The sliding glass door sits ajar, smoke wafting out into the chilly night. A couple girls in bikinis shriek and laugh loudly as they race into the house, goose-pimpled and wet.

Lo jiggles the knobs to a glass cabinet. Crystal bottles line about seven shelves, filled with amber liquid. Every lavish party starts the same. Lo beelines for the most expensive alcohol in the house and impulsively craves the taste of the different brands.

"It's locked," I tell him. "Can you stick to your own bourbon tonight?" His flask stays in the waist of his belt that matches his red and black suit.

"Hold on." He departs for a second, vanishing around the corner, and I pretend to be interested in a still life painting on the wall. Better to look fascinated by apples and pears than like a lonely loser.

Lo returns moments later with a safety pin.

"Lo," I warn as he starts to wiggle it into the keyhole. "We just got here. I don't want to get kicked out."

"You're distracting me," he says.

Visions of high school parties swim to me. Lo creeping down the cellar of a kid's house—a kid who invited *everyone* in his grade. Those parties happened far too often. Lo would drink the vintage wines and imported scotches, the angered host dragging him out by the shirt. Lo stumbling to stay upright. Me, exiting the bathroom with flushed cheeks, only to hurry after my only friend.

I don't like repeating mistakes, but sometimes, I think we're both forever stuck on a turntable.

Even with the smokers' chatter by the stove, I hear the *click* of the lock. The glass doors swing open, and Lo's eyes light up. Watching him delicately touch the bottles with hungry anticipation reminds me of my desires.

Which is why I blurt out, "You want to do it in the bathroom?" My voice remains small and timid, not yet a confident, sexy girl that I'm sure fills Lo's dreams. It's hard to be her when Lo isn't a conquest I sleep with and then ditch.

"Huh?" Distracted, he gathers the best liquors in his arms and sets them on the granite counter beside me.

"After you drink, do you want to go to the bathroom to . . . " I trail off, fearing the fatal blow of rejection.

He pops the crystal plunger on a bottle and tips the liquid in a glass. "I thought I rocked your world," he says. "Unless I imagined you saying it. You were making all kinds of noises, so it was hard to tell."

My elbows blush as I remember the scandalous acts before we left. "You heard incorrectly. I don't think it was possible to form actual words."

He smiles and then takes a languid sip from his liquor.

"But," I continue, "we've only done it at the apartment or on the yacht."

He looks back to the depths of his drink. "Is that something you have to have?" he asks. "I didn't think location was a big fucking deal." He grimaces at his biting tone and then throws the rest of the liquor back in his throat. He refills the glass quickly.

I open my mouth but end up looking like a fish trying to breathe air. Where we have sex shouldn't matter, but there's an allure to doing it somewhere deviant. Always has been. "Okay." The one word does not properly answer his question or his rudeness.

He clenches his jaw, fingers tightening on the glass. "I'm stuck in this suit anyway. Unless you want to cut a hole for my—"

"No." I hold up my hands. "You're right."

"And in case you've forgotten, *Laura*," he emphasizes X-23's real name. "It's my fucking birthday." He raises his glass. "Which means this trumps *that*." He eyes my nether region.

"You're so much like Julian it's scary." I use *his* superhero's real name. Both can be moody, irritable jerks and then do a flip and be the sweetest guys ever. You just have to catch them at the right time, the right moment.

"Wrong. I have both my arms." Hellion lost his arms fighting Sentinels in *X-Men: Second Coming*. Madison Jeffries created metal hands for Hellion, now a new signature part of his wardrobe, but Lo ditches those because it hinders his ability to hold a flask.

My eyes dart nervously around the kitchen, half expecting Thomas Jefferson to pop up and berate Lo.

"If you don't want to stand here, go hang out with Connor."

"You trust me?" I wonder.

"I sincerely think that Connor is like an amoeba. He probably wouldn't even notice if you hit on him."

I want to mention my theory about Connor crushing on Rose,

but Lo will probably make a snide remark about her. I'd rather not start a fight by having to defend my sister while she's not here.

"What about other people? Do you trust me with them?"

He gives me a sharp glare. "I don't know. Now you're making me think I should be fucking worried." He's in a foul mood. I'm not sure what put him there. Maybe the familiar atmosphere brings bad memories and he wishes we stayed home. Or maybe he'd rather be drinking with his father and smoking a cigar than be here, celebrating in a strange house with strange people that mean nothing to him.

"I'm irrationally freaking out," I say. "The same way you're kind of being an asshole."

Lo tips back his drink, downing the fiery alcohol in one gulp. He wipes his mouth with the back of his arm. He hides any and all expression and gestures to me with his fingers. I hesitate and then sidle to his side. Before I reach him, he sets a kiss right on my nose. And then my cheek. My neck.

I smile at the tender, quick pecks. His arms swiftly swoop around me, pulling me fully to his body, his movements lighter than air, rocking on our feet as though we have no real balance. His lips finally find mine, and the kiss lasts longer, sweeter. After a long, dizzy moment, he retracts and puts his thumb to my bottom lip. "How about this?" His husky, low voice takes my breath. "Just repeat this phrase whenever you feel the urge to jump some other guy's bones." His mouth brushes my ear. "*Loren Hale fucks better.*"

I gape.

"Good, huh?" He winks and steps away. I immediately want to grab him back, hold his hand and tug him to my chest. Instead, he finds his glass.

I can't believe I'm envious of dishware. I clear my throat, collecting my thoughts. "That'll work, but I'm coming up with a different mantra."

"And what's that?" His lip quirks, but the bottles call out to him. And his eyes flicker away from me.

"I will not cheat on Loren Hale."

Lo inspects the cabinet. "I like mine better," he says, distant. He plucks a triangular shaped bottle off the shelf, and despite my lust for him and my worry for his mental state, I leave him to binge.

Gradually, I brace the crowded living room, where the lights dim and the Halloween colors strobe. I spot Connor beside the crackling fireplace, surrounded by a large group of people chatting over each other, as though he's the focus of the party. He interjects a couple of times, but more people talk *to* him than him needing to talk back. All plans whoosh out of my head, and even the idea of vying for someone's attention sounds both exhausting and terrifying.

Before I can look away, Connor catches my eye and waves me over. My gaze traces the hippies who stagger, even with bare feet, and I shake my head. I belong in the shadows and the cobwebs. Connor clearly lives in the spotlight.

Frown lines crease his forehead, and he mutters something quickly to his friends before surprisingly detaching from the herd and heading to me. His cape billows behind him, but he pushed his mask to the top of his thick, wavy brown hair.

"You know," Connor says, "they don't bite. Dreadful company but relatively harmless."

"I know," I say. "I just don't like large groups. Usually I just . . . dance when I go to parties." What a big fat lie, but I'd rather not add *and have sex* to the statement.

"You never know, one of these pirates may be a future investor that you need in your back pocket."

"Don't let me stop you." I motion to the talkative groups. "Go find a future millionaire."

His feet stay cemented. "Where's Lo? Did you lose him again?"

"He's in the kitchen and probably going to get us kicked out. I thought I'd take a tour of the house before then." Hopefully I sound as bitter as I feel.

"Why would he get us kicked out?"

I shake my head, clearing away the sudden judgment. "Nothing. It's fine."

A shirtless firefighter saunters past us, sweat glistening on his bare chest like he's saved someone from a burning building. *I will not cheat on Loren Hale*. Nope, not even with a sexy firefighter.

"Hey, Connor." Batman walks over carrying a rare beer in this place. "I didn't think you would show here. Darren Greenberg's party is supposed to have free helicopter rides."

"Flying in puke doesn't sound that appealing, and I thought there would be food here."

"Yeah, Michael went cheap this year. I thought he was going to re-create a scene from *Evil Dead* in the front yard. Instead, he went for D-list zombies." Batman glances at me. "You look familiar. Do I know you?"

I *really* look at him this time but come up blank. Usually the only people that recognize me and I can't place are the ones I've slept with.

"No, I don't think we've met," I tell him.

"This is Lily," Connor introduces. "She's a friend."

Batman slaps Connor's shoulder. "Good job, man." What does that even mean? He glances at my bare stomach with a hungry gaze. Oh. I cross my arms. He then notices my costume. "Hey, Wolverine!"

I don't even try to correct him.

"We should go find all the superheroes here and try to fight some fucking evil together."

"Her boyfriend is around here somewhere. He's part of X-Men too."

Batman looks a bit crestfallen. "Boyfriend, huh?" His eyes narrow to slits. "I think . . . I think I do know you. Do you ever go to The Cloud? It's a club downtown."

Before I say a word, I see him formulating the answer. Amusement flashes across his features. Immediately, my gut reaction kicks in and I bolt away from both of them, hoping Connor will follow. One guy spotting me and claiming we had sex is a weird coincidence. Two guys—Connor will think something's wrong with me.

I stop in the foyer, blocked by a pack of people watching Fred Flintstone slide down the curving bannister.

Connor touches my shoulder, and I spin to face him, glad to *not* see Batman by his side. "I would adopt your methods at avoiding douchebags, but I'm guessing running away doesn't make many friends."

I relax. He thinks I flee to avoid jerks like frat Kevin and Batman. Truth be told, I'm not even sure if these guys are the assholes in the situation. I slept with them, acting exactly how they perceive me to be. Trashy.

"I'm not in the market for many friends," I tell him.

"I figured. Should we find your boyfriend? Make sure he doesn't puke on anyone."

"He rarely pukes."

"That's good. Does he ditch you a lot at parties?"

"He didn't ditch me. I left him in the kitchen."

He holds up his hands, coming in peace. Then I lead the way, and when we reach the glass cabinet, a guy in nothing but a white button-down and socks realigns the bottles with an irritated scowl.

208 · KRISTA RITCHIE and BECCA RITCHIE

Uh-oh.

"What happened?" Connor asks, though I'm sure he's deduced the obvious.

Tom Cruise from *Risky Business* takes out a skeleton key. "I found some asshole drinking my uncle's liquor. Shit costs more than a car." *Uncle*. He must be Thomas Jefferson's cousin.

"Did you kick him out?" Connor keeps calm while my pulse spikes. What if they pulled Lo outside to beat him up or humiliate him . . . or worse?

"Nah, my brothers wanted to get his name first. They're all out back." Tom Cruise holds up a bottle with residual amber liquid. "He's surprisingly coherent. I would be knocked out if I drank as much as this kid."

I don't wait for anything else. I dart for the back door, praying that Lo keeps his lips sealed. He has a way of saying the exact wrong things to instigate a fight. Most of the time, he does it on purpose.

I shouldn't have insisted on attending a party. When I noticed the shift in his mood, I should have offered to go back home. He didn't want to be here.

My boots sink into wet grass, and I pass the pool that glows a deep orange. Half-naked girls bob in and out of the water. Lo isn't among the crowds that group off into small clusters with drinks nestled firmly in their hands.

Connor touches my shoulder and nods towards the side of the house. "Over here." Has he already seen him? Or does he know where they interrogate unruly guests? I push back spider webs and black streamers, walking closer to the east side of the mansion.

People are sparse here, and the night sky whistles while yelling overlaps the soft hum of music.

"For the hundredth fucking time, the cabinet was open! Maybe you should check your locks before you throw a party."

Lo. We found him, but his inciting words only bring fear to my heart.

"We don't give a shit about your excuses!"

Another guy adds, "Who the hell are you and what bastard invited you here?"

"That bastard would be me," Connor says as we come into view.

A rock lodges in my throat. Lo stands cornered against the stone siding of the house. Four guys dressed in dark green, long sleeve Under Armour shirts and light green surfer tanks carry indignant scowls—as well as hard shells on their backs, dressed as Ninja Turtles.

Even in orange-lit light, I make out the red plume burgeoning on Lo's cheek.

Someone hit him.

I run towards Lo, all sensibility flying out of my brain.

One of Thomas Jefferson's Ninja Turtle cousins grabs me around the waist before I reach my boyfriend.

"Hey!" Lo and Connor yell in unison.

"Why the hell would you bring this trash to our uncle's house?" The purple-bandana Donatello asks as I struggle to break from his grip. I kick out, my legs flailing in the air, but he holds tightly as if I'm a sack of bones.

Connor steps forward. "What are you, back alley thugs? Let her go, Matt. Then we can talk."

The few other clusters of people in the yard begin to watch. Through my struggle, I spot a Tinker Bell, a Peter Pan, a green-clad superhero and Dobby, the house elf. The green-clad superhero edges forward, and just when I think he's coming to my rescue, Matt releases his hold on me, and I finish the distance to Lo.

He quickly places two hands on my cheeks, inspecting the length of my body with his gaze.

"I'm fine," I tell him, more worried about his state. "Stop fueling them."

His eyes harden, his cheekbones sharpening, which turns his lips into a pout. "Just get behind me."

"Lo." I panic, my chest constricting.

"If something happens," Lo breathes as he pushes me back. "Run to Connor's limo. Don't wait for me, okay?"

"No." My eyes bug. "Lo, please—"

"This kid owes us forty grand," Matt sneers, turning the spotlight back on Lo and off Connor. Why would Connor even help us? It may damage his reputation beyond repair.

"I'm not giving you a cent," Lo spits. "How the hell was I supposed to know the liquor was off limits? There wasn't a sign."

"It was *locked*," says the blue-bandana cousin.

Lo opens his mouth again, and I pinch his arm, shooting him a glare. We need to leave, preferably together. He clenches his jaw and thankfully shuts up.

Matt steers his heated glower back to Connor. "Do you think we're going to overlook this because you're Connor Cobalt? You realize that anyone else would be blacklisted by now." *Oooh, blacklisted.* Lo and I are probably crossed off all lists in the affluent Philly circle. If it wasn't for Connor, we wouldn't have even passed the doors.

"Blacklist me, then," Connor says. "This is a terrible party. You didn't even bother to serve food."

Matt's head jerks back in surprise. "You're going to choose them over us?"

Connor nods, his muscles tensing. "Yes. Let's see what we have here. Net worth of maybe"—he scans the mansion behind me—"twenty-five million combined." He points to Lo and me. "Calloway and Hale. That's every fucking soda can in your house and all your little nephews' and nieces' diapers. Billions. So yeah, I'm going to side with the two people that make your inheritances look like chump change."

I gape, not expecting any of that, mostly about Connor being our friend in a few days. He collects people, and Lo and I are gold nuggets in his jar. It's been so long that anyone has stuck up for us that I slide past the superficiality in his motives. Having an ally is nice. Desperate, yes, but no one said Lo and I are perfect either.

Matt and the other Ninja Turtles look stupefied, trying to process our wealth and our last names. Then he laughs in cruel amusement. "Well then, I suppose with your *means* you'll have no problem taking that pacifier out of your ass and reimbursing us for what you drank."

Lo's expression grows dark. I put my hand in his, hoping he's not about to be belligerent and argumentative. I trust Lo to stand down with me here, but once I leave, anything can happen.

"Fuck you," Lo curses.

Connor cuts in before one of the cousins raises a fist to *make* Lo pay it. "Will your uncle really care? Forty grand is nothing."

"He drank a car, Connor," Matt says in disbelief. "That's more than some people make in a goddamn year! Yeah, he'll be pissed, and Diaper Rash over there can easily afford it. Pay up, or we're going to find *collateral* until you grab your fucking checkbook." They eye me, and I back up into the cold stone. Lo glances over his shoulder, all sharp lines, and when he feels that I'm safe, he steps forward.

No! I lunge and grab his wrist.

"Lily—"

"He can't pay it," I defend.

"*Lily*," Lo warns. "Don't."

I seal my lips, not about to spill Lo's personal life to strangers.

His father put him on a stringent allowance, tying up his bank account and pooling in money on a monthly basis. He supervises every transaction, calling Lo when there are any big purchases. That four-thousand-dollar champagne at the Italian restaurant plus his other expenses wiped him clean this month.

And if he overdraws, Jonathan Hale will throw a fit.

"You really expect me to believe that, sweetheart?" Matt says. No, he wouldn't.

Connor, for the first time, looks concerned. He keeps edging backwards, glancing around to find reinforcements in case this gets ugly.

"I can—I can do it. But my checkbook is in the car with my purse," I say. If I have to take the heat for a forty grand charge, then I will. I can easily blame it on a dress for the Christmas Charity Gala, citing that I stained the one I already bought. The only problem: I didn't bring any money. With no pockets and an affinity for ditching purses, I left the house with nothing but my plastic blades and knee-high leather boots.

"Matt!" A tall, tanned guy jogs over to us. He wears a green leather jacket and carries a bow with a quiver of arrows strung to his back. I recognize him as the green-clad superhero from the sidelines. Dark green paint streaks across his eyes like a mask and disheveled brown hair accentuates the hard lines in his jaw. He looks manly, powerful and pissed. His costume probably helps, but I have a feeling the self-confidence is all him.

He stops a few feet from our stand-off with the Ninja Turtles and focuses on the purple-bandana cousin. I'm ready for him to shake his fists at Matt, threaten him with his strong build, something that Lo has avoided.

The green-clad superhero says, "Hey, I just talked to some girl. She said Michael wants you guys to come in the house. He needs you to break up a fight in the basement. They're knocking into shit."

My mouth slowly falls. So . . . he's not here to help us. I'm an idiot.

Matt rubs the back of his neck, his eyes flickering to us before he nods to the other Turtles. "Go. I'll take care of this." The cousins sprint off towards the pool.

"The girl said that Michael wanted all four of you."

Matt huffs. "Can you do me a favor, Ryke? These two owe my uncle forty grand." He points to me. "This girl says her checkbook is in the car. Follow them and get the money from her."

"Yeah, no problem."

My stomach drops further. Now we're going to be tailed by Matt's superhero friend who looks fit enough to tackle me and pin me to the grass. Maybe not Lo. Definitely me. Probably Connor . . . Great.

The evil Turtle disappears around the corner and Ryke shifts his attention to us. "Where's the car?" He turns his head, and I catch his profile: unshaven jaw, slender nose, brown eyes that melt into honey. He's something I would normally pursue without question. I shake off the thought, especially since he's friends with Thomas Jefferson's cousins.

"This way." Connor leads us to his limo.

Lo slips his hand around my waist, bringing me close. Ryke walks ahead of us with Connor, and Lo burns holes into the superhero's back. Besides the fact that Ryke is working as Matt's errand boy, I wonder if Lo feels threatened. Did he see me eyeing him? I'm not so sure. Ryke also stands a good inch above Lo, probably six-foot-three, and carries himself with that extra assurance, exuding a strong sense of masculinity. Lo does too, but there's a small difference. I can barely place it. Where Lo is all sharpness, this guy is hard-lined. Like ice versus stone.

I blink, trying not to focus on Ryke's handsomeness. Not at a time like this.

Five paces out and Lo plucks his flask from his belt, drinking again.

"Is that even your booze?" I ask, pissed that he's drowning another situation with liquor. But I guess I just spaced out a little—one second from imagining Ryke's abs. So I can't be too critical.

He wipes his mouth with his hand. "Maybe."

Ryke looks over his shoulder every so often. His eyes dart between us, his expression too enigmatic to understand. If Matt trusts him, he can't be any better than the Ninja Turtles.

Maybe I can cry instead of paying him. Don't guys get really uncomfortable when girls start sobbing?

"So what are you supposed to be? Robin Hood?" Connor asks.

"Green Arrow," I correct before Ryke can.

Ryke looks back, and he scrutinizes my costume, his intrusive gaze heating my body. "You know Green Arrow?" he finally asks, meeting my eyes.

"A little," I mumble. "DC comics aren't really my thing." I like the underdog stories, the kind where any average person can be a superhero. Peter Parker, mutants—they know a little something about that.

"Only losers read DC," Lo adds. Okay, I wouldn't go *that* far.

"I don't read comics," Ryke confesses. "I've just seen *Smallville* on television. What does that make me?"

"A prick."

Ryke's eyebrows shoot up, surprised by the hostility. "I see."

"For the record," I interject, "I don't agree with Lo. I'm not a comic book elitist." Anyone can read comics, and if you don't it's perfectly okay to enjoy the characters in other mediums.

Lo makes a point to roll his eyes at me.

Ryke ignores my comment and turns to Connor, who has gone

quiet. "Why are you with these two? Aren't you usually surrounded by a pack of people trying to kiss your ass?"

"I'm broadening my social reach."

As we near the car, I realize I need to formulate a plan. But my
brain short-circuits with each panicked breath. We step onto the
street and the wind churns, blowing my hair. Connor's limo hugs
the curb.

"Where the hell is your car?" Ryke asks, eyes flickering cau-
tiously to the house.

"Right here." Connor knocks on the door and Gilligan, his
driver, pops open the lock.

I motion for Lo to climb in before me. He sways on his feet,
needing no other encouragement. When he's safely on the leather
seat, I begin to relax. Somewhat.

"Where's your purse?" Connor asks. And then his eyes gradually widen. "Wait, you didn't bring a purse, did you?"

"I-I . . . " I avoid Ryke. Is he going to shake me down? Hit me?
His broad muscles tense, and I shrivel back in fear.

"What did you do?" Connor asks, horrified.

I open my mouth, but as I look up, I realize he didn't address
me. He glances from Ryke to the lawn where Ninja Turtles sprint
out the door, dodging motionless zombies and heading straight
for . . . us.

Twenty-two

"G et in the car," Ryke urges.

I hop in too fast and whack my head against the metal frame. I curse under my breath and rub the welt, ducking further inside. Lo lies on the longest seat, eyes closed and cradling his flask like a teddy bear. I sit beside him and rest my hand on his ankles.

Connor enters and, surprisingly, Ryke follows suit. He slams the door and locks it. "Drive!" he yells.

Gilligan speeds down the suburban street, and the Ninja Turtles race after our getaway limo, their figures visible in the brightness of the taillights. When we gain more and more distance, they slow to a stop and fade into the darkness.

I spin back, facing Connor and Ryke.

Connor says, "Let me guess. There was no fight inside the house."

Ryke watches Lo wheeze in an unconscious sleep. "I made it up," he admits, sounding detached. "Is he okay?"

"Wait." I hold up my hands. "What's going on? Why did you help us?" He was standing on the sidelines watching the drama play out. He could have easily stayed there, not made a move, not intervened. Instead, he created an elaborate lie to get the Ninja Turtles inside and us to safety. Random acts of kindness do not exist in my world. The only answer that makes sense—he wants to be friends with us, choosing a billion dollar net worth over twenty-five million like Connor said.

For the first time, Ryke unfastens his gaze from Lo. "You think I could stand around and watch Matt drunkenly grab a girl?"

"Lots of people would," I mumble. His brows scrunch into something hard and dark, making me more reserved and cautious.

"Yeah? Then people fucking suck." He glances back at Lo, who hugs his flask. All of a sudden Ryke leans forward and snatches the flask from Lo's fingers. He unscrews the cap and rolls down the window.

"What are you doing?" I say, frantic. I jump to the other seat and try to pry the flask back. "That's not yours!" I struggle to reach for the alcohol, so he won't dump out the liquid onto the dirtied roads.

Ryke effortlessly holds the flask away from me, but I angle my body against the open window, blocking him from any sort of exit. He stares at me like I've suddenly mutated into a lizard. "What's your problem?"

"That's *not* yours to trash!"

"Yeah? I take it that's your boyfriend?"

I glare, not saying a word otherwise.

Connor watches curiously but only observes.

Ryke swishes the liquid. "This," he says, "caused all the fucking drama today. So I'm doing him a favor, you a favor, and everyone else in this fucking limo a favor by tossing it out." He goes for the window again, and I spider the door, my arms stretched out to stop him. He places a hand above mine—his body so close that I feel the rise and fall of his ribs against my chest. Oh God . . .

He tries to pass me by extending an arm towards the window, but I knock it away. Amber liquid splashes over the both of us. And I fight against him for the flask, but I end up dousing us in more alcohol. To end the struggle, he pins my arms to the cushion. "Stop," he forces.

I glare at his hold. "How is this any different than Matt grabbing me?"

His jaw hardens to stone. "I'm trying to help your boyfriend." With this, he eases off and rests his back against the seat.

My bare stomach is slick with alcohol, and heat rises to my face at the remembrance of my actions. I pick up Lo's empty flask and slide onto my seat, my eyes still narrowing in distrust at Ryke. "Who are you?"

Connor's eyebrows shoot up. "You don't know him?"

I glare. "Should I?"

"This is Ryke Meadows, captain of the track team. Michael and Matt are on it as well."

I inhale a strained breath. "So"—I turn my heated gaze on Ryke—"those are your track buddies?"

"Yeah," Ryke says. He glances at Lo again and leaves his place to sit on the other side of my boyfriend.

"He's fine," I nearly shout. I know how to take care of Lo. I've been in this situation plenty of times to understand when he needs a hospital and when he needs water and a bed.

Ryke doesn't take my word for it. He puts two fingers to Lo's neck, checking his pulse.

Connor nods to me. "You knew he was drinking their expensive booze the whole time, didn't you?"

Ryke's brows cinch, and with the paint across his eyes, his expression looks even darker and angrier than before. "You didn't stop him?" He shakes his head in disapproval.

A surge of guilt assaults me, and I hate it. I hate him for making me feel this. I've done everything I can to protect Lo from himself without being hypocritical. "I tried." I warned Lo not to, but I couldn't force him to stop. Not when I wanted sex as much as he craved alcohol.

"And does he always drink this much?"

What's with the interrogation? I bite my lip, not able to form the words that boil. "It's his twenty-first birthday." Most people end their twenty-first passed out drunk, but Ryke looks as suspicious as before. He sees through me just like the sex worker had.

"That's bullshit," Connor says. "Lo hasn't attempted to hide his problem from me. I've *never* seen him without booze."

I turn my head from their judgment and tighten my hand on Lo's ankle. "I just need to get him home." *Wake up*, I want to scream at Lo. He left me here to clean his mess. Again.

Connor drops the subject and the limo silently bumps along the badly paved city streets. I feel Ryke's sweltering emotions, his breathing heavy as he tries to come to terms with the situation. Every time I catch a glimpse of him, he looks like he could punch a wall. Or more accurately, go for a run.

When the limo slows outside of the Drake, I crawl beside Lo and hook my arms underneath his, lifting his heavy body against mine.

"Lo," I whisper. *Wake up!* I can barely carry him into a shower. How the hell am I supposed to drag him to the elevator? Asking for help happens to be a foreign phrase for me, so I spend the next couple of minutes struggling to upright his body and scoot him towards the door.

Connor and Ryke climb from the limo and then my door whips open. Connor sticks his head in from outside. "Lily, move. We'll carry him."

"No, Lo wouldn't want that."

Ryke lowers his head into view. "And most guys wouldn't

want to be carried in by their girlfriend either." I take that as a personal insult, even though he may not mean it as one.

"He's not even coherent to care," Connor says, as if that settles the matter. I can see I'm not going to win this one.

I slide from the seat, bracing against the cold Philly air. And Connor dips into the limo. "You take his feet."

Ryke positions himself outside the door, and they exchange directions to each other until Ryke is able to scoop Lo into his arms, carrying him rather easily. I wish Connor was the one to hold him. Something about Ryke puts me on edge.

Nevertheless, he cradles Lo. The picture should be comical since Lo wears red and black spandex, looking like a wounded X-Man. But I imagine Lo waking up and seeing Green Arrow assuredly holding him in his arms. He would freak out. And not in a fan-boy kind of way.

"Watch his head," I instruct as we walk through the revolving doors.

"I have him." Ryke marches into the lobby without breaking a sweat.

Even in the elevator, I watch Lo closely, upset at the course of events. I've never allowed someone else to carry or help him. That job has been mine for as long as I can remember. And maybe I have been horrible at it, but at least he's still alive, breathing. Here. With me.

At the door, I find my keys and lead them into our place. My nerves jump again when I realize this may be the most testosterone to ever cross the threshold of my apartment. Maybe not. I did have that moment where I brought two guys home.

"You can put him on the bed." I lead Ryke into Lo's room and motion to the champagne comforter. He sets him down. While I untie Lo's boots, Ryke scans the decorations, the Comic-Con posters, the photographs and the tinted cabinets. The way he looks off—it's strange, as though he's never seen a guy's room before.

"You two live together?" Ryke picks up a picture frame from the desk.

"She's a Calloway." Connor leans a hip on the door frame, arms crossed over his chest.

Ryke says, "That doesn't mean anything to me."

"My dad created Fizzle," I explain.

"I know, that explains why Connor's hanging around the two of you, but that has nothing to do with you two being together." He puts the frame down.

Connor raises his hand. "Just to clarify, I actually kind of like these two. Never a dull moment."

Ryke shrugs off his leather jacket that's soaked in alcohol. "So you're in a serious relationship with Lo?"

"What does it matter to you?"

His face twists in irritation. "Are you always this defensive with people who save your ass?"

Yes. Instead of admitting my faults, I answer his previous question. "He's a childhood friend. We just started dating, but we've lived together since the start of college. Satisfied?"

"That'll fucking do," he says, picking up another frame.

Connor asks, "What time do you think Lo is going to be awake? He promised me that we'd go to the gym tomorrow."

I sigh. "Promises from Lo are like bars at 2 a.m.—empty." I open the desk drawer and find three bottles of Advil. I toss the bare container in the trash and dump four pills from the second bottle into my palm. Hurriedly, I fill a glass of water from the bathroom and place it beside the bed with the capsules.

"You do this a lot," Ryke states.

I shut off the lights, not meeting his eyes, and usher them into the living room. I wrap my body in a cream cotton blanket, hiding my hands that have begun to shake. While they choose the couch, I curl up in the red suede recliner.

Ryke soaks in the atmosphere from the cushions, inspecting the light fixtures, the unused fireplace and the Warhol-inspired polar bear prints. It's like he's constructing a person out of our things. I don't like it.

"You both should leave. I'm kind of tired," I say softly.

Connor stands. "Okay, but I'll be here in the afternoon to pick up Lo for the gym. He may not keep his promises, but I collect on all offered to me."

Ryke stands just as Connor leaves through the door. He continues to glance around, his eyes flitting over the kitchen, the bar stools, the bookshelves . . .

"Are you planning on stealing something?" I ask. "We really don't have that many valuables here. You should try my parents' house."

Ryke's face contorts. "You're something, you know that?" His eyes narrow. "Just because I'm staring at your fucking lamp doesn't mean I'm going to hijack it."

"If you're not taking mental pictures to come back later, then what the hell *are* you doing?"

He cocks his head to the side and stares at me like I'm truly a moron. "I'm trying to get a sense for who you are." He points to the fireplace mantel where a crystal vase sits, a housewarming present from Poppy. "Rich." He nods to the liquor bottles that litter the kitchen counters. "Alcoholic." How can he form that conclusion from a few bottles?

My nose flares. "Get out."

His eyes continue to narrow. "Does it hurt—hearing the truth? Has anyone told it to you before?"

I rarely ever become this worked up, but my chest rises with something foreign and furious. "You can't look at *things* and understand us!"

"Yeah? I seem to have struck a chord. And I'm pretty sure it's because I'm right."

"What's your problem?" I spit. "We didn't ask for your help. If I knew you were going to be such a . . . " I growl, not able to form complete words at this point.

"A gorilla?" he banters. "A monkey? An ape?" He takes a step closer to me. I could punch him. I have *never* felt such hostility towards someone before.

"Leave me alone!" I shout, almost whining. I *also* hate the tone of my voice.

"No," he says adamantly.

I clench my teeth, suppressing the urge to stomp my foot like a weirdo. "Why?"

"Because if you thought Lo was in serious trouble, I don't think you'd do a thing about it. And that fucking pisses me off." He looks me over. "So deal with me." He moves backwards to the door. There's a huge part of me that agrees with Ryke. I don't know how to help Lo without hurting myself. And I'm too selfish to find a solution to his problems.

"I don't ever want to see you again," I say, honest and truthful.

"Well, that sucks for you," Ryke tells me, turning the knob. "I'm fucking hard to get rid of." With this, he leaves. And I want to scream. He's that concerned about Lo's well-being that he's willing to see us a second time?

The door closes, and I try not to think about him. Maybe he said empty threats to force guilt on me. No one would inject themselves into another person's business like this.

Then again, he stopped a fight that was not his to end. Clearly, he's the type of guy to stick his nose where it does not belong.

Twenty-three

As Ryke continues to plague my mind, I waste the rest of the night on porn and toys and drown in sweat and natural highs. We should have stayed home for Lo's birthday like he wanted. I wish we had, and I won't make the same mistake next year.

Every time I cuddle in my sheets, willing slumber, tears bridge and they flow uncontrollably. Being in a *real* relationship was supposed to fix the kinks in our lives. It should've made our problems easier. We no longer have to pretend. We can be ourselves. We're free from one lie. Isn't this the part where our love overcomes our addictions? Where our problems magically solve from a kiss and a promise?

Instead everything has trickled into the gutter. Lo drinks. I screw. And our schedules overlap and bypass too often, becoming more destructive than healthy.

No one told me you can love someone and still be miserable. How is that possible? And yet, the thought of walking away from Loren Hale collapses my lungs. We've been friends, allies, for so long that I don't know who I am without him. Our lives intersect at every possible junction, and separating sounds like a fatal, irreparable cut.

But something is so wrong.

My wrist aches by the late morning, but I still pop in another DVD. The buzzer rings as I plop on my mattress. *No.* I am in no mood to entertain Connor. Also, I may jump his bones. My body stays riled, and I desperately need Lo. But his actions last night deserve little reward. Even if withholding hurts me more than him, he isn't getting *any* anytime soon.

The buzzer lets out another aggravated wail. Great. Lo is still passed out.

I crawl from my sheets, throw on a T-shirt and sweatpants before I slam my thumb on the speaker button. "Hello?"

"Miss Calloway, I have a Mr. Cobalt here."

"Send him up."

I make coffee, hoping caffeine will make Connor look like an ugly hobbit that's too ghastly to pounce on. Though, Frodo is kind of cute.

"Was that the buzzer?"

I nearly drop the cream.

Lo rubs his eyes, walking wearily to the cabinets, scavenging for saltines and bloody mary mix. His hair looks wet from a shower, and he only wears a pair of running pants that hang very low on his hips.

My body tightens, and I turn away just as his eyes meet mine.

"Hey." He puts a hand on the bareness of my neck, brushing back my hair.

"Stop," I choke. I lengthen the distance between us.

I watch familiar remorse cloud his features. He looks me up and down, from my sweaty legs to my clothes that stick to my body, and my hair that's tangled and damp.

It must look like I've been having sex.

He places a hand on the counter to keep his body upright, like the wind knocks out of him. "Lily—"

A fist bangs on the door. "Loren Hale!" Connor calls. "You better wake up. You promised me gym. I want gym."

Lo reluctantly leaves my side and lets him in. "You're on time," he says flatly, going back to the kitchen.

"Always am." He watches Lo grab a bottle of vodka from the freezer. "You know, it's barely noon. Brain cells generally don't respond well to alcohol this early. Gatorade is the better option."

"He's making a bloody mary for his hangover." My defense spurted out before I could stop it.

"What she said," Lo adds, not making me feel any better about covering his problem. *Don't think about it.* He pops open a V8 and starts fixing the drink. Connor says something about electrolytes.

I stare off and imagine hands pressing to the countertops on either side of me, caging me in. The faceless, nameless guy touches his warm lips to my neck, sucking. Fingers slip underneath my tee, and then they head to the hem of my sweats, edging closer, tingling—

"Lily, sound like a plan?" Lo asks, worry creasing his forehead.

I blink. "Huh?" I rub the back of my neck, trying to cool off but my thoughts set me ablaze.

Lo clenches a blue Gatorade. What happened to his bloody mary? Did Connor really convince him to switch? He sets it down and comes to me, noticing my shaky hands. "You okay?" He reaches out to touch my face, but I turn my head and separate. His whole body tenses at the rejection.

"Fine," I say. "I'm going to take a shower."

"Are you coming to the gym with us?" He sounds worried.

"I wasn't planning on it." Each step away from Lo makes my body throb. My willpower starts dying out. I need him. I want him. I am seconds from crumbling and taking him for myself.

Swiftly, he catches my sides in two hands. He leans down to

my ear. "Please come." His husky voice sends me to bad places. I hold in a noise. "I'll make it up to you there." He whispers exactly what he wants to do to me at the gym. I can't say no to this. I can barely say no to anything. He's buying his forgiveness through my weakness. It's like me screwing up and sending him a gift basket full of expensive whiskey.

I nod and mumble something about a shower first. My feet carry me to my bathroom, and I wash my hair and the sweat.

Lo knocks on the door. "Do you need me?"

Yes. But I think I can hold out until the gym. I hope I can. "No."

I sense him lingering by the door. He won't apologize for last night, even though he must know he fucked up. I wait for him to ask if I slept with some other guy, but he never does. And then I hear his footsteps pad away. After showering, I change into a pair of nylon pants and a baggy shirt.

When we arrive at the gym, Connor chooses to spend his time at the lower body machines next to a series of flat-screen televisions. He pushes weight down with his feet, using his thigh muscles for strength.

Across the open room, I sink to the floor beside the Pec Deck machine. Lo grips two handles attached to weights and brings them to his chest and back out.

I am through trying to avoid Lo's touch. In the car, I spent the entire time hugging the door to make a point, and the divots in the road practically vibrated the seats, killing me. "Can we do it now?" I ask, rolling my high socks that awkwardly rise above my ankles.

"Isn't the anticipation a part of the fun?"

"Sometimes." I pull my knees to my chest and catch Connor pausing his workout to argue with another guy over the television remote. "We should ditch him." It's the easiest solution to our problems. He's the interloper, the guy forcing us to confront our problems, to truly stare and see them for what they are. I don't want to think about any of it. I also blame Ryke for planting guilt-ridden seeds in my head.

"He's okay," Lo says, bringing the handles to his chest again. He lets out a long breath and releases. "He's probably the biggest prick I've ever met, but he's not perfect, even if he thinks he is."

I pick up a couple of dumbbells, avoiding the stink-eye from two girls on StairMasters. I guess accompanying your boyfriend to the gym and watching him work out is considered lame. I crunch them in my arms, which happen to be the weakest of my four limbs. Minutes pass and I let them drop in my hands.

I take another seat. "Are we ever going to talk about last night?"

He grimaces as he brings the weight to his chest one more time. Then he takes his fingers off the handles and wipes his forehead with a towel. I see the wheels spinning in his head. "What is there to say?"

"You drank that guy's liquor."

Lo rolls his eyes dramatically and rises from the bench to add more weight. "I've done that before. What makes now so different, Lil?"

"You're not in high school anymore," I say. "And . . . and you're with me."

The weight clinks together and he sits back down. "Do you want me to stop drinking?" he asks seriously. I do. Why would I want him to continue his descent towards something horrible? He can die from this. He can pass out and never wake up. Before I muster the courage to say the words, he adds, "Do you want to stop having sex?"

No. Why does that have to be a stipulation? I guess because it's not fair that I pour my thoughts and energy and time into sex while he has to withdraw from alcohol.

"Look," he says, realizing I can't answer. "I drank a lot. You masturbated all night. I mean, I assume you didn't cheat on me." He waits for me to refute and I shake my head, telling him I didn't. He nods and looks a little relieved. "It was a bad night. We've had plenty of those. Okay?" He returns to the handles.

I stare dazedly at the ground. "Sometimes I think we're a better fake couple."

He stiffens. "Why do you believe that? Is the sex bad?"

"No . . . I just think it's easier." We should go back to the way things were. We didn't fight as much. We allowed our schedules to be different and to cross occasionally. For the most part, we separated our addictions, and now they intertwine too much to juggle.

"No one said being in a relationship is easy." He doesn't go back to the handles.

My body aches. I wish I had the fire in my heart to stand up, to walk over to him. To put my hands on his chest and wrap a leg around his waist, straddling him on the bench seat. His breath falls short and he asks, "Lily?" But he doesn't stop me. He lets me lean in, my hips sinking into his. I kiss the base of his neck while his restraint lessens, and he groans. He becomes excited underneath me and throatily tells me to meet him in the locker room.

A damp towel hits my face, and I jolt back to the living. Lo raises his eyes accusingly. "Dream of me?"

My arms flush. "Maybe." Hopefully I'm only transparent with Lo.

"You're supposed to say *yes*." His eyes twinkle in amusement.

"Yes," I say with a smile. "Can we do it now?"

He swings his legs off the bench and grabs his Gatorade. Excitement swells inside my body and instantly extinguishes when he stays seated. "It'll be better if it's spontaneous, Lil."

I frown. "Are you . . . are you scared to do it in public? We won't get caught. I'll make sure of it and—"

"I'm not scared," he assures me. Just to prove his point, he kneads his hand in my hair and then kisses me aggressively, full of eagerness and promise of something more. His tongue slips into my mouth, and a small noise escapes me.

He pulls away with a satisfied grin. "Soon." *Yes.*

He walks towards the lower body machines near Connor but stops when he notices me permanently frozen to the floor. His kiss has turned me to stone.

"Are you coming?" *Soon apparently.*

"Shouldn't I let you have boy time?" I'm the intruder, the needy girlfriend who hangs around. It's hard to know the proper protocol for moments like this since we've always been each other's only friend.

Lo considers this for about two seconds before he grimaces. "Fuck that. Come on." He motions for me with two fingers. I don't think he's being overtly sexual, but *good God*, he can't do that to me right now.

I look up, just as he spins around, and glimpse a fragment of a smile.

Lo takes a machine next to Connor, and I grab a yoga mat and spread it on the ground near them but far enough away that I'm not smothering Lo.

I'm not a complete idiot. I notice the way he's dragging out having sex with me, and a part of me wonders whether it's to heighten the tension or to limit me, to try to see if I can have less sex throughout the day, to help me fight my addiction.

I have no idea which, but I lean towards the latter.

The guys in the gym are transfixed by a soccer game on the flat-screens. I vaguely pay attention to it, but boredom sinks in. My gaze drifts to a golden skinned man on a forty-five-degree machine. He holds a bar above his head and brings his legs up in a "crunch" position.

I lie on the yoga mat, staring at the ceiling, and shut my eyes. He rests a hand beside my head, hovering. His body weight suspends above me. He peels down my pants *with* my panties and kneels between my legs. His hands creep towards my thigh and he cups the place between . . .

My body shudders and my eyes snap open. Oh my God.

"YESSSS!" The whoops and hollers cause my face to flame, even if it's because a soccer team scored another goal.

Connor's gaze transfixes to Bloomberg Television, a business channel. At least he missed me zoning out like a freak. But Lo has his eyes set on my body. How long has he been staring? Does he know I'm not dreaming about him anymore?

I spring to my feet, unable to wait any longer. He'll either have to follow me into the locker room or I'll find a way to appease myself *without* cheating.

"I'll be back," Lo tells Connor. He races after me.

I relax. Maybe this isn't easy, but we'll have to make it work.

Twenty-four

I t's inhuman to require a general science credit for all majors. In two years, I'll forget everything I learn anyway, and my plans don't involve going into business for some pharmaceutical company. When will I ever need to know about mitosis? And if I have to read one more case study about Drosophila—the fancy word for fruit flies—I may seriously consider switching to Fungi, Friends and Foes.

But the ingeniously named course has a horrible rating on RateMyProfessors.com. A student review called the instructor a hard-ass for making everyone memorize the scientific names of *all* fungi discussed. And my brain can barely retain the names of my neighbors. Now I'm stuck in another ring of hell: Biology 1103 for Non-Bio Majors, meaning the scientifically challenged. It doesn't make the class any easier; it just allows more students to share misery.

Library lights dull as time ticks on, tugging my eyelids down and down and down. I yawn, about to employ Connor's study technique and buy a Red Bull. Maybe I should make flashcards.

So far I've only been distracted once, and it wasn't even to fantasize about the cute guy with glasses two tables away. Some student beat a Fizzle machine to death when it refused to deposit his Cherry Fizz. He gave up after realizing the big plastic box is indestructible—at least against a pair of Vans.

Lo texted me twice. The first to ask if I'm going to be home to drive him to the liquor store. The second to tell me to pick up condoms. I almost choked on my Diet Fizz with that comment, never believing we'd be so intimate and comfortable about it.

At the end of my long table, a girl in a navy Penn sweatshirt leans across to whisper to her friend.

"Do you see him?" she hisses. "He's walking this way. Oh my God."

The tiny, muscular blonde with a Gymnastics hoodie cranes her neck, trying to look past the eight foot bookshelves.

"Don't be so obvious, Katie," the girl hyperventilates.

Who the hell could be good-looking enough to incite such dramatics? Now I'm curious. I bite the end of my pencil and glance around, not seeing what they do. Damn. Less subtly, I lift my butt from the uncomfortable wooden chair and angle my body to peek *around* the bookshelf. Unless this guy is a ghost, he's acquired my favorite superpower and literally vanished into thin air.

"Who are you looking for?"

I jump, my spine hitting the wood slates with a *thunk*. Uh . . . I lean back and look up as he towers above me. They cannot be talking about *him*.

Ryke, aka Green Arrow, has a hand on my table, a smug look plastered to his face. He must know I was trying to spy on him— but that was before I knew the hot mystery guy was the same one who carried my boyfriend into my apartment.

The athletic girls press their noses to their notebooks, taking pretty obvious glances at him. He follows my gaze and bridges the gap between our chairs, but he turns his back on them. They shoot me the *worst* looks imaginable.

"I think your friends want you," I tell him, staring at my textbook.

To appease me, he actually rotates. "Katie, Heather."

Katie acts surprised. "Oh. Hey, Ryke! I didn't notice you there."

"You guys have practice today?"

"Yeah, conditioning. Will you be in the gym?"

Ah, yes, they know each other through athletics; it all makes sense now. Since I don't necessarily belong to any group at Penn, especially one that involves bouncing balls or tumbling in the air, Ryke's allure is quite lost on me. Maybe he dazzles them when he stretches his quads.

I glance at his calf muscles, sadly hidden beneath jeans. *I will not cheat on Loren Hale, especially not with Ryke.* I really need to stop thinking about other guys. It's not as if Lo isn't enough. He is, so far, but when there's someone else lingering, my mind starts wandering to sinful places.

"I'm running outside today."

"That's too bad. Well, if you ever want to work out together, you know where we are."

He nods and then shifts back towards me. *No. Go away.* He skirts around to the other side of the table, and for some reason, I think he may obey my mental order. Instead, he scrapes a chair and sits down. He leans in, setting his elbows on the wood.

And I lift up my textbook to block his view.

Seconds pass and he puts his hand on it, the spine thudding to the table. "I need to talk to you."

"And I don't want to talk to you." I go to lift the book again as a blinder, but he slides it towards his body, taking my textbook hostage.

"I have to study," I say in that screechy tone.

"Do you always whine?"

I glare. "Do you always insult people when you want something?" I wish Lo was here. He'd be able to shoo this guy away without a problem. Why don't my words have the same effect?

"Only you," he muses, flipping through my book and shutting it. "Biology? Are you a freshman or something?"

I blush. "I put off some of my core credits." I reach out to snatch the book, but he jerks it away from me again.

"I'll give this back to you after you hear me out."

"Is it about alcohol?"

"No."

"Is it about Lo?"

"Not entirely."

"Are you going to be mean?"

He leans back, his chair creaking, and lets out a short laugh. "I don't know. I could be, depending on the direction of this conversation. How's that?"

Good enough. "Fine." I motion for him to continue and then cross my arms over my chest.

He catches the haughty movement and manages to stifle a smartass comment, cutting to the point. "When I was at your apartment, I saw your posters from Comic-Con. I'm a freelance writer for *The Philadelphia Chronicle* and they're paying me to go to the convention. Thing is, I have no idea what to expect or what it entails or even what to do."

I figure out the rest. "And you thought we may know?" I didn't expect him to ask me *that*.

"I was hoping I could talk with Lo about it."

My eyebrows shoot up. "You want to talk to my boyfriend? About Comic-Con?" That's not weird. "Is this really about comics, Ryke?"

"You think I'm lying?"

"Kind of, yeah."

He rolls his eyes. "Look, I'm a journalism major. I'd rather talk to a primary source about Comic-Con than quote from Wikipedia and blogs."

"I thought you said you needed help learning what Comic-Con entails, not a quote." Ha! I caught him in his lie.

Ryke doesn't even flinch. "That too." He rubs his lips in thought. "Look, maybe I can at least borrow some of his comics and he can give me some highlights of characters and conflicts."

I stare at him, still skeptical. "You said this wasn't about Lo's problem, right?"

"You mean his alcohol addiction."

I glower. He's pushing it. I go to stand up and leave. Screw the bio book—he can have it. Ryke quickly extends his hands to stop me.

"I'm sorry. I can be insensitive sometimes."

I stay in my seat, waiting.

"This isn't about alcohol."

"Do you have a crush on him or something?"

Ryke jerks back in surprise and cringes. "What? Why the fuck would you think that?"

"I don't know." I feign confusion. "You keep asking about *his* comics. *His* advice about Comic-Con. You do realize, I have comics too and *I* went to Comic-Con with him."

He groans. "Why do you have to make this so difficult? I'm asking for help. From you, from Lo, from whomever knows the difference between whatever costume you were wearing and Wolverine."

"There are a lot of other people that can help you." I will continue to distrust Ryke. Literally, his responses grate on every nerve in my body. It's impossible to be attracted to someone that shrivels my insides.

"I don't want their help. I want yours."

Before I make sense of that, my phone buzzes on the table.

Ryke glances at the name in the text box. "Lo," he says. "Maybe you can ask him if it's okay."

"He will say no," I shoot back.

"You don't know that."

"*You* don't know Lo," I retort and click into the text.

> Can I watch porn with you tonight?
> You clock more time with your
> remote than me. Jealous.—Lo

I clutch my phone to my chest, hoping Ryke didn't catch a peek. My elbows blush anyway.

"You're turning red."

"It's hot in here," I mumble and clear my throat. "I don't know what more to tell you."

"Say 'yes, Ryke, I'll help you this one time since you stopped Matt from beating the shit out of my boyfriend.'"

My eyes narrow. "How long are you going to hold that over my head?"

"Forever."

I sigh heavily, realizing this is not going to end like I want it to. "Lo may yell at you. He may call you rude names until you leave."

Ryke lets out another short laugh. "Yeah, I think I can handle him." He tilts his head. "Do you think he can handle me?"

"You do realize that sounds sexual," I blurt, my eyes widening in regret. Why did I just say that?!

"And maybe you have a perverted mind."

I can't argue with that, but I have officially roasted into a new shade of red. To ignore my embarrassment, I go back to the issue at hand. "You're not allowed to mention alcohol. If you do, you're gone."

He nods. "Fair enough."

Maybe Lo will find a way to deter Ryke. If anyone can skillfully kick someone out of our apartment, it's him.

I scroll through the calendar in my phone. "What day were you thinking?"

He stands and stuffs *my* biology book into *his* backpack. "Right now."

I gape. "I'm *studying*, Ryke."

"Really. That's what you were doing?" He rubs his jaw. "I could have sworn you were people-watching and eating the end of your pencil."

I glare. "You've been spying on me?"

He slings his backpack over his shoulder. "I was observing you. Don't get so pissy about it. I just needed to make sure you were in a good enough mood to hear my request." He nods to the exit. "Shall we?"

I stand up in a huff, gathering my notebooks and shoving them into my backpack. "I don't understand why we have to do this right now."

He scoots his chair into the table. "Because, Lily Calloway, you seem like the type of girl who will *never* return my calls." He motions for me to follow with his fingers, as though I'm a pet dog. "Let's go."

I inhale a strained breath, silently throwing darts into Ryke Meadows' face. His self-confident swagger rubs me wrong. In fact, I'd rather not be rubbed by him at all. At least Lo will know what to do with him. *That,* I hold on to.

Twenty-five

We agree to meet in the lobby of the Drake since we drove in two separate cars. When I walk in, I'm not surprised to see him waiting by the golden elevators. My bio book rests under his arm, and for the first time I allow myself a good look at Ryke. Without his Green Arrow costume, he appears slightly older, especially with a stubbly jaw and tanned skin. Underneath his white track shirt, I'm sure lies very toned and very lean muscles. He has a face that could force girls to their knees, but so does Lo.

I can't imagine the two of them squaring off. Ice vs. Stone. Sharpness vs. Hardness. Cold vs. Hot. They're different, yet somehow, they're still alike.

Ryke presses the button when he sees me approach. "You look like you're going to vomit."

"I'm not," I mumble a stupid reply, thankful that the elevator doors burst open and slice the awkwardness. I slide in and hit the top floor. When they close, Ryke spins around and faces me, positioning himself in front of the doors, as though hoping I won't bolt the second they break apart.

"I lied," he starts.

My jaw unhinges. "Wha . . . " This was a bad idea.

"I'm not actually going to Comic-Con—"

"I knew it!" I should have listened to my gut. "Get out."

He tilts his head with a frown at my asinine order. "We're on a fucking elevator. In fact . . . " He presses the emergency stop, and it rumbles to a halt. Oh my God. He's going to murder me! I spring to the buttons to restart the elevator, but he shields my passage by extending his arms and then lightly pushing me back.

"Let me out!"

"I need you to listen to me," Ryke starts. "I am a journalism major. I do write for *The Philadelphia Chronicle*. But I have no intention of going to Comic-Con."

"Then why—"

"Because I want to help your boyfriend, and I needed you to get me at least this far so I could explain the rest."

My defensive barriers start rising tenfold. "We don't need your help! I can take care of him." I point to my chest. "*I've* taken care of him my whole life."

"Yeah?" Ryke's eyes narrow heatedly. "How many times have you watched him pass out? Tossing a few aspirins isn't helping him, Lily. He has a fucking problem."

My cheeks burn, and I take in his words very carefully. It hurts to see Lo drink so excessively. It hurts to watch him depend on one drink after another, and I constantly fear the day where it becomes too much. But I always bury those worries with carnal pleasures and a natural high. My voice softens. "Why do you want to fix him so badly?"

Ryke stares at me with more empathy than I thought he was capable of. "My father is an alcoholic, and I don't want Lo to turn out like him. I wouldn't wish that on anyone."

I ask a question that has been plaguing me for some time. "How can you know Lo's an alcoholic? You don't know him. You've seen him once, on his twenty-first birthday, and he was passed out more than he was awake."

Ryke shrugs. "I can just tell, especially with the way you became possessive over his flask. He'd be truly pissed if someone wasted his expensive alcohol, wouldn't he?"

He would. I bite my nails. "I don't know what you want me to do."

Ryke edges forward. "Let me try to help him."

I shake my head. "Lo won't let you."

"I figured as much, and that's why I can start by hanging around you guys, getting to know him."

The pieces start adding together. "Comic-Con. You want to keep up the lie to grow closer to Lo so you can try to influence him. You want *me* to lie?" I'm not sure this will work. We've already allowed Connor into our lives—another person may unsettle an already off-kilter balance.

"Yeah," Ryke says. "I want you to lie to your boyfriend so that he has a chance to get better. You think you can do that, Lily? Or are you going to be fucking selfish and let him continue this destructive path? One day, he may never wake up. One day, his body may shut down. And you're going to think back to this moment and wonder why you didn't agree to this proposition—why you didn't try something *else* to help your boyfriend."

I stumble back, punched in the gut. "I don't want him to die," I murmur.

"Then do something about it."

I nod out of impulse, but I haven't processed what this means in the long run. That I'll have to lie to Lo. Can I do it? My brows scrunch in thought. I think I can. Lo has more to lose if I don't try. Surviving another debacle like Halloween sounds less and less likely, and I struggle to help Lo because of our relationship and *my* vice. No second party has ever offered aid before. And if Lo was given the same deal to help me, would he take it?

I know he would.

I look back up at Ryke. "I still don't like you."

"I'm not very fond of you either," he admits and hands me my bio book.

"What did I do to you?" I frown. Why doesn't he like me?

He presses a button and the elevator groans to a start. We rise. "You're too skinny. You whine too much. And you enable an alcoholic."

I purse my lips. "I'm already regretting this." But I'll suffer through Ryke's mean comments if it gives Lo a chance to get better.

"I warned you that I'm not easy to get rid of."

I thought he was exaggerating. The elevator doors slide open, and I lead him to my apartment even though he knows the way. The thought is as unsettling as the looming situation. The last time he was here, Lo had been unconscious to the world. Moments ago, I hoped Lo would find a way to kick him out, now I have to defend Ryke, who has proved to be an annoying force in my life.

I unlock the door and toss my jangling keys in the basket.

Lo calls to me from the bedroom. "Lil, we're going to watch *Blow Hard*, and I'm going to fuck you better than . . . " He trails off to read the label on the back of the DVD while my eyes bug, not willing a peek at Ryke by my side. ". . . a group of pierced thugs. Huh . . . "

"Lo!" I yell.

"I don't like that one either," he says. I hear the sound of DVD cases clattering together.

Ryke clears his throat beside me, and I glimpse at him for a millisecond, catching sight of his raised brows at me. Can this get more awkward?

"Or would you rather I sucked every part of you, love?"

Oh my God.

If Ryke's uncomfortable, he doesn't let on. Between the two of us, *I'm* the one shrinking back. After only a second, Lo emerges from the bedroom. He wears nothing but a pair of jeans, the band of his boxer-briefs peeking from the waist. On a normal day, I'd take in the ridges of his abs, the curve of his muscles that seem to lead towards something much lower and much more sinful. He would flash those bedroom eyes and tease me for thirty minutes. Then he'd lift me in his arms and carry me to his mattress. He'd draw out every movement, every look, every*thing* to excite my body and electrify my nerves.

Instead, he freezes in the space between the hallway and the kitchen. His face sharpens, and his muscles cut into rigid lines.

I open my mouth to introduce Ryke, but Lo ignores me and sets an ice-cold glare on him. "Who the fuck are you?"

Ryke takes the words with ease. "Green Arrow."

Lo's face contorts in confusion.

He doesn't remember what happened. I step forward and come to his side. "He's from the Halloween party," I say. "He helped stop the fight." *And he carried you home.*

Lo nods. "Thanks then." He shifts to me, keeping his back to Ryke. His voice lowers so Ryke can't hear. "We're on a schedule, Lil. You shouldn't have brought him to the apartment."

I frown. "You're not going to ask me why he's here?"

His eyes flicker hesitantly to Ryke. "Right now," he whispers, "I'm more concerned with satisfying you."

"I'm okay," I tell him. "This morning was good enough."

"Are you sure?" His brows furrow. "I only came inside you twice."

I swallow, sensitive spots throbbing. Well *now* I'm not so sure. But I have to try to wait. "I can hold out."

He puts two fingers underneath my chin and tilts my head up. "I don't know if I believe you." He takes a step forward, causing me to take one back, repeating the movements until my spine hits a bar stool. I grip it behind me, and he pins me against it with two hands on the counter.

244 · KRISTA RITCHIE and BECCA RITCHIE

"We have company," I remind him.

"Like I give a shit," Lo whispers. He kisses me hard, stealing my breath, and my back arches to meet his pelvis. His hand slips into my jeans pocket.

Ryke says, "Lily."

I immediately separate my lips from Lo's, and I lean back into the stool to try to avoid his touch.

Lo clenches his teeth, and his head whips to Ryke. "Clearly, I'm trying to fuck my girlfriend. So leave."

"Look, you can do whatever you want to her later." He sets his hard gaze on me for extra reinforcement. This is where I should agree and peel away from Lo, but his fingers slip into the band of my jeans, sliding underneath my panties in the back. He has a hand planted firmly on my ass.

"Lo," I warn. "He asked us for help, and we owe him a favor . . . "

He squeezes, and my knees nearly buckle. He keeps me standing by pinning his weight against me. "You really want to entertain this guy?"

Obviously not, but it's the right thing to do. Before, we would have shooed him out of the door, distancing ourselves from everyone in sight. Being alone, together, that's our thing. Adding a new person into the mix—that's something we haven't quite figured out yet.

With his other hand, he unbuttons my jeans.

"Lo!" I shriek. He's trying to make Ryke so uncomfortable that he flees, but what I've come to understand about the guy, he's impenetrable to all offenses. Somehow, I disentangle Lo from my body and button my jeans, my neck heating as I create distance from him.

I stand between Lo by the kitchen and Ryke by the foyer, wondering what the hell I'm supposed to do now.

Lo angles his body so he has a good view of Ryke. "You're still here."

Ryke scrutinizes Lo, trying to figure him out from afar. "Lily said you both would help me with research on Comic-Con."

Lo takes this in. "She agreed to this?" He looks down at me. "That's unlike you."

"I owe him."

Lo's jaw locks as his eyes flicker to Ryke. "And you can't come back later?"

"I'm here now. What's the big deal?"

Lo scowls at him like he's a moron. "You're cock-blocking me, that's the big fucking deal."

I want to disappear. Like right now.

Ryke glances at me and then tilts his head at Lo without a shadow of insecurity. "Have sex with her later. I'm not stopping you." He inches closer. "Lily, you want to show me your comics or should I go find them myself?"

Lo interjects. "Hey, I don't know you. There's no way in hell you're going to be alone with her."

"Lo, it's fine," I tell him. Really, I have *zero* desire to do anything sexual with Ryke, and I'm pretty sure the feeling is mutual.

Ryke inspects Lo once more and then he nods. "If I was you, I'd probably be the same way. Some strange guy creeping in with your girlfriend—I get it. It's weird."

"That's an understatement," Lo says flatly. "I make out with my girlfriend, you stand there. I put my hand down her pants, you stand there. I tell you I'm going to fuck her, you stand there. What am I supposed to make of that?"

My heart beats wildly, and I've lost the ability to breathe. I must be dreaming. Yeah, this is a dream. I'll wake up soon, but obviously not soon enough.

"That I'm a self-assured guy that likes to get what he wants, and right now that's information about Comic-Con. Pretty simple, right?"

Lo takes this in.

To nudge his thoughts, I say, "I'll grab a few *New X-Men* comics. Stay here." I don't give Lo the option of backing out. I disappear into his room, sprinting around to try and gather some issues. After I collect a handful, I rush out to the hallway.

Lo has crept into the kitchen, where he opens a cupboard for a glass. When I pass Ryke by the sink, the guy gives me a look like *help me.*

I'm trying, I mouth.

Try harder, he mouths back.

I flip him off in a knee-jerk reaction, and he rolls his eyes. I set the comics on the counter beside him and then fill the space in the kitchen between Lo and Ryke.

Lo closes the fridge, plopping an ice cube into his whiskey. When he leans an elbow on the counter, he eyes me like *come here.* He'll probably wrap an arm around my waist and let me sink my body into his.

No, Lily. I shake my head at him and wade in the center, unsure and uncomfortable.

His face sharpens at the rejection, and he directs his hate onto Ryke. "What do you need to know?"

He shrugs. "Anything."

"Ever hear of Google?"

"You mean that little search engine on that thing called the internet? No, I've never heard of it before. Can you explain that to me too?" He flashes a dry smile.

Lo grits his teeth and looks at me. "Why is he here again?"

"He's writing an article on Comic-Con, and we owe him a favor."

Lo inhales sharply. "Fine." He starts rattling off X-Men characters, mutant powers and how they fit into Earth 616, way too quickly for *anyone* to understand.

"Wait, wait." Ryke holds up his hands. "What the hell is Earth 616?"

Lo already looks frustrated. He downs half his drink, and Ryke's body tightens, as though each time Lo takes a sip is a bullet to his chest. His reaction actually makes me sidle to Lo and try something else.

I stand on the tips of my toes and whisper in his ear, "Hold me."

Obligingly, Lo sets down his drink and wraps two arms around my hips, leaning my back into his chest. The public display should embarrass me, but Ryke ignores our affection like we're just standing around.

I cut in, "Earth 616 is the Marvel universe."

"That's not too hard to understand," Ryke says.

One of Lo's hands creeps beneath my shirt and stays on my stomach. I am a horrible, horrible person. I should push him off and stay focused on the conversation, but if this deters him from drinking, then maybe it's okay.

Lo says, "Not all Marvel comics take place in Earth 616."

Ryke cocks his head. "Now I'm confused."

I try to explain. "It's used to denote Marvel's primary continuity. There's a string of comics that all fit together in sequential time . . . " I feel something cold on my lower back and stifle a gasp.

Lo runs an ice cube on my skin, teasing . . . and probably hoping Ryke will take a hint and leave. *Concentrate, Lily.*

I clear my throat. "Then there are other comics that will take the characters and screw around with them. These comics do *not* fit into Earth 616." He slides the cube up my spine, my skin cold and prickling. Oh God . . . "Like *Ultimate X-Men* . . . it . . . "

The cube melts away and Lo rakes his fingers along the same

wet trail. I tuck a piece of my hair back. ". . . It doesn't fit in with any of the other *X-Men* comics. The same way *The Ultimates* don't fit in with the *Avengers* line, even though they're about the Avengers."

Lo takes a small sip of his drink, and at first, I think my efforts aren't helping, but he pops an ice cube out of his mouth, not even hiding what he's doing from Ryke. A hand flies to my eyes, creating a blinder against any sort of judgment and awkwardness. Lo says to Ryke, "They're alternate universes."

"What's better, the main line or the alternate universes?"

"They're just different."

The ice shocks me, and I flinch from Lo. I spin around and set my hands on his chest. *Stop,* I mouth.

His lips find my ear, and I have a feeling he's glaring at Ryke as he whispers to me, "I'm going to take you so hard, you're going to come with every thrust. And when you're swollen and wet, all it's going to take is me inside of you. I won't even have to move for you to cry out." *Yes.*

No! I try to focus even though my legs quake in desire. I keep my palms on his chest and push him back into the counter, away from me.

He clasps my wrists and devours me with his gaze. I would have put a hand on his shoulder and forced him to his knees by now. And he would willingly hold on to my thighs, spreading my legs open. *Focus.*

Ryke goes to the fridge. "Which do you guys read?"

Lo mouths to me, *Ignore him.*

I shake my head and break his hold on my wrists. "We both read Earth 616."

Just as Ryke returns with a Diet Fizz, Lo picks up his glass again. I guess now that I've left his arms, he's free to drink. Great. If I told him to stop, he'd shoot me one of those looks like *maybe you should stop having sex*. Right now, that sounds close to torture.

"You can take those comics," I tell Ryke, thinking of a new solution quickly. "And you can stop by and return them when you're done."

Ryke actually looks impressed that I created a decent lie for him to come back.

Lo glares at me, his fingers tightening around the glass. "I don't think it's necessary for him to take our comics. He can sign up for an online subscription." Ryke's whole master plan involves becoming friends with Lo. According to him, the relationship will somehow help Lo stop drinking. I don't understand it completely, but if he's been around alcoholism, then I trust he knows more than me on good solutions.

"Don't be rude, Lo," I say.

He downs the rest of his drink. *No, no, no.* Before he can make another, I grab his wrists.

His eyebrows cinch. "Lily . . . " I've never told him how I feel about his addiction, and I can see the wheels spinning in his head, wondering if I'm about to fuck with our well-oiled system.

I'm not. I place his hands on my breasts, and his lips upturn in a crooked smile. He shifts both hands. One goes underneath my shirt, the other hooks around my shoulders, drawing me to his body. My back stays to Ryke, and as Lo kneads my breast, my willpower poofs into nothingness.

"I'll bring these back tomorrow," Ryke says. "Have fun fucking." Oh my God.

Lo says, "You can keep those. Think of it as a gift for helping us at the party." Translation: *We're even.*

"I'd feel better returning them. Thanks for the invite, Lily." *Way to throw me under the bus.* The door shuts, and he's gone.

For a second, I realize Lo may have teased me in front of Ryke *only* to kick him out. And now that he has left, Lo may go to his vice and stop feeding mine. My fear lasts a single moment. Lo starts to make good on his promise and slams my back into the fridge. He's going to take me hard.

He pins my wrists above my head. I try to move my body to meet his, but he puts considerable distance between us.

"Lo," I whine, breathing heavily.

"You want me to fuck you?"

"Yes," I moan and try to reclaim my hands. *Touch me!*

He edges closer, his body melding into mine, but he stretches my arms even further above my head.

"Lo." I want to undo his pants. I want him to rip off my shirt. Instead, he keeps teasing me in this locked position.

"I understand that you felt like you owed this guy, but after this, we don't owe him a thing, okay?"

I try to find words to refute, like *he's nice.* He's not. *He's lonely.* He's not. "He means well." I land on a truth and squirm underneath him. "Lo, please." I need him. Now.

"Did you fantasize about him?"

I cringe. "What? No." Is he worried I like him? "I think every word out of his mouth made me dryer and dryer." How's that for dislike?

"Then what's this about, Lily?" He uses one hand to hold my wrists together above my head and then the other to unbutton my jeans.

"He . . . uh . . . " I can't concentrate! "He asked me about comics . . . and . . . "

Lo tugs my jeans down, and I easily step out of them. The cold hits my flesh and I ache for Lo's warmth. "This is really about comics?" he questions, disbelieving.

"I . . . uh . . . forgot . . . condoms," I say, my mind reverting to sex.

"If you're on the pill and you haven't fucked anyone else, we should be fine."

I nod quickly. "Can I have my hands back?"

"No." He rubs his fingers on the outside of my panties, not pushing in. I shake beneath him. "So when he returns," Lo says, "are you going to kick him out?"

"What?" He stops the friction between my legs. *No, no, no.* "Lo . . ."

"I want to know if he's really here for comics, Lily. Is that the last time we're going to see him?"

I bite my lip, and he sees straight through me.

"What'd you do?" he breathes, his hands tightening on my wrists. The pressure feels better than it should.

Telling the truth will be a defeat I do not want to claim just yet. So I think on my toes. "He wants to write an article about us . . . about what it's like to be the children of consumer moguls. And I said yes because I owed him, and I knew . . . I knew you wouldn't agree because he has to follow us around. So I thought the Comic-Con lie would help introduce him to you . . ."

Lo stares at me with cold, narrowed eyes, and he drops my hands, taking four steps back from me. "He has to follow us around?"

I nod. "I'm sorry. I should have asked you—"

"You know why I would have said no?" He points to his chest. "I hate having to hide alcohol. You don't get it because sex is something we do in private."

I frown. "Like you mauling me in front of Ryke? That was private?"

Lo shakes his head. "The most he'll think is that I'm a horny guy, Lil. He won't connect that you're a sex addict. And I don't need him fucking writing about our problems in a published article for my father to see."

"It's for a class grade," I lie. The article doesn't even exist! But it's the best excuse I have to validate Ryke hanging around us. "He won't publish it."

"And you believed him when he told you that? It's bullshit."

"It's not!" I refute, my eyes welling with tears. I've never tried this hard to guide him towards a good place, and it's breaking me apart inside. "ImsorryImsorryImsorry," I slur.

His face shatters and he closes the space between us. "Hey . . ." His voice softens. He holds my cheeks and wipes the tears with his thumb. "We can tell him that we're not interested anymore."

I shake my head and choke on a sob. "No . . ." Why can't this be easier? I want to be able to tell Lo to stop, but he won't. No matter what I say, he'll keep drinking. This feels like my only option.

"Why not?"

"I made a promise," I say. "Please . . . let me . . . let me keep it." These emotions need to end. I start to drown in them, and so I focus on things that always make me feel better. I kiss him lightly on the lips.

He kisses back. And then his lips leave mine. He has a hand on the back of my head, and he stares at me like we should talk more, but I'd rather do other things.

I unbutton his jeans.

"Lily . . ." he says, very softly.

I unzip and yank them down. "Don't speak." I'm about to drop to my knees, but he grabs my elbow.

"Lily . . ." His amber eyes glass over. Is he about to tell me to stop?

I frown in confusion. "What?"

After a long moment, he whispers, "Nothing." He releases his hold, and I watch his cheeks sharpen to ice. My knees hit the floorboards, and I pull down his boxer-briefs in a systematic routine. He keeps his hand on the back of my head, and I try to forget the sadness in his eyes, the kind that can call on silent tears.

I try to remember the passion, the fire, and for this moment, I make sure to drown him in pleasure.

Twenty-six

O ur relationship is dangling on thin strings that threaten to tear. I feel it. I'm sure he feels it as well. His biggest worry was being able to satisfy me, but that's hardly a problem. Our selfishness wedges between us. Neither of us is willing to give up what we love for each other. Not yet. And I'm not sure what it's going to take to let go of our addictions.

By Sunday, a thunderstorm confines us indoors, and Connor drops by unannounced—for no reason at all other than to share a beer with Lo. I'm starting to believe he likes hanging around us. After arguing who would win a game of chess, Lo and Connor crack out a board and play between chatter and sips of beer.

I flip through a *Cosmo* magazine on the chair, reading about new sex positions. I realize what's important to me may not be important to other girls. And I'm okay with that. Sex is something I genuinely love. In my case, probably too much.

Rain patters against the windows, and I ignore texts from my sisters about missing the luncheon. I also find Ryke on Facebook and send him a quick message about the new lie. When I scroll through my phone, I see his response.

And he bought it?—Ryke

I type back. Yeah. I think so.

"You shouldn't make that move," Connor tells Lo, pointing to his rook. "There's clearly a better one."

Lo takes his fingers off the rook and scrutinizes the board set on the coffee table. A new message pops up.

Is he drinking right now?—Ryke

Beer.

Connor leans forward in the chair opposite the couch, hunching over the pieces. He points to the bishop. "That's the better move."

"How about you play your own game, and I'll play mine?" Lo shifts the rook.

I glance down at Ryke's word bubble.

I'm coming over.—Ryke

My stomach churns. Lo never really accepted the idea of Ryke following us around, but I burst into tears, so he hasn't denied the idea either, for my sake. Everything just feels strained and messy.

I send: *Now?*

See you in twenty.—Ryke

I internally groan.

Connor slides over a measly pawn. "Check."

"What?" Lo gapes. "But that . . . Oh." He rolls his eyes. "There's no way for me to win, is there?"

Connor smiles as he picks up his beer. "I'd say you could win the next one, but you won't."

Lo forfeits by flicking over his king.

And then the buzzer chimes. I stiffen. Can he be here already? No. He said it would take twenty minutes, not twenty *seconds*. Right? I glance back at the messages and realize he never specified. Oh, I'm so not ready for this.

I shake off nervous jitters and go to the foyer. I feel Lo's eyes on me all the way there.

"Want another beer?" Lo asks Connor.

"Sure."

Lo stands and acts casual as he opens the fridge in the kitchen. I press the button on the speaker box. "Hello?"

"Miss Calloway, Rose is here to see you."

I relax and press the button. "You can send her up."

"Rose?" Connor heard the security attendant's voice.

My eyes widen. I forgot Rose dislikes Connor. "Uh . . . yeah."

Amusement swims in Connor's bright blue eyes. "She's not going to be pleased to see me."

Lo hands him a beer and finds his seat on the couch. "Join the fucking club. She hates me, and yet she keeps torturing herself by showing up here."

"Don't be rude," I warn both of them. At the end of the day, she's still my sister and I love her no matter what any boys say.

Lo mumbles something into his . . . whiskey. He must have just switched. I worry that I'm not trying hard enough like Ryke says, but the only way to stop him from drinking is to become a needy girlfriend and make him focus on my addiction. So far, it has only put tension in our relationship.

I'm afraid that he's going to start resenting me for keeping him from something he enjoys.

So I let him drink his whiskey until an abrasive knock pounds on the door. With two deep, motivational breaths, I turn the knob. "Hey."

Rose stands with a sopping umbrella. She shrugs off her fur coat, revealing a high-collared black and white dress that fits her slender frame. Her normally straight hair frizzes on the sides and sticks out in strange places.

"It's hailing," she says with scorn.

"Really? I thought it was just raining."

"It was until I stepped out of the car." She comes inside and places the umbrella in the corner and hangs her coat on a hook. I wonder how much longer I can stall her by the foyer to lengthen her inevitable view of Connor.

She runs her fingers through her hair. "Do you have coffee?"

"Yeah, I'll get you a cup." I lead her towards the kitchen, but she detaches halfway there, her head whipping over to the adjacent living room.

"What?!" she shrieks. "Lily Calloway, you did not invite *him* over here without telling me first."

Lo interjects, "Last time I checked, Rose, your name wasn't on the lease agreement. You don't have a say in who comes over to *our* apartment."

Rose turns her back on the guys. "What is *Richard* doing here?" she hisses.

"He just showed up." I hand her a steaming mug and place my palm on her back, guiding her to the living room.

Lo flashes her a dry smile. "Does that remind you of someone?"

"Shut up," Rose snaps. "Do not compare me to *him*."

Connor rises like a good prep school boy, and Rose stands her ground while I grab my magazine and scoot in beside Lo. I've circled some of the positions I want to try with red magic marker like the Spank Me Maybe, Mission Control and Wild Ride. Lo points to the most submissive of the three, a picture of a guy pulling the girl's ponytail as she straddles him backwards, and Lo whispers, "Later."

If only Ryke would *not* show up today.

Lo sips his whiskey.

On second thought, maybe it's a good thing he is.

I glance back at Connor and Rose and realize they've been pretty much silent. They just stare at each other for a really, really long time, as though talking through their eyes.

"Is this what smart people do?" I whisper to Lo.

"They must have some superhuman telepathic power that we don't have." He adjusts so my head rests against the hardness of his chest, the warmth enveloping me further. I kinda, sorta, really want them to leave so Lo can take me in surprise.

"Is this still about last year?" Connor asks with a growing smile. "Just because you didn't know Williams wrote *Ethics and the Limits of Philosophy* and *Problems of the Self* doesn't make you a stupid person. Lots of people don't know him."

Her chest puffs out, looking more ruffled than when Lo pushes her buttons. "I know Freud, *Connor*. I knew Williams influenced him. Had someone on my team not sneezed, I wouldn't have been so distracted."

"A sneeze? You're going to blame your loss on an allergy problem?"

Rose holds up a hand to his face, as if pausing the argument, and sets her icy gaze on us. "You both really can't be friends with this asshole. Actually"—she points at Lo—"I believe *you* can, but you, Lily, really?"

Lo smirks. "Keep it coming, Rose. You're just making me love the guy more." Oh jeez. And to make matters more complicated, Connor looks amused by the continuation of this madness. He sticks his hands in his pockets, at ease.

"What happened to Charlie and Stacey?" she questions. *They never existed.*

"They moved," Lo lies easily. "Transferred to Brown a month

ago. I'd let them know you said goodbye, but they wouldn't care. They didn't really like you." And there goes our scapegoat with one new fib.

Rose glares. "That's real cute, Loren, considering they didn't even know me."

"Wait, Charlie who?" Connor asks.

"You wouldn't know them," I say.

He looks offended. *For real?* "I know everyone."

I open my mouth, at a loss of how to reply to *that*.

Rose snorts. "You're always the same, Connor, raising yourself on some prodigious level. I bet your biggest dream is to kiss the ass of Bill Gates."

Just when I think Rose's comment has penetrated Connor's cool, calm, know-it-all exterior, his thousand-dollar smile widens. He takes a step forward, threatening to breach Rose's safe space.

Lo whispers under his breath, "Protect your balls, Connor."

I'd agree, but Connor has proven to hold his own so far. He cocks his head at her. "Says the girl whose clothing line just got dropped by Saks." He inspects her tailored dress. "Is that piece extinct yet? Or can your *two* customers go buy it at Plato's Closet?"

Lo bursts into laughter, and I sink deeper into his arms. This is not good. At all. Rose has longer and sharper claws than me, able to defend herself quite effortlessly.

"Shut up, *Loren*," she says first. Then she places a hand on her hip. "So you read the newspaper, Connor. Congratulations, a well-informed citizen of Pennsylvania. Let's throw confetti and have a parade."

"Or you could go out with me tonight."

What?! Lo chokes on his alcohol. I gape, my jaw permanently unhinged. Rose. He just asked out Rose, my sister. I saw this coming, did I not? "Ha!" I say to Lo, poking him in the arm.

He bites my shoulder and murmurs, "She hasn't said yes yet."

Oh. I'd like Rose to give Connor a chance. If anyone can verbally keep up with her, he can. But she pushes men away as much as I used to lead them in.

Her body language stays closed off—her face as icy as before. "That's really funny. Nice joke." *Oh no, Rose, he's not joking.* I want to tell her that this isn't some cruel trick to make fun of her. She has guards up so she won't get hurt. It's easier to be cold than to feel the sting of disappointment.

"It isn't one," he tells her, taking another step. Her feet stay cemented to the floor, a good sign. "I have tickets to *The Tempest*."

I chime in, "Rose, you love Shakespeare."

She shoots me a look to stay out of it. I press my lips together, but I see her mind reeling at his proposition. Rose scrutinizes Connor. "So you have two tickets for *tonight*? This is obviously a pity invite."

"How could you think that?" he rebuts. "I don't pity you in the least. I'm inviting you because I happen to have two tickets that will go unused if you don't accompany me. I bought them for my mother, but work came up, and she can't go."

"Why take me?" she asks. "You know *everyone*. I'm sure you can manage to find some rich man to schmooze."

"True, but that's not the company I feel like sharing tonight. I'd rather take you, a beautiful, intelligent girl from Princeton."

Rose peruses Connor with beady eyes. "And this isn't a pity invite?"

"I already said it wasn't. Maybe you should get your hearing looked at. I wouldn't want to beat you unfairly in the next Bowl tournament."

She rolls her eyes. "Please, you wouldn't be able to beat Princeton even with a cheat sheet."

"Says the girl who got distracted by someone's nasal sensitivities."

"You're so weird," she says. Her arm drops off her hip and her stance finally loosens. *Yes!* He takes one more step, officially inches from her, the closest I've seen her to a man—or child—in a long, long time.

Lo whispers to me, "Are we in an alternate universe?"

I nod. "Yep, we've definitely left Earth 616." *And I love it.*

"So here I am," Connor continues, "about to waste front row seats—"

"Wait, you can't see anything in the first row. The stage blocks your view. Everyone knows that."

"Did I say first row? I don't think I did." He tilts his head. "You really need to get those ears checked, Miss Calloway." Oh, that was sexy. I will be the first to admit that. He takes out his wallet and hands her the tickets, which I presume are labeled for the third or fourth row, not the first.

Rose barely glances at them since Connor has infiltrated her safe space. She breathes all heavily and her cheeks start to flush. Aw, my sister is actually affected by the guy. It's like a once in a lifetime happening.

She hands one ticket back to him. "Pick me up at seven. Don't be late."

"I never am."

Rose rolls her eyes and then turns to me. "I have to make a stop at Poppy's house, but I wanted to see how you're doing."

"Fine," I tell her. "I haven't gotten my econ test back, so I'm not sure how well I'm doing in class yet."

She sips her coffee and sets it on the table. "With my help, you'll do better on the next one."

"I'm still her tutor," Connor says.

"No you're not," Rose tells him. "I have familial rights to this one." She points at Lo. "You can take that rodent."

Lo flips her off.

"Very mature," she says flatly and glances at her pearl-colored watch. "I need to go. I'll tell Mom and Dad you miss them, but it'd be better if you attended next Sunday's luncheon. They're starting to ask questions that I can't answer." She kisses my cheek and surprisingly meets Lo's gaze. "You too, be there." With that, she struts out in a dignified, Rose manner.

Gotta love her.

"You're crazy," Lo tells Connor. "I thought you were just a little insane for wanting to hang out with Lily and me, but now, you're certifiable."

The buzzer rings.

The silence afterwards sits heavy and unbearable. If Rose left, only one other person could be waiting in the lobby.

"Did she forget something here?" Connor asks.

Doubtful. I go to the door and buzz in Ryke. I also unlock the door and send him a quick message to just walk in. When I plop back beside Lo, something separates us. Unidentifiable and intangible. Lo senses my openness towards the situation, towards accepting Ryke and the article. For the first time, we stand on two different pages.

I know letting Ryke into our lives will complicate things. It'll be harder for me to disappear without questions. It'll be harder for Lo to drink without being chastised like a child. But it's too late to go back now, and I wouldn't want to.

"Who is it?" Connor asks.

"Ryke." I explain the article with the fewest details, and when the door clicks open, I shut up about it. Ryke enters, eyes pinging to each of us. He has sealed the comics in a Ziploc bag to avoid rain splatter, but *he* needed protection from the thunderstorm. He drips on the carpet like a wet dog, his white shirt glued to the ridges in his chest. His jeans stick to his thighs, and he runs a hand through his soaked hair, pushing back the brown strands.

"Can I use your dryer?" he asks, already pulling off his shirt.

Oh my God. I look away, and Lo closes the *Cosmo* magazine and tosses it at my face so I'll stop gawking. He stands. "I'll show you to the machine."

As Lo passes to the laundry room, Ryke lifts his eyebrows at me like *see, he was nice, making progress*. Yeah, I'm not so optimistic. Ryke nods to Connor. "How's it going?"

"It's going," he says.

At this, Ryke follows Lo out of view.

Connor scrolls on his iPhone, my mind drifting to what happened with my sister. "About Rose . . . "

"Yes?"

"I like you, Connor. I do, but I also know you're a social climber. I may look small and not put up much of a fight when it comes to words, but I'd find a way to hurt you if you hurt her. She should mean more to a guy than a paycheck and a last name."

Connor pockets his cell. "Lily," he says. "If I wanted to date for a last name, I'd have a girl on my arm every single day. I would never be single." He leans forward. "I promise you that my intentions are pure. And I think it's sweet you're looking out for Rose, but she's more than capable of taking care of herself, which is one of the many reasons why I want to pursue her."

"What's another reason?" I test him.

He smiles. "I won't have to taxingly explain to her menu items in a real French restaurant." He knows she's fluent? "I won't have to explain financial statements or dividends. I'll be able to discuss anything and everything in the world, and she'll have an answer."

"What about your philosophy on wealthy girls? Aren't we all the same? We want to find some Ivy League guy and do nothing with our lives?"

Connor's lip twitches, suppressing a smile. "I also said something about probably marrying that type."

I don't see where he's headed with this. "Rose is *not* that kind of girl. She's talented and driven and determined—"

"I said I would *probably* marry the type, not that I wanted to."

Oh. I realize that Connor Cobalt will ace any test I give him—the downside to quizzing an honor student.

Ryke and Lo return, and surprisingly, one of Lo's black T-shirts fits Ryke perfectly. And he wears a pair of Lo's jeans, the thighs a little tight, but other than that, they fit as well. Neither guy says a word, the tension eking from their stiff postures. Lo settles back beside me while Connor offers up his chair to Ryke.

Ryke nods in thanks and takes a seat. Connor drags the red recliner closer to our little group, and the rumble of the dryer fills the short-lived void.

Connor turns his attention on Ryke and says, "So you're writing an article about children of tycoons. I assume you forgot to ask me."

Ryke teeters back on two legs of his chair. "Must have slipped my mind." He flashes a dry smile, avoiding my gaze.

"Then I accept."

Ryke's eyebrows shoot up. "You accept?"

Lo interjects, "That sounds perfect. You should just write about Connor. He's a willing participant, and your story will have a happy ending. Everyone wins." He squeezes my shoulder, and I stiffen, not sure how Ryke's going to cover this one.

"No, I don't like it." *That's* his lie? I roll my eyes. I shouldn't have expected something better.

Lo rubs his lips. "Then you're not going to follow Connor too?"

Ryke briefly looks at Connor, who sits with his ankle on his knee, so preppy that you could snap a picture and put him in a

J.Crew catalogue. "No offense, Connor, but I'd rather not hang around ass-kissers all fucking day. If you're with Lo and Lily, I'll write about you. That's all I have."

"I already accepted," Connor tells him.

Lo hasn't. He laces his fingers in mine. "Are you going to ask me questions?"

"Do you have something against them?" Ryke wonders. "Question-phobic?"

Lo glares. "I just don't have a warm spot in my heart for people who pry."

"Yeah? Well that kind of goes against my profession." He points to his chest. "Journalism major. Asking uncomfortable questions is my forte." I can believe that.

Lo glowers at the ceiling. "Then I have full discretion to ask you anything personal. How's that for a stipulation?"

"Sounds fair."

Lo doesn't need to tell me that he hates the situation. His icy posture says it all. I understand his hesitation. There's an underlying judgment that comes with surrounding ourselves with other people. We've been cut off from snide glances and hateful words like *slut*, *drunkard*, *loser* for so long that he fears going back to that place. The one where his father smacks the back of his head, wondering why his kid just fucked up by staying out all night drinking. The one where a prep school girl slanders me as diseased, dumb and dimwitted.

I can't gauge my strength. I just hope I'm resilient enough to stand against ridicule in order to help Lo.

"It'll only be for a couple of months," I tell Lo. "The semester is almost over."

"It's fine." He finishes off his glass of whiskey and stands to go make another.

Ryke gives me a hard look that I can't respond to since Connor sits one chair over. At least Connor busily texts on his phone. Suddenly, he stands, slipping his cell in his coat pocket. "I'll see you guys later."

"Where are you going?" Lo asks from the kitchen.

"I have to figure out what I'm going to wear tonight."

"Are you serious?" Lo snaps. "You're going on a date with the devil. All you need is some pepper spray and a fire extinguisher."

Ryke nods to me. "Who's he talking about?"

"My sister Rose."

"Huh." He watches Connor go to the foyer.

"She's a fashion designer," Connor tells us. "She's going to judge me on what I wear." With this, he waves us goodbye and heads out the door.

I hear the clink of bottles, not sure the steps to take. Ryke whispers to me, "So you've been distracting him with sex?"

I blush. "Is that bad?"

"No," he admits, "but it's not entirely working, considering he's making"—he leans farther back on the chair legs to peek at the kitchen—"whiskey straight." I kind of hope Ryke falls.

And just like that, the wooden legs slip beneath Ryke and his back slams on the rug.

I laugh so hard my chest hurts.

"It's not fucking funny," he tells me, picking himself up and stretching out his arms.

"Yes it is."

Lo comes back with a full glass of whiskey. "What is?" He sits on the other side of the couch, an entire cushion separating us.

"He fell off the chair," I say.

Ryke switches to the recliner, a much safer choice. And then he nods to Lo. "What's with the whiskey?"

I can tell Lo wants to glare at *me* for putting him in this position, but he resists. "I don't see how that question relates to your article." He sips the dark amber liquid.

"Background," Ryke says evasively. "You didn't answer me."

"I wasn't planning on it." He takes another huge swig, not even grimacing as the sharp alcohol slides down his throat.

Ryke rubs his lips. "What's your father like?"

"Are we really starting this now?" Lo snaps.

"No time like the present."

He downs the rest of his drink way too quickly and stands. "Do you want a beer or something?"

"I'll take a beer," I say as Lo disappears into the kitchen.

Ryke shakes his head at me like that's a bad move.

"Cancel my order," I call to Lo.

"Ryke?" Lo asks. "Last chance."

"I'm fine."

I whisper very softly to Ryke, "You're annoying him so much that he's drinking *more*."

"I see that. Let me handle it."

I try to trust him, but he's doing a poor job at breaking through Lo's tough exterior. When Lo returns to the living room, we both glance at the newly filled glass in his hand, the liquid nearly black.

Lo takes his seat. Far away from me. I dislike it immensely.

He watches Ryke as he sips the liquor. He licks his lips and says, "You seem awfully interested in my whiskey. Are you sure you don't want a glass?"

"No, I don't drink."

The muscles in Lo's jaw twitch. "You don't drink? Not even beer?"

"No. I had a rough patch in high school. I drank and drove, which ended in a totaled car, a broken mailbox, and angry neighbors. I haven't tasted alcohol since."

"Driving was your first mistake," Lo tells him.

"I disagree." Ryke nods to the liquor in Lo's hand. "That was."

"Well I'm not you, am I?" Lo says with bite. "If you're expecting some sort of story where I turn into *you,* then you're going to be disappointed. What you believe about me is probably right. I'm a rich asshole who has *everything.* And I like it." I hear his father in his voice, and it scares me. Maybe this wasn't such a good idea.

Ryke's face hardens to stone. And his eyes narrow in empathy, which I'm sure Lo does not appreciate. "Let's start with an easier question then. How'd you two meet?"

"Childhood friends," Lo tells him. "You want to know if I took her virginity too? I didn't. Some prick beat me to it."

"Lo!" I grab a pillow, about to hide behind it.

Ryke keeps his challenging gaze on Lo. "That's interesting." He finds the loss of my virginity interesting—that's just great. "Did you lose your virginity to her?"

Lo drinks at this.

Ryke rolls his eyes. "I'll take that as a yes. Is she the only girl you've ever been with?"

I interject, "I don't see what this has to do with *anything.*"

"No," Lo says, ignoring me. "I've slept with other girls."

"I wasn't talking about sex."

Lo holds Ryke's stare. "Long term, yeah. Same for her."

I wonder if Ryke is adding up all the years that I've enabled Lo, helping facilitate his addiction. When his eyes flicker to me with a sliver of contempt, I know he probably is. I can change things now. It may hurt our relationship, but I've found a way.

I crawl over to Lo and press my shoulder against his. He finishes his drink, and before he stands, I wrap an arm around his waist, keeping him here.

His cold eyes cut me, and he whispers lowly, "I'm *not* in the mood." He disentangles my hands from him and steps over my feet to go to the kitchen. I sit back like he socked me in the gut.

"You okay?" Ryke whispers.

Tears build. "I don't know what to do," I mutter.

"If I come over there, will he strangle me?"

My eyes burn. "I'm not even sure anymore."

Ryke tests the waters and plants his butt on the cushion next to me. "You're doing a decent job, Lily. I just don't understand why you haven't tried sooner." *Because we have a system that cannot be disrupted.*

"He's not hurting anyone," I try to defend in a small whisper. "He's *never* hurt anyone, Ryke."

"Seems to me he's hurting you."

I shake my head. "*Me?* No, I'm fine."

"Then why are you crying, Lily?"

I wipe the traitorous tears, and Lo enters without a drink but carries Ryke's bundle of dry clothes. He throws them on his lap.

"It's time for you to leave." Lo won't even look at me.

Ryke stands tensely, holding the clothes. He edges towards Lo and whispers to him, "Your girlfriend is upset, Lo. Can't you see that?" He's trying to guilt him into sobriety. I doubt that'll work.

"Don't act like you know her."

"I know her enough."

"You don't know *shit*. You'd be fucking spinning if you did." He motions to the shirt that Ryke wears. "Keep my clothes. I don't need them."

"Fine. I'll see you soon." With this, he makes his exit, the door slamming shut.

Lo wipes his mouth and says, "I'll be in my room."

My chest caves. We should talk, but what do I say? *Lo, I wish you would stop drinking.* And he'd say, *Lily, I wish you'd stop having so much sex.* And then we'd look at each other and wait for the other to say *okay, I'll change for you*. But there'd be silence so deep and cutting that I'd feel ripped open and bare. There's no coming back from that.

I respond in the only way that makes sense to me. "I'm sorry for putting you in that situation. I'm really, really sorry, Lo."

His muscles tense and he runs a hand through his hair. "I want to be alone right now. We can have sex in the morning, okay?" He leaves me. And I sink into the couch and listen to the ticking of an old, expensive clock on the bookshelf.

I curl up in a blanket, so hollow inside.

Minutes pass before I actually start crying, the messy tears that scrunch up your face and cause snot to run.

At least no one can see me, but I know I'm not alone in my misery.

Morning sex is hard and rough and so emotional that my head starts whirling. I'm so dizzy by the end of it that I rush to the bathroom and vomit in the toilet.

"Lily," Lo calls, pulling up his boxer-briefs as he hurriedly enters the bathroom. He kneels behind me and rubs my back. "You're okay. You're okay." He says it like he's trying to convince himself.

I dry heave for a full minute before I calm down, my trembling hands gripping the toilet bowl.

"What happened?"

I keep my back to him. "I was dizzy."

"Why didn't you say something?"

"I don't know," I murmur, my voice raw and scratchy. I stand to brush my teeth. I shakily find my toothbrush and some paste.

"Lily, talk to me," he says from behind me. He sets a gentle hand on my hip while I spit into the sink.

When I finish, I turn around and lean my backside against the counter. "Do you want to break up?" I say bluntly.

His breathing shallows. "No. I love you, Lil." He holds my hand. "Look, I'll try harder. We both will." I'm not surprised by the sudden proclamation. We fight one minute and then try to make up the next. It's why we've lasted so long. And I suppose, the fear of losing each other is always stronger than the pain we cause.

"Try harder to do what?" I want clarification of where we stand.

"I'll drink more beer. Ryke was pissing me off yesterday, so I chose hard liquor." He pauses and eyes me hesitantly, about to turn the tables. "Lily . . . I love having sex with you, but the past two weeks, you've been crazy. I can barely even think."

"I know. I'm sorry." But I've been like that to stop him from drinking. I guess we need to work on fulfilling our compromises, which means I need to stop trying to force him to be sober by diverting his attention elsewhere.

Ryke will be disappointed, but this is the best I have without shoving Lo away. I need him more than he needs me. His vice is a bottle of whiskey. Mine is his body. So when we fight, I'm the one who loses out in the end.

"Do *you* want to break up?" he offers me the same out.

It'd be easier to let him go, to return to our regular rituals, but now that I've had him, I can't imagine not being swept in his arms and being fulfilled to the highest degree. He's my drug that I gladly consume, and I think that's what he fears most. He enables my addiction. Always has. And the longer we're together, he always will.

"No," I whisper. "No, I want to be with you."

He draws me close and kisses me on the forehead. "We'll do better." His lips brush my ear. "Next time you feel sick, please tell me."

"I will."

He tilts my chin up and kisses me on the lips, urging my mouth open. His tongue slips in for a second and then he breathes, "Let's do it right this time." He scoops me up in his arms, and I hold him around the neck, gladly about to erase all the bad moments and replace them with good.

Twenty-seven

"Can you zip me up?"

Lo fixes his tie and then rests a hand on my hip. I try not to focus on the way his fingers press into my side. We *just* had sex and took showers. I do not want to show up to Rose's fashion show with ratted hair and flushed cheeks.

He zips my dress to the collar, and the touch ripples my skin. "You okay?" he asks.

"Yeah." I smooth my hair, which reaches my shoulders, trying to satiate the nervous jitters in my stomach. I struggle to think of an instance before middle school where I willfully introduced any friends to my family. In part, it was probably because Lo has been my only companion for some time.

A buried, vile part of me almost wishes Rose and Connor never met. Or that I wasn't his friend first. Anything so that my two worlds don't have to collide—my family and my college life. Connor knows things. More than even Rose, and I fear we made a mistake in not scripting lies for our new friend. But how was I supposed to know that Rose of all people would find Connor Cobalt's personality attractive? My luck is like a perfect storm.

At least I wasn't selfish enough to destroy their relationship before it started. That would have been mean.

With Ryke following us to events, it doubles the stress. At any moment Connor or Ryke could let something slip to my family, and everything could be ruined. More than that, I feel overwhelmed by letting my family see another part of my life. I compartmentalize for a reason, and now everything seems utterly messy and complicated. If Lo feels the same, he doesn't let on. I watch him casually check the cards in his wallet before sliding it into his pocket.

Someone knocks on the door.

"Are you decent?" Connor's voice muffles from the other side.

Lo opens the door, and Connor stands there, wearing his own thousand-dollar suit and an equally expensive smile. "We need to leave. I don't want to be late."

"We'll be an hour early," Lo complains. "We can wait around a few minutes."

I follow them into the kitchen, where Ryke sits at the bar, typing on his cellphone.

"I want to see Rose before the show starts," Connor confesses. "She sounded nervous this morning."

"She is," I say. "She's mostly worried about no one showing up." I even called her. Mostly to talk about Connor, but she wouldn't really give me any details on their theatre date other than he'd acted exactly how she thought he would. Whatever that means. They're still going out, so I can only presume that it went well. Hopefully they didn't talk too much about Lo and me. I need to find time to tell Connor that Rose is unaware of certain aspects of our lives. Like Lo's constant drinking.

"I told her that I have it handled, but she chooses not to believe me," Connor says. Small wrinkles crease his eyes in discontent, an emotion I've yet to see from the unflappable Connor Cobalt.

"Who'd you call?" Lo wonders before eyeing Ryke at the bar. Even with days where Ryke asks Lo questions, he keeps him at a distance, answering back with sarcasm or disdain. And now that

I am no longer a driving force in actively diverting Lo's attention from alcohol, Ryke wastes no opportunity to glare at me. I can do nothing right.

"The owners of Macy's, Nordstrom, H&M and some lesser known department stores will be there. It'll be a full house." Connor glances at me. "Don't tell her about who's going to be at the show. There's no point in making her more anxious."

"I won't."

Ryke stands from the bar, slipping his phone into his suit pocket, his wardrobe just as expensive as Connor and Lo's. For some reason, his tailored suit catches me off guard. I expected him to be on an athletic scholarship, but by the fit and fine fabric, the suit clearly is name brand. Possibly Armani or Gucci. Which means he has money. Lots of it.

I realize I haven't asked Ryke much about his personal life. Lo meant to, but he gets so irritated that he usually walks off.

Before Ryke can shoot me a scathing look, I find a good question. "What do your parents do?"

Connor puts his hand on my shoulder. "Talk and walk. We're running late." We're really not, but Connor Cobalt's definition of *late* is much different than mine. We leave the apartment with Connor in the rear, practically pushing us out.

Ryke sidles next to me, but Lo remains closer on my other side. "My mom doesn't work. I come from some family money."

Connor neurotically checks his watch again, and I press the lobby button on the elevator. "From your dad?"

"Yep," Ryke says. "I don't live with him. It's always just been me and my mom."

My chest swells at the news, and I can't tell if it affects Lo or not. He looks utterly blank by the revelation.

"Divorce?" I wonder. Lo swoops his hands around my waist and I lean back against his chest. My eyes shut as I feel the pump of his heart and the warmness of his weight. I wish he'd lean me over and . . . *no, Lily.*

"Yeah," Ryke says. "It was pretty messy. They were supposed to have joint custody of me, but my mom won full in the settlement."

"Have you ever met him?"

"I have," Ryke admits, somewhat detached like he's dealt with all of this before and come to terms with it. "He'd send me gifts all the time, and my mom would throw them out. But she let me meet him every Monday since I can remember. He seemed like an okay guy, but I have years of my mom telling me some . . . pretty horrible things about him. Stuff that she shouldn't have been telling me so young. After a while I stopped seeing him, and I stopped loving him too." Ryke glances at Lo. "What about you?"

"What about me?"

"Aren't your parents divorced?"

"I live with my father," Lo says flatly. "He's the greatest dad in the fucking world. Sorry yours couldn't have been better."

Ryke's face hardens. "You have a good relationship with him?"

"The best."

I stare at the ground, my stomach rolling at his biting tone.

"Your girlfriend doesn't seem to agree."

"Stop psychoanalyzing her movements," he shoots back. *Yes, please stop.* Especially because I have to cross my ankles to focus on something other than sex at the present moment.

The elevator dings. As soon as my mind rights itself on a proper course, a sudden wave of anxiety crashes into me. Bringing Connor and Ryke to the fashion show feels like doom. I'll end up trading these overwhelming emotions for fantasies and carnal highs. That sounds better than this creeping anxiety.

We head to the limo, and by the time we reach the venue, I've concocted ten different scenarios with Lo in the backseat, and

I've spaced out approximately five times. Lo notices my fantastical departures, but I'm sure no one else does.

The spot between my leg pulses, eager to be relieved, but I avoid facing any unease so I torture myself with these images. Of Lo on me. Of Lo in me. Of him whispering to take me. It's so stupid.

I'm here for Rose.

And yet, I can't stop.

I ball my hands, forcing myself to concentrate on the present moment.

I'm here.

Nowhere else.

An elevated runway sits in the middle of the room and white plastic chairs line both sides, no one here except photographers, publicists, models and stylists. Most run off to the back room, where I'm sure Rose busily dresses the models. Daisy is probably being fitted right now in a silk day dress for the everyday kind of girl. I should go see them, but I want to do something else, something I know is wrong in this current time.

"Lo," I whisper, clutching his bicep. I look at him with shallow breath and bedroom eyes. *Please, come with me. Please . . .*

"Can you wait until we go home?"

Ryke catches those words just as Connor dials Rose's number and wanders off. "What's wrong?" he asks me.

"Nothing." I shoot Lo a warning look. "I'll be right back." I go to leave for the bathrooms, and Lo catches my wrist.

"You need to try," he tells me.

"Like you're trying?"

Lo puts his lips to my ear and whispers, "I *am* trying. I've only had beer today. You know this."

I can't imagine not fulfilling this need right now. It hurts too much. It's all I can think about. And if Lo won't help me, then I'll help myself. Without cheating. I disentangle from him. "I don't want to sit through the show like this. We have time."

"What is it that you need to do?" Ryke asks me. I hate the hard tone of his voice, as though I'm one step away from killing Lo by causing him stress, by handing him a glass of alcohol, by watching him drink without reproach.

I glare. "It's none of your business."

"Hey," Ryke says. "I was just going to ask if I could help."

My cheeks heat. "*You* can't."

"Jesus, someone woke up on the wrong side of the fucking bed."

"Don't *you* talk about me in a bed," I retort, being nonsensical and irrational.

Lo grabs my wrist. "Lily, stop."

"You're defending *him*?" I gape. "Really, Lo!"

Lo whispers heatedly in my ear. "Do you hear yourself right now? You're not thinking right."

I shove Lo off my chest. "You both are assholes," I say, looking between them as they stand side by side. Dapper, handsome, ice and stone. I hate them. I hate *me*. "I don't even know why I agreed to any of this." To being with Lo. To letting Ryke follow us around. If I stop and *think* for two seconds, maybe I'll understand that I'm projecting all of my anxiety from the fashion show onto them. And it's unfair, immature and cruel. But I don't want to think. I just want to *do*.

I inhale sharp, sporadic breaths. I need to go. Now. I race to the bathroom, a lot faster than Lo, and head into the men's room rather than the women's. A guy in his thirties sees me through the mirror as he relieves himself. He curses and zips up his fly. Confidence inflates my body—the need to do this surpassing everything else.

I pick a stall without saying a word to him.

Lo walks in, not even glancing at the guy. He sets his sights on me, only me, and looks as though he wants to devour me whole or maybe choke me. *Yes.*

He slams the stall shut behind us and roughly grabs my wrists. He spins my body so my backside rubs against his pelvis and places my palms on the tiled wall. My back curves in an angle, my feet just outside of the toilet.

"You want this?" Lo growls, his hand slipping underneath my dress, his fingers finding the wettest spot.

I gasp, my eyes rolling back. *Please.*

He wraps a hand over my mouth, muffling my moans as he pushes his fingers in and out. My palms slip on the tile, and I almost knock my head into the hard wall, but Lo has a tight hold on me, keeping me on two feet.

He thrusts inside, and I lose myself to the pleasure, to the bliss, to the hardness of him. My breathing sharpens in my throat, and he never slows. He slams against me, as though telling me I've been bad. And I take it with bated breath and headiness.

When we're done, he pulls his pants up to his waist and buttons them while I try to find my panties around my ankles.

"You okay?" Lo asks, brushing my sweaty hair off my face.

"I think so." Why did I have sex here? Everything I just did surges into my head and my heart, and I inhale weighted breaths. Why did I do this? What is wrong with me?!

When we exit, he washes his hands, and then leads me out. Luckily, the show hasn't started, but the room is filled to the brim.

I slip into a front row seat beside Connor, avoiding Ryke.

"I should go see Rose," I say.

"There's no time." Connor glances at his Rolex. "The show will start in fifteen minutes."

"Oh."

I try to blink away the guilt that knots my stomach. My hands shake, and Lo reaches over and clasps them. I spot the worry in his eyes, but I try not to hold on to it. I'm okay. Everything is going to be fine.

I look up and see Poppy walking down the aisle with a wide grin and Sam on her arm. My stomach does a full somersault. They scoot in and she comes over to greet me, kissing me on the cheek. "There are so many people here!" she exclaims. "Rose should be so proud."

"Where's Mom?" I ask, my heart pounding to the fast-paced rhythm of the music.

"She's coming. Dad was on the phone, so they stopped outside for a second." She glances at Connor and Ryke. "Who are your friends? Oh, is this Charlie?" She focuses on Ryke, who wears a confused expression.

"No, Charlie moved," I lie. "This is Ryke. He's a friend from Penn, and that's Connor Cobalt."

Poppy momentarily forgets Ryke as Connor rises to shake her hand and then Sam's. "It's nice to meet you both." His good looks and words have officially hypnotized Poppy. She nods while he talks about Fizzle to Sam, trying to bring up familiar conversation. I can't tell if this is Connor's normal bout of schmoozing or if he's adding on the extra charm to embed himself further in Rose's good graces.

When Poppy detaches herself from Connor Cobalt's magnetic hold, she whispers to me. "This is the boy Rose is seeing?"

"Yep."

Poppy smiles. "She did well."

"Yeah, but she probably thinks she can do better."

Poppy laughs and then touches my arm. "We're sitting a few seats from yours. I'll see you after the show." She hesitates. "And Lily, I'm glad to finally meet your friends."

I smile, but it hurts. Because deep down, these friends may as well be bought and paid for.

Poppy and Sam go find their seats, and I settle in mine with a weight heavy on my chest. The only thing that takes my mind off of it is sex. And once I start focusing on photographers, especially the scruffy one in the corner, my body starts to switch again.

I've trained myself to self-medicate with sex for so long that stopping seems so unfeasible, like trying to break a high-speed train before it crashes into a cement wall. So I'll crash. I'll splinter and break. But it'll feel damn good going two hundred miles an hour beforehand.

That's all I concentrate on. The thrill, the high and endorphins from rocking against another body. Any body. Hopefully Lo. No other thoughts enter my mind and my knees practically bounce in earnest hunger.

People dip into their chairs as the time ticks by, and I can faintly hear Ryke asking Lo about Daisy's modeling career. I don't hear the answer, too fixated on the way the photographer holds his camera. His muscles flex and I imagine him holding me instead. *Stop.*

I inwardly groan and rub my sweaty palms on my dress. I'm a junkie who needs another hit, and I hate that the quickie in the bathroom didn't satiate me. I've already fucked up. How angry will Rose be at me for not going backstage? *Stop.*

I don't want to think about that.

The lights dim. "Lo," I breathe. "Lo, I need to . . . " I can't say it, but the tone of my voice speaks for me.

"The show is about to start, Lil," he whispers. "You have to hold out."

I don't know if I can. I squirm in my seat, battling the cravings for my favorite natural high.

And then my parents start to enter. Ryke rises and stretches his arms. "Hey, I'm going to go to the bathroom before the show starts." He's going to the bathrooms, where *I* want to go. Lo's brows bunch, staring at him until he disappears.

I cross my legs, sweat gathering on my skin. I can't do this. I need someone . . . I need to relieve this . . . I stand.

"Lily," Lo protests, jumping up with me. "Lily, *your sister.* Think about Rose."

"I can't," I whisper, bolting towards the exit, leaving Connor between three empty seats. His usual content expression has fractured. He looks pissed.

Lo says, "Think about afterwards, Lily. *Please.*" I'll feel horrible. Yes. But I can't stop my feet from moving, or my breath from hitching. There's a place so deep down, a compulsion that must be sustained. I need this. I need it more than breath, more than air, more than life itself.

It's a stupid thought. One that makes no right-around sense. But it's what drives me.

I pass my parents as they look on with confusion. Lo stays back to spout off some excuse, and I head outside. In the freedom of the city. In the parking lot where the cars line up like black dots.

I unlock Nola's Escalade that my parents I'm sure used to get here. Thankfully she's not inside. I slide in the backseat and hike up my dress. Before I do anything, the door opens, and Lo crawls in. He coarsely grabs my ankle and yanks me towards him. I'm lost to these feelings.

I'm lost to him.

When I come down from the high and after the stimulating hormones leave, everything rushes back and tears begin to burn. "What's wrong with me?" I choke. I start to dress quickly, finding my bra littered on the Escalade floor. Lo moves at a much more sluggish pace, and he looks sick to his stomach.

"Lil," he says softly and reaches out to touch my hand. I pull back instantly, too frantic and shamed for such comfort.

"No, we have to go before it ends. Maybe she won't notice . . . " As I open the car door, people already begin to pool out into the darkened parking lot, swinging gift bags in their hands. What? It's over? I missed the entire thing?!

"Lily . . . " His suit jacket is draped on his arm, and he hesitates a moment before placing a hand on my shoulder.

"Did you know the time?" I question. "Why didn't you stop me?"

"I tried," Lo breathes. He swallows hard, pained. "Lil, I tried about five times."

"What?" I shake my head. "I don't remember that. I don't . . . "

"Hey, hey, it's okay . . . " He brings me to his chest, wrapping his arms around me in a cocoon. "Shhh, Lil, it's okay."

No it's not.

I should have stopped the first time. Why did I convince myself that this would be worth a high? I push him off, the guilt almost suffocating me. "No, no, I've got to apologize." I slide my feet into my heels, trying to focus. It'll be okay. I'll make up some lie about food poisoning and then say a few *sorrys* and smooth everything over.

It'll be fine.

My heart beats as loud as the crowd pouring through the glass double doors. I don't have to walk far to find my parents. They're already heading to the car with Poppy and Sam in tow.

They laugh and Poppy shows a picture to my mother on her Blackberry. When Poppy notices me approaching, her face falters and the expression passes between the four of them. My presence has sucked all joy from their features.

"I-I," I stammer. "I didn't feel well. I had stomach cramps and was really dizzy. I don't think I ate enough. We thought there might be food in the car."

284 · KRISTA RITCHIE and BECCA RITCHIE

My father turns to Sam, completely ignoring me. "I have a Fizzle report you should see." He ushers Poppy's husband away and gives Lo a long glare as he passes by.

I evade my mother, who is probably searing me with a look that could freeze over Florida. That leaves Poppy.

"Honestly, I didn't feel well. I would never miss Rose's fashion show." The lie burns my throat.

Poppy's eyes rise to my hair and I subconsciously flatten the wild strands. Lo touches the small of my back and I jerk away again.

"Your dress is wrinkled," my mother tells me coldly before setting her eyes on Lo. "Maybe try to control your hormones during family events." *What? No.*

"Lo didn't—"

"No, you're right," Lo interjects and I stare at him dumbly. "I'm sorry. It was the wrong time. It won't happen again, Samantha."

My mother processes his words for a small moment before she nods slightly. With pursed lips she passes us for the car. Poppy remains, disappointment coating her eyes. "Rose is inside, but I don't think she wants to talk to you right now. Give her some time to cool down."

Poppy leaves before I can say anything else. Not that I have anything other than another pathetic apology.

I can't wait until tomorrow. It hurts too much to not at least confront her. I start towards the building but Lo grabs my wrist.

"What are you doing?"

"I have to talk to her."

"Did you not just hear Poppy?" Lo says with wide eyes. "Let Rose calm the fuck down. Unless you want your heart ripped out." Maybe I do. Maybe I deserve it.

Connor pushes open the glass doors with his shoulder, his

hands preoccupied with texting. I bolt for him, and when he looks up, his face darkens.

"How is she?" I ask, glancing past him for a peek.

He steps in front of me, blocking me from any visual or entrance. "Not happy," he says, his voice tight.

"Where's Ryke?" Lo wonders with a frown.

"He left. He was sick."

"I think it was something we ate," I say.

Connor's eyebrows furrow in disbelief. "Was that before or after you left to screw in the car?"

I stumble back from the blow to the gut. My shoulders hit Lo's chest and this time I let him wrap an arm around my waist.

"Hey, back off, Connor," Lo warns.

Connor barely blinks. "I've been around you both long enough to know that the bathroom breaks aren't for synchronized bladder attacks. Which is fine. Your sex life is frankly none of my business." He glances back at the building and then looks to me. "You should go," he suggests.

"I want to apologize first."

"Why?" Connor's tone stays flat and edged. I've insulted him or disgusted him in some way. The one person I thought was unable to be repulsed by me.

"She needs to know I'm sorry."

"She sold her line to Macy's and has an offer from H&M," Connor tells me. "Don't ruin that by trying to make yourself feel better. Just leave, Lily."

I don't know what else to do. So I take the advice and disappear.

The next day I try calling Rose's cell almost every hour with no luck. After my tenth attempt at reconciliation, I toss the phone onto the floor and scream into my pillow. This is why I don't do family functions. This is why I don't have friends. I disappoint *everyone*.

My door opens and I turn my back on Lo, who shuffles inside. "She'll forgive you, Lil. Maybe not me . . . but definitely you."

I cringe. My mother thought his spiked hormones ruined the night, but it was all me. I hate that he's taking the blame this time.

Lo sits on the foot of the bed and tentatively places a hand on my ankle. Instantly, I pull away and rise to the headboard. "I don't . . . " I mutter.

His eyebrows bunch together in concern. "Do you want to quit?" And what? Be celibate? I don't even know what quitting sex means. How do you quit something that's engrained in human nature?

"Maybe. No. I don't know." Should I get rid of my porn? But what will happen a week from now when I realize this won't work? I'll just have to rebuy my entire stash. Not worth it.

"I'll support you in whatever you decide," Lo tells me.

Guilt stops me from having sex. Literally driving all of my hormones into a state of perpetual chastity. I bury my head into my knees. I need to make a decision, but I've been ping-ponging between choices. It was one mistake, spurned from being around my family. I just have to separate myself again. Distance. Once I apologize to Rose, I'll back off and everything will return to normal. Clean and compartmentalized.

"I'm going to talk to Rose," I decide. "Then we'll have sex."

He kisses my temple. "I'll be here, love." He nibbles my ear.

I grab a pillow and playfully whack him in the chest. He smiles but respects my wishes and stops from sexily wrestling it from me. In part he looks a bit relieved. I know I haven't been the best company, all mopey and self-involved.

I slide from the bed. I'm going to confront her now when I have the chance. Tomorrow she'll be back at Princeton and I'll be too busy trying not to fail my classes to drive and see her. "Do you think she'll let me in?"

"Tough call. Depends if she finally got laid," Lo says.

I give him a hard glare and he holds up his hands in peace. I'm proud that my sister hasn't given up her V-card to just anyone.

Quickly, I brush my hair, grab my coat and leave Lo in the kitchen, where he starts fixing himself a mild afternoon drink. On the way to Villanova I try to formulate a speech, but by the time I get to the house, everything flutters away.

I dodge the staff that mills around the mansion and climb the grand staircase towards Rose's old room, where she stays when she visits. I knock a couple of times before the door swings open. As soon as her yellow-green eyes hit me, her lips purse and her entire body goes rigid like she's practicing to be a guard for the Queen of England.

"We need to talk," I say, glad that the door hasn't hit me in the face yet. That's something.

She continues to block the entrance into her room. I'm obviously unwelcome in her sanctuary. I've really screwed up this time. "What is there to talk about? You had sex with Loren during my fashion show. I'm done being surprised or hurt or shocked, Lily," she says, removed from the drama.

"I'm *sorry*." I touch my chest. "You don't know how sorry I am. I promise I'll be a better sister."

Rose shakes her head, brows furrowing. "Stop, Lily. I'm tired of your promises. You'll always choose Lo. And the two of you will never give a shit about anyone else. You're selfish, and unless I want to go through life constantly disappointed, I've learned to accept that character flaw. You should do the same."

Her cellphone rings in the background and she glances back,

still not offering to let me inside. "I have to go. It's Macy's." She shuts the door before I can even utter the word *congratulations*. Maybe I should have started with that.

I contemplate her words on the ride home, and wonder if she's right. If accepting the fact that I'm selfish and unable to change will help heal the guilt.

If not—maybe sex will.

Twenty-eight

make an effort to call Rose more often. For the most part she
answers and gives me updates on Calloway Couture. Sometimes she's short with me, but it's better than slammed doors.
While I try to heal my relationship with Rose and ignore the rest
of my family, Lo spends time with Connor at the gym.

Ryke continues to follow us around, and since the fashion
show where—for one strange moment—Lo and Ryke seemed to
band together, they've been much more cordial. Ryke has pretended to scribble notes for his fake article, but he usually tries to
understand Lo. Last night, they started talking about their experience with nannies. One of Lo's used to drink strawberry mar-
garitas and was sloshed by noon. Apparently Ryke had a similar
situation, only his nanny let him sip her mimosas and bloody
marys. He was only nine.

I pull a brush through my wet hair while Lo rubs a towel
through his. Shower sex. Classy.

I almost can't remember why I was so worried about my lifestyle. I'm more than capable of making everything work.

Today the professor posted the econ grades online. As usual,
Lo refuses to divulge his grade, but I earned a C+, which is practically an A+ in Connor's mind. He insisted on celebrating. Only

for Connor Cobalt can achievements wipe slates clean. Lo some-how squirmed back into his good graces too. After the fashion show stunt, I thought we'd be *blacklisted* from any events with Connor. But I think it all comes down to Rose. His one human weakness happens to be my sister. And if she's forgiven me, then she's probably ordered him to do the same.

I'm still trying to untangle my hair when Connor arrives with Ryke. Lo leaves to answer the door and I snap one of the comb's teeth. *Really?* How is that even possible? I've finally acquired a superpower—indestructible hair. Super lame.

My door stands open as I search for another comb. Or better yet, an actual brush to tackle these knots. I hear the guys in the living room, but they must not realize it because their conversa-tion turns from the best pizza joints in Philly to *me*.

"Whose idea was it to ditch the fashion show?" Ryke asks.

"Is this for your article?" Lo wonders.

"No, just curious."

"I wanted to fuck her. So I did. And didn't you ditch the show too? What's your excuse?"

"I have a hot girlfriend that I wanted to fuck," he banters. "No, really, I had food poisoning from that taco stand around the corner."

"We eat there all the time," Lo says. "I've never been sick." Does he think Ryke's lying? He has no reason to. Actually, he probably *wishes* he could have stayed to witness my demise.

"Then maybe it was bad milk in my cereal. I don't fucking know," he says exasperatedly.

Connor cuts in. "It was really your idea, Lo?"

I close my eyes, hoping Lo rejects some of the blame.

"She wasn't exactly saying no." *Okay, I thought that would feel better.*

"It takes two to make love and only one person to make a mistake." Connor must turn to Ryke as he says, "Write that down."

"It's all up here." I imagine him pointing to his head.

"Do you have any friends?" Lo wonders in an easy tone. "We have to be seriously grating on you by now."

"Lily, definitely. Connor, maybe. You're okay."

"Well you're not my type of company either, Meadows," Connor says casually, not offended.

"I'm definitely writing that one down for the article."

"You should just quote everything I say, and I expect my name in the headline. Like 'Children of Tycoons, featuring Connor Cobalt, an upcoming entrepreneur to look out for.'"

"I'll consider it, but my professor doesn't like ending things with prepositions. So I think I'll end it with, 'featuring Connor Cobalt: You'll want to kiss his ass.'"

"Perfect," Connor exclaims.

I finally find a brush stuffed in my sock drawer and finish battling the knots. When I brace the kitchen, I see Lo pouring a glass of scotch. I sidle up next to him and he wraps an arm around my waist.

Ryke mouths, *Distract him.*

I shake my head. I am done trying to force Lo to do anything, not at the expense of our relationship.

Ryke flips me off, and Connor's too stuck in his cellphone to notice. I stick out my tongue at him—really mature, I know.

Lo grabs my chin and turns my head towards him. "Did you just stick out your tongue at him?" He wears an amused grin.

I shake my head. "Nope."

"She did," Ryke rats me out.

"He flipped me off!" I refute.

Lo kisses me on the lips, shutting me up. Oh . . . When he

breaks, his warm breath hits my ear. "I love you." My heart flutters at the words. Before I can reciprocate, his phone vibrates on the counter.

I catch a glimpse of the screen, my stomach dropping. "Maybe you shouldn't answer it."

Lo takes the phone and presses the receiver to his ear. "Hey, Dad." He walks towards the bedroom for privacy.

To preoccupy my mind, I go to the fridge and find a Cherry Fizz, popping the can. I remember I owe Connor a thousand bucks for passing my econ exam. I'm not in the mood to fish out my checkbook right now, but I'll plan a search for it later. It may very well be hiding underneath my bed. Or in a random purse.

"Connor," I say, "can I pay you later for our bet?"

One of Ryke's eyebrows arches. "What bet?"

Connor distractedly answers and texts at the same time. "A thousand dollars on whether or not she would pass her econ exam. And Lily, I don't want your money."

"Oh . . . "

"However, I'd love a favor." He has yet to look up at me.

Ryke lets out a short laugh. "You *would* choose favors over cash."

Connor doesn't argue.

"What kind of favor?" I ask.

"When you feel up to it, I think you should work for your sister. It doesn't have to be now. Maybe sometime in the spring. She's looking to hire an assistant at Calloway Couture, and I know she'd love for you to be involved."

My stomach sinks. "As much as I'd like to be working with my sister, I know nothing about fashion."

"That's why you're an *assistant* and not running the company."

"That doesn't sound fun." *And how will I be able to take sex breaks?* I can't believe that's all I can think about: how to schedule in porn, how to sneak Lo through her offices, how to find time to feed my desires.

"Well, you lost the bet, so you owe me."

"Can't I just pay you?"

"No, that's too easy."

I sigh, wondering if I'll be able to squirm out of the deal as it approaches later in my life. Probably not, but by the time it happens, maybe I'll be okay with my decision. So I nod. "Okay. I'll be her assistant sometime in the future."

"Near future." He types something in his phone and then stands. "I have to take this." He presses the cell to his ear and heads into the living room. Leaving me alone with Ryke.

I hop on the counter by the cabinets and face him.

Ryke glances over his shoulder at the hallway where Lo disappeared. "Does he like his father? I can't tell."

I shrug. "It depends on the day."

He turns back to me. "What's he like?"

"Jonathan Hale?"

Ryke nods.

"Lo doesn't talk about him with you?" I've managed to dodge their boy outings by having breakfast with Rose the past week. I enjoy it more than I'll let on.

"Not much," Ryke says. "Sometimes, he curses his father out, and then other times, he talks about the guy like he's a god."

Sounds about right. "It's complicated."

"How so?"

"Look." I lower my voice. "I know you're not really writing an article, so you don't need to ask these things."

Ryke rolls his eyes. "I fucking know that, Lily. I'm asking because I'm genuinely curious. No offense, but I care about your boyfriend more than I care about you."

I squint. "Are you sure you don't have a crush on him?"

He groans. "Seriously, Lily?"

"What? It's an honest question. You're obsessed with Lo."

"I'm not *obsessed*. Don't use that word. I'm just curious. I want to know him. Why do I have to be *in love* with him to want such a thing?"

I shrug. "I don't know. It's weird." I can't make sense of the strangeness. I feel like it's there, but it's not connecting. "Are you sure there isn't something more?"

"No. There's not. Just go back to my first question. How's Jonathan Hale complicated?"

I focus on that and open my mouth, trying to form words to describe an enigmatic man. He doesn't physically hit Lo, but he's not earning any Father of the Year awards either. In one minute, Jonathan can wrap an arm around him and call him a great son. And then next, he can spit out hateful words. Lo's mood fluctuates with his father's temper, and whenever he interacts with him, you can see a switch. I assume that's where Ryke's concern originates.

After I fail at describing Jonathan aloud, Ryke changes questions. "Do you talk to him a lot?"

I shake my head. "He makes an effort to ignore me unless he wants to blame someone for Lo's poor grades. Otherwise, I steer clear of the Hale household."

"Has he remarried?"

"No. He brings a lot of girls over at night." After Lo's mom left when he was a baby, Jonathan hired a nanny and started dating again. The number of women stumbling out of the house in the morning, wearing the same dress as the night before, grew exponentially as the years ticked by.

When I was sixteen, I remember shoveling scrambled eggs into my mouth while Lo tried to unlock his father's liquor cabinet. Jonathan overslept after a night of his own debauchery. A woman in a slim black dress carried her red pumps and shuffled through the kitchen. She refused to look at us, instead keeping her sight on the door like it was a finish line in a 5K race. And I had a sudden urge to bolt up from my chair and pull her aside. To ask her if she liked the thrill of one-night stands as much as me. To talk and gossip about being two girls completely in control of their bodies. At the time, I felt closeted, like a slut with a secret. But I stayed in my seat, letting her leave and fantasizing about what she might have told me.

I don't know if Lo realizes that I learned about one-night stands from his father's numerous flings. I hope not. And I'd never tell him.

I return my focus back on Ryke, who watches me too closely, as though reading my expression for his answers.

Lo enters the kitchen with a clenched jaw and a pocketed phone. Oh no.

"Everything okay?" Ryke asks.

"Fine," Lo says unconvincingly. He grabs his jacket off the chair and a bottle of bourbon from the counter. "Let's go."

Ryke and I exchange looks of worry, and we both follow Lo in close pursuit.

The necklace I gave Lo thumps against his chest as he dances with me. I touch the arrowhead and he clasps my hands in his. He plants a light kiss on my cheek before distancing himself. I reach out, but he's already gone, delegating himself king of the bar stool.

He orders a slew of drinks while sweat gathers at the base of my neck, and I solo-dance on the floor, shedding off insecurities with the hypnotic music. I keep glancing back at the bar.

Each time, Lo holds a new drink. I've evaded the phone call topic because Connor and Ryke always hang around him, and I'd rather not broach the subject in front of them.

After three shots of tequila for Connor and Ryke, they head to the bathroom, and I grab my chance to speak to Lo alone.

"Hey." I nudge his shoulder and slide onto the nearby stool. Distracted, he stares at his glass of amber liquid—his mind far away from here. "What did your father want?"

Lo shakes his head and cups the glass tighter. "Nothing."

I frown and try to push away the hurt from his unwillingness to share. The rejection stings, but it may just be the wrong time. He catches my despondence and looks back towards the bathrooms to make sure Ryke and Connor aren't returning soon. Then he twists his body towards me. Our knees knock together, and I have a sudden urge to lean in closer, to intertwine our legs and feel his lean muscles against my body. *This is serious*, I remind myself, pushing away those selfish thoughts.

"It was about my mom," Lo confesses. All dirty images evaporate, being replaced by sheer concern. "Somehow, he found out I contacted her." Lo pauses and rubs his lips in deep thought. "He told me that she wanted nothing to do with me." My chest constricts. "He told me that she doesn't deserve to think about me or to even hear my voice." He lets out a short, bitter laugh. "He said she was a fucking cunt."

I cringe.

He runs a hand through his hair. "Lil, I think . . . I think I agree with him." Wrinkles crease his forehead in utter confusion as he struggles to make sense of his warring emotions.

"Your mother left you," I say. "It's okay to be angry at her. It doesn't make you him."

His lips press together as he processes my words, and I wish I had more to offer. He leans forward and kisses me lightly on the temple, a small *thank you*, before he turns around on his stool and flags down the bartender for another drink.

She pours bourbon in a Riedel glass and slides it into his hand.

"How long before you want to go to the bathroom?" I ask.

"I don't know. My bladder is pretty big. I could wait at least another couple hours," Lo says. He smiles into his glass, and I give him a sharp look.

He hooks his foot under the rung of my stool and slides it forward. Oh wow. My hip knocks into his, and he snakes an arm around my waist, melding me to his side. This is kind of nice. I feel his hand run up underneath my shirt and rub the soft skin on my back.

I start dreaming about having sex right *here*. Lo taking me across the bar in a sultry heat. Fucking on a bar.

It'd be like our addictions making love.

His lips tickle my ear. Back to reality. "What are you thinking?"

I think he knows because he smiles and nibbles my ear.

"Get a room," Connor exclaims, sidling up beside me while Ryke sits down beside Lo.

"Or better yet," Ryke says, "a car."

"How about Connor's limo?" Lo asks with a smile. "Do you think your driver would mind?"

"I would mind," Connor tells him. "You're charming, Lo, but not enough to make me want to sit in your—"

"Stop." I cringe and cover my ears. Gross. Guy-talk. No.

All three of them laugh, and I wave down the bartender. "What do you want?" Lo asks me.

"Just a beer."

He nods and lets me order for myself. I slide my fake ID to the bartender, and she hands me a Blue Moon.

"You don't want to go in those bathrooms," Connor tells Lo. "They're disgusting. I think I might call the CDC when we leave. You need a hazmat suit just to walk in there."

Lo grins at me and raises an eyebrow. No! Connor is just being over dramatic.

"You rarely venture into smoky clubs," I tell Connor. "I'm sure you're just not used to a place that doesn't have a bathroom attendant and complimentary mints after you pee."

"I've lowered myself to these standards before, but there are some places no human being should go."

Lo smiles into another big gulp from his drink. I let the issue drop but plan to sneak into the restrooms later to make my own conclusions.

After a couple more drinks, Lo starts asking Ryke questions and I struggle to hear over the cacophony of sounds: drunken college students, newly blasting music, and Connor practically yelling into his phone as he talks to my sister.

"Yeah! I'd wear a peacoat!"

What? Is Rose asking him for fashion advice? The world really has gone mad.

He grimaces. "I can't hear you! Hold on!" He presses his palm to the speaker. "Lily, can you save my seat?" Before I can agree he's hopping off the stool and charging towards the door. Connor Cobalt doesn't push his way through bodies; he saunters into the masses and waits with an impatient scowl before people part and make man-made paths for him. I smile in amusement and turn back to place my coat on the stool.

But a blonde rushes to take it before I can claim the spot. Oops.

"I don't have any siblings," I overhear Ryke say. "It's been pretty much my mom and me since I was a kid."

Lo shifts, uncomfortable by the topic of *mothers*, especially after his phone call with his father. So he redirects the conversation. "How did you get into running?"

I'm surprised Lo chooses to ask questions and not be evasive like usual.

"When I was little, my mom put me in a lot of races. She told me it was either tennis or track, and I picked track." He laughs to himself. "I have a thing for running towards finish lines." I can believe that.

"That's funny," Lo says bitterly, "my father always tells me that I run away from everything."

"Do you?"

Lo's cheeks sharpen, his lips forming a pout.

"Forget it," Ryke says quickly. "You don't have to answer that."

"How much of what I'm telling you are you going to exploit?" Lo asks.

Ryke frowns. "What are you talking about?"

"The article," Lo reminds him. "I'm expecting to be in the tabloids by the end of the semester."

"I wouldn't sell you out."

"Isn't that what they all say?" Lo turns back to the bar and orders another drink. To me, he asks, "Want another beer?"

I shake my head. What I really want doesn't reside at a bar, but Lo has jumped into the rabbit hole of self-involved drinking. I can't pry the shot of whiskey from his fingers, and he's had enough liquor to forget about my problems.

"We need to toast," he tells us and holds up his drink in salute. "To Sara Hale. For being a fucking bitch." He throws back his shot and I steal a glance at Ryke.

His eyes narrow to hard stone. "Maybe you should switch to water."

"If I'm bothering you, you can always run *towards* the door."
He takes his next shot in hand.

Ryke tensely leans back and shoots me a wide-eyed look like
do something.

No, I mouth. There's nothing I can do. I see the end of the
night. Lo wants to pass out. He wants to reach that point so he
can drown his feelings. No matter what I say, he'll continue to do
it. Even if I plead and scream and beg Lo to stop, he won't.

I wouldn't.

He needs to wake up by himself, and nagging Lo will only
push him from me. That's not what I want. Or what I need.

Ryke shakes his head at me in disapproval and watches as Lo
curses his mom again in a more callous toast.

"Can you not?" Ryke spits.

"What's it to you?" Lo watches the bartender help someone
at the other end, waiting for her to return to this side.

"I generally don't like toasting to *bitches* and *whores.*"

"No one's making you," Lo retorts.

Ryke looks distressed as he runs a hand through his brown
hair. "I know you hate your mom—"

"Do you?" Lo spins towards him.

"Let's go dance," I tell Lo, tugging on his arm. He jerks away
from me and glares at Ryke on the other side.

"You don't know me," Lo sneers. "I'm sick of you acting like
you understand what I'm going through. Did you live in my
house?"

"No."

"Did you watch the cops take away my bed because my mom
claimed it belonged to her?"

Ryke rubs his jaw. "Lo—"

"Did my father grab your neck"—Lo places a hand on the
back of Ryke's, bringing him close—"and tell you, 'son . . .'" He

pauses, only inches separate their faces, and something intangible circulates in the air, a tension so thick I can hardly breathe. ". . . 'Son, grow the fuck up.'"

Ryke refuses to back down. He meets Lo's challenge, not deterring from his sharp gaze. He even goes one step further and sets a gentle hand on the back of Lo's neck. "I'm sorry," Ryke breathes with so much hurt that it takes me by surprise. "I'm so fucking sorry, Lo. I'm here for you now. Whatever you're going through, I may not have experienced it, but I'm right here."

And just like that, Lo takes his hand off Ryke, the strangled moment passing. What kind of response did Lo expect? A fight? Another verbal showdown? Something other than compassion—that's for sure.

Lo flags down the bartender and acts like nothing happened. Like Ryke never offered to help in some giant immeasurable way.

"Let's go dance," I try again.

He avoids my gaze. "I'm busy. Dance with Connor."

The bartender slides over another small glass. Should I leave him alone? Ryke drinks from a water bottle and watches him carefully. He'll stay here with Lo. I'll just . . . go. Maybe he'll remember me and follow after a while.

When Connor returns, I convince him to dance with me—the chaste, friendly kind with more than twenty inches between our bodies. Occasionally I glance back at Lo, but he drinks silently, staring off at the towering racks of bottles behind the bar. The only difference is the burger in his hand, which gives me some relief. At least the food will soak up some of that liquor.

I try to relax and concentrate on the pumping music, drifting away from Lo and his worries. The *bump bump bump* of the bass carries me.

In the pit with other bodies bouncing up and down, I lock onto wandering eyes, and for a brief moment I connect with another guy. The clandestine looks set my blood ablaze and it takes all of my energy not to follow them subconsciously.

After our sixth song, Connor looks back to the bar and someone takes an invitation to dance against my backside. His hands linger on my hips. I don't see his face, and in my head I imagine it being Lo or maybe Prince Charming. Someone other than Mr. Reality.

I close my eyes and float on the idea. The hand moves across my belly and then up underneath my shirt. Past the soft flesh of my abs and onto my padded bra. My breathing shallows and I sink back into the body.

I feel a hand tightly grip my wrist and yank me forward. I stumble into a chest as he wraps an arm around my shoulders in a brotherly way. "Go grope someone else," Connor tells the guy calmly, but his hand tightens on my elbow. It was real? Not a fantasy?

My body heats and I refuse to look at my handsy dance partner. He mutters something under his breath and walks off. I steal a glance at the bar, but Lo is now in a heated conversation with Ryke, waving his burger around so wildly that lettuce falls out of the bun.

Connor puts his hands on my shoulders and makes me face him fully. "Lily," he says, a rare drop of concern on the edge of his tongue, "what the hell is going on?"

I want to shrink in place. This wasn't supposed to happen. Not when Lo is already spiraling. My throat becomes swollen and just as I'm about to mutter the stupidest lie in the world, Ryke saves me.

He bounds over with a water bottle in hand and a scowl creasing his eyes. "Lily," he snaps. "I need your help." He points to the bar. "Lo is going to be piss drunk in five minutes. You need to tell him to switch to water. Every time I say a word about it he throws back a shot of whiskey just to spite me."

"He's eating a burger." Is defending Lo engrained in my DNA?

Ryke stares at me, dumbfounded. "Don't do this right now. *He* needs his fucking girlfriend. This is not going to be like Halloween, okay? I'm not carrying him up to your apartment unconscious." He rubs the back of his neck with a shaking hand.

I take a shallow breath. "I'll go try." I push past people and slide into the empty bar stool beside Lo.

He barely acknowledges me, but he says, "Just when I was starting to like that fucking prick."

"What did he do?"

"He doesn't take a hint. I don't want to talk about my parents. I don't want to talk about his mother when I don't have one. I don't want him to badger me about drinking." He takes another shot. "What the hell is this article on anyway? Two rich kids with silver spoons in their mouths? Or two spoiled brats who became destructive fuckups?" Lo's words spill out clear and coherent. He rarely slurs, but there's an edge to his voice that comes with drinking a lot, and I hear it tenfold.

"I don't think he's asking about that stuff for the article," I say softly, "maybe he just wants to get to know you."

"Why?" Lo asks with furrowed brows as if it's completely foreign for someone to befriend him.

"He cares about you."

"Well he shouldn't." Lo orders another drink as he pops a French fry in his mouth.

"Maybe we should leave."

"No. This place has good liquor and food."

I wait for the sexy smile or maybe a flirtatious joke but he's consumed with what's in front of him. And I just sit off to the side. Even if I take off my shirt and fling off my bra, he'll keep that glass in his hand. He'll drink until everything melts away. So I keep my clothes on. The only tactic I have in my arsenal is completely worthless.

"Ryke carried you home," I let out the truth. "At the Halloween party, you passed out and he had to carry you up to our apartment."

His face twists in hundreds of emotions, and he settles on something blank and foreign.

"Do you really want him to carry you home again?"

"I'm not drunk," Lo refutes, finally looking at me. His eyes ice over. "Not by a long shot. I'm even too sober for this conversation."

I feel rooted to this bar stool. Like if I slink away it will implode. "You're scaring me," I murmur.

His gaze softens a fraction. "I'm fine, Lily. Honestly." He keeps his hands to his liquor and fries, not touching me in comfort. "I'll let you know when I'm ready to leave, and it'll be before I pass out."

My chest clenches. "I'm going to go dance with Connor."

Lo nods and doesn't try to stop me as I leave the stool.

I find Connor and Ryke lingering by a high table near the dance floor. "And?" Ryke asks instantly.

"He says he's not drunk."

Ryke gives me a disgusted look. "Yeah? No shit, Lily. He's got a problem! He's going to fucking tell you he's sober."

"What makes you an expert?" I shout back. "So you quit drinking, that doesn't mean you know how to fix Lo!"

"You're right," Ryke says. "This is beyond me. He needs professional help."

Tears gather. "Stop." I want Lo to be helped. I do, but I can't imagine a world where he's torn from my life. What will become of me?

"Anyone with a heart would care, Lily," Ryke says. "So the better question is why don't you?"

The punch to my stomach knocks me back. It hurts too much to breathe, and the hardest part is trying to defend myself to *me*. I do care. I've kept Lo from sitting behind a wheel. I've made sure he returns home in one piece. I've protected him. From everyone but himself.

I glance at Connor as I try to wrack my brain for the right words, but for the first time he's become silent. Avoiding my gaze by peeling back the label to his beer bottle. He agrees with Ryke?

I let out a short laugh that borders on a choke. "I guess I'm just a terrible girlfriend." And I believe it. In more ways than one.

I push through the sea of bodies, not having the heart or stomach to watch Ryke and Connor's reactions. My hand shakes like a junkie needing a fix and my head spins from all the lights. I stumble over plastic cups and brush against someone on my way to the bathroom.

The stalls line up in a single row, doors ajar and empty. I lean over a sink, writing scrawled in permanent marker all over the basin. *Wash up. Tina was here! Use Soap, you dirty wench! Blow me.*

The door creaks and I glance over. A nameless guy with a face like a wolf, scruffy chin and dark eyes, saunters in. Is he the one I accidentally brushed up against? I don't break his gaze, and he takes the invitation.

His hands linger on my hips questioningly, and I brace the porcelain basin in response. Rough kisses press into my neck and for a moment it feels better. It feels like it could be okay again. When my jeans lower and the cold air prickles my skin—I jolt awake.

"No." *I will not cheat on Loren Hale.* No matter if anyone tells me how bad of a person I am.

He doesn't hear me or doesn't take the hint. Hands grab my ass, only a thin layer of fabric between him and me and scoring. Fuck.

"No," I say louder, employing the one word I've always avoided.

His hands slip beneath my panties and I try to turn around and pull away. But he pushes against me hard, and my stomach slams into the sink, nearly taking my breath. "Stop!" I struggle and try to kick out, but I'm all skin and bone and he's all brawn and hunger.

Tears fall down my cheeks as I try and scream, but the thumping music bleeds into the bathroom, drowning out my pleas.

What do I do? What the fuck do I do?!

Maybe I should just take it. Get it over with. Act like I want it. Convince my body that it's another pursuit. Make it okay. Make myself believe it's some fantasy.

My tears dry up and I try to fight one last time, only to be slammed against the basin. I cough hoarsely.

Time to pretend, Lily. Make believe. It's what you're good at.

Just as I close my eyes, the door crashes open.

"Get the fuck off her!" Screaming. Terrible screaming. And the pressure behind me leaves. I'm numb, but I subconsciously pull up my jeans, covering myself like this is any other night.

I look to my left, and Ryke grips the guy by the arms, fighting against his drunken, hostile movements. The guy swings. Ryke ducks, and then slams him into a stall. The guy falls hard into a toilet bowl, his forehead hitting the porcelain lip, and his legs splay out the door.

Ryke clenches him by the shirt, lifting him up. "What the fuck is wrong with you?!" he screams. But I feel like that question should be directed at me.

Connor steps in front of my transfixed gaze, but I stare past his eyes.

"Where's Lo?" My voice is small and not my own.

"He's still at the bar," Connor says softly. "Lily." He waves a hand in my face. "Lily, look at me."

I do, but I don't. I've never changed my mind after I invited someone to have sex with me. I've never been hurt by my addiction. Not like this.

Ryke kicks the guy in the groin and then bangs the stall door on him.

This is all wrong. Lo should be here, not Connor and Ryke.

"I want to go home," I murmur.

Ryke puts a hand on my shoulder and steers me out of the bathroom and away from my attacker—or at least a guy who doesn't understand the word *no*. A frown weighs down his face. "I need to go find Lo. Connor, will you . . . "

"I've got her."

Ryke's hand leaves me only to be replaced by Connor. He guides me, and I float away from the bar, outside, and into the backseat of Connor's limo. Connor finds a water bottle in the cooler and places it in my palm.

"Why did you come into the bathroom?" I ask. I should have sealed my own fate once I stormed off.

"You were acting strange all night, Lily. I was worried, so I told Ryke we should check on you."

The car door opens, and Ryke enters with a wobbling Lo. He staggers but manages to duck underneath the frame before hitting his head. He collapses onto the seat across from me, and immediately shuts his heavy eyes, drowning in a sea of darkness, silent and void of turbulent thoughts.

Ryke climbs in beside him, shutting the door and giving

Connor's driver the order to go. I envy Lo so much right now for his peaceful, temperate sleep, the kind that shields the world's dissonance, if only for one night.

Ryke checks his pulse and then nods to me. "Are you okay?" A welt grows on his cheekbone like the guy elbowed him.

I blink away tears. "I asked for it."

Ryke's face contorts, like I physically impaled him. "What? Why would you fucking say that?"

Connor covers his eyes with his hand so I can't see his reaction. If Ryke looks this wounded over something bad happening to me, I'm sure it's not good.

"I let him touch me," I say. ". . . but then . . . then I changed my mind. I think it was too late by then." My hands shake. I wish Lo could hold them. My knees bounce. I wish he was awake. I wish I didn't need him this much, but I love him. I sniff as tears spill. "It's my fault. I gave him the wrong impression."

Ryke gapes. "No means no. I don't care when you fucking say it, Lily. Once it's out there, it's out there. Any halfway decent guy would have backed off."

My heart clenches. If Lo finds out this happened while he was at the bar, it'll crush him. I won't inflict that type of pain on Lo. "Don't tell him."

"He needs to know," Ryke says.

I want to scream back about how wrong he is, about how the information will tear Lo apart, not strengthen him, but something sensible pulsates in my head, telling me to listen. I never do.

"This will kill him," I choke. "You're not helping!"

"You can't keep this from him, Lily. Think about how much pain he'd be in if he found out and *everyone* knew but him? And he will. Don't kid yourself."

Maybe he's right. I disintegrate into the seat, surrendering to Ryke's unapologetic glare. I wipe the rest of my tears with a quick swipe and stare out the window. The limo quiets for the rest of the ride. No one talks. Not even as Ryke carries an unconscious Lo up to the apartment. Not when I close his bedroom door, locking him in for the night.

When it's just the three of us left, Connor is the first to break the silence. "I'm going to make some coffee. If you want to go to bed, I understand, but I'd like to talk to you."

I don't deserve friends, but I try to hold on to them because I fear the blackness and emptiness that wait if I let go.

"Can you make me hot chocolate?" I ask.

"Even better. You could use some calories."

I sink into the recliner, snuggling into a warm blanket, and watch Connor mill about the kitchen like he owns it. I imagine if I ever had a brother, Connor would fit the perfect mold. A little conceited but deep down, even below his people collecting habits, he has a warm heart.

Ryke slouches on the couch. "Should I call your sisters?"

"No. They'll just worry."

Connor returns with a tray of coffee and passes me my mug of hot chocolate. "It's too late. I already texted Rose."

"What?" I squeak.

"She's on her way."

Twenty-nine

Rose is coming over.

The words still haven't fully sunk in. They sit there, along with the rest of my drifting thoughts, but they translate into something numb and foreign. I cup a steaming mug of hot chocolate, taking small sips in the wake of the quiet.

Connor says nothing. Ryke says nothing. They're two statues on the couch while I curl into the chair.

An abhorrent place inside of me wonders how to lie to Rose. How can I concoct a new deceit to hide Lo's unconsciousness and my maybe-assault? With two witnesses who will vouch for the night, I have no thread to spin my tales. Cold, blistering reality sets in, and I feel no dread, no sense of loss that I expected would come after all these years of lying to Rose.

I'm just empty.

The speaker box buzzes, and Connor rises to ring Rose inside. The movement shifts my gaze up, and I see Ryke, his ankle perched on his other knee. He stares distantly at a lamp, fingers to his lips. The light catches his brown hair and flecks of his brown eyes that shimmer with gold. He's enchanting, but right now, no man can hypnotize me.

And then he turns his head a fraction and sees me watching.

"What are you thinking?" I ask.

"What it would be like"—he pauses—"to be him."

I look away, my eyes burning. "And?" My voice shakes. I wipe a fallen tear, forcing the others back with a strong inhale.

When he doesn't reply, I glance at him again. He stares, haunted, at the ground, as though picturing the alternate reality. Does it really look that bad? The door closes, and we both flinch, waking from the reverie.

I pull a woolen blanket tighter around my body, hiding beneath the soft fabric. I lose the courage to meet my sister's gaze, and I listen to the familiar clap of her heels on the hardwood. The noise dies off as she steps onto the living room rug.

"Why didn't you take her to the hospital?" Rose accuses.

"It's complicated," Connor says.

"It's not complicated, *Richard*," she spits. "My little sister was just attacked. She needs to be checked out."

I take a small breath and risk a glance. Wearing a fur coat and chapped lips from the chill outside, her usual cold demeanor has been undeniably fractured with something more human. She cares. I've always known that, but others wouldn't be so quick to see it.

"I'm okay," I tell her, believing it too. "He didn't get that far."

To avoid a surge of emotion, she clenches her teeth hard, staring at me like I've suddenly come undone. But I don't feel how she sees me. I'm okay. Honestly.

"I'm okay," I repeat, just so she understands.

Rose holds up a finger to pause the talk. She turns to Connor. "Where's Lo?" She clears her throat, choked.

I chime in, on an automatic setting. "He's asleep."

"Unconscious," Connor corrects me.

Ryke stands. "Connor and I found Lily. Lo was . . . " *drinking himself to sleep*. He shakes his head, more upset than I thought possible. "I'll go check on him." Ryke pads off. And then there were three.

Rose looks back to Connor. "What was Lo doing?"

"Nothing," I cut in. "Honestly, it's fine. I'm okay. He's okay. You guys don't need to be here." We can handle this. We've handled so much already. How is this any different?

Rose ignores me and waits for Connor to answer.

"He was drinking at the bar, getting wasted."

Rose shakes her head almost immediately, disbelieving. "No. He doesn't drink that much anymore, and he wouldn't leave Lily. They're *always* together."

Connor frowns. "Are we talking about the same Loren Hale?"

I suck in a breath. "Stop," I say. "Please! It's fine." But it's like they've put my voice on mute. My head spins. Is this what free-falling feels like?

"I think I know him better than you," Rose says. "He's been dating my sister for three years."

I crumple into the chair, seeing the wrecking ball smash apart my life before it happens.

"Then one of us has been fed wrong information. The Lo and Lily I know have been dating for two months."

I crawl further into my blanket as their accusatory eyes pierce my body.

"Lily," Rose says in a high-pitched voice. I'm scaring her. "Explain."

Don't cry. I swallow. "I'm sorry," I start. "I'm sorry." I bring my knees to my chest and press my forehead to them, hiding the tears that brew. I sense her condemnation, her hatred and spite at the world I've constructed for her to trust. A girl who has done nothing but love me unconditionally.

"Lily," she breathes, her voice soft and near. She places a hand on my cheek, smoothing back my hair. I look up, and she kneels in front of me, not as betrayed as I imagined. "What's going on?"

I want to paint a picture for her—a torrid, restless picture that spans across three long years—but spilling truths hurts more than constructing the lies. I focus on the facts. As an intellectual, maybe Rose will accept them.

I rest my chin on my kneecaps and stare past her. It's easier. "Three years ago, Lo and I made a deal to pretend to be in a relationship. We wanted everyone to believe we're good people, but we're not." I look away. "We started dating during the boat trip to the Bahamas."

Rose tenses and picks her words carefully. "Lily, what do you mean about not being good people?"

I let out a short, crazed laugh. Why is it so funny? It's not. None of this feels right. "We're selfish and miserable." I lean my head back. Being in a real relationship was supposed to fix everything. Our love should have mended all the pain and the hurt. Instead, we're met with more complications, more consequences, more frowns and furrowed brows.

"So you closed everyone off?" she questions. "You built a fake relationship to hide away from the rest of us?" Her tone sharpens, beyond hurt, but when I look at her, I see fear and pain and sympathy. Sentiments I do not deserve. "It doesn't make sense, Lily. You're not a bad person, not enough to cast us away and play make-believe with your childhood friend."

I cringe at everything. "You don't know what I am."

Rose glances over her shoulder. "Leave us," she tells Connor. He doesn't hesitate before disappearing down the hall. Swiftly, Rose spins back and clasps my hands in hers. I try to jerk away.

"Stop," I say.

She holds tighter. "I am right here. I am not going anywhere."

Tears well up. She should leave. I've tortured her enough.

"Look at me," she pleads.

Hot tears scald, sliding slowly down my cheeks in fiery lines. I can't meet her gaze.

"You cannot get rid of me, Lily. Nothing you do or say will make me leave. If you don't tell me now, then I'll hear of it in a year . . . "

"Stop," I cry.

". . . three years, five years, a decade. I'll wait for you to tell me." She's crying—a girl who never cries, who squirms at the sight of tears and a wailing baby. "I love you. You're my sister. That will *never* change." She squeezes my hands. "Okay?"

Everything surfaces. I break into sobs, and she rushes into my arms, holding me tightly on the chair. I don't say I'm sorry. I have spoken enough empty apologies to last a lifetime. This has to mean something.

I break from the embrace first, but we share the recliner, sitting close. She keeps her hand in mine, waiting while I form what feels impalpable. "I . . . I always thought something was wrong with me." I swallow, my mouth cottony. "I try so hard to stop, but I can't. And being with Lo, I thought it'd make everything better. I thought there would be no more bad nights, but it's just a different kind of bad."

Her breath goes. "Is it drugs?"

I let out another short laugh, tears dripping. "I wish; then it'd make more sense." I inhale. "Don't snicker, okay?"

"Lil," she says. "I wouldn't."

"Lots of girls would." I meet her eyes. "I started having sex when I was thirteen." I tuck a piece of hair behind my ear, feeling small all of a sudden. "I've had more one-night stands than birthdays . . . " I open my mouth, ready for the next wave of truths but I stick to those.

"You think you're slutty?" she wonders with a frown. "I wouldn't judge you because you lost your virginity so young." She lifts my chin with a finger. "One-night stands do *not* make you a slut. Sexuality is a part of human nature. No woman should be slandered for experiencing it."

"It's more than that, Rose." Although, I could have used her empowerment years ago when I tossed and turned in bed, believing I should wither away before I touched myself, that masturbation was something for the boys. All the young girls said as much. They avoided the word, shunned those who so much as mentioned it, as though only guys can be the ones to touch girls' aching flesh. Now it seems so ridiculous.

"Explain it to me," she says.

"I've chosen sex over family functions hundreds of times. Even when I know it's wrong, I keep doing it. Before I was with Lo, I used to convince myself that I'd stop all of the time. The next morning, I'd pop up another porn site. And I'd start all over again." My arms tremble. "What does that sound like to you?"

Her eyes stay wide in thought. "You're addicted."

I wait for her to laugh or to convince me that I made it all up.

"Lily," she says, very softly. "Do you know how this started— why you're like this?" Her cheeks concave. I read her thoughts. *Were you molested? Abused? Touched by some distant uncle of ours?* I've sat and wondered for hours if I've repressed some traumatic event, but I always come up blank.

"Nothing happened to me. I just started. It made me feel good. And I couldn't stop." Isn't that how most addictions begin?

"Oh Lily." Tears build in her eyes again. "You were assaulted . . . does this play into your addiction somehow? Has this happened before?"

"No, no," I say quickly, trying to bed her tears. My eyes already start burning again. "This is the first time, and it's partly

316 · KRISTA RITCHIE and BECCA RITCHIE

my fault. I . . . I sent the guy the wrong message. I've never been monogamous before, and this is the first instance that I've slipped up."

Rose's clutch tightens. "No," she forces, jostling my hands in hers. "You are so wrong, Lily."

"You don't understand—"

"You're right. I don't understand your addiction, not yet. It's very new to me, and I'm still trying to process it, but if you said or gave him any sort of impression to go away, then he should have listened."

Ryke said the same thing. "I should feel upset about it," I say. "This should change me in some monumental way, shouldn't it?" But why do I feel so numb?

"I think you're in shock," Rose murmurs. "Do you need to see someone? I have a good therapist." She scans the room for her purse.

"No, I don't want to go to a shrink."

"So you want to live like this? You don't want to try and curb your addiction?"

I shrug. "I'm okay." Or at least, that's what I've convinced myself. "Lo is here. As long as I have him . . . "

Her eyes suddenly darken and I see the gears clicking in her head. She's far too smart to let something as big as this go unnoticed. "You said you both were bad people. You're helping each other keep secrets, aren't you?" And then it hits her. "Oh my God, Lily. He *never* stopped drinking, did he?" When I don't answer, she leans back in the chair, touching her lips. "Why hadn't I noticed? He said he stopped partying because you didn't like it. That was all a lie."

"We're okay," I say for the millionth time.

"No, you're not!" she shrieks. "You're not okay. He got wasted at a bar and passed out while a guy assaulted you!"

My face cracks. "It's okay," I whisper. Tears flow full-force now. The waterworks pour while I stare at my hands. "This system works. I know you don't see it, but it does." I wipe my eyes but they keep coming. "And . . . and everyone's better off. Lo and I, our addictions only affect each other. And we've learned to deal with it."

Her mouth falls. "You think pushing your family away is the better option? This affects us. No matter what you choose, Lily. You know why? Because we all *love* you. Dad asks about you every day because he knows you won't answer his calls. Mom has a stack of self-help books on her dresser. Want to know what they're about?"

I shake my head. Not really. This is going to hurt.

"How to reconnect with your daughter. How to build relationships with your children. You affect them. Your addiction affects them. Missing parts of our lives isn't a solution, it's a problem."

I understand what she's telling me. I hear the words, and they make a great deal of sense. But what's my alternative to satiating this addiction? Getting help? Kicking it? How do you eliminate something that's a part of life? I can understand being sober, but abstaining from sex? It's unnatural.

Rose must see me processing because she adds, "You start with counseling and someone who has been through this before."

"I want to wait to talk to Lo," I tell her. I'm not sure I'm ready to give up my crutch, even though I know it'll make everyone else happy. I hate myself for it, but stopping sounds beyond my reach. "I'm going to go to bed." Mechanically, I rise from the chair.

She follows suit. "I'm spending the night. I'll be on the couch to give you some space."

"You don't have to stay. Really, I'm . . . " She gives me a sharp glare and I rephrase my automatic response. ". . . I'll be okay."

She nods and tucks my flyaway hair behind my ear. "I know you will. I'll see you in the morning, Lily." Before I pull away, she wraps her arms around me, squeezing harder, holding tight. "I love you."

I almost start crying again, but I bottle the feelings. *I love you too.* "I'll be okay," I murmur. With this, I disentangle from her and glide to my room. My head has finally separated from my body.

Thirty

I t takes me hours to shut off my brain and fall asleep, to stop the endless tracks where I bounce between justifying my actions and condemning them. Sometimes I think Rose is right, that maybe therapy would be good for me. But some medical physicians barely even consider sex addiction a real thing. What if I end up at the mercy of a shrink who scorns me and makes me feel even more worthless?

Plenty of other reasons bomb my mind, keeping me firmly on a destructive loop. And when I finally wake, I watch the red glowing numbers change on my digital clock. Weighed down by a strong force, it feels too strenuous to lift my numb body from the mattress.

I hear Rose crack the door and peek into my room every so often, but I feign sleep and she slips out just as quickly. So much has changed in the past twenty-four hours that I'm struggling to grasp on to something familiar. Lo, my one constant, will no doubt hear about the events last night. I wish they would come from my lips, but it's already mid-afternoon and I still can't pry myself from the sheets.

Curtains encase my room in total blackness, refusing to let in a shred of light. The only source belongs to my glowing phone as

I search Tumblr for naughty photos, but it only makes me sick to my stomach. I don't stop. Not until the door opens. I quickly click off the screen and close my eyes, pretending to be asleep.

Concentrating on the footsteps, I wait for Rose to leave again. The door closes, and I let out a breath before returning to the pictures.

"You're a terrible liar."

I jump at the deep, hollow voice and quickly yank the dangling cord on the lamp. The room illuminates and Lo squints in the dark. Eyes pink and swollen, and hair matted like he's been pulling at it in distress. They must have told him what happened. As I assumed.

He stays firmly against the wall beside my dresser, putting a great deal of distance between us. I try not to overanalyze what it means, but it hurts regardless.

"I've managed to fool everyone this long," I say under my breath. "What gave me away?"

He licks his bottom lip before saying, "I asked Rose if you had your TV on. She said it was pitch black in here. So I knew you must have woken up and turned off your porn." Almost every night I fall asleep to videos playing in the background. Most of the time on mute.

"That doesn't make me a bad liar," I refute softly. "That just means you know me too well." I slide up on the bed, resting against the oak headboard and pulling my knees to my chest. "I had to tell Rose everything."

"I know." His expression stays inscrutable, not letting on if it bothers him. So I make the leap myself.

"I think it will work out. She doesn't seem like she'll tell anyone else. And she said that she'd give me as much time as I needed." That's what she was getting at, right? "And with Rose, that could be forever. So we'll just move on from last night and everything will go back to normal." I give a self-satisfied nod to seal the proclamation.

But Lo doesn't reciprocate my confidence. He clenches his jaw and tears well up, turning his eyes to a puffier pink. "Do you really think I can just move on?" He chokes. "Let it go like any other fucking day?"

Oh . . . "We have to try," I say in a small voice.

He laughs sadly and it cracks and dies short. He wipes his mouth and lets out a breath. "Ask me."

"What?"

His eyes flicker up to me and they turn into cold steel. "Ask me why I drink."

A lump lodges in my throat. We don't talk about our addictions. Not outright. We bury them with booze and sex and on the occasion where we feel lost we return to the nostalgia of comic books.

Fear steals my ability to form words. I think I know the answer, but I'm so terrified of changing the structure that we have in place. My constant. My Lo. I selfishly don't want that to end.

"Goddammit, Lily," he says through clenched teeth. "Just fucking ask me!"

"Why?" The word knifes me.

A tear escapes and he says, "Because I can. Because when I was eleven years old and tasted my first drop of whiskey, I thought it'd bring me closer to my father. Because I felt empowered." He touches his chest. "Because I never hit anyone. I never drove. I never lost a fucking job or lost any friends that mattered. Because whenever I drank, I didn't think I was hurting anyone but me."

He takes a shallow breath and rubs a shaky hand through his hair. "That is, until last night. Or maybe for the past two months. Or forever. I don't know anymore."

I strangle my sheets in my fists and try to remember to inhale.

"I'm okay." I cringe. "I'll be okay, Lo. You didn't hurt me. It was just a mistake. A bad night."

He pushes off the wall, gaining confidence from somewhere, and sinks down on the edge of the bed. Still far from me. His eyes pierce mine as he says, "You're forgetting that I know all the tricks, Lil. How many times have you repeated those words to yourself, hoping they'd come true? I do the same thing to justify every shitty night." He scoots forward and I've petrified, going still as a piece of wood. His fingers graze my bare kneecap and his face cracks like it's painful to touch me. "But I don't want any more bad nights with you."

"Did Rose put you up to this?"

"No." He shakes his head. He gently rests his hand on my leg without looking so tortured, and I let out another strained breath. "I should have been there. I should have stopped the guy. I should have held you in my arms and told you that everything was going to be okay even if it wasn't. That was my job, no one else's."

"Where does this leave us?" I ask. *Please don't leave me*, I selfishly think. It may be one of my more abhorrent thoughts yet. I bury my head in my arms as the tears avalanche. I can feel him leaving me, drifting away like a breeze.

"Hey, look at me." He touches my arms and tries to untangle my cave. I tilt my chin up after he succeeds. He crosses my arms and keeps his hands tight on my elbows, his chest so close to mine.

His eyes start watering again, and I'm suddenly terrified of what he's about to say.

"I'm an alcoholic."

He's never said that out loud, never admitted it in that way.

"My father is an alcoholic," he continues, tears spilling down his cheeks and onto my arms. "I can't just will it away like some fairytale. It's a part of me." He rubs my tears with his thumb. "I love you, but I want to love you enough that I *never* choose alcohol over you. Not even for a moment. I want to be someone you deserve. Who helps you rather than enables you, and I can't begin to do that until I get help for myself."

I hear only one thing. *Rehab.* He's going to rehab. Far away from me. I am proud. Somewhere, deep down, I know I'm proud. But it's hiding behind fear. He's going to leave me. Two things have held me together thus far. Sex and Lo. They never used to mix, but losing both at the same time feels like someone ripping off a vital organ and refusing to hook me to a machine.

"Lily!" Lo shakes me a few times, his voice frantic. I can't make sense of anything until his lips touch mine. He kisses me and tells me to "breathe" over and over.

I inhale a large gasp of air, and my head spins like I've been drowning underwater.

"Breathe," he coos. He rests his hand on my diaphragm, and I've somehow made it onto his lap.

I clutch his shirt, silently wondering if I can guilt him to stay. No, that's wrong. I know that's wrong. I swallow hard.

"Talk to me, Lil. Where's your head at?"

"When are you leaving?"

He shakes his head. "I'm not."

Tears burst. "What? I-I . . . " That doesn't make sense. He just said . . .

"I'm going to detox here."

I find myself shaking my head anyway. "No, Lo. Don't stay here for me . . . please." I push his chest.

He gathers my hands. "Stop," he forces. "I've already argued with your sister about this. I'm staying here. I'm giving this a shot, and if it doesn't work, then I'll go. But if I can be here for you and for me, then I have to try."

"Isn't it dangerous to detox here?"

He rests his chin on my head. "Connor hired a nurse. I'll be fine." I hear the fear in his voice. He's about to eliminate alcohol completely from his life. He hit his rock bottom.

Have I hit mine?

I can't think about helping Lo detox and doing the same myself. So I'm going to focus on him, and then when he gets better, I'll worry about me.

That seems right.

Thirty-one

Lo has been sober for a full week. The first couple of days were the worst. The nurse hooked him up to an IV so the fluids could rehydrate his body. He has to be on vitamins to replace the nutrients lost by alcohol and eat a particular diet to get rid of the toxins. I've also hidden the coffee pot so he doesn't get addicted to caffeine in the process. Regardless, he went through bouts of vomiting and sweated and shook and complained in angry screams until Ryke threatened to duct tape his mouth. That made him laugh.

Today, Lo asks to drive my BMW to Lucky's for Thanksgiving. Every year, I spend the day with my parents and Lo goes to his father's place, but beforehand, we eat a pre-turkey dinner at the small diner. It's not as fancy, but the comfort food tastes better than the small portions and strange foams our parents' chefs prepare.

He holds my hand in the middle console and steers the car down the busy Philly street, one palm on the wheel. His fingers tremble and he shakes them out and clenches them once before placing them back.

"Is it like riding a bike?" I ask about driving.

"Easier," he tells me. "There's no gear shift in your car. All I really need to know is how to flick on a blinker." He teasingly

326 · KRISTA RITCHIE and BECCA RITCHIE

taps the blinker and it makes a clicking noise. He takes his hand from mine and slides it on my thigh.

He's devoted his time to me, using my addiction as an outlet I suppose to forget about his. It's worked, for the most part, but sometimes I see the longing in his eyes, the itch to return to his usual routine since I wade in mine.

Lo parallel parks, and I feed the meter. The bell chimes as we enter Lucky's, Lo holding the door open from behind me, his long arm extending above my head. Everything looks how I remember from last year. Orange and yellow streamers drape from the ceiling, a lazy fan whirling in the center of the small establishment. Booths with red crackling vinyl backs line the left side by the windows. Someone drew a feathered turkey with washable paint on the glass and added bright multicolored words, *Happy Thanksgiving*, for all to see. The familiar cranberry and garlic mashed potato scent permeates in the air and old couples at tables drink coffee and smile.

I stare at a pair for a long moment, their gray hair short and nearly identical. They bicker about a spill on the man's shirt, and the woman leans over to help him wipe it up. I want that to be us. I want to grow old and yell at Lo for dribbling coffee. I want him to be *my* forever. For the first time, he may be on the right path towards reaching that. I can only hope I'll join him too.

There's one noticeable difference to our yearly tradition—*they* wave us over to a booth by the window.

We slide in on the right side while Connor, Rose, and Ryke fill the left. My sister looks like a million dollars in her high-waisted skirt and cream chiffon blouse, a diamond necklace shaped like a water droplet tight on her collar.

"Is that new?" I ask.

She touches the jewel, her cheeks reddening as much as mine would. I can't help but smile.

"I bought it for her," Connor exclaims, his arm draped on the top of the booth behind her.

I squint. "Why?"

"No reason," Connor says. "I saw it and I thought she'd like it."

Rose tries really hard not to smile, but she can't quite hide it.

Lo groans. "You're making me look bad." His hand rises on my thigh and dips towards the inside. Lo gives me things that I like much better than diamonds or flowers.

Ryke wads his straw paper. "You've never given Lily a present like that?"

"No, she'd rather I give her something else than a necklace."

"Like what, Loren?" Rose looks like she could rip out his throat.

Lo is about to take the challenge. "Like my tongue on her—"

"Oh my God!" I shriek, scooting away from Lo and into the wall of the booth. I grab a menu and shield my face from everyone.

Ryke laughs under his breath, but I think my sister is about to launch herself at all the guys and scratch them with her nails.

Connor whispers in her ear, "He's just picking on you."

"She's a sex addict," she whispers back just as fiercely. "He shouldn't be joking around about this."

"I can hear you," Lo says flatly.

I peek at Ryke since he's the one person I haven't confronted since my addiction has spread from Rose to Connor and from Lo to Ryke. Yes, he told Ryke. I have no idea how it came out. Maybe in his confessional about needing to get sober. Our addictions intertwined so much that it was too hard for Lo to talk about his without bringing up my dependence on sex.

Ryke doesn't even look at me. He's mouthing something to Lo. I read his lips. *I'll tell them.*

I glance at Lo and he nods to Ryke in approval.

I frown. "Tell them what?" I ask Lo.

"Nothing," he lies, motioning for me to return to him. I set down the menu and slide back into his arms, and the waitress comes by to break up my sister's whisper battle with Connor.

We order the turkey dinners and waters, and I'm left to wonder what secret Lo and Ryke share about me. It could be anything. As the waitress traipses back to the kitchen, Rose turns to Ryke and fishes out a crisp white envelope. "I couldn't find your address anywhere, so I was unable to send this to your house." She passes him a Christmas Charity Gala invitation. "Is Ryke a nickname? It wasn't showing up in any directory."

"Middle name," he says, distant. He pulls out the cream card with gold cursive lettering. "I can't go." He barely even gives it a chance.

"Why not?" Lo questions, obviously hurt by the notion. If anyone has been a rock since he decided to become sober, it's been Ryke. He's practically his unofficial sponsor. I know he really wants Ryke there, especially since his father will be attending. "Is it the article? You're supposed to be finished with that thing soon, aren't you?"

"No, I submitted the article weeks ago." He finally escapes the lie. "My professor gave me an A."

"Send me a copy," Connor says. "I'd love to read it."

"Sure." He'll probably "forget" to email him the article for the next few weeks until Connor stops asking.

"Do you have plans or something?" Lo asks. "It's the day before Christmas Eve. You can still spend time with your mom if you go." I've never seen him like this—pleading for someone else in such a transparent manner.

Ryke nods. "Okay. Yeah, I'll make it work. Thanks, Rose." He folds the envelope in fours and stuffs it in his back pocket.

Lo relaxes, and he glances at the bathrooms. Does he want to go have sex? He turns to me, as though reading my mind, and whispers softly, "I have to use the bathroom for real. Don't let Ryke eat my food if it comes." With this, he kisses my cheek and disappears towards the blue doors.

I sink into the seat, hot from the three pair of eyes bearing down on me.

"Lily," Rose starts, sitting forward. She clasps her hands. "Lily, I've been thinking a lot lately, and I really want you to come live with me when the semester ends. There's more than enough room in my apartment, and—"

"What about Lo?" I frown and shake my head. "I can't leave him like this. And I go to Penn."

"You can always transfer," she reminds me.

Ryke turns to her. "Lo has it under control."

Her yellow-green eyes puncture him. "He's sick, Ryke. He needs to concentrate on himself, and he's not going to be able to do that if he's concerned about Lily's well-being. I want him to get better, *but* I want her to get better more. So pardon me if I'm looking out for my sister's best interest."

"And I'm looking out for Lo's. He wants to try it this way first. Look. It's worked for the past week—"

"Yes, he's sober, but is Lily any different? Has she started going to therapy or weaned off sex?"

"You guys, please stop," I say, my voice lost to their heated ones. They do not need to be discussing my sex life at Lucky's. I may never muster the courage to come back here.

"He has a plan," Ryke retorts. "You need to trust that he loves Lily."

He has a plan? Is this what they were talking about?

"What sort of plan?" Rose wonders. *Yeah, what sort of plan. And why did no one tell me?!*

"He's going to start limiting her and gradually decrease her use of porn."

I gape while my sister nods in approval.

"What?!" I shout. I'm more disturbed by the fact that Lo talked about our sex life with Ryke of all people. "Tell me you didn't discuss this with Lo." I already see the answer. The moment Ryke projected himself into my life at the library, telling me he would help Lo, I took the opportunity. I told him about Lo's addiction. And if he gave the same offer to Lo, I know he would take it.

Ryke unabashedly meets my gaze. "He told me most of your dirty secrets."

"Oh my God," I mumble, looking frantically over at Rose like *what do I do?*

She glares at Ryke for me. "That's personal."

"Yeah? Well guys talk just like girls do. Maybe you should remember that before you go down on someone."

Connor cuts in. "All right, everyone needs to cool down right now. I think people are beginning to stare. Come on, Rose." He lifts her up by the arm. "Let's go outside for a minute."

She tensely rises from her seat but points at Ryke. "I'm glad you're here for Lo, but I swear, if you hurt my sister—"

"Rose." Connor ushers her from the booth.

Ryke says, "I wouldn't intentionally hurt anyone."

Connor gives him a look. "Just stop talking."

Rose starts rambling, and Connor finds the right reply each time, keeping her sane as they take a breather. At least she found a date to the Charity Gala this year who isn't gay.

Around the same moment, the food arrives, and only Ryke and I are left at the table to eat it. Neither of us touches our plates.

"I don't want to be limited," I tell him. "This isn't about me right now."

"It's always been about you," Ryke says. "If you would have told me from the start what kind of deal you two struck and what kind of lives you lived, I wouldn't have been so upset with you when you stopped helping Lo. I apologize for that."

"He needs to concentrate on himself," I remind Ryke.

"Lily . . . " He puts his elbows on the table and leans in. "You two have done everything together. You've been through every step of your lives with the other by your side. In order for this to work, you can't be regressing while he's moving forward."

My frown deepens. The way he phrased that—it makes it seem like he'll change into a different person. That he may become someone new, someone that does not fit into my life anymore. Maybe he'll outgrow my rituals and find a person that shapes his new routines. I don't like that future, but I want one where he's better.

"Do you understand what I'm saying?" he asks.

"Okay." I nod. "Okay, I'll try."

He stays tense.

My brows bunch. "You don't believe me, do you?"

"No, but the admission is nice to hear."

I glare. "I can fight."

"I guess we'll see how hard." He leans back. "And Lily . . . I sincerely hope you fucking surprise me."

I do too.

Lo has been kind enough to gradually limit me. No hardcore sex in the past week. I threw out *half* my porn videos yesterday, but the desire still lingers. Instead of compulsively filling it, I pop a few sleeping pills so I'll pass out before thinking about sex. Nighttime is the worst. My endorphins rise and all I want to do is straddle Lo in some nefarious way.

But I try. I have to.

I'm scared to be alone. I'm afraid I'll start touching myself or I'll call a sex worker out of impulse. I've been so paranoid that I've skipped most of my classes. I think I'm going to have to re-take three out of five in my schedule. It's better than cheating on Lo and cheating on myself.

Lo barely sleeps. He tosses and turns in the middle of the night, even waking me from my pill-induced slumber. I keep wait-ing for his withdrawals to lessen, to be easier, but they never are. Sometimes I wonder if he's going to have to fight this forever. And then I realize, I may have to fight that long too.

I accompany Lo and Ryke to the track field. Mostly because I hate being alone, and Rose has final exams this week. I finished mine yesterday. Well, sort of. I didn't even come in for my Biology and Managerial Economics class. I'm expecting an F, but at least I have the option of a "redo." I just may be in college for an extra semester.

I sprawl out on the bleacher and play with a new camera that Rose bought me. I've never had a hobby other than sex, but tak-ing mindless pictures has filled a small void. I snap a few as the guys stretch in the grass. Both wear long-sleeved shirts and track pants, and as they laugh and banter, I catch a photo of them smil-ing at the same time.

They look alike. Both have brown hair, even though Ryke's is a little darker. Both have brown eyes, even if Lo's are a bit more amber. Ryke's tan has started to disappear in the winter, and his skin starts to resemble Lo's Irish hue. They could be brothers, but Ryke has broader shoulders, a stronger jaw, and thinner lips.

When they start running, Ryke takes off in a quick sprint, and Lo chases after him, catching up within seconds. They race fast and hard, their legs pumping and their sneakers pounding into the black track. Ryke stays two paces ahead of Lo, more trained, but Lo holds his own.

They run as though nothing can stop them. I watch Lo, and I start to see a new future. It's there, still blurry, but it looks brighter and better.

I just wonder if it still includes me.

Thirty-two

Some days aren't good. Hours before we have to arrive at the hotel for the Christmas Charity Gala, I suspect this will be a very bad one.

Lo slept maybe thirty minutes last night, and he paces around the room until he calls Ryke and talks to him for a couple hours. Nothing seems to calm him, and I think it may be from the conversation he wants to have with his father—the one where he admits that he's trying to be sober. But I also worry it's something else.

Before he goes to the kitchen, he snaps at me twice when I bring up college. I asked him what he got in Managerial Econ—which I promptly failed. And he told me to worry about having to retake it in the spring and stop being so nosy. He wouldn't be so mean if something wasn't wrong.

Rose applies my makeup at my vanity. I already wear my plum dress with lacy long sleeves. Rose actually bought the velvet sapphire dress, even though she tried on ten more after it. The Gala works in two parts. One, the dinner where we all sit around a round table and are served five courses. Then business types will go to the podium and thank everyone for their generosity for the night. After which will be the reception where people will drink cocktails and walk around the grand ballroom to chat and socialize.

When I go with Lo, we usually stand by the bar and try to ask the server the most embarrassing questions to see what will happen. It's obnoxious and probably rude, but it passes the time. This year, I plan on wandering aimlessly. Which doesn't sound much better.

In prompt Connor Cobalt fashion, we arrive a full hour early. Ryke straightens his tie and nervously looks around the bare room, mostly filled with servers as they adjust red rose center pieces on the tables and finish stringing icicle lights.

"Have you been to an event like this?" I ask.

"Yeah," he admits. "Not this social circle though."

Lo fidgets more than usual. He runs a shaky hand through his hair. "I need a drink." He rubs his eyes and groans.

"You're okay," Ryke assures him. "Hey, what's bugging you?"

"Nothing," Lo says in annoyance. "I really don't want to talk right now. No offense, but that hasn't helped all day. I just have a pounding migraine."

I reach out for his hand, and his eyes meet mine. Something bad stirs in me. "You want to . . . ?"

"No," Ryke says to both of us. "No."

I glare at him. "Not that it's any of your business—I went a full day without watching porn." I leave out the part where I spent the entire afternoon in bed with Lo. And we weren't sleeping.

"Congratulations," Ryke says dryly. He gives Lo a stone-cold look. "You're avoiding."

"I'm helping her."

"You know you're not."

I'm helping him, I want to refute. But Lo has already made his choice. His hand slips down the small of my back and he guides me out of the room and towards the hotel lobby.

He pulls his wallet from his pocket. "One room," he tells the receptionist. I rock on the balls of my feet. *Yes.*

. . .

Now that my high has vanished, my whole body feels sore. He took me from behind, much harder than usual, and I liked it. When it happened. I regret the position, his intensity, and giving him the idea to be here in the first place.

"What time is it?" Lo asks, grabbing the clock on the nightstand. "Fuck." He hurries off the bed, the comforter on the floor, the sheets twisted in odd ways. "Get up, Lil."

I lie with my head on the pillow, unmovable. Maybe I can disintegrate into the sheets.

Lo leans over the bed and tilts his head so he stares directly at me. "Get. Up." He tosses my dress at my face.

I hold the fabric and straighten to a sitting position. I try to tug the material over my head, but my sore arms barely allow me the strength.

Lo hops into his pants and then finds his white button-down.

I wish we could stay here, but that would have been old Lily and Lo. We're improved now. I struggle with the fabric and finally poke my head through the hole of my dress. And then, I see the open mini-fridge. *Maybe not that improved.*

"Lo . . . " My voice sounds small.

He pockets a mini-bottle of tequila. Why is he doing this? Everything was fine. Wasn't it? Except for this morning and this afternoon and now . . .

"Lo, have you been drinking?"

He doesn't meet my gaze. "It's fine. I'm not going to drink at all tomorrow. I just need something—"

"Lo!" I shout, springing from the bed, sans underwear. I struggle to steal the liquor from his pocket, and he clenches my wrists tight.

"Lily, stop!"

"You stop!"

We wrestle standing up until we fall on the bed. He pins my arms on either side of my body.

"Lo!" I shriek. "You can't just give up like this!" It's my fault. Deep in my heart, I know I led him here. It was all me. I burst into tears, adding to the dramatics of the night. And he gently eases off of me.

"Please stop," he chokes. "Lily . . . " He lightly kisses my lips, my cheek, my nose, my eye and chin. "Please, it's okay. I'm okay."

"I did this," I cry.

His lips return to mine, and he tries to make me focus on the kiss rather than my pained thoughts. If I was right in my own mind, maybe I would throw him off. Maybe I would tell him to stop. Maybe I'd do something that would benefit both of us instead of continuing our destructive cycle.

His fingers slip into me, and I clutch the sheet and wrap an arm over my eyes, which alternate between something good and something bad.

He replaces his fingers with his cock, and I let out a sharp gasp at the sudden fullness. His lips find mine again, and he kisses me as he rocks slowly, as though telling me everything is right, everything is okay. He's here. I'm here.

That's all we need.

It's our greatest lie.

I stand numbly in the elevator as it drops towards the first level and the grand ballroom. We've missed the dinner portion of the Gala, and I almost want to ditch the reception and go to the Drake to curl in my bed and wallow. But I'd rather find Rose. I need her.

Lo loops his tie around his neck, staring at the numbers as we descend. Wide space separates us, and so does the emotional sex and his drinking. I couldn't stop him from downing that little bottle of tequila or pocketing another one. If the alcohol made him at ease, it doesn't show. His muscles tense, and his neck barely moves, locked straight ahead.

"Where are you going when we get down there?" I ask.

"I need to talk to my father." His eyes narrow at the glowing numbers.

"Maybe you should find Ryke first."

"That's not necessary."

I swallow hard, and the elevator dings, the doors sliding open. Lo walks briskly towards the ballroom, and I struggle to keep up with his long legs. I skid to a stop by the door, struck by the bright, twinkling chandeliers and busy room with people milling about *everywhere*. A Christmas tree towers in the center, draped in gold tinsel with apple ornaments. Two screens on either side of the stage remind everyone of the benefactors of the event. *Hale Co.* and *Fizzle*. I pass a server who carries a tray of pink champagne.

Lo plucks one off, downs it in one gulp, and sets it back. I can't leave him. Not like this. I weave in between bodies and mutter "excuse me" hundreds of times, trying to tail Lo. He strides towards a certain spot with purpose and determination, ice crystalizing his amber eyes.

"Lo," I say, grabbing out, but his hand drifts away from me.

I'm afraid to look for Rose or Ryke in the crowds because I may lose sight of Lo. Just by glancing over my shoulder, he gained considerable distance ahead of me. By the time I catch up, he stands in front of his father, who wears a tux and a stern expression.

I stay an arm's length away, close enough to hear every word.

"Have you been avoiding me?" Jonathan asks. "You usually stop by on Wednesdays."

"I've been going through some things."

Jonathan scrutinizes his son. "You look fine."

"I'm not fine," Lo admits. He shakes his head repeatedly, and his eyes grow glassy. "I'm not fine, Dad."

Jonathan's eyes flicker to his surroundings, and he says, "This isn't the place, Loren. We'll talk later."

"Something's wrong with me," Lo tells him. "Do you hear me? I'm telling you that I'm not okay."

Jonathan downs the rest of his whiskey and places it on a nearby high table. After he rubs his lips, he edges closer to his son. My breath hitches, and I stay frozen in place. "Are you trying to embarrass me?"

Lo's hands shake and he balls them into fists. "You know that I drink, and you don't give a shit."

"That's what this is about?" Jonathan's face contorts. "Lo, you're a fucking twenty-one-year-old man. Of course you drink."

"I pass out," Lo says. Why is it so hard for Jonathan to understand that Lo has a problem? And then it dawns on me. Maybe because Jonathan hasn't come to terms with his own.

"So have many before you. It's natural for kids your age to abuse alcohol."

"I can't go a day without a drink."

Jonathan's lip curls. "Stop trying to find an excuse for your mistakes, and own up to them like a goddamn man." There's a difference between abusing alcohol and being dependent on it, and if he understood that, he'd realize Lo fits the latter.

I step forward and reach for Lo's hand, but he jerks away from me.

Jonathan has found another glass of whiskey from a server. He sips and nods to me. "Have you put these thoughts into my son's head?"

I shrink back from his scathing glower.

"I've known this since I was a kid," Lo tells him. "She didn't have to say anything to me."

"I highly doubt that."

An arm wraps around my waist. I jump and meet Rose's concerned gaze. I fall into her hug and try not to cry into her shoulder.

Ryke, breathless as though he ran here, slinks up to Lo's side and puts a hand on his arm. He doesn't even look at Jonathan. "Come on, Lo."

Rose tries to tug me away, but I shake my head and stay firmly here. Something's wrong. I see it in Jonathan's face. He pales beyond his natural Irish hue and almost drops his whiskey. "What are you doing here?" he says to Ryke.

Lo frowns. "You know each other?"

Jonathan lets out a small huff. "You didn't tell him?" he says to Ryke. His eyes flicker back to the ballroom where people begin to stare. He shakes his head in annoyance and finishes off his whiskey.

Lo shifts his weight. "Tell me what?"

"Nothing," Jonathan says with a bitter smile. He sets down the glass and meets Loren's gaze once more. "So is this what you wanted to say to me? You wanted to blame me for your problems and stomp around like a child?"

Ryke keeps his hand resolutely on Lo's shoulder, supporting him in a way that I can't.

"No," Lo says softly. "Maybe if this was a story about my teenage years, I'd have done something like that. I just wanted to say that I'm going to get sober." His eyes cloud, and a single tear slides down his cheek. "I'm going to rehab. And when I come back, I may not see you all that much."

He's going to rehab. He knows this can't work—us, together, while he tries to avoid alcohol for good. I can barely breathe. He's leaving. For how long?

Jonathan inhales sharply and glares at Ryke. "Did you put him up to this?"

"No," he says. "It's news to me."

Jonathan looks back at Lo. "You don't need to go to rehab." He mutters, "This is fucking ridiculous." He shakes his head. "I'll call you tomorrow, okay?"

"No, you won't," Lo tells him, more tears threatening to fall. "I won't answer, and I'll be gone by then."

"You're fine!" Jonathan shouts, silencing half the ballroom. He glances over his shoulder, as though just realizing his sudden outburst. He inches forward and speaks lowly. "You're fine, Loren. Stop this."

"He's not okay," Ryke interjects. "He's telling you that he's not okay." My whole chest is on fire, and my head keeps spinning. The only reason I'm still standing is because Rose has her hand intertwined with mine, and if I fall, I don't want her to drop with me.

Jonathan ignores Ryke. "Why are you crying?" he says to Lo, half in repulsion and half in something more human.

"I don't know," Lo says, his nose flaring as he tries to repress the silent tears.

Jonathan grabs the back of Lo's neck and brings his face right into his. "Think about this," he pleads with a sneer, shaking Lo.

People definitely start looking now. Lo tries to break the hold, putting his arm on his father's, but Jonathan's grip is too tight, his fingers pressing into the tender part of Lo's skin.

"Stop," I say, trying to rush forward, but Rose pulls me back.

Ryke grabs Jonathan's arm and pries it off of Lo, who stumbles in a daze. "What is wrong with you?" Ryke shouts at Jonathan. "No, you know what? I know what's wrong with you. You never fucking change. Go back to believing you're a great fucking man, but I won't let you ruin Lo's life."

Why does he sound like he knows him?

"Is this Sara's doing?" Jonathan asks. "Where is she?" His eyes dart around the ballroom, looking for Lo's absent mother.

Lo parts from both Jonathan and Ryke, staring between them to try and understand their relationship. Clearly, it goes beyond anything we imagined.

"She's not here. She doesn't even know I've been talking to Lo," Ryke exclaims.

Jonathan's face twists in pain. "So you took it upon yourself to tear my family apart? After all that I've tried to do for you?" His eyes flash hot. "I could have shunned you, but I let you have a father." *Wait, wait, wait . . .*

"I didn't want one," Ryke says.

Jonathan clenches his teeth. "You will *not* turn my son against me, do you hear me?"

"What's going on?" Lo asks. "What the fuck is going on?"

From behind Jonathan, Connor appears and whispers in his ear. Jonathan nods and then says to Lo, "This is not the time. We'll talk later." With that short goodbye, Connor ushers Jonathan away to end an even bigger scene.

"Meet me in the hall," Lo tells Ryke, not even looking his way.

I follow with Rose. Too many things swim in my head for me to focus. Tears keep falling—the source unbeknownst to me. Maybe from Jonathan's sharp words. Maybe from Lo's rehab proclamation. Or the strangeness between Ryke and Jonathan.

We stop in the hallway of the hotel, the carpet a tacky diamond pattern and the wallpaper a shiny gold color, both dizzying my flyaway mind.

"Who are you?!" Lo yells at Ryke. "Don't fucking lie to me anymore!"

"Calm down," Ryke says. "Give me the chance to explain, please. You deserve every answer."

"How do you know my father?" Lo asks. "How does he know you?"

Ryke holds out a hand, palm down, as though trying to keep the peace. "Sara Hale is my mother."

Oh my . . . Jonathan said something about being a father to Ryke. Is that why the divorce started? Sara cheated and became pregnant with Ryke?

That would make Lo and Ryke half-brothers.

Lo staggers back and raises a hand to pause the argument while he sorts out his thoughts. And then he looks up with furrowed brows and says, "You're a bastard child?"

Ryke cringes in hurt, and he shakes his head once, so terse and pained that a tear flows from his eye.

Lo points to his own chest with a trembling hand. "I'm the bastard?"

Ryke nods once.

Lo lets out a strange choking sound, and I try to step forward, but Rose holds me back again. Lo wipes his eyes with his arm and inhales strongly. "Give me your license," Lo immediately demands.

Ryke pulls his wallet from his back pocket and slides out the card. Before he hands it to Lo, he says, "You're still my brother. It doesn't make a difference who wasn't supposed to be here."

"Just give it to me."

Ryke hands it over, and Lo scans the name. His jaw locks, sharpening his cheeks to ice. His hand quakes as he reads the card. "*Jonathan Ryke Meadows*." Lo lets out a crazed laugh and he flings the license back at Ryke. He leaves it on the carpet. "What did you say your mother did?" Lo feigns confusion. "Oh yeah? She lives off your dad." Lo bites his bottom lip and nods.

"Lo . . ."

He sets his hands on his head. "Fuck you," Lo sneers. "Why didn't anyone tell me? You're Jonathan's *son*. Sara Hale is your mother, but she's not mine, is she?"

"My mom filed for divorce when Jonathan got another woman pregnant with you. I was just born."

Everything that his father told him is a lie. No wonder Sara hates Lo and cursed him on the telephone. He's the product of adultery and her failed marriage. I try to move towards him once more, but Rose keeps pulling me back.

Lo is crying heavily. "Sara took my bed to give to you, didn't she?"

"I didn't know it was yours."

"My dresser, my fucking clothes, she took them from the settlement and gave them to *you*." Lo presses fingers to his eyes. "Why keep this from me?"

"There are legal issues . . . " He steps closer to Lo. "I didn't even know you existed until I turned fifteen. My mom let it slip in one of her rants. I visited Jonathan all the time at country clubs. And I didn't lie when I said I stopped seeing my father. I felt weird about him, especially when I started getting sober. I felt like I could see right through him." He sniffs, trying to hold back emotions, but it's hard because Lo is a mess. And Ryke's eyes grow red and puffy.

"You knew about me for *seven* years? And you didn't think to meet me?" Lo frowns in deep hurt. "I'm your brother."

"You were also the thing that tore apart my parents," Ryke says, his voice shaking. "I spent years resenting the idea of you. My mother hated you, and I loved her, so what the fuck was I supposed to believe? And then I went to college, and I gained some distance from her. I started thinking things through, and I came to peace with you. I'd leave you alone. You'd be some sort of wealthy prick that Jonathan Hale would raise. And then I saw you." Ryke nods to himself, his eyes welling. "I saw you at the Halloween party and I knew who you were. After I learned about your existence, Jonathan would show me pictures of you, always asking if I wanted to meet you. I never did."

Lo looks pained. "Why did you?"

"I saw what would have become of me if I was raised by him. And I regretted *everything*. I blamed you when you were just a kid dealt a shitty hand of cards. I wanted to help you . . . for all the years that I sat by. I knew what he was like. I listened to my *mother* talk about the things he said to her—horrible, disgusting things that were sometimes just as bad as a punch to the face. And I knew you were being raised by that. And I didn't do a god-damn thing." Ryke's voice breaks. He shakes his head.

"So you saw me," Lo says. "Am I as pathetic as you imagined?"

"No. You're kind of an asshole, but so am I. We really must be brothers."

Lo chokes on a short laugh. "Why'd everyone keep this from me?" He takes a step back and Ryke's hand falls off his shoulder. "What are the legal matters?"

Ryke swallows. "In the settlement, my mom has to keep quiet about the name of your mother and she has to retain Hale as her surname or else she loses everything she won in the divorce." Ryke must have taken Sara's maiden name: Meadows.

"Why?"

"So your father won't go to jail. Your mom was almost seven-teen. She was just a minor, and my mother could have turned him in, but she signed papers that censured the truth. And if she changed her mind, then all the money would go to charity and she'd lose out."

Lo's face twists. "Did he rape her?"

"No," Ryke says quickly. "No. Sara said a lot of bad things about Jonathan, but she never said that. I don't think he loved your mom, or else he would have found a way for her to be in your life. I think it was . . . a one-time thing." He runs his hand through his hair. "I think she walked . . . " He struggles to finish the truth. "I think she walked away from you. I don't know why she chose to have you, but she did. And I know she didn't want to keep you after."

Jonathan raised Lo, when no one else wanted him.

As the words sink in, Lo's hands tremble and his chest barely rises to accept breath. "It was just easier for everyone if I didn't know, right?"

"I wasn't sure if Jonathan ever told you the whole truth," Ryke professes. "But when you met me, I knew he hadn't. You had no recognition of who I was."

"Why couldn't you tell me up front?" Lo asks. He points to his chest. "I deserved to know."

"You did. You're right," Ryke says. "But you're not well, Lo. I wanted to help you. So I made up a couple lies to be close to you. I even had to ditch Rose's fashion show because Lily's father showed up. I've met him. He knows me, and I didn't think you were ready to find out the truth."

My father knows? He had the answers the whole time. I can barely process this.

Ryke edges closer. "I was afraid if you found out, I'd push you to a dark place. Can you understand that?" His eyes flicker to me. "I think you can."

Lo rubs his eyes again. He can't stop crying. I see the hurt coursing through him like jagged tidal waves, crashing and crashing until he loses breath and focus and drowns beneath the rapids. He screams into his hand—angry, pained, pissed.

He slowly drops to his knees and puts a palm on the carpet.

"Lo," Ryke says, bending to him. He tries to help, but Lo swats him away with wild, watery eyes.

"Where's Lily?" he asks, frantic. "Lily!" He whips his head. "Lily!" he cries, searching for me.

Rose finally lets me go, and I run into Lo's arms. He holds me tightly and cries into my shoulder, his body heaving. "I'm here," I breathe. "It's okay." When I look up, I see Ryke and Rose exchanging hesitation.

I understand now. They're afraid of our closeness. We're not good together.

Not yet anyway.

He clutches onto my dress, and he cries until there are no more tears. I try and pray to hold mine back—to be strong for him. He whispers to me, in a dry voice, "I feel like I'm dying."

"You're not." I kiss him on the cheek. "I love you."

After a few more minutes, we rise and silently walk outside to the valet with Rose and Ryke close behind. I convince them to leave us alone in one of the cars, but they're going to meet us at the Drake.

Lo slides into the Escalade first. And then me.

"The Drake," I say, not even looking at the front seats. The car starts moving, and I turn to Lo, who has a hand covering his eyes.

"I don't know what to do."

"You're going to rehab," I say assuredly, even though a pain weighs on my chest. I know this is the right thing. For both of us.

"I can't leave you." He drops his hand. "It could be months, Lily. I don't want you with another guy . . . "

"I'm going to be strong," I tell him, taking his hands in mine. I squeeze. "I'm going to go to therapy."

"Lily . . . " His pained voice sends daggers to my heart.

"I'm going to move in with Rose."

He shuts his eyes and more tears spill.

I keep from crying. I swallow. "I'm going to transfer to Princeton, and I'll be waiting for you when you return."

Lo nods a lot, letting the news sink in. "If that's what you want . . . "

"It's what I want."

Lo licks his lips and leans a shoulder against mine. "I'm sorry about today. I shouldn't have done that in the hotel room. I . . . I was upset, and it had nothing to do with you. I . . . "

"What is it?" I frown. What could be so bad that he threw back mini-bottles of alcohol, breaking his short sobriety that meant a great deal to him, to me, and our friends . . . his brother.

"Penn sent me a letter this morning." He pauses. "They've kicked me out."

"What? They can't kick you out. You haven't done anything wrong. We'll go to the Dean—"

"Lily, I haven't gone to half my classes. I've failed almost every one. I have a one-point-something GPA. They can kick out people that don't meet their academic standards. They warned me last year, and I didn't give a shit."

"What?" I squeak. I knew something was wrong, but I thought he had been pulling better grades than *me* at least. "So . . . so you'll go to Princeton with me. You can transfer. They'll let you in with your last name."

"No." He shakes his head. "No, I'm not going back to college. It's not for me, Lil."

I process this. "So what are you going to do?"

"I don't know," Lo says. "How about get healthy first?"

"That works," I murmur. "What about your father? Lo, if he finds out, he'll take away your trust fund."

"He won't find out. I've already called admissions and told them not to contact him."

I exhale in relief.

The car rolls to the curb. "We've arrived, Mr. Hale."

I stiffen. That voice—that voice did not belong to Nola.

The driver shifts slightly, and I see the gray whiskers, feather hair, and glasses perched on a beak nose.

"Anderson," Lo says tensely. Anderson, Jonathan Hale's driver, the guy who has been known to rat us out. "Please don't tell my father . . . "

"Have a nice night," Anderson says with a fake smile. He spins back to the front, waiting for us to leave.

We do, and in my heart, I know that everything is about to change.

Thirty-three

After a short conversation, we agree to spend the night apart. I stay with Rose at the Drake, and Ryke takes Lo to his apartment on campus. I only learn that his father calls him in the morning because Rose relays the information.

He gave him the ultimatum we avoided and feared our whole lives. Go back to college, set your life straight, or else your trust fund will disappear. Months ago, Lo's choice may have been different. He may have opted for college, transferring to Princeton or Penn State, going back into a familiar routine in a new setting. But I think we both realize that some things are worth more than a fancy lifestyle and padded wallet.

At breakfast, while I pick at a bowl of oatmeal in the living room, I'm not surprised when Rose tells me that Lo stepped away from the money. She says it's the most heroic thing he's done in his life. The irony is that he's not saving some damsel in a castle, he's not rescuing a baby from a burning building—he's helping himself. Maybe a little bit to save our relationship, but mostly for him. And that's the best reason there is. Beneath my fear, I am so, so proud.

In a few days, I'll need to find the same bravery.

My sister sets a hand on my shoulder. "He's coming over to grab some of his things. They're leaving at noon."

Pressure sits heavy on my chest, but I nod anyway. We also agreed that he should go to rehab as soon as possible. We're afraid we'll change our minds, that we'll convince each other it's not the right step and that we can work it out together. We can't. We've tried that, and it ended with Lo drinking tequila in a hotel room and me pulling him against my body.

Rose scoots next to me, and I make room for her on the couch. "How are you doing?" she asks, gathering my short hair and braiding the strands.

I shake my head. I have no words. In one night, Lo lost his trust fund, learned his father lied to him and that he has a brother. We're so connected that I feel the hurt from the deception as if it was my own.

How could Jonathan lie to Lo for so long? I want to despise him for holding back the truth, and yet, I can't. He loves Lo. More than anyone will admit. He loves him so much that he decided to raise Lo instead of abandon him. He fears the thought of Lo going off to rehab, of learning that he failed as a father and that his son may move on without him. I think there's a part of Jonathan that believes Lo will return home for money, that he'll come back to him when he realizes the hardship of the working class. Maybe Lo will. Or maybe he'll finally say goodbye to his father and never turn back.

"It'll be hard at first," Rose tells me, tying off my braid. "When's the longest you've been away from him?"

I shake my head again. "I don't know . . . a week, maybe." It seems completely absurd, but it's true. It's like we've been married our whole lives, and now we have to separate. I know it's for the best, but the hurt still festers like a new wound.

Rose rubs my back, and I spin to face her fully. She looks at me with more concern than I thought possible. In the end, it was not a boy who helped me.

It was my sister.

I hold her hand and say, "Thank you." Tears build. "I don't know if I can do this without you." Rose and I agreed to keep my addiction quiet from our parents and sisters. It's not something that people can easily accept or understand, and I don't want to spend my days justifying these compulsions. If Rose also thinks it's for the best, then I must be making a sound decision.

"You'll be able to. Not now, but you'll get there."

"I'm scared." My throat hurts. I inhale a strained breath. "What if I cheat on him? What if I can't wait?"

She squeezes my hand. "You will. You're going to get through this, and I'm going to be there every step of the way."

I wipe my cheeks and then wrap my arms around her, hugging for a long, long time. To say thanks, I'm sorry and . . . "I love you," I whisper.

She strokes my hair. "I love you too."

I stand on the sidewalk outside of the Drake. Snow flurries kiss my cheeks as I wait for Lo. People dress in nice church clothes, heading to Christmas Eve mass or service. Tiny lights wrap around lamp poles, and wreaths with suede red ribbons hang on the outside of our apartment complex. The city stays in a celebratory mood while my heart clenches with each beat.

Ryke's black Infiniti hugs the curb. He tosses in Lo's duffel bag and closes the trunk.

Lo has sleepless circles underneath his weary eyes, and he looks beaten and tired. Three feet separate our bodies, and I wonder who will close the space first—if at all.

"What do we say?" I breathe. "Goodbye?"

"No." He shakes his head. "This isn't goodbye, Lil. I'll see you." I don't even know which rehab he's going to. Ryke won't tell me the address, but I have to trust that it's a safe place and maybe imagine it's not very far away.

I give him a weak smile, desperately trying not to cry. But once I see a tear slide down his cheek, it's over for me. I sniff. "Don't change too much," I tell him. I fear he'll return and won't fit within my life anymore. He'll grow beyond me while I stay stagnant and alone.

"Only the bad parts," he says. He takes the first step forward. And then another. And another. Until our shoes touch, until his thumb strokes my cheek. "I'll always be yours. No distance or time apart will change that, Lily. You need to believe that."

I place my hands on his firm chest and skim my fingers over his arrowhead necklace.

"I never wanted to leave you here"—his chest constricts underneath my palms—"and put you in pain, Lil. You have to know that . . . that this is the hardest thing I've ever had to do." He licks his lips. "It's harder than saying no to my father, than rejecting the trust fund, this, right here, *kills* me."

"I'll be okay," I whisper, trying hard to believe the words.

"Will you?" he says, doubtful. "Because I see you crying and thrashing in bed. I see you screaming for someone and praying to God for the pain to end. And I'm responsible for that."

"Stop," I breathe, unable to look him in the eyes. "Please, don't think that."

He opens his mouth, and I think he's going to let me off the hook. He's going to tell me that I can cheat on him and get a free pass. Instead, tears flow and he says, "Wait for me." The words come out choked and pained. "I need you to wait for me."

Someone put him up to this. I glance over my shoulder, and Rose has her hand over her mouth, her eyes wide. I look at Ryke, and his hard gaze says nothing.

This was Lo's idea.

354 · KRISTA RITCHIE and BECCA RITCHIE

He knew the only way for me to truly fight is if I have something to lose.

I try to form a response, but my throat closes for words.

Lo draws me close and wraps his arms around my shoulders. "I love you." He kisses me on the forehead and detaches from me, leaving me speechless and broken on the curb. He nods to Rose. "Take care of her."

Rose says, "Take care of yourself."

He nods again, and I wait for him to glance back at me.

He doesn't.

"Lo," I call.

He has a hand on the car door frame. And he hesitates before looking my way.

I open my mouth, wanting to express all of my feelings at once. *I love you. I'll wait for you! You're my best friend and my soul mate and my lover. I'm so proud of you. Please . . . come back to me.*

His lips upturn in a hopeful smile. "I know."

And with this, he slides into the car and shuts the door. The Infiniti pulls onto the street.

And down out of sight.

BONUS CHAPTER

—

Retelling of Chapter 32

Loren Hale

ily looks as numb as I want to feel. The elevator descends to the grand ballroom for the Christmas Charity Gala. I can't even rest my eyes on Lil.

Can't glance over to wonder if she's okay. I have flashes of us together in the hotel room, and I know I hurt her, somehow. I know she's not okay. I shouldn't have fed into her desire to fuck. I shouldn't have been that rough. *Can't take it back.* Can't rewind time. I tried to erase it for a moment.

The mini-bottle of tequila I downed lingers like acid in the back of my throat. Everything is building. Amassing.

Crushing.

I stare straight ahead. Muscles searing.

She deserves better.

She shouldn't be with me—not *this* me. The me who'd let my bad day become her worse one. The me who'd drag her so low with me—but I don't know what life is like without Lily. She's . . . she's my best friend.

She's my world, my soul.

She's the thing buried inside me that deserves to be held gently. That deserves to see the light. I know that.

I know that.

"Where are you going when we get down there?" she asks quietly.

"I need to talk to my father." I sound harsher than I mean to be, especially towards her, and I watch the glowing numbers, my unblinking eyes burning.

For a moment there, I did believe I could get sober without rehab. Without leaving Lily behind. But *can't can't can't* seems to be my motto. I *can't* rewind time.

I *can't* hack college.

I *can't* be the man Lily needs.

I *can't* be the man that I should be. That I hope to be. Not yet.

And maybe I am a fool—that I even want to try, that I even think *maybe* this could work. I'm a guy who *can't*. A guy who maybe never *could*. But I won't be a guy who never will. I will try. I have to see.

For her. For me.

For us.

Once the elevator doors slip open, I only think, *find him.* Find my dad. There is cowardice in me. Shitty, unbecoming *cowardice* that could eat the fragile determination I just built. Determination born from hurting the person who means everything to me. How long have I hurt her? How long will I keep hurting her?

It has to stop.

It has to be put to rest. I need off this track. And we just need a new beginning—and God, this might be the only way.

Nothing stuns me or halts me. Not the fancy chandeliers. Not the pricks in suits. Not the enormous Christmas tree decorated in an obscene amount of gold tinsel. Not the stage with the big projected screens that read *Hale Co.* and *Fizzle.*

The only thing that briefly stops me is alcohol. I pluck a flute of pink champagne off a tray. Downing the thing in one gulp.

Wishing for the taste of bourbon, I grimace but keep moving. Lily trails after me as I snake through hordes of socialites.

I want to hold her hand.

I want to bring her close.

I want to turn away and leave with her. *I can't.*

It takes everything in my wretched, god-awful body to avoid her. When she's all I really want in this second. This moment. This world.

I have to see this through. While I cling to this fledgling perseverance, my stride lengthens as I spot my father in a crisp tux among other older white men. All cupping glasses of whiskey.

"Lo." I barely hear Lily as she falls further behind me. *I'm sorry, love.* It hurts. Everything fucking hurts.

As soon as my dad notices I'm on a path towards him, he shoos the other men away. My face feels brutally set. Like if I shift my jaw or my narrowed eyes, I might break.

He might break me.

His stern expression is what I've always known. I'm not cowering, not as he asks, "Have you been avoiding me? You usually stop by on Wednesdays."

"I've been going through some things."

He scrutinizes me, up-down. "You look fine."

My eyes burn hotter. He really thinks that? He can look at me and think I'm okay? I want to scream but the words come out leveled. "I'm not fine." I shake my head repeatedly, more emotion climbing. "I'm not fine, Dad."

He briefly glances to the left, to the right. Taking in the few onlookers. Yeah, we're in a public place that represents *his* company. Hale Co.

My future, right?

"This isn't the place, Loren. We'll talk later."

There is no later. "Something's wrong with me," I tell him like this is life or death—and it feels like it is. It feels like if I don't do this now, it's over. "Do you hear me? I'm telling you that I'm not okay."

I don't imagine him hugging me.

I don't imagine him nodding and saying, *We'll get you help. You want it. I have the means. Come on, son. I love you, son.*

I don't imagine the impossible.

Apathy courses deeply through my veins, and I never thought some father-son heart-to-heart would change his volatile demeanor or his mind.

He downs the rest of his whiskey, throwing the alcohol into the back of his throat. I watch him place the glass on a nearby high table. My muscles are so stiff they're vibrating for release. For me to turn and run away.

I stay.

After he rubs his lips, he edges closer to me. "Are you trying to embarrass me?"

I clench my vibrating hands into fists. Just so they'll stop shaking. "You know that I drink, and you don't give a shit."

"That's what this is about?" His face contorts. "Lo, you're a fucking twenty-one-year-old man. Of course you drink."

"I pass out."

"So have many before you. It's natural for kids your age to abuse alcohol."

I don't listen to him. Even if I love him, I don't listen to him this time. "I can't go a day without a drink."

His lip curls. "Stop trying to find an excuse for your mistakes and own up to them like a goddamn man."

Lily is behind me. She reaches for my hand, and I jerk away. It's a knife in my chest. But I can't hang on to her while I'm facing him.

He's whisked another glass of whiskey from a server's tray. He sips and nods to Lily. My pulse spikes the second she's dragged into this. He glowers at her. "Have you put these thoughts into my son's head?"

She shrinks backwards.

I speak louder. "I've known this since I was a kid. She didn't have to say anything to me." *Keep her out of this.*

"I highly doubt that."

I grind my teeth, but words are caught in my acidic throat. Once I see Rose embracing Lily with an arm around her waist, my pulse slightly eases. *Rose is here.*

Ryke suddenly slinks up to my side. He's catching his breath like he ran over to me, and I feel him rest a hand on my arm. The comfort in his touch is something I'm never going to get from my dad.

Ryke breathes, "Come on, Lo."

I'm watching my father, and I can't move. My dad has gone ashy white, his clutch loosening on his whiskey. The way he's staring at Ryke unsettles every assured thing inside me.

But I know I'm not in *The Sixth Sense*. Ryke isn't a ghost. He's a real person.

A real person that my dad recognizes.

My suspicion is confirmed when my dad finally says, "What are you doing here?"

I frown. "You know each other?"

My dad lets out a small huff. "You didn't tell him." He's speaking only to Ryke, and something brews inside me. Something dark and molten. People are watching. My dad can see, and he downs the last of his second whiskey with a grimace.

Is anyone gonna clue me in here?

I shift my weight. "Tell me what?"

"Nothing," my dad says with a bitter smile. As he sets down the glass, his sharp eyes return to mine. "So is this what you wanted to say to me? You wanted to blame me for your problems and stomp around like a child?"

I could press him about his connection to Ryke. I could forget my plans. I haven't spoken them out loud yet. I could turn back now and let that fragile determination crumble underneath me.

Ryke never takes his hand off my shoulder. His palm rests easy. Not heavy. Not like lead but like something careful, understanding. Ready.

Ready to be there for me. I know he's here for me.

And as I stare my dad in the eye, I don't hate him as much as I hate who I am. "No," I say softly. "Maybe if this was a story about my teenage years, I'd have done something like that. I just wanted to say that I'm going to get sober."

I want to be someone I can love.

And I'm going to try.

BONUS PLAYLIST

Songs

"Wildest Moments" by Jessie Ware

"Habits (Stay High)" by Tove Lo

"Lost in My Mind" by The Head and the Heart

"On the Rocks" by Grieves

"Let It Go" by Fossil Collective

"Trembling Hands" by The Temper Trap

"Pasadena" by Modern Skirts

"Two Fingers" by Jake Bugg

"Worthy" by Jacob Banks

"Life Is Hard" by Edward Sharpe and the Magnetic Zeros

"Animal" by Miike Snow

"Lose Your Soul" by Dead Man's Bones

"Pleasant Street / You Keep Me Hanging On" by Tim Buckley

BONUS TEXT MESSAGE THREADS

AUGUST
10:04 A.M.

LILY: SOS! We need a GOOD excuse to bail on the next Sunday luncheon. Like an adamantium-strong excuse. Impenetrable!

LILY: Rose keeps texting me about it

LILY: OMG she won't stop!! 😱 Lo, you there?

LILY: Didn't you have a 9 a.m. class too? I'll meet you on campus somewhere

LO: Just woke up

LILY: Just now?

LO: Late night, love. Remember? Or did you get dicked too hard by pizza face?

LILY: that's mean, Lo

LO: What else am I supposed to call him?

LILY: his name

LO: Which is??

LILY: idk . . . I never asked. We just hooked up after we met at that dorm party and then kinda left each other. But there are NICER names than pizza face. He just had acne. Lots of people have acne.

LO: Or he had herpes. You should prob go get checked out

LO: I'll come with you

LO: meet you soon, love

LO: Love? 😟

LILY: Okay but later. I have another class soon.

LILY: AND ROSE KEEPS TEXTING! I don't know what to tell her

LO: We got food poisoning and can't go tomorrow. Done.

LILY: The luncheon is on Sunday

LO: I know. It's always on Sunday

LILY: Today is Thursday, Lo.

LO: huh

LO: just tell Rose we're not going because we have plans with Charlie and Stacey. And they're way more fun than her.

LILY: What if she asks about our plans? Like dates and times and then shows up? And then she realizes there is no Charlie and Stacey??

LO: right okay

LO: we gotta use something that appeals to your sister

LILY: fashion? We went shopping

LO: no, she'll ask why she's not invited

LILY: I got it! College. It just started back. We're busy studying. For VERY important exams. We're trying to do better this year.

LO: Perfect, love 🖤 See, you didn't even need me

LILY: that's not true. I always need you, Lo

LO: I'm leaving the Drake. Going to meet you on campus.

LILY: !!! 🎉

LO: Let me know when you get out of class

LILY: I will, about to go in ✋

LO: ✋

SEPTEMBER
1:32 P.M.

LILY: new phone! Checking the texting quality. How's it performing?

LO: the same as the other phone. But your texts are the best, the prettiest.

LILY: are we practicing flirting for when we pretend?

LO: do you need practice?

LILY: Idk. You wanna sext?

LILY: For practice! For our pretend relationship. Never mind, I take back my offer. I take it right back very quickly! Please don't respond to that.

LO: you sure, love?

LILY: I'm sure. I'm sure.

LO: okay. Wish I went to the phone store with you. Feels like you've been gone forever.

LILY: I know, I hate it. You wanna go watch Thor in theaters again? I think it's still playing.

LO: 1000% and we should take pictures with our popcorn. Gotta get proof that we were there

LILY: that we were there together? So we can send them to Rose as relationship evidence?

LO: that too

OCTOBER
9:24 A.M.

LO: you remember how it felt this morning? Having me inside you? You want a repeat?

LILY: Repeat x3

LO: How about Repeat x5?

LILY: yesyes maybe I should bail on the new tutor today?

LO: no, go meet whatever his name was. I'm doing a store run first 🥃

LILY: Connor Cobalt. Best name ever

LO: Not in the history of ever. It's okay

LILY: Name someone with a better name.

LO: Lily, my love, Calloway

LILY: Stop 😊

LILY: Seriously, Lo, name a better name than Connor Cobalt

LO: I did. Lily Calloway.

LO: I love you, Lil

LILY: I love you too, Lo

4:40 P.M.

LILY: so much traffic today

LO: you going to hold up the new tutor?

LILY: hope not. He might fire me as his tutee before I even get there

LO: over my dead body

LILY: I wish I could apparate. Or teleport.

LO: me too. I'd teleport to you.

LILY: If we think really, really hard, maybe we can psychically connect and teleport to each other.

LO: I'm trying

LILY: Me too. Superpowers aren't kicking in 😔

LO: just think about the sex from this afternoon and it'll make you feel better, love

LILY: you mean wetter? Repeat x5 sex is the best sex

LO: 😈

8:33 P.M.

LO: *Missed call from Lily*

8:34 P.M.

LO: *Missed call from Lily*

8:36 P.M.

LO: *Missed call from Lily*

8:37 P.M.

LILY: Where are you? I just walked into the apartment. The tutor is with me btw to help me cram. You okay?

NOVEMBER
1:12 P.M.

LILY: How's Calloway Couture doing?

ROSE: Fine.

LILY: I'm really sorry, still. You know that?

ROSE: It's okay. I'm just busy, Lily.

DECEMBER

A WEEK BEFORE THE CHRISTMAS CHARITY GALA
9:04 A.M.

LILY: I'm skipping.

LO: skipping class?

LILY: I don't want to be here, Lo.

LO: come home, love

LO: But we just had sex, so maybe we shouldn't have it again for a few hours.

LILY: I know. I don't want anything.

LILY: I mean, I do want sex, but that's not why I'm coming home. I just want to be with you.

LILY: Without sex.

LO: we can finally do that binge watch of all 7 Harry Potter movies now that Deathly Hallows Part 2 is out. What do you say, love?

LILY: YES!

LILY: Hold on. Almost tripped walking and texting across campus

9:08 A.M.

LILY: How are you feeling?

LO: like shit, I guess

LO: I'm craving a drink prob as much as you're craving for me to fuck you

LILY: yeah

LO: It'll be better when you're home. You on your way?

LILY: In the car now.

LO: 🖤

ACKNOWLEDGEMENTS

First and foremost, we want to thank all of the people who supported *Addicted to You* over the course of its creation. Family, friends and the greatly adored and revered and beloved in our hearts: fellow bloggers and the bookish community, we owe all of you the biggest thanks and giant hugs. Whether they are virtual or real, they mean the same to us.

For anyone suffering from an addiction or feeling as though they may have one, acknowledging the problem is the first step, talking to someone can be the next. It's important that as female readers, as women, we empower each other. Sex addiction for women is a tricky subject. There's a fine line between being a destructive sex addict (as in Lily's case) and merely exploring sexuality. By being aware of that line, we can support other females in their sexuality, not shame them. We're all sisters, and we're excited to start celebrating that bond we all inherently share. And for any boys reading this book, we love you too! Thanks everyone!

Krista and Becca Ritchie are *New York Times* and *USA Today* bestselling authors and identical twins—one a science nerd, the other a comic book geek—but with their shared passion for writing, they combined their mental powers as kids and have never stopped telling stories. They love superheroes, flawed characters and soul mate love.

VISIT THE AUTHORS ONLINE

KBRitchie.com
KBMRitchie

Ready to find
your next great read?

Let us help.

Visit prh.com/nextread

Penguin
Random
House